A DEATH IN JERUSALEM

AN ADAM LAPID MYSTERY

JONATHAN DUNSKY

LION CUB PUBLISHING

A Death in Jerusalem

Jonathan Dunsky

Copyright © 2022 by Jonathan Dunsky

Cover designed by Deranged Doctor Design (DerangedDoctorDesign.com)

Cover Photographs © Neo-Stock (man); rasika108/Shutterstock (street); Janis Smits/Shutterstock (clouds); Kamenetskiy Konstantin/Shutterstock (running man back view)

Published by Lion Cub Publishing.

ISBN: 978-965-7795-21-7

Visit JonathanDunsky.com for news and information.

BOOKS BY JONATHAN DUNSKY

For Froumit Tandet

1

Spools of barbed wire barricaded the street. Behind them stood a row of helmeted policemen, truncheons in hand. They looked ready for war but offered no resistance as our vanguard cast the obstacle aside.

How many were we? Five thousand? More? A pulsing column of men and women. Teenagers too. All dressed warmly against the Jerusalem winter. Our shoes made rainwater jump from the puddles left by an earlier downpour. The banners rippled in the wind. The chanted slogans ricocheted between the buildings on either side of Ben Yehuda Street. The yellow stars some had pinned to their coats shone like memorial candles in the early evening light.

As I marched near the front of this swarming mass, the voice of Menachem Begin resounded in my head: *"I call upon Mr. Ben-Gurion, do not commit this act. You are placing a bomb under the house of Israel, which may come crashing down on its inhabitants. I say this for the blood that was spilled in Majdanek and Auschwitz, and so you would not have to bow your head before the gentiles. Therefore, I say to Mr. Ben-Gurion: There will be no negotiations with Germany. On this matter, we are ready to surrender our lives."*

A second string of police officers was ahead, this contingent larger than the first. Their steel helmets glistened, their truncheons as black as death. A barrage of garbage rained on their heads, hurled by youngsters who had climbed bordering rooftops. The policemen huddled, their bodies tense. Their expressions were determined, their gazes fierce. The hands gripping the truncheons flexed. The air crackled with the threat of violence. Yet these cops, like their predecessors, made no attempt to block our advance.

"There is no sacrifice we won't make to thwart this scheme," continued Begin's voice between my ears. *"Mr. Ben-Gurion has stationed policemen, and in their hands is tear gas made in Germany, the same gas that suffocated our forebears. He has prisons and concentration camps. Ben-Gurion may be older than me in years, but I am older than him in resisting an evil regime. And this I declare: Evil confronts a just cause, and it will shatter like glass against rock."*

The demonstration had taken place in Zion Square, a short distance from Frumin House, where the Israeli parliament, the Knesset, held its sessions. The right-wing Herut party had arranged the demonstration, but many of the attendees, like me, could not be counted among its ardent supporters. I had come to Jerusalem because my heart had urged me to. Because I could not imagine doing nothing while my government sought approval for the unthinkable.

A series of Herut officials had given speeches, each excoriating the government and its desired policies vis-à-vis Germany. But if not for the leader of Herut, Menachem Begin, it likely would have ended there. The demonstration would have fizzled out. The anger would never have erupted.

But from the moment Begin took up position behind the microphone, from the second he opened his mouth, I could feel a charge building inside and around me. As though with each fervent word, a giant spring was slowly being coiled ever tighter under the feet of the spectators. All eyes were fixed upon Begin's small, unprepossessing form. He did not look like a man whose voice could ring with such emotion. Not a man who could move thousands with his intonation and gestures. Yet his oration was like a tidal wave of emotion and indignation—penetrating, stirring, irresistible, demanding action.

"If need be, I shall renew the war," Begin said, referring to the violent campaign he had waged as commander of the Irgun against the British when they had occupied the Land of Israel, but now with Ben-Gurion's government as his enemy. *"And in this war, we will be accompanied by the spirit of the millions of all countries, from the ovens and the gas chambers, who have commanded us: No negotiations. A boycott on Germany for all time."*

And right at the end, after he had primed the thousands who hung on his every word, he lit the fuse by calling on us to not be afraid, to march on the policemen who stood between us and the Knesset.

By that time, I needed little prompting. The blood was surging fast and hot through my veins. The number tattoo on my arm burned like a cattle brand. My skin vibrated with rage that had gradually built up over the past few weeks, ever since the newspapers first reported preliminary contacts between the government of Israel and its counterpart in West Germany.

The discussions revolved around one issue: reparations from Germany to Israel. Reparations for the Holocaust. For the millions who had perished. For the survivors who were forever damaged. For the invalids, the tormented, the haunted. And for expropriated Jewish property for which no heir survived. Because the Germans had not merely killed individuals. They'd eradicated whole families, entire communities. They had wanted to murder us all.

And now, January 7, 1952, less than seven years after the Holocaust ended, the government of the Jewish state sought approval from the Knesset to abandon its policy of boycott against Germany and enter into direct negotiations with it.

Never mind what it said about the Jewish people. That we would be willing to set a price on our dead brethren. On my wife, daughters, mother, sisters. On my best friend. And on all the rest.

Ever since the newspapers broke the story, Israel had been in turmoil. Large segments of the public—the majority, I believed— were dead set against direct negotiations. Opposition came from both ends of the political spectrum. From Herut on the right, to

3

Maki, the Israeli Communist Party, on the left. But Mapai, Israel's ruling party headed by Prime Minister David Ben-Gurion, was in favor, and it exerted great pressure on its coalition partners to back it.

In recent days, impassioned rallies and marches against negotiations were held across the length and breadth of Israel. The Chief Rabbi expressed his disapproval, as did a range of artists and academics. Partisans and resistance fighters from the ghettos portrayed negotiations with Germany as a betrayal of the dead. Some claimed such negotiations would pave the way to the rearmament of Germany, to a third world war and another Holocaust. A poll conducted by the newspaper *Ma'ariv* revealed that eighty percent of its readers opposed the government's position.

At that moment, the Knesset debated the issue. Later, tomorrow perhaps, would come the vote. Aye, for direct negotiations with Germany, and all it entailed morally, politically, historically. Or nay, to maintain Israel's righteous position that Jewish blood was not for sale, and that Germany could not purchase our absolution with cash or goods.

The newspapers predicted that the government would prevail. Despite the overwhelming opposition. Despite the dead millions. Despite the shame it would bring upon Israel. Unless the government came to realize that the people would not have it.

At the corner of Ben Yehuda and King George, we met our first resistance. A police inspector with a megaphone ordered us to disperse. When that didn't work, a firetruck unleashed a torrent of water at us. A man flew backward through the air after receiving a direct hit. People slipped and fell. Others dropped to their knees, shielding their heads. A large banner held aloft by two women was ripped from their grasp.

A powerful blast rammed me in the shoulder, spinning me like a dreidel. I tumbled into the man behind me, and together we crashed to the wet road. I landed badly, smacking my head.

For a second, all was black. Then sight returned, and with it my other senses. My forehead hurt. My jaw ached. Around me, jets of water stabbed into the demonstrators. There were shouts and yells. Cries of pain. Curses at the government and the police.

"*Kapos!*"

"*Judenrat!*"

"Gestapo!"

"Traitors!"

My hat had flown off. My hair was plastered to my scalp. My clothes were drenched. Water dripped into my eyes, streamed down my collar, pooled in my shoes. But it didn't cool me one bit. I was burning up on the inside.

They would not stop us. We would make our voices heard.

I pushed myself to my feet and, bent low, arms raised before my face, took a step forward. Around me, people kept coming and falling before the water. I did too, banging my elbow so hard on the asphalt, I thought I had broken it. A few dozen meters away stood Frumin House, where at this moment, the debate raged.

For a few minutes, the water held us off. Then the tank ran out. The firetruck, out of its liquid ammunition, sped away. The same police inspector who had ordered us to disperse now switched to begging. In a choked voice, he beseeched us not to destroy our dear country and its democracy.

No one paid him any mind. Not even me, despite having once been a policeman myself. Soaked and dripping, I had but one goal: the Knesset. I had to reach the Knesset.

"Onward," someone shouted, and we obeyed, surging down King George Street toward Frumin House. No longer a tight, orderly column; now a disorganized mob. Not all the demonstrators joined the advance, but hundreds did. All of us driven by a conviction that an abomination was about to take place, and that we had a duty to our dead families and friends to stop it.

Frumin House was just ahead. The Knesset hall was on the ground floor. The windowpanes glowed with light. There, beyond those windows and walls, the fate of our country, of our people, was being decided.

Before us stretched a cordon of cops, more than two hundred

strong, their faces made hideous by gas masks. The cops stood shoulder to shoulder, like a Roman phalanx. The shouts of the demonstrators, in Hebrew and Yiddish, bounced against their formation like projectiles. Beside me, a woman shrieked that she had lost her entire family in Treblinka. She implored the cops to stand aside. To not defend this evil government. To not take part in this desecration of the dead.

I shouted too, though what I don't remember. I only know that I uttered each word with such force that it seared my vocal cords as it burst from my mouth.

Then came the stones. A fusillade of them arching through the air. Mostly launched by a cluster of teenagers atop a hillock of earth across the street from the Knesset.

Some of the stones landed short of the policemen. Others found their mark. Two cops went down after being struck on the helmet. Others sustained body blows. The cars of the ministers parked outside Frumin House suffered their share of damage. Windshields and side windows disintegrated. Dents pocked the doors and roofs.

Several stones went long, or perhaps found their true target. They soared over the officers and into the Knesset. Windows shattered. Glass sprayed. A manic cheer rose from the crowd.

The demonstrators charged, with me among them. An avalanche of bubbling anger. A sharp command sounded from somewhere ahead. A flurry of round black objects swooped toward us. They detonated upon hitting the street, spewing acrid gray fumes.

"Gas!" someone screamed, and numerous others took up the cry. "Gas! They're using gas!"

The word was laden with several million meanings. I imagined my loved ones suffocating in the gas chambers. Others must have done the same. People wailed hysterically. Others snarled imprecations at the cops and at the government. Yet others simply looked stunned that Jews would employ such a weapon on each other.

For a stitch of time, there was wild panic. But, of course, this was not the gas the Germans had used to kill millions. Not a deadly gas at all.

Within seconds, my eyes were stinging and watery. My throat blazed. Every breath was painful. Through the blur of flooding tears, I saw people retching, coughing. One man vomited. But nothing worse than that.

Our advance halted, but only temporarily. The wind picked up, clearing away much of the gas. And the use of it, nonlethal though it was, inflamed us further.

We charged. I had no weapon. I had not come here to spill Jewish blood, but to protest the selling of it. All I wanted was to reach the Knesset. To shout my objection right in the prime minister's face.

The other demonstrators, sharing my purpose, were similarly unequipped for battle. But propelled by a mindless rage, they slammed headlong into the wall of masked officers. They knocked policemen to the ground, battered them with booted feet, pummeled them with naked fists. The cops returned the favor, using their truncheons with growing ferocity. Casualties mounted on both sides. Here, a protester lay unconscious in the street. There, two policemen carried an injured comrade to the safety of Frumin House. To my right sat a dazed man with a yellow star on his breast and blood streaming from his temple. To my left, a grimacing police officer limped in retreat.

The skirmish was messy, chaotic, close-ranged. The lines of cops and demonstrators weaved into each other. Thuds of truncheons against flesh. Shouted curses. The banging of stones against walls. The breaking of glass. The howls of the injured. A maelstrom of sound punching my ears.

More tear gas, and the battle subsided. The officers pushed us away, hauling some of the demonstrators into police cars. Smoke seeped through the broken windows of the Knesset. Ambulances wailed in and out. Medical crews tended to the injured or evacuated them to the hospital.

The smoke cleared again, and the battle resumed. Yells and grunts and cries sliced through the air. Blood mingled with rainwater on the road. Jewish blood spilled by Jewish hands in the capital of the

7

country that was the culmination of two thousand years of Jewish prayers.

A few members of Knesset emerged to peer at the fighting. Those in the opposition yelled at the police to stand down. Others simply looked horrified.

And so it continued. Jews fighting Jews. The cops motivated by their wish to maintain order and enforce the law. I, like the rest of the demonstrators, propelled by a sense of wrongness so acute it threatened to rip my soul into shreds. To strip me of my hard-won identity as a proud independent Jew, strong and honorable, equal among nations, and reduce me to my old unbearable identity, the one from Auschwitz—that of the powerless slave who had failed to protect his family.

For if we agreed to accept reparations from Germany, if we even entered into negotiations on that issue, it meant that the dead could be quantified in dollars or marks. That the crime could be redressed monetarily. And it couldn't. Not for all the money in the world.

The next few minutes passed in a blur, during which time I was driven entirely by fury. Everything else, all traces of thought and rationality, had deserted me. Around me, the fighting raged, shifting like the sea, back and forth. We pushed toward the Knesset, and the cops pushed us back. More and more people were injured or arrested. Stones and glass fragments littered the street. Fallen banners and signs lay trampled. I don't remember striking anyone, nor being struck, but when I slipped on the wet road and fell to my knees, I saw that my knuckles were bruised, and my body ached in numerous places.

I raised my eyes to the sky, and there, at the tip of a pole on the roof of Frumin House, the flag of Israel shuddered.

At the sight of that blue-and-white cloth, the tide of anger that had engulfed me receded partway, and the ensuing void instantly filled with bewilderment and shame. I gazed at the mayhem around me and couldn't fathom how it had come to this. These demonstrators were regular men and women, good citizens, law-abiding by nature. But they, and I, had raised our hands against our fellow Jews and against the Knesset, the shrine of Jewish sovereignty after centuries of exile and longing, of persecution and displacement, of pogroms and genocide.

This was an abomination. Similar to what the government was trying to do. This wasn't why I had come to this land, not why I had fought in the War of Independence and nearly died when an Egyptian soldier put two bullets in me. The Nazis would have loved seeing this, us fighting among ourselves. It had to stop.

A few meters to my left, a young man was bent over a fallen policeman, punching him repeatedly. "Enough!" I yelled, catching the demonstrator unaware with a hard shove that sent him sprawling. I showed him my fists when he turned on me with a snarl. "Enough," I yelled again. "No more."

The demonstrator fixed me with a hard stare. For a tense moment, I thought he would lunge at me. But then he blinked, and a look of what might have been shame flitted across his face, and he muttered something I didn't catch and turned away.

I knelt beside the policeman. He had lost his helmet and gas mask in the melee and was bleeding from the nose and mouth. His eyes were closed, but he was breathing, and his pulse was strong and steady. I was about to get him some help when I sensed rushing footfalls behind me. Before I could whirl, a devastating blow slammed into my kidney. A flash of scorching pain exploded up my side, robbing me of breath. Gasping, I crashed down on top of the injured policeman, banging my forehead on his.

An instant later, my hands were wrenched backward, and a ring of cool metal wrapped itself around each of my wrists. Someone slapped the back of my head. "You son of a bitch, you're going to jail for what you did to him."

I opened my mouth to protest, to explain that I had not beaten this policeman, when from the corner of my eye, I caught a black object streaking toward me. I identified it as a boot just before it connected with the side of my head. Then a dark, impenetrable cloud descended upon me, swallowing up my consciousness, choking off all sensation and thought.

9

2

I came to in the back of a police wagon. I was lying on the hard floor between two benches that were bolted down. Sitting on them were several other men, all handcuffed, some showing signs of minor injuries. The air was thick with the pungent aromas of cooling sweat and wet clothes, with an undertone of fresh blood. My head throbbed as though someone had given it a violent shake, and there was a coppery taste in my mouth. I must have bitten my tongue when I got kicked in the head. My vision swam, dark spots dancing before my eyes. My body was pressing down on my cuffed hands, which were sending sharp stabs of pain all the way to my shoulders.

With a groan, I flipped over onto my stomach. The pain in my arms subsided. The floor of the jouncing vehicle felt cold against my cheek. Someone asked if I was all right. "Yeah," I mumbled, which seemed all the speech I was capable of. The fogginess enveloping me began to recede, but then the police wagon went into a pothole, and my head was bounced up and then back down onto the floor, and I was out again.

Next time I awoke, I was lying on a metal cot with a mattress so thin it could only be described as emaciated. Uncomfortable, but I'd slept in harder beds. Much better was the fact that I was no longer handcuffed. A few inches before my eyes was a concrete wall, pitted and scratched and stained. Slowly, I raised a hand to my head to touch the spot where I'd been kicked, and immediately regretted it when pain flared down my face.

Hearing voices, I raised myself on my elbows and swiveled my head to the other side. I was in a jail cell. Made for two men, but with five crammed within its walls. Two of my cellmates were sitting on the other cot; the other pair stood puffing on cigarettes, blowing smoke through the bars into the hallway beyond.

All four of my cellmates displayed signs of recent violence: cuts, abrasions, bruises, torn clothing. They were in the middle of a raucous conversation—mainly lambasting Ben-Gurion, the government, and the police—so it took them a minute to notice I was awake.

"You're up," one of the smokers said, a lanky man with receding dark hair. "How are you feeling?"

"Like I got kicked in the head. Which is exactly what happened."

"A cop?"

"Yeah. How did I get here?"

"From the police wagon, you mean? You walked. Kinda. A couple of us had to hold you up. Not so easy with handcuffs, but the bastards wouldn't take them off until they put us in this cell. I told them maybe you needed to go to the hospital, but they said there weren't any available ambulances, so they'd let you sleep it off. But if you feel you need to see a doctor, I can holler for the guard."

"No. Don't. I'm fine." I came to a sitting position and sat for a moment with my eyes closed, fighting a spell of dizziness and wondering if what I'd just said was true, and then decided it probably was. My head still ached, but the world had stopped somersaulting around me.

"Good," the man said. "We were starting to get worried."

"I told you he was all right," said the other smoker, shorter and stouter. "Way he was mumbling in his sleep, he couldn't have been too far gone."

"I was talking in my sleep?" I asked. "What did I say?"

"Nothing any of us could understand."

An exaggerated sense of relief flooded me. As if I might have let slip some intimate secret, though what that secret might have been, I couldn't say.

"You were speaking Hungarian," the stout man said. "I recognized the language, but none of us speaks it."

"Where are we?"

"Jerusalem. There are a few dozen of us here. They took the rest to other jails. Probably worried we'll riot."

"The rest?"

They filled me in on the news, gleefully delivered to them ten minutes ago by a spiteful guard: The demonstration had ended following the arrival of reinforcements that included army units. None of the demonstrators had made it inside the Knesset. Hundreds had been arrested.

"How many wounded?" I asked.

The lanky man scowled. "Also hundreds, I'd say. A good many of them cops."

He said this with bitter pride in his voice, and two of the others echoed it. I said nothing. Before my eyes hovered the battered face of the cop I'd tried to help. I wondered how he was doing.

"Any dead?"

"Probably not," the lanky man said. He no longer sounded proud, just surly and glum. "They would have told us, I think."

I let out a breath. Lines had been crossed that day, by both sides, but at least no one had been killed.

Testing my legs, I walked to the back of the cell where there was a tiny sink and a toilet. My legs were a bit rubbery, but they managed to bear my weight. I unzipped my trousers and grimaced as I filled the toilet bowl with red. Blood in my urine, and plenty of it. I hoped my kidney hadn't suffered any lasting damage.

At the sink, I gulped several mouthfuls of tepid water and splashed my face and hair. The wound on my head stung like a fire, but I doused it over and over, trying to clean it as best I could. There wasn't a mirror, so I couldn't see how I looked. Judging by how wretched I felt, that was probably for the best.

I studied my hands. One fingernail was partially torn, and the knuckles on both hands were heavily bruised and aching. I shut my eyes, took a deep breath, and tried to conjure up the faces of the men I had punched. No face appeared. The fog of battle had blotted them from my mind. I supposed that, just like not being able to see my own face, that was also a blessing.

Feeling a little better, I returned to the cot. The lanky man lit a fresh cigarette, which made me crave one of my own, but a search of my pockets yielded nothing. The pack I'd been carrying—an almost full one—was gone. Even worse, so was my wallet.

I looked on, under, and around the cot. Nothing but bare mattress and dirty floor.

"What is it?" the lanky man asked, and grunted when I told him. "Probably lost them during the skirmish."

That seemed improbable. The cigarettes and wallet were in separate pockets. One of them might have fallen out. But both?

All four of my cellmates swore they had not seen my lost possessions. "We were here together the whole time," the stout man said. "If any of us had tried to steal from you, the others would have seen him."

Which left another possibility. But not one I could do anything about.

The lanky man offered me a cigarette and lit it for me. Then I and the others exchanged names and places of birth and residence. The two smokers had been born in Poland. A third man in Slovakia. The fourth in Estonia. All but the Estonian had come to the Land of Israel before the war. Following the German invasion of the Soviet Union in 1941, the Estonian had joined the partisans and endured four years of harsh fighting. All four had lost most if not all of their families in the Holocaust. Just like I had.

They hailed from all corners of Israel. From Rehovot in the south to Nahariya in the north. The one from Slovakia lived in a kibbutz in the Negev. Another a stone's throw away in Jerusalem.

"I can't believe they would do this," the kibbutznik said, and made it clear that by *they* he meant the government when he cursed Ben-Gurion and a few of the ministers by name.

"What did you expect?" the lanky man said. "Ben-Gurion has always tried to curry favor with the gentiles. Been doing it for years. That's why he called us terrorists when we fought against the British."

"You were in the Irgun?" I asked him.

"Lehi. We and the Irgun drove the British out of here, you know. With very little help from Hagannah and Ben-Gurion. He always thought that by being nice and docile, the gentiles would simply bequeath us a country. It's not surprising he would be willing to take money from Germany. The man has no morals."

"We won't be getting any money," the man from Rehovot said. "The Germans will never pay, no matter what promises they make. Just like they did after the previous war. Ben-Gurion is a fool."

The Rehovot man had been in the Irgun, and he and the lanky man began exchanging stories of ever greater daring from their days of resistance to the British, stories that seemed to grow ever more fantastical with the passing minutes.

They ran out of wild tales after a while, and the conversation returned to the matter of Ben-Gurion's perfidiousness. But it didn't last long. Guards came and removed the two Poles and the Slovakian to another cell. I and the Estonian stayed. His Hebrew was bad, and he was not the talkative type anyway. We were spared the awkward-ness of silence when a guard shouted, "Lights out!" and we settled in our cots to sleep.

3

A little before noon the next day, a guard escorted me to a stuffy interrogation room with depressing gray walls and no windows.

"Wait here," he said, depositing me in a wooden chair before a metal table. On the other side stood another chair, this one slightly taller. Maybe it was an interrogation trick, designed to make the suspect feel smaller than the interrogator. Or maybe the police, low on budget like Israel in general, used whatever furniture it could lay its hands on.

I did not have to wait too long. Twenty, twenty-five minutes at the outside. Then the door opened, and inside strode a police inspector trailing the scent of cologne.

He was medium height and trim, with close-cropped rigid black hair that had started thinning, making the top of his head look like an overburdened pincushion. He had an austere face: narrow, with a humorless mouth and a nose like a dagger blade. His uniform had been meticulously pressed, the crease in his trousers as sharp as his nose. A no-nonsense expression molded his features into a disciplinarian cast. He sat in the other chair and did not waste time on pleasantries.

"I'm Inspector Kulaski. You're Adam Lapid?"

He didn't look at me when he said this. Rather, his eyes were directed at the wallet he'd placed on the table. My wallet. The one I'd noticed was missing the previous night. The one I'd guessed was in the hands of the police. The one from which he now extracted my identification papers. He glanced at them as though seeing them for the first time, then flicked his eyes at my face. They were knowing eyes, the sort some interrogators learn to cultivate. The kind of eyes guilty men wilt before.

"Yes," I said. "That's me."

"Your address?"

I told him, and he jotted it down in a small notebook and set his pen beside it. I noticed that the inspector's nails were clipped very short.

"You know why you're here?" he asked.

"In this room?"

"In this jail."

"I took part in the anti-reparations demonstration yesterday."

"That's not the reason. Thousands of citizens took part in that demonstration. Nearly all of them spent the night at home. You're here because you assaulted a police officer. You broke his nose and knocked him unconscious. He had to be hospitalized."

"I was trying to help him."

He arched a thin eyebrow. "You thought his teeth were crooked and were trying to straighten them for him? You knocked three of them out, you know."

"That wasn't me," I said, and told him about the man who had punched the fallen policeman and how I had made him stop.

Kulaski's lips twitched in the weary amusement of a man who had heard it all before. "That's a nice story. Only it doesn't fit the facts. Another officer saw you in the act."

"Is he the cop who kicked me in the head?"

"He's the one who arrested you. How he did it is immaterial."

"He made a mistake."

"He saw you with his own eyes."

"The wounded cop was lying on the ground, bleeding. I crouched

16

next to him to see what his condition was. The policeman who arrested me must have thought I was the one who hit his colleague."

Kulaski gave me a look that suggested he was actually considering my version of events. After a moment, he said, "But that wasn't you, you say. You actually scared that guy away, didn't you? You saved that policeman from greater harm." The inspector's tone was studiously neutral. He was good. A worthy interrogator knows that sometimes you need to show the suspect that you might end up buying his story. It will loosen his lips and likely lead him to incriminate himself further.

"That's right," I said.

Kulaski picked up his pen and held it poised over his notebook. More acting. "You can describe the assailant, then?"

"Can't the wounded policeman describe him?"

"His memory is a bit hazy, what with being hit numerous times in the head. So, can you describe the assailant or not?"

I could. In detail, in fact. A sketch artist would have been able to paint an accurate portrait of him based on my recollection. Accurate enough that the man would be easily identifiable and at high risk of being brought up on serious charges.

"No," I said. "I'm afraid not." For I did not wish for that man to be tried and imprisoned. In all likelihood, he was a good man. A regular citizen driven mad by memories of his dead loved ones and his deep shock at the possibility of negotiations with Germany. Just like I had been.

Kulaski leaned back, tilting his head a tick to the left. He regarded me with what looked like genuine puzzlement. I knew well the reason for it. I had surprised him. He had expected me to deliver a made-up description of a nonexistent assailant. To attempt to send the police on a wild-goose chase. He would have written everything down, pretending to believe me and encouraging me to be as specific as possible. Then he would have questioned me repeatedly on my description until I had stumbled, forgotten what lies I had told him and uttered some inconsistency. Once I did, he would have used that slip to hammer me as a liar, make me see the futility of further denial, and extract a confession out of me. Not that he needed one with a policeman bearing witness to my guilt, but nothing beat a confession.

I knew what he planned on doing. I had used the same technique myself when I'd worked as a police detective in Hungary before the war. Before the world went mad and my life was upended and scraped hollow.

Recovering from his surprise, Kulaski lowered his eyes to his notebook before raising them back to me.

"Things will go easier for you, Adam, if you tell me the truth." His voice was as soft as a petal now, and he used my first name. Adopting a friendlier, more intimate attitude, inviting confidence. Another technique I had used to great effect.

"That's what I've been doing, Inspector."

He shook his head as though saddened by my obstinacy. Then his face hardened again.

"You know the penalty for assaulting a police officer?"

I shook my head.

"You're looking at more than ten years in prison. Hard time."

"I didn't do it."

"So you keep saying. But my witness says otherwise."

"Ask him if he actually saw me hit his colleague, or if he just assumed I did."

Kulaski pressed his lips. A trio of small lines curlicued at the center of his forehead. I was proving to be a harder nut to crack than he had anticipated.

Then it was his turn to surprise me: "Mr. Lapid, are you a member of Herut?"

"Why? Is that a crime?"

"It soon might be."

"What do you mean?"

"Word is that the government is about to outlaw Herut following their attempted putsch yesterday."

"That wasn't a putsch," I said, my heat rising.

"No? What would you call it?"

"We simply wanted members of the Knesset to know how we felt before they voted."

"By throwing rocks? Smashing windows? Trying to break into the Knesset? By injuring cops?"

I fumbled for the right words, thrown off balance by the shift in the conversation. Because what had happened yesterday had rattled me just as much as it had those members of Knesset who had stepped out of Frumin House to gawk at the fighting.

Kulaski, sensing my discomfort, pressed his advantage. "What would you have done if you'd made it past the courageous cops who stood in your way, huh? Would you have burned down the Knesset, beaten the ministers, killed them?"

"No." My voice was shaking. I cleared my throat and repeated more firmly, "No."

But did I know this with certainty? I was sure I wouldn't have done any of those things, but could I say as much about the others? Could their grief and outrage have driven them to such acts? The very notion seemed outlandish, but things that had been unimaginable until recently were now a grim reality. A day ago, I would have scoffed at the idea that ordinary Israeli citizens, with me among them, would storm the Knesset and do battle with police officers. A few weeks ago, I would have reacted similarly to any suggestion that the Israeli government—my government—would contemplate negotiating with Germany over reparations.

But both these things had happened. So who could say what else might have occurred?

"Adam," Kulaski said, drawing my attention back to him. His tone was soft once more. "I can tell that you didn't plan to do what you did yesterday. I can see it in your eyes. It happened in the heat of the moment, didn't it? Any judge will understand that and take it into account. But you must tell the truth first. Otherwise, things will go very badly for you, and I'd hate to see that happen."

I looked at him. At his slate-gray eyes now slightly rounded in feigned concern. Yes, he was good. But he didn't quite manage to mask the contempt he held me in.

I thought of revealing that I'd once been a policeman myself, but I doubted it would yield any benefit. I also weighed the option of giving him the name of Reuben Tzanani, my longtime friend, who was a policeman in Tel Aviv, or the names of other cops with whom I'd come into contact since my arrival in Israel, but I didn't think it would do much good. Reuben would vouch for my character, but he was too low ranked for his opinion to carry much weight. As for the others... well, they might not find the notion of my striking a policeman in a fit of rage as far-fetched as I would have liked to believe.

"Just come clean, Adam," Kulaski said, leaning halfway across the table, his hands wide apart and turned up in a show of friendliness and openness. "Get it off your chest. You'll feel better, I promise. Be honest, and things will go easy for you. Just tell the truth, and you'll probably get probation."

I almost smiled. This was another trick. Designed to get me to confess. Done right to a credulous suspect, it was remarkably effective. I wondered how many innocent men got sent up because they fell for it, thinking they found an ally in their interrogator and deciding it would be easier to simply go along with his suggestion, not knowing they were setting themselves up for a hard fall.

"I'm not about to confess to something I didn't do," I said. "Yes, I protested yesterday, and I'm proud of it. It was the right thing to do. But I did not throw rocks at the Knesset, and I did not strike that policeman. I did my best to help him."

Kulaski shook his head and sighed, and it seemed he wasn't acting this time. He genuinely regretted my refusal to confess, though this was likely due to selfish considerations rather than concern for my welfare. No policeman likes working harder than he has to.

He shed all pretense then, his expression once more that of a drill sergeant. He planted an elbow on the table, pointing a finger at the center of my face. His voice was as tough and abrasive as rough stone. "You think you'll be able to get away with this? Weasel out somehow? Let me tell you something: You haven't got a prayer. No judge will believe your nonsense. You'll be locked up for years."

He didn't say these words so much as hurl them at me; and with them, spittle sprayed from his lips. A few drops landed on the table between us like the first explorative salvos of an artillery bombardment. A few more clung to his lips, though he didn't seem to notice. I thought I recognized the cause of his anger. Cops are a close-knit bunch. They stick by one another. Hurt a regular citizen, and you'll likely find yourself in some trouble. Hurt a cop, and you're inviting the fires of hell upon yourself.

"I didn't do it," I said. "Just talk to the arresting officer, will you? Ask him specifically what he saw. He'll tell you he never saw me hit that fallen cop."

I hoped that would be the end of it, at least for the time being. Kulaski would rise from his chair and go talk to the cop who arrested me, and I would be in the clear. At least for this particular offense.

But Kulaski didn't rise. He stayed in his chair and sneered at me. "I don't need to talk to him again, you idiot. I already have his written statement. You think he'll change it for you? After what you did? You were there. You took part in that attack on cops. And judging by your hands, you hit quite a few of them."

My knuckles. He was pointing at my bruised knuckles. Reflexively, I pulled my hands back and under the table. As guilty a gesture as I could have made.

"So I don't give one sliver of a damn if you're the one who punched that specific policeman," he said, his eyes blazing with fury. "It makes no difference to me. You're guilty one way or the other. You and all the rest of that rabble. If I could, I'd dump the lot of you in the darkest, dankest cell I could find and throw away the key. The others might get off easy, but I'm going to make sure you don't. You get it now?"

For a few seconds, I couldn't speak. I'd known I was in trouble the moment I woke up in the cell, but I hadn't imagined it would be as serious as this. Kulaski was right. The chances that the cop who arrested me would change his story on my behalf were minuscule, even if his memory supported my claims. Because cops have no mercy for someone who harms a fellow officer. I knew that from personal experience.

So yes, I got it then. I got it like a mallet blow to the back of the head. And I felt a cold stab of fear at the center of my stomach, digging and twisting deep inside me.

"So you got two choices," Kulaski said. "You sign a confession right now and save us all a lot of time and effort, and I won't ask the judge to give you the maximum sentence. Or you can keep on being stupid and stubborn, and I'll make sure you go away for as long as the law allows. And I'll pile on whatever additional charges I can. You'll be a grandfather by the time you get out."

"I don't have children," I mumbled, not really thinking about what I was saying.

"Good. So no one will visit you in prison."

I looked at him then. At his fevered cheeks and ferocious eyes. At his taut jaw and compressed mouth. And I knew that he meant every word. That he would see his threat through. This was more than professional ardor on his part. This was personal to him.

My mouth went bone dry, and my lips felt chapped. Panicked thoughts bounced inside my head, making it hard to construct a proper reply.

Sign the confession, a small, defeated, yet enticing voice inside my brain whispered. *Just sign it, or you're as good as dead.*

I tried to ignore it, but it kept on whispering like a thousand snakes, injecting venom into my mind.

Under my sleeve, my number tattoo began to itch. I didn't dare scratch it because my hands had started to tremble, and I didn't want Kulaski to see that. I dug my fingers into my thighs, but that didn't stop the tremors.

The idea of being locked up for years, of becoming a prisoner again, terrified me. Whatever prison they'd put me in would be a picnic compared to Auschwitz, but I would still be deprived of my freedom. I would still spend my days behind fences and barbed wire and have guards order me about. My heart stammered in my chest at the prospect.

Kulaski, with long years of experience, chose that moment to produce a folded piece of paper from his pocket, spread it on the table, and held out his pen.

"Sign it!" he said, with almost obscene satisfaction.

The paper had my name on it. Along with a bunch of other words. I didn't bother reading it all. I knew what it was. A confession. Already typed. All that was missing was my signature.

I took the pen. I lowered my eyes to the paper. At the bottom was an empty space. Waiting just for me. A simple flourish of my hand and it would be done. Like a man with a noose around his neck kicking away the chair on which he stands.

For a moment I didn't move. Then I raised my eyes, looked squarely at Inspector Kulaski, and hurled the pen as hard as I could to my right.

It bounced against the wall, dropped to the floor, and rolled a couple of times. When it stopped, so, it seemed, did everything else. All movement, and all sound too. Neither Kulaski nor I shifted or even twitched. We simply stared at each other, eyes fixed as though with rivets, like two cowboys about to draw their guns and fire. The air in the interrogation room seemed to gain substance and weight with our silence. It pressed against me like damp clothes.

I was the one who broke the silence. "I'm not signing anything you give me. Don't bother trying to persuade me." I spoke with calm assurance, but it was a false front. I knew well the gloomy nature of my predicament. I was in a deep pit with slick walls and no toeholds, and I had no idea how I'd be able to climb out. Not with Kulaski standing above me, ready to shove me back down.

Kulaski shrugged, refolded the unsigned confession, tucked it in his pocket, and tapped the table with his hand. Then he smiled. A smile of wolfish anticipation. An eagerness for revenge. "Fine. We'll do it the hard way. I'm going to relish seeing you get the maximum sentence. And after the sentencing, I'll make sure they put you in the worst place possible."

"Cut it with the games," I said, still terrified but also angry and tired of his crap. My hands had stopped trembling and instead were now clamped into tight fists. "We both know you'd have done it anyway. You're a cruel son of a bitch, aren't you?"

Kulaski looked on the verge of exploding. He jerked his mouth open to reply, but a knock on the door forestalled him. "What is it?" he barked.

The door swung open, and a police officer stuck his head in. "Sorry to disturb you, Inspector, but there's a telephone call for you."

"Tell whoever it is I'll call them back."

"It's the deputy commissioner."

Kulaski frowned. He tapped the table again and stood, needlessly smoothing the front of his shirt. "I'll be back shortly," he told me. And to the officer: "Stay here. And don't talk to him."

He was gone no more than five minutes. When he returned, he brusquely ordered the officer to return to his post. Then he went to his chair, sat in it, and wouldn't meet my eyes. When he finally did, he said nothing for a long while, and his expression kept twitching, making it difficult to guess his emotions.

"Who are you really?"

"I'm Adam Lapid," I said, baffled by the question and the change in Kulaski's demeanor.

"I'm not talking about your name. I'm talking about who you know." He said it like an accusation.

I had no idea what he was talking about and said as much.

His slitted eyes made it clear he did not believe me. The corners of his mouth were pulled down at a resentful angle. He delivered his next words with obvious effort, as though every single one of them pained him. "It's your lucky day, it seems. You're free to go."

I didn't move, unsure if I'd heard him correctly. Was this another one of his tricks? Some devious ploy he'd orchestrated with the other officer? Had there really been a phone call? And why would the officer lie about the deputy commissioner being on the line?

Kulaski shouted, "Are you deaf? I told you you're free to go. So go on, get the hell out of here!"

Still uncertain, I pushed my chair back and stood. I paused for a second before reaching for my ID and wallet, thinking that this was the moment in which he'd pull the rug from under my feet and laugh in my face.

But he didn't. He stayed quiet as I picked up my papers and returned them to my wallet. Then I checked the money compartment. Six liras. Less than what I'd had the prior evening.

I said, "The officer who arrested me, did he give you your cut?"

"What cut?"

"Ten liras are missing from my wallet. Don't tell me you didn't get any."

His jaw tightened. "You'd better watch it, understand?" The threat had plenty of bark but no bite. For some mysterious reason, I was inviolate. At least for the time being. It gave me a frisson of satisfaction varnished with a delicious dash of juvenile recklessness.

Putting the wallet back in my pocket, I said, "I hope he threw some cigarettes your way, at least. The pack he took off me was more than half full."

Then I turned and went to the door. The cool handle was in my grip when he said, "This isn't over, Lapid. You mark my words."

I could tell by his face that he meant it as much as a man could mean anything. If the opportunity to harm me came his way, he would grab it with both hands. A trace of the fear I'd felt before wormed its way through my intestines. I did my best not to show it.

"So long, Inspector. It was an absolute joy talking to you."

And with that, I opened the door and stepped out of the room, leaving him alone with his unquenched thirst for my destruction.

4

Within ten minutes, I was at the gate. As I waited for the guards to open it, I gazed up the wall with its barbed-wire topping and beyond it at the dreary winter sky, and I wondered again how I came to be standing there, a few seconds from freedom.

I no longer believed this was a ruse. There had been a telephone call, and it had been the deputy commissioner on the line. But why would he telephone anyone about me? And why would I be let loose? I'd never met the man, didn't even know his name. I doubted he knew mine.

A biting wind tore at me as the gate swung open. I stuck my hands into my pockets but didn't duck my chin into my collar. I was walking out of this jail with my head held high.

I didn't look back as I stepped over the threshold between incarceration and liberty. I had no sense whether I was being watched. Maybe Kulaski's eyes were trained on my back like a sniper's sight. Or maybe he was inside the building, seething and fantasizing about locking me up.

Outside, I paused for a moment, unsure of where to go. I was unfamiliar with this part of Jerusalem. Then a car horn honked, and I turned in its direction in time to see the door of a blue Morris Eight swing open and a man climb out of it.

He was bald with a fringe of light-brown hair. His eyes were also light brown and shielded by a pair of horn-rimmed glasses. His face was round and pudgy and sprinkled with freckles. I had nearly busted his jaw three years before and had never regretted it. Neither of us had forgotten the incident or forgiven each other's role in it. But that didn't mean we hated each other.

"Hello, Shmuel," I said.

"Good day, Adam." Shmuel Birnbaum wasn't smiling. His cheeks were tinged red by the cold. Further chill seemed to emanate off him in my direction. "I trust you had a pleasant night."

"I've had worse."

He expelled a low grunt. "Get in. Let's get out of here."

As he started the car, I asked, "Do you have any cigarettes?"

"No." His tone was flat, and he clipped the end of the word as if with a hatchet.

We drove for a few minutes in uncomfortable silence. He seemed to know the way. His work as a columnist for the newspaper *Davar* must have involved frequent visits to Jerusalem.

"What are you doing here, Shmuel?" I asked when he stopped to let a quintet of rowdy boys cross the street.

"I came to spring you out of jail. Though I'm far from sure you deserve to be sprung. I heard what you did to that policeman."

"That wasn't me. It just looked that way." I explained what had happened.

"Is that the truth, Adam?"

"Yes. I swear it."

His lips twitched into what might have become a half-smile if he hadn't killed it in its infancy. "Do you know how many people have sworn to me over the years and how many of them were lying through their teeth?"

"Dozens, hundreds—I don't know. It's part of the job, isn't it? Yours as well as mine."

"I haven't counted, but it just might be that the majority of those who swore most fervently were being dishonest."

"Then count me among the virtuous minority. I'm not lying to you, Shmuel. I did not put that cop in the hospital."

"But you did take part in the assault on the Knesset. You struck other cops?"

I didn't answer, just looked through the side window at shopfronts whizzing by.

"Have you lost your mind, Adam? How could you?"

I spun around to face him, incensed by his tone and words. "You dare ask me that? After what you've been writing these past few weeks? All the columns praising the government and ridiculing all those opposed to negotiations with Germany?"

"I haven't ridiculed anyone."

"Yes, you have, Shmuel. And quite sharply, too. As though their moral position has no merit whatsoever."

"I never belittled the ideological stance of those opposed, just some of the arguments they present. Such as saying that we're legitimizing Germany as a country by agreeing to negotiate with it."

"We are," I said.

He shook his head. "If only we were so powerful. In truth, we are a tiny, weak, inconsequential country. Our tradition may say that Jerusalem lies at the center of the world, but that's hardly the case today. Not in the realm of global politics, in the struggle between East and West. You know what does lie at the center of that struggle, Adam?"

"I have a feeling you're about to tell me."

"It's Germany. A quick glance at a map of Europe can tell you that. That's where the line between the Russians and the Americans stretches. The Americans and their allies want West Germany on their side, to serve as a bulwark against the Soviets. To do that they first have to allow Germany back into the family of nations. This will happen regardless of what Israel says. In fact, it's a process that's already underway."

"But it will speed things up if Israel makes a deal with Germany, right?"

"Perhaps. But not by all that much."

"Are the Americans pressuring Israel to negotiate with Germany? Is that why the government is doing this?"

"Whatever gave you that bizarre idea?"

"Some say Ben-Gurion always tries to curry favor with the great powers. Before 1948, that was Britain; now, it's America."

"If that were true, Ben-Gurion wouldn't have made Jerusalem the capital of Israel in the face of worldwide opposition. Jerusalem was supposed to be an international city, remember? Not a part of Israel at all. But Ben-Gurion decided otherwise and moved the seat of our government to Jerusalem. If he hadn't, your little riot yesterday would have taken place in Tel Aviv."

A policeman was directing traffic on Jaffa Street. Birnbaum stopped as instructed. The car engine throbbed and rumbled. The wind whisked a newspaper across the hood and away. The heavens uncorked, and rain spattered the windshield. Birnbaum started the wipers. The policeman waved us forward.

Birnbaum said, "Let's see, what else does our loyal opposition say? Ah yes, that West Germany is full to the brim with Nazis, while East Germany has been utterly de-Nazified. Now they're all wonderful communists, not a Jew-hater in the bunch. They would be happy to assist us financially if only we came to our senses and stopped supporting the imperialists. Of course, East Germany has never shown the slightest willingness to acknowledge, let alone pay for, Germany's crimes against the Jewish people; only West Germany has."

· "The communists differentiate between West and East Germany, not Begin."

"You're right; he doesn't. Begin believes every German is a Nazi, every German is a murderer. He said as much in his speech yesterday, didn't he? The bloody *meshuggeneh*."

"I thought you admired him," I said.

Birnbaum shot me a stern look. His newspaper, *Davar,* was the unofficial party newspaper of Mapai, Ben-Gurion's party. Expressing even mild approbation of Menachem Begin was likely to cause him serious problems with his employer.

"You know my views well, Adam," he said. "Begin and the Irgun fought bravely against the British. He's perfectly suited to lead a resistance group. But as a politician, as a statesman"—he let out a laugh —"that would be a joke. No, I take that back—it would be a tragedy. You know what Begin's problem is? He's drunk on his own rhetoric, a victim of his own pathos. But he was smart enough not to personally participate in the march on the Knesset. While you and the rest of his disciples were outside bashing policemen's heads in, he was safely inside the Knesset, delivering his most outrageous speech to date, calling Ben-Gurion a hooligan, a murderer, a fascist. Tell me, Adam, do you believe Ben-Gurion is a murderer and a fascist?"

"I don't know what I think of Ben-Gurion anymore."

"And do you believe every German is a Nazi? Every single one of them?"

"I know that there are former Nazis in the West German government, some holding high offices. I know that millions of Germans served in the Wehrmacht and the SS, and millions more supported them. Do you think they suddenly had a change of heart, that they stopped hating Jews a mere seven years after trying to exterminate us?"

Now it was Birnbaum's turn to stare out the window and not utter a sound. A few minutes later, we exited Jerusalem and were on the road to Tel Aviv. The Jordanians controlled a section of the road near the fort of Latrun, where several frontal assaults by the Israeli Defense Forces during the War of Independence had ended in calamity. Therefore, one needed to take a circuitous route to get from Jerusalem to Tel Aviv, making the trip long and arduous.

"How do you think the world will view us taking compensation from Germany for all the dead millions?" I asked while Birnbaum maneuvered the Ford around a horse-drawn wagon that was trundling down the mountain road.

"It's not compensation; they're reparations."

"Don't split hairs. You know what the Germans are calling it? The *Wiedergutmachung*. You know what it means, literally? To make good again. You understand? The way the Germans see it, by paying us, they're expunging their guilt, wiping the slate clean. You're granting them absolution for the murder of six million Jews!"

Birnbaum snapped his head toward me. I had never seen him so livid. Not even when I had punched him in the jaw. In my peripheral vision, I saw a massive dark shape rushing toward the windshield.

"Watch it, Shmuel!" I shouted, and he slammed on the brakes, sending the car into a skid, our front bumper barely missing the rear of a truck.

The tires scrabbled for purchase on the wet road, and the car felt weightless beneath me. I was sure we were going to flip over. The car veered closer to the lip of the road. Beyond it gaped the craggy maw of the mountainside, its teeth made of sharp rocks and gnarled trees, plunging down into a deep and deadly gullet.

Birnbaum wrestled with the wheel, a shrill yelp piping from deep in his chest. As the drop filled the windshield like a panorama of death, he jammed on the brakes again. The car lurched, bucked, stalled. The front wheels no more than a revolution or two before the road gave way to nothingness.

We sat mute for several long moments, both huffing as though surprised to still be drawing air. My heart was doing a wild, drunken dance. A delirious, crazed dance of life.

I glanced at Birnbaum. His mouth hung open, and his chest heaved. His hands gripped the wheel so tightly his knuckles shone through his skin.

"You okay, Shmuel?"

He blinked, closed his mouth, and let go of the wheel as though it were a live wire. Then he faced me again, and his expression was so fierce that I instinctively edged backward.

"Don't you ever—and I do mean ever—suggest that I'm absolving the Germans for what they did to our people." His voice wasn't raised, which somehow amplified the indignation in every word he shot at me. "Do you think that because you were there and I wasn't, because I only lost cousins and uncles and not siblings and children like you did, that I'm not outraged by what the Nazis did? That I'm prepared to forgive them for money? Is that who you think I am?"

"That's how the Germans see it," I said.

"We can't control what they do or what lies they tell themselves. But rest assured, none of us is ready to forgive them. Not Ben-Gurion or any of the ministers, and not me either. And if the Germans think they'll be able to buy our forgiveness, they're deluding themselves. We'll never forgive them for what they did, and we'll never forget it. And we won't let them, or the world, forget it either."

"It's wrong, Shmuel. It's setting a price on the dead. It's doing deals with murderers."

"Would it be better to let the Germans keep everything? All the property they stole? For the murderers to also be the inheritors? And what of the survivors? You know how many of them live here in Israel? How many of them are hurt physically and mentally? Shouldn't the Germans bear some of the cost of treating them? Of helping them rebuild their lives?"

"Some of the cost, but not all, right? There's no way the Germans will agree to pay what they should. Even if we put aside the six million they murdered, for whom there is no price."

"You're right; they won't. I doubt it will even come close. But it will be more than nothing, which is what we'll get if Begin has his way."

"How much is it going to be, do you know? Rumor says the government is willing to settle for three hundred million dollars. With six million dead Jews, that comes to fifty dollars a head. Quite a bargain for the Nazis, isn't it?"

"That's what the negotiations are for. But Israel will demand much more than that."

"That's good to know. I wouldn't like to think our government values Jewish life so cheaply."

Birnbaum didn't rise to the bait, though I could tell it took an effort for him to maintain his cool.

I raked a hand through my hair. All this talk about money had left the taste of death in my mouth. I couldn't believe this was reality and not a demented nightmare. And God, how I wanted a cigarette!

I said, "Why is the government so adamant on doing this now?"

Birnbaum didn't answer right away. He looked straight ahead and chewed on his lip, evidently mulling his reply. When he turned my way again, the anger was gone from his face. He looked exhausted and worried.

"I'll tell you why, Adam, but you must swear not to repeat it to anyone. If this became public knowledge, it might cause panic."

"All right," I said. "You have my word. What is it?"

"Everyone knows Israel's economy is in a bad state. But very few people realize how dire the situation really is. Reserves of foreign currency are close to depleted. It's becoming almost impossible to secure credit because there are serious concerns that Israel will not be able to pay off its debts. To put it bluntly, we are on the brink of collapse, of not being able to provide the most basic needs of our citizens. I'm talking about clothing, heating, food."

"Things can't be that bad," I said.

"I'm afraid they are. It's just that so far the government has been able to hide the worst of it. But in a few months we'll be facing a catastrophe. And more Jews keep arriving in Israel, most of them with nothing. Some in the government have suggested halting or limiting immigration, but Ben-Gurion won't hear of it. He says that Israel is the home of any Jew who wishes to come here, no matter how poor, old, or sick. In short, Adam, Israel has no choice. We need these reparations, and we can't get them without talking to the Germans directly. The government appealed to the Americans to act as intermediaries, but they refused."

I glared at Birnbaum. "Funny how none of this came to light six months ago when we had an election. Of course, the government also kept secret the fact that they were talking to the Germans. Ben-Gurion wouldn't be prime minister if it was known at the time."

"You can be as cynical as you like, Adam, but Ben-Gurion has always had Israel's best interests at heart. If it became known how terrible things are, the Arabs might decide to renew the war. And then where would we be?"

"You've known all this for a while, haven't you?"

Birnbaum hesitated, then nodded.

"Yet you didn't report it in your column."

"It would have harmed Israel."

"And Ben-Gurion," I said. "It often seems the two are interchangeable in your mind."

Birnbaum tilted up his chin. "Sometimes I don't report news that can cause greater harm than good. You should know that better than anyone. I did it for you more than once."

He was right; he did. Though, of course, that was hardly the equivalent of covering up for the government. But I saw no point in telling him that. He knew it full well.

The rain intensified, rattling on the roof and hood. Birnbaum started the car and resumed driving down the road. He went slowly, visibility reduced to near nothingness.

For a long while, the only sounds were the rain, the hum of the engine, and the rapid swipe of the windshield wipers. Then we left the mountains and began the long flat ride across the plains toward Tel Aviv. The rain let up, and the sun pierced the cloud cover. Shafts of golden light beamed down on the countryside, giving it a fresh, wholesome sheen. Blankets of weeds and wild grass and squat thorny bushes bent and dipped in the wind. Rainwater streamed through meandering channels in rich muddy soil. Vibrant colors swayed and swirled on the horizon like a rainbow trying to piece itself together.

It was a beautiful country. A country I had bled and nearly died for. A country I loved. I wasn't sure how I'd feel about it if it took money from Germany.

I said, "How do you know they'll pay? The Germans, I mean."

"They'll pay," said Birnbaum.

"How can you be sure? Germany owed money after the First World War and never paid it. Why should it be different this time?"

"Ben-Gurion believes Konrad Adenauer, the West German chancellor, is sincere in his willingness to pay reparations."

"And if he changes his mind?"

Birnbaum threw me a look that suggested he'd gotten tired of me. "Then Begin and you and the rest of the rabble who stormed the Knesset yesterday will have the pleasure of reminding us of our mistake till the end of time."

With that, a curtain of silence descended between us. Silence and something more: an apartness, a rift, a chasm. Similar to the one that now split the part of Israel that supported the government's position from the part that opposed it.

I was surprised to realize how sad this made me. The nature of my relationship with Birnbaum was one I had never bothered to define. We weren't friends. We met or spoke rarely, and only when one of us desired something of the other. I, information related to whatever case I was working on; he, a potential story to write about in his column.

On two past cases, I had availed myself of his contacts and the bottomless reservoir of information stored within his bald head. On both occasions, I had provided him with an exciting story in return. Twice he had resisted his natural inclinations and agreed to keep my name out of the paper, though he couldn't understand my desire for anonymity.

I liked his wit and intelligence, and I respected his curiosity and relentless hunger for stories, despite being a victim of said hunger. During Operation Yoav, in the War of Independence, I had stormed an Egyptian position and taken two bullets in the process. While I lay unconscious in the hospital, Birnbaum had sneaked into my room, armed with a camera.

When I discovered that my face had adorned the pages of *Davar*, I had sought Birnbaum out and introduced his jaw to my fist. He'd thought he was doing me a service by publicizing my heroism and could not fathom my reaction. Most people would have killed to be extolled in his column.

Birnbaum could have reported me to the police. Instead, he took his beating with dignity, recognizing that he'd overstepped the mark, yet never regretting it. He considered a punch a good price to pay for a juicy story.

He also developed a keen interest in me. He'd learned that I'd been in Auschwitz and had heard rumors of what I'd done in Germany in the aftermath of the war. He tried to persuade me to tell him my story but took it in good stride when I refused.

He was a good man. Despite being dead wrong about negotiations with Germany. I wanted to bridge the gulf that now gaped between us.

"Thank you for talking to the deputy commissioner," I said, thinking that some gratitude might do the trick. "I didn't know you had that kind of pull."

"I don't," he said without taking his eyes off the road. "Not for something as serious as assaulting a police officer."

We were almost in Tel Aviv by now. The low, misaligned skyline of the first Hebrew city reached pitifully for the heavens like stubby baby fingers pursuing a fleeting dream.

"Then how come you were waiting for me outside the jail?" I asked.

"I wasn't the one who spoke with the deputy commissioner, but I am the one who got you out. I hope I won't regret it."

"I don't understand."

"An acquaintance of mine spoke with me yesterday. He asked if I could recommend a private detective. Someone trustworthy. Foolishly, I thought of you. I telephoned that café you spend so much time in, to see if you were available, but the proprietress told me you'd gone to Jerusalem for the demonstration. I telephoned again this morning, and she told me you hadn't come in, though you said you would. She was worried about you. By that time, I'd heard of the assault on the Knesset. I made some calls and learned you'd been arrested, and why. Then I made what may turn out to be one of the most ill-advised decisions of my life: I decided to help you go free."

"How?"

"My acquaintance is the one with the pull. I told him of your predicament and asked him to intercede on your behalf. It wasn't easy to persuade him. When he heard that you'd beaten a policeman, he wanted nothing to do with you. But I vouched for your character, told him he wouldn't find a better detective, and called in a favor he owed me." He gave me a glance of steaming disapproval. "You now owe me a favor, Adam. And don't you dare forget it."

"All right, I won't," I said. "But who is this man? How does he have such influence?"

"His name is Baruch Gafni. Is the name familiar to you?"

I shook my head. "Never heard of him."

Birnbaum sighed, disappointed with my ignorance. "Gafni is not only a wealthy man, with factories and businesses in various spots in Israel, he is also a council member of Tel Aviv. Some believe he has a shot at being the next mayor."

"Let me guess: he's a member of Mapai."

"Indeed he is."

"So Gafni has influence in the ruling party, and the deputy commissioner knows this. He also knows that it would be Mapai who'll pick the next commissioner, so when Gafni calls to ask a favor, the deputy commissioner goes along with it. Is that about right?"

"To your infinite fortune, yes."

"What does Gafni want with me? Why does he need a detective?"

"I'll leave it to him to tell you. But if I had to guess, I'd say it has something to do with his daughter."

"What about her?"

Birnbaum's expression was grave. "She's dead."

5

Birnbaum parked before a wide three-story building with tall windows and no balconies.

"Do try not to mess this up, Adam," he said, in the weary tone of a disillusioned father who expects very little from his son. "You're not off the hook yet. A single phone call and you're liable to find yourself back behind bars."

In the loving care of Inspector Kulaski, I thought, my insides knotting.

"I'll do my best to not fall short of your recommendation."

"Good luck, Adam," Birnbaum said with a sigh, then reached for the ignition key to start the car.

I was surprised. "Is that it? You're not going to make me swear to tell you the whole story when I'm done?"

"Not this time."

"How come?"

"I don't see any public interest in the story, whatever you may find."

"So that's it, then?"

"That's it," Birnbaum said. "This is one of Gafni's factories. He's expecting you."

Earlier, I had asked Birnbaum how Gafni's daughter had died, but he said it was up to Gafni to tell me, if indeed her death was the reason Gafni wished to meet me. I got the impression that I was about to take an audition. Only if I passed would I be given the information I'd need to carry out my assignment, whatever it might be.

I opened the door and was about to exit the car when a question came to me.

"Shmuel, is it true the government intends to outlaw Herut?"

"Why do you ask? Are you a member of Herut, Adam?"

"No."

"Good. I won't ask if you voted for them, but if you did, keep it to yourself. Don't let Gafni know."

"You haven't answered my question. Will they be outlawed?"

"There are rumors that some of the ministers are pushing for it. Ultimately, it will be Ben-Gurion's decision."

"Will he do it?"

"I hope not, but I don't know. He won't if he uses his brain, which he usually does."

"Why do you say that?"

"Because if you outlaw Herut, you turn it into an underground organization with Begin as its leader. Like I told you before, Begin is perfect for such a role. He'll be far more dangerous to Ben-Gurion and the country than if he remains a regular politician with a modicum of public support."

I nodded. Birnbaum's logic made sense, though I still worried. "I hope you're right about Ben-Gurion, Shmuel. I really do."

"I think he'll do the smart thing. Why don't you try to follow his example from now on, eh?"

I got out and closed the door without replying and waited as Birnbaum started the car and drove off. I searched my pockets for my cigarettes before remembering that they'd been pilfered by a cop with sticky fingers and a foot made of steel. I looked around for a kiosk or a store, but there was none. I considered going around the corner but decided it would be best to meet my savior and see what he wanted of me as quickly as possible.

The building had a large metal door. Heaving it open, I was hit by the ear-thumping rumble of machinery. I stepped over the threshold and into the smell of leather, oil, and cloth. Past a short vestibule was a vast hall with two rows of support columns dividing the space into roughly equal thirds. About thirty people worked there. Some were seated at sewing machines, others toiled with needle and thread, and others still were affixing buckles and zippers and testing their handiwork. They were making handbags, suitcases, valises, wallets, and other items in that vein. Along one wall were samples of finished products, all neatly arranged on tables or hanging on pegs. I was no expert, but they looked like quality products.

A thickset woman was walking among the employees, looking very much in charge. I told her Mr. Gafni was expecting me. She pointed to a staircase. "Second door on the left."

I followed her instructions, the aches and pains of yesterday's battle flaring with each step I ascended, and soon found myself before a small desk occupied by an attractive blonde secretary, somewhere in her mid-thirties. I gave her my name and purpose, and she told me to wait while she inquired whether Mr. Gafni wished to see me now or at all.

She went through a door into what I presumed was Gafni's office and returned less than a minute later with the good news: Mr. Gafni had decided to grant me an audience. I was to go right in. She did not offer me coffee or anything else. Perhaps she was busy.

I entered an office with large windows overlooking the production floor below. The windowpanes must have been thick because the noise of machinery was but a murmur. Behind a desk stood a man wearing a well-fitting gray suit and a conservative dark tie. A white handkerchief peeked neatly from his breast pocket. Mr. Gafni, I presumed.

He was on the short side and carried some extra weight. It showed in his face, which was as round as a ball, and on the underside of his chin, which drooped like a sagging floor. A small rectangular mustache did little to offset the overall softness of his features, but based on what Birnbaum had told me about him, I imagined that softness belied a sturdier core. His hair had deserted the front half of his scalp. The bare skin gleamed pink. The hair that remained was taupe and short. Deep lines gouged his forehead, lending him an air of distinguished thoughtfulness. I pegged his age at fifty, but I might have been off by three or four years either way.

He surveyed me with a pair of small eyes the color of bitter chocolate. I could tell I was making a lousy impression. Not that this was any surprise. My clothes were streaked with dirt. The collar of my shirt was torn. I hadn't shaved since yesterday morning. And based on how poorly I'd slept in recent weeks, and last night in particular, I must have looked haggard. Most likely, he was regretting his call to the deputy commissioner and wondering whether Birnbaum had lost his mind. Could the slovenly creature before him really be the resourceful detective Birnbaum had assured him I was? The role of the deranged beater of policemen suited me better.

It occurred to me that it might be worthwhile to say something to improve my negative image. Perhaps thank him for talking to the deputy commissioner? But I feared that would only make things worse.

Instead, I said, "I'm sorry about your daughter, Mr. Gafni."

His expression changed abruptly. Before, it had been critical and judgmental. Now, he looked as though he'd been gut punched. It lasted but an instant, though. Then he was eying me with undisguised suspicion.

"How do you know about my daughter?" He had a faint Eastern European accent. Russian or Lithuanian, but he'd left there a good while ago, maybe in childhood.

"I asked Shmuel Birnbaum why you wanted to see me. He speculated that it might have something to do with your daughter. He said she had passed away but wouldn't give me any details."

Gafni nodded and ran a hand over his mouth. He appeared to be trying to hold his emotions in check. Though whether it was sadness over his daughter or irritation at Birnbaum for informing me of her death, I couldn't say. He gestured to one of two chairs that stood before his desk. "Perhaps you should sit down, Mr. Lapid."

It appeared that I had passed the audition, or at least the initial part.

"Would you care for something to drink?"

I said coffee would be nice, and he called to the secretary and told her to fetch some. While we waited, both of us seated, he continued to appraise me, and it was clear he didn't know what to make of me. He didn't say one word until the secretary arrived with my coffee and left, shutting the door behind her at Gafni's request.

Gafni did not have coffee himself. I took a few sips from my cup, enjoying the warmth that spread around my midsection. The coffee wasn't real; real coffee was hard to come by in Israel and cost a pretty penny. This was the chicory variety the government rationed out. It was a poor substitute for the real thing, even when you laced it with sugar, which was also rationed, and this particular cup was no exception. If Gafni was as wealthy as Birnbaum had said, he likely possessed the real thing, unless he was one of the virtuous few who abstained from shopping on the black market. Maybe he didn't wish to waste any of the good stuff on me.

I set my cup on the desk and leaned back in my chair. "Is there anything you'd like to ask me, Mr. Gafni?"

His eyebrows twitched. "Ask you?"

"You're wondering if you can trust me. I don't blame you. Having to get a man out of jail before you even met him does not inspire confidence."

A small smile spread across his mouth. "Are you always this direct, Mr. Lapid?"

"It gets me where I'm going faster. Here's the situation as I see it: You have a certain problem, and you wish to employ a private detective to solve it for you. You don't know any detectives yourself, so you asked Birnbaum for a referral. He's written extensively about crime, so you figured he would know someone. He recommended me. So far, so good, but then you learned that I'd been arrested for beating a cop so hard he had to go to the hospital. Birnbaum persuaded you to pull some strings to get me out, and you did, which tells me your problem is painful, personal, and urgent. Otherwise, you would have searched for another detective, one who wasn't facing serious charges. How am I doing so far?"

"Go on," Gafni said, which I took to mean I was right on the money.

"Still, you can't help but worry that I'm not the right man for the job. Like I said, I don't blame you. So I thought maybe you'd like to ask me some questions that might ease your mind. But before you do, I'd like to tell you a few things: I did not put that cop in the hospital. Another demonstrator did that. But I did take part in the demonstration yesterday in Jerusalem, and I did fight with cops outside the Knesset. I'm not proud of the latter, but I am of the former. I think it's wrong for Israel to negotiate with Germany. I think it would be wrong to take money from it. I suppose you feel differently."

"You're damn right I do. Israel could use these reparations. There's no good reason not to take them."

The last thing I wanted was a repeat of my argument with Birnbaum. I dug my fingernails into my palms and said, "So we know where each of us stands on this issue. Now, do you have any questions for me?"

"I do," he said. "First question: Do you support the Herut party?"

"That's none of your business."

He blinked. "I thought you were trying to set my mind at ease."

"I am, but I don't approve of politics-based hiring. That's how they do things in dictatorships, like Nazi Germany."

A flush invaded his cheeks. "You're getting dangerously close to being thrown out of this office and back into a jail cell, Mr. Lapid."

I took a breath, berated myself for my childishness, and said, "I apologize, Mr. Gafni. I was out of line. I appreciate your concerns. You're an official of Mapai. You're worried that if I learn anything embarrassing about you or your family, I'd share this information with members of Herut. You have my word that won't happen."

"I noticed you haven't answered my question."

"That's right. And I'm not going to."

"Are you always this stubborn?"

"More often than not. It's part of why I'm good at my job."

"So I'm simply supposed to trust you, is that it?"

"You're going to have to trust somebody. It might as well be me."

Gafni scrutinized my face for a long moment. Then he burst out laughing. It was a short laugh, born more out of surprise than humor.

"You're strange, you know that? Any other man would have just said 'No, Mr. Gafni, sir, I don't support those dirty fascists of Herut. I voted Mapai, and all my family too.' But you're different. You have principles and you stick to them, even when you may pay dearly for doing so. I respect that."

I didn't feel worthy of praise. Mostly, I felt stupid for not lying through my teeth. My head throbbed where the policeman had kicked me. I might have been thickheaded, but evidently not enough.

"Any other questions?" I asked.

Gafni rubbed the sides of his chin with thumb and forefinger. He looked contemplative and sad. "Do you have any children, Mr. Lapid?"

I shook my head.

"But you did, didn't you? I can see it in your face."

This wasn't a subject I wanted to talk about. Not with him, not with anyone. But I said, "I had two daughters. Both died in the war in Europe."

"I'm sorry to hear that," he said.

His commiseration made me uncomfortable. As if I was being forced to share something private and painful, to expose a part of me that was raw and vulnerable and bleeding. Yet, hadn't I, mere minutes ago, expressed my own condolences for his loss?

Perhaps Gafni sensed my emotional state, for he did not wait for a reply. He settled his forearms on the edge of the desk and intertwined his fingers. He looked determined and certain—a man who had made up his mind.

"I don't need to ask you anything else, Mr. Lapid. I want you to do a job for me."

6

"Her name was Moria," Gafni said. "She was twenty-three years old. A little over a month ago—on December 6—she was found dead in her apartment in Jerusalem."

"How did she die?" I asked.

"Pills. She took pills."

"Suicide?"

"According to the pathologist, she swallowed more than twice the amount it would have taken to kill a woman of her size. Moria was never one for half measures. It was one of the only things in which she took after me."

He said that last bit with a crooked little smile on his mouth, but his tone was that of hopeless regret.

"And you believe the suicide was staged? That Moria was murdered?"

"What? No. Why would I think that?" Gafni looked as though I'd suggested cats were capable of flight. "There was no sign of violence or a struggle. The police did not hesitate in ruling it a suicide. Here, I have a copy of their report. You can read it yourself."

The report was three pages long. It stated that Moria Gafni had been found dead in her apartment at three thirty on the afternoon of December 6, 1951, and that she had died around noon of the same day. Empty pill bottles were found by her bed. The pills had come from the hospital where Moria Gafni had worked. The police found a suicide note next to the pillow, written in the dead woman's hand, though for some reason, the message therein had not been recorded. The woman who discovered the body stated that the door to the apartment had been locked when she arrived. There was no sign of any disturbance inside. No hint of violence. A clear-cut suicide.

I put the report on the desk. "If you don't suspect foul play, why do you need a detective?"

Instead of replying, Gafni reached into his inside jacket pocket. His hand came out holding a folded piece of paper. "This is the note Moria left."

I unfolded the paper and read the message written across it in black ink. "Are you sure this is Moria's handwriting?"

"Yes. I recognized it instantly."

It was possible someone had coerced Moria into writing this note, but my instincts doubted it. The writing was precise and neat, the product of a steady hand. This wasn't written by a woman beset by roiling emotion or under a threat more terrible than imminent death.

In addition, if the note had been written under duress, or if it had been forged, the killer would have crafted a depressed and unremarkable farewell. Something along the lines of "I can't go on anymore" or "I see no point in carrying on living." Instead, the note was decidedly cryptic and its tone aggressive rather than desolate. The killer would have wanted the note to settle all questions regarding Moria's frame of mind and her decision to end her life. But what it did was the opposite: it raised questions. And unanswered questions arouse curiosity and invite scrutiny. The exact things a murderer would least want.

I read the note again, pondering its hidden meaning. "Who is the person Moria refers to?"

"I don't know."

"What about the other bit, what she regrets doing?"

"I don't know that either. There's a whole lot I don't know. That's why you're here."

I lowered the note and looked at him. He appeared to have aged ten years in the space of a minute. Grief can do that to a man. Sometimes, it can kill him too. Often this doesn't happen all at once. Rather, the sorrow worms its way into your marrow and drains the life out of your body drop by drop until nothing is left. It was possible that Gafni was in the grip of such a process and that he sensed on some level that it was happening.

He said, "My daughter and I weren't on the best of terms. In fact, we hardly had contact with each other these past few years."

"Why?"

"That doesn't matter."

"It doesn't? You're sure about that?"

"Yes, I am," he said, stressing each word.

I dropped the matter. There are ways of making a man talk when he's not inclined to, but I was pretty certain none of them would work. And I still needed to tread carefully around Gafni.

I said, "What is it you want me to do, Mr. Gafni?"

"You read the note. What do you make of it?"

"It's deliberately vague, which is strange. Moria could have named the person, but she chose not to."

"Why do you think she did that?"

"Impossible to say. Perhaps the police can find out."

"The police don't get involved unless a crime has been committed."

"I'm sure they'll make an exception if you ask them."

"Perhaps, but I don't think that would be appropriate." He paused and cleared his throat, struck by the absurdity of his statement. I was living proof that he was quite willing to ask the police to bend the rules when it suited him. He made a vague motion with his hand. "The police have enough on their plate as it is. Protecting the Knesset, for example."

I ignored the barb, recognizing it for what it was: a reflexive jab by a man unaccustomed to being on the defensive. I had no doubt he

47

could have mustered the resources of the police to dig into his daughter's life, to, perhaps, decipher the meaning of her suicide note. The fact that he had decided not to, that he'd opted to engage a private detective instead, spoke volumes.

I looked him right in the eye and let him have it like a kick to the heart. "Maybe Moria was referring to you."

"No!" Gafni slammed a fist on his desk, making a pen jump. He shook his head resolutely, as though to emphasize his assertion. "No, I don't believe that for a second."

But he clearly did, and for quite a bit longer than a second. And the possibility, however much he wished to discount it, had been burrowing ever deeper into the nethermost regions of his mind, likely infecting his dreams and his waking thoughts as well. Perhaps that explained the heavy bags under his eyes, the haunted look within them. I could empathize. I was well acquainted with nightmares.

This was likely the reason he refused to tell me what had torn him and his daughter apart. Whatever the secret was, he couldn't rule out the possibility that it had ended up pushing his daughter to suicide. A man could go crazy doing battle with such thoughts.

"My daughter didn't kill herself because of me," Gafni said firmly. "Why would she? Last time I saw her was over three years ago."

I thought of my own daughters. How much I missed them. How their absence was a gaping wound at the center of my soul. If they were alive today, I could not imagine anything that would keep me from seeing them for three whole years. Yet Gafni, who did not strike me as a man who'd let anything stand in his way, admitted to just that.

"I did my best to improve our relationship," he said, speaking quickly and disjointedly. "I wrote to her, bought her things, helped as much as I could... I spent a lot of money, Mr. Lapid. A lot of money. More than she... The couple of times we spoke on the phone, I tried to arrange a meeting, but she wouldn't let me near. No matter how much I begged her, no matter how much I spent, she..." He paused, out of breath, a man trying vainly to cast off his mantle of guilt. "That note—I can't get it out of my head. Whenever I close my eyes, I see those three lines shining in lurid red and yellow. I need to know what that note means. I need to know why Moria wrote it. I need to know why she killed herself." His voice was rough with anger now, the raw kind an injured animal might feel. He growled the next words. "I need to know who made her do it."

"And if you know, what then? What will you do?"

He didn't answer right away. He collected himself by smoothing down his jacket lapel and lacing his fingers. "I don't know. Sometimes, most of the time, I just want to know what happened."

"And other times?"

"Other times," he said simply, "I think I'd like to kill him."

The second option was what worried me, as did the casual tone in which he'd voiced it. But at least he didn't lie to me. That made it better. It meant there was a smaller chance he'd actually go through with it. At least, that was what I told myself.

He said, "You asked me before what I want you to do. Well, now you know. I want you to find out why Moria killed herself, and I want to know the identity of the man in the note."

And if you end up killing him, I thought, *I will bear part of the blame.* Then again, if this mysterious man was responsible for the death of Moria Gafni, he deserved to be punished. He... a sudden thought hit me.

"If it's a man at all," I murmured.

"What was that?"

"I was just thinking that it might be a woman. Moria's note doesn't make it clear either way."

Gafni's brow furrowed. "I just assumed—"

"I did too. But maybe we were both wrong."

"I don't see that it matters, do you?"

His expression was neutral, as was his tone, and I felt a shiver slither its way up my spine. It was one thing to contemplate killing a man; it was quite another to do the same to a woman. At least, it was that way to me. If Gafni was of a different persuasion, he might be more inclined to violence than I wished to believe.

49

I did not relish the role of his bloodhound, but what choice did I have? If I turned Gafni down, I would likely find myself at the nonexistent mercy of Inspector Kulaski. Furthermore, as the father of dead daughters, I related to Gafni's pain. Their estrangement notwithstanding, he obviously still cared deeply for his daughter. The questions surrounding her death were a constant torment and would remain so as long as they went unanswered. And besides, the content of Moria's suicide note both intrigued and troubled me. I was curious to learn the truth hidden behind her opaque message, and I feared that truth might prove even more terrible than Moria's early death. The possibility that Gafni might try to avenge his daughter worried me, but I figured I could deal with it later, when—if—I got to the bottom of all this.

So I would take on this assignment. But before I did, there was one thing I needed to say: "Are you sure you want me to do this, Mr. Gafni?"

His cheeks bunched as he pressed his lips. "Do I look like a man who's in the habit of second-guessing himself?"

"Not in the slightest. But there's something I want you to consider. If I go digging into Moria's life, I might uncover things that would stain the image you have of her. Things you would in retrospect prefer never to have known. Are you sure this is what you want?"

"Yes," he said. The word was unequivocal, but a twitching muscle near his right eye betrayed his fear. "Whatever it is, it would be better than not knowing."

Words he might live to regret, I thought, but I accepted them with a nod. "All right," I said. "Now tell me what you can about Moria."

He shifted awkwardly, likely because he didn't know as much as a father should. Just the basic, general facts. Her address, her birthday, that she'd moved to Jerusalem in December 1946. That she'd never been married and had lived alone. That she'd worked as a nurse. He didn't know any of her friends.

"They weren't at the funeral?" I asked.

He shook his head. "I wanted the funeral to be small and private."

Of course he did. A daughter's suicide brought shame and embarrassment, precisely what Gafni wished to avoid. That was why I was sitting here in his office.

I asked about his family, and he said Moria had been his only child. Her mother had died some years ago. He hadn't remarried.

Next we talked about money, a topic that Gafni was more comfortable with. When we'd discussed his daughter, his posture had been tight and closed. Now he was relaxed, in his element, luxuriating in his financial superiority. He was a wealthy businessman, while I, in my worn, soiled clothes and heavily scuffed shoes, looked the quintessential hired hand, teetering on the edge of destitution.

With a show of self-satisfied largesse, he announced that he did not expect my remuneration to be limited to my freedom. Handing me sixty liras, he asked if that would be sufficient, in a way that made it clear that he expected it would. I said it would be fine.

"How long do you think this will take?" he asked.

"Impossible to say. I'll report to you in a week, would that work?"

He assured me it would, then asked if I thought I would be spending nights in Jerusalem or going back and forth each day.

"I'll stay there, probably."

He nodded thoughtfully, retrieved his wallet, and counted out twenty more liras. "For a hotel," he said. Then he handed me a key. "To Moria's apartment. I assume you'll want to pay it a visit. I paid the rent till the end of next month. I need some time to decide what to do with her things."

"Did you take anything?"

He shook his head. "I was meaning to, but not yet. I haven't been there since the day the police called me to tell me she'd died."

Upon my request, he gave me a photograph of his daughter, taken when she was sixteen. He was right: she looked nothing like him. Moria had springy dark curls, deep-set soulful eyes, and a large mouth with plump lips. Her smile showed a sliver of teeth and seemed to hint at secrets, or perhaps that impression was the product of what I knew of her fate. She wasn't beautiful, yet still pretty in the way girls on the verge of womanhood often are.

Still in a generous mood, Gafni decided to see me out. As we were crossing the outer office, with the blonde secretary at her desk arranging papers, he asked, "I trust you'll start right away, Mr. Lapid?" A demand posed as a question.

"I'll head to Jerusalem first thing tomorrow," I said.

We exited the office, descended the stairs, and halted at the entrance to the production hall, where the machines still clamored.

"Look at that," Gafni said, gesturing with his arm. "The newest of these machines is over ten years old. They keep breaking down, and it's getting harder to fix them. But here in Israel, they're the best we can get. In the meantime, do you know what's happening in Germany? The country is filled with modern factories with top-of-the-line machinery, pumping out quality products they sell all over the world, including to countries that fought against the Nazis. Some are calling it an economic miracle."

He paused, waiting for a reaction, but I gave him none. The incredible economic revival of Germany was hardly news. The news-papers had been reporting it for at least a year. I read these reports with impotent resentment and an involuntary awe that never failed to leave me ashamed. Germany, at least the western part of it, had managed to rise from near ultimate destruction and resurrect its economy in record time. As someone who had witnessed the devasta-tion of Germany soon after the war, I could scarcely believe it.

How had they done it? The only answer I could come up with was that the Germans had simply shifted the focus of their immense talents. From blitzkrieg to business; from industrial slaughter to industrial production. Germany's newfound prosperity enraged me. It screamed injustice. Why did this nation, so soon after committing so many heinous crimes, deserve such good fortune? And why, at the same time, did Israel find itself sinking ever deeper into poverty and want?

Gafni said, "The reparations the Germans will give us won't be just money. Mostly, they'll pay us with goods, finished products, and modern machinery factories like mine need." His lips were parted and moist, and I could see greed glistening in his eyes like blood-drenched pieces of silver.

I couldn't speak or move a muscle. The shock was too great. This was the first time I'd met a person who supported negotiations with Germany for personal rather than national interests. Then Gafni looked once more at his toiling employees, and the paralysis evaporated, and in its place came a bone-deep tingling, a flash of heat in my throat and face, a clenching of the muscles in my arms and hands.

The urge to hit him was sudden and powerful. I pictured my fist connecting with his plump face, breaking teeth, crushing bone, splitting skin. I was on the verge of succumbing to uncontrollable anger, the kind that had engulfed me yesterday outside the Knesset.

"Hello, Baruch," a man's baritone sounded from behind me, yanking me back off the ledge. As Gafni began turning around, I forced my teeth apart and unfurled my fists, pressing my fingers against the sides of my trousers to keep them from bunching up again.

"Arye," Gafni said, with a deep frown. "I didn't think we had anything more to discuss." His jaw was clenched. His eyes flicked from the man to me and back again.

"I forgot a copy of my proposal in your office. I thought I'd drop by and get it," the man said, then paused, waiting for an introduction that Gafni failed to deliver.

He was forty-four or five. A handsome man in an expensive suit and coat, just under six feet and on the thin side, with a full head of black hair, a solid jaw, a high forehead, and clear blue eyes that might have been more at home on a child's face. Those same eyes were now probing me with evident curiosity, taking in my weary face and dirty clothes.

A few more seconds passed; then he flashed me a suave smile and reached out a hand. "Arye Harpaz."

"Adam Lapid," I said.

He pumped my hand, giving it a good, solid squeeze. Assertive, yet not overbearing. His handshake seemed to say, "A lesser man might have tried to crush your hand, but I'm confident enough to not need to."

"It's a pleasure to meet you," he said. "What line of work—"

"Come, Arye, let's go to my office," Gafni interrupted. "Mr. Lapid was just leaving." It was another command in camouflage, this time posing as a fact, and I felt the urge again, a vibration in my fingers. I tamped it down, muttered a quick goodbye, and ducked out of the building.

Out on the sidewalk, I let out a shaky breath, then swore in Hungarian. That was close. Much too close. I needed to keep my head. I couldn't allow myself to lose control. Not if I wanted to stay out of jail.

I marched away, hands in pockets to ward off the afternoon chill. The sky was an ominous pewter, the cloud cover low and thick. The air carried the sharp smell of both recent and imminent rain.

As I walked, I tried to squash my anger, but the memory of Gafni's amoral selfishness was like gasoline poured over a righteous fire. I told myself it didn't matter, that Gafni's position on the question of reparations meant nothing. He was a client. I didn't have to like him. In fact, it was probably better that I didn't.

I turned north at the nearest corner and found a kiosk. I bought a pack of cigarettes, tore it open, and put fire to one of its inhabitants. I sucked in the smoke as though it were oxygen, staring blankly at the buildings across the road, seeing little past my black thoughts.

When the first cigarette was down to its filter, I used it to light a second before tossing the remnant into a gutter. The smoke had dulled the edge of my fury, but I was still simmering. I hated the thought of working for a man like Gafni, someone who was willing to sell out his people's honor for private gain. I'd had unscrupulous, even criminal clients before and had managed to give them service and take their money without it bothering my conscience all that much, but doing the same for Gafni made my skin crawl.

I told myself I was overreacting, but it didn't seem to do much good. Maybe I'd become impervious to logic and good sense. Birnbaum would likely have said so.

I blew out a mouthful of smoke and watched it dissipate. That made me think of another smoke, thicker and blacker and smelling like death, smoke from tall brick chimneys under a Polish sky, and I clenched my eyes shut and shook my head, wondering if I was going crazy.

Then something occurred to me, and I plunged a hand into my pocket, grabbed my wallet, and from it took out the photograph Gafni had given me. I stared at Moria's smiling face, frozen at sixteen when her world was brighter and more optimistic, when the possibility of self-annihilation was unthinkable.

Looking at the photograph, I tried to do the impossible, to read into the girl's future, into the years that had passed since this picture was taken, to uncover what had led Moria to decide to swallow those pills and end her life.

Of course, the answer was not there, but something nearly as important was. A lifeline. A way to reconcile my distaste for Gafni with the necessity of pursuing this case. For as I gazed at Moria's girlish face, I decided I was working for her, not her father. It was her truth I was chasing. If there was justice to be had, it would be for her.

Nodding to myself, I took a deep breath and let it leak out of me in a single even flow, growing calmer and at greater peace with myself. After one final glance at the photo, I returned it to my wallet and put the wallet back in my pocket.

Then I got out my notebook, flipped to the page on which I had copied Moria's suicide note, and by the dim winter light and the red glow of my cigarette, I read her final message again.

I hate you for how you made me feel. I hate you for what you did to me. I hate you for what you made me do.

7

I could have done with a shower and a change of clothes, but I had eaten nothing since the measly breakfast the Jerusalem jail had provided, and my apartment offered little but the prospect of bare cupboard shelves and an empty icebox. I had neglected my shopping over the past week as the day of voting in the Knesset neared, and I'd found myself increasingly preoccupied, or perhaps dominated, by the larger issue at hand.

I was hungry, and I knew just the place where I could get something good to eat. Besides, Birnbaum had said Greta was worried about me, and I wanted to set her mind at ease.

By the time I got to Allenby Street, a fine, delicate rain had begun falling. I paused before a bulletin board rife with posters growing soggy and dark with the rain. Most of the posters decried the government's desire to negotiate with Germany. Some announced various protest events: an assembly of partisans, a march of communists, a gathering of Herut supporters. I wondered if the latter would be allowed to take place.

Half of the tables at Greta's Café were taken. Greta herself was seated behind the serving counter. Her eyes widened when she saw me, first with relief, then with concern. She rose to her feet. "Adam, what happened?"

She was wearing a thick woolen dress that loosely draped over her wide frame. Greta was a big woman, with a heavy bosom, thick arms, and a large head of salt-and-pepper curls. Her face was wide and lined, her hands wrinkled by years of washing dishes and preparing food. Her café was aptly named, for she was the heart and soul of her establishment. It was her character that made the café a sanctuary in the heart of Tel Aviv. My favorite place to be. I despised myself for causing her worry.

"I'm all right, Greta. Just a few bumps and scrapes."

"Were you at the Knesset yesterday?"

"Yes."

"Was it as bad as they say?"

I rubbed the side of my jaw. "Can I get something to eat first? And some coffee?"

She nodded, and I withdrew to my table at the rear, but not before I looped an arm over the counter to grab the chessboard and box of pieces Greta kept there for me.

At my table, I set up the board—white pieces on my side, black on the opposite—a matter of convention, nothing more, for I played both colors. This was a habit I'd picked up after the Second World War, though its origin lay squarely in it.

I wasn't a good player, but that wasn't the reason I chose myself as an opponent. It wasn't victory I craved, but a few minutes of idle mental time, and a bout of lightning chess against myself was the best way I knew to achieve that.

Two dozen or so moves into the game, Greta appeared with the coffee and a plate bearing a large sandwich and a scattering of vegetables.

"Is that blood on your collar?" she asked, setting down the dishes.

"Yes." I nudged the chessboard aside and tugged the plate closer.

"Yours?"

"Probably. At least part of it."

She clucked her tongue, then smiled indulgently like a mother at a reckless child who'd skirted disaster for the umpteenth time. "Enjoy your meal, Adam." She left me with the food. Glorious Greta, she was curious as hell, but she would give me all the time I needed.

The coffee was as wonderful as always, the vegetables crisp and fresh, the sandwich simple yet filling. With each swallow, I could feel my tiredness abate and my anger recede further. Once I'd finished eating, I resumed my game. Black won decisively.

Greta cleared the dishes, then sat down across from me.

"So tell me," she said. "Just how awful was it?"

"It wasn't pretty. What have you heard?"

"That Begin threatened to overthrow the government."

"That's not true," I said, perhaps too quickly.

"That he called Ben-Gurion a tyrant, that he suggested citizens stop paying taxes, that he swore he and his men would make any sacrifice to stop Israel from negotiating with Germany."

I wished I could deny it, but Begin had said all that.

"That he said this would be a war to the death."

I kneaded the back of my neck, where knots had started to form. "Yes. He did say that."

"That he ordered his followers to storm the Knesset."

I shook my head, glad for the opportunity to balance the scales a little. "No. He never gave such an order. He asked us to appeal to the policemen as Jews to not raise their hands against us. To tell them we were fighting for the nation's honor. He never said we should fight them. That was an unplanned eruption of emotion."

Greta looked at me for a long moment, and I imagined that she was thinking much the same as I was, that Begin was well aware of his oratory skills, that he could sense the crowd's agitation, that he knew, or should have known, what acts his speech would inspire.

Greta said, "I heard on the radio that King George Street looked like a battlefield, that hundreds of people got hurt."

"That sounds about right."

"And that some of them were injured pretty badly."

I thought of the unconscious policeman I had been wrongly accused of beating. "Some of them, yes. There were ambulances.

Plenty of them."

Greta's expression was closed to me. Like the door to your home after someone changed the locks without you knowing. "You took part in the fighting?"

"Yes," I said, not shying from her gaze. "I didn't plan to. I went to Jerusalem to demonstrate, to express my opinion, not to fight anyone. But somehow I ended up near the Knesset, trying to push past the cops to get inside."

"To do what?"

A jolt of panic flared in my stomach, surged up my chest, and curled around my neck like a garrote. Of all people, I needed Greta to understand, to not judge me too harshly.

"To get the Knesset to vote against the government's plan to negotiate with Germany," I said, my voice coming out choked and squeaky. I added in a rush, "They can't do that, Greta. They just can't. It's wrong, a sin. It's an insult to the dead. To my... to my..."

I couldn't continue. My lungs felt cramped, my airways clogged. It was difficult to draw breath. Hot tears pricked my eyes, a million tiny burning needles.

Greta reached over and grabbed both my hands in hers, enveloping them like warm gloves. "I know, Adam. You don't have to say it."

I lowered my head and bit back a cry, my eyes overflowing. Greta released my hands, and I heard her chair scrape across the floor. Then she was beside me, hands on my shoulders, and I knew she'd positioned her body so as to block me from view of the other patrons. The scents of cooking oil, salt, margarine, and coffee wafted off her. The comforting smells of a homey kitchen.

I dried my face with my hands, the salt of my tears stinging the small cuts from yesterday's battle. I looked up at her. "I wasn't trying to overthrow the government, Greta, but to save Israel's soul. You understand, right?"

She nodded, her strong fingers pressing into my shoulders, ten firm anchors keeping me from drifting into uncharted waters.

"I know why you did it, Adam. Why you felt compelled to do it.

But I so wish you chose another way." She patted my shoulders. "Why don't you go wash your face? I'll bring you another coffee, and you can play another game."

When I returned to my table, face clean and dry, I found that Greta had already refilled my cup. She was at the other end of the café, chatting with a customer. I sipped some coffee and drew the chessboard toward me. I moved the pieces around as fast as I could, no time for thought or strategy, just instinct. Black won again.

I sat back and looked around the café. Six other patrons other than myself. Five men and one woman. The woman laughed at something her companion said. At another table, one of the other men was busily scribbling in a notebook. Two of the others were talking in Yiddish, each armed with a cigarette. Greta served them coffee, and one of them said something that made her wag her finger at him.

A man entered the café, one of the regulars, a Russian guy who worked as a bank teller. He called to Greta, "Turn on the radio. They say Ben-Gurion's going to give an address."

Bulky and encased in weathered wood, the radio monopolized a shelf on the wall behind the serving counter. An ancient contraption, it had come into Greta's possession as a result of her softheartedness. A customer who was down on his luck had given it to her in lieu of settling his tab. I'd advised Greta against the exchange, pointing out that a radio of such vintage could be had for half the outstanding debt. But Greta had accepted, on the grounds that to refuse would hurt the man's feelings, which was more important than money, especially given the fact that he'd frequented the café for many years.

"Did you at least check it's working properly?" I'd asked.

"He assured me it does," Greta had replied.

And the radio had worked properly. For five whole days. After this brief grace period, it began showing its age by supplying an incessant hiss as an accompaniment to all broadcasts. Sometimes the hiss was loud like a snake sibilating in your ear; at other times, it was but an indistinct susurration, like a gaggle of distant busybodies sharing gossip. In either case, it was irritating to the point that the radio saw gradually less and less use. These days, it was turned on only when one of the patrons requested it, and usually not for very long.

Greta shook her head, suggesting in her mild tone that perhaps it would be better to read about Ben-Gurion's address in tomorrow's papers. She pointed out that the radio's performance deteriorated on cloudy days.

But another patron seconded the first's request, and soon the woman and her companion voiced their support as well. Surrendering to their will, Greta turned one of the large knobs on the radio's front, and the crackle of static burst from the speaker as the machine roused itself to life.

Then came the all-familiar hiss, and over it, and only somewhat more pleasant, the nasal, strident voice of David Ben-Gurion, prime minister of Israel, with his Polish accent and distinct clipped enunciation. It was not the voice of a statesman, not the tone of the founder of a country. But then Ben-Gurion had none of the outward characteristics of a leader. With his five-foot-one frame, his bald dome of a head fringed by unruly hedges of white hair, his sausage of a nose and near invisible lips, Ben-Gurion had the appearance of a hapless grandfather rather than the man who, against all odds, had led his tiny nation to military triumph and renewed independence.

His was an elusive, hard-to-define charisma. He did not have Begin's eloquence, nor his gushing fervor. He was not blessed with the good looks of some of his young generals. He did not possess the easy charm of a socialite. He dressed simply, his tastes were humble, and he always looked unkempt, even in a suit and tie. Yet, despite all these shortcomings, Ben-Gurion had been the foremost leader of the Jewish Yishuv during the British Mandate of Palestine, and as prime minister, his domination of Israeli politics was near complete.

"Yesterday," Ben-Gurion said, "a nefarious hand was raised against the sovereignty of the Knesset. An attempt was made to destroy Israeli democracy. It was proclaimed that Israeli policy would not be decided by the people's representatives, but by men of the fist and the political murder."

Greta looked at me. Her expression was angry. I felt like burying myself out of sight of the world. The prime minister of Israel, a man I admired despite everything, was talking about me.

Ben-Gurion went on to explain that the previous evening, a wild and incited rabble made up of communists and former Irgun members had attacked the Knesset and assaulted the policemen ordered to protect it. Over one hundred officers had been wounded.

The man who had fomented this revolt, as Ben-Gurion called it, was Menachem Begin. He had incited the crowds in Zion Square. He had declared a "war to the death" against the Knesset and the government. Ben-Gurion stressed that, despite the danger posed to the Knesset by Begin's followers, he had ordered the police to refrain from using their firearms; and he praised the brave policemen who, without exception, had followed this order, even when many of them lay injured in the street.

Ben-Gurion was angry now, and this sharpened the grating qualities of his speech. Yet his outrage was more controlled, less flamboyant than Begin's, and I couldn't help but think of Birnbaum's observation: that Menachem Begin was better suited for the role of a resistance commander than that of a statesman. Fiery passion was a prerequisite of the first, but the second called for a calmer, cool-headed attitude.

To whip up a crowd into a frenzy, one would pick Menachem Begin. But to run a country, and to successfully prevail upon assailed policemen to not use deadly force in the face of serious physical harm, choose Ben-Gurion.

All were silent in Greta's Café as the prime minister spoke. The only sounds were his voice and the underlying hiss of the radio. The other patrons either stood to move closer to the radio, or sat forward in their seats, drawn toward the prime minister's voice.

Ben-Gurion said that he took the treasonous threats made by Begin with the utmost seriousness. That he did not underestimate the courage of Irgun members, nor their willingness to pay a heavy personal price for their beliefs. And that he knew full well that he was the prime target of these threats. But he assured the public that the State of Israel had the means to safeguard its democracy and to thwart any prolonged terroristic activity. That even if ministers and members of Knesset became targets for assassination, the security forces would be able to maintain order and the rule of law.

He concluded by promising the citizenry that despite this serious threat, Israel would remain a free and democratic country, and that any attempt to undermine the sovereignty of the Knesset and the government would be squashed without compromise.

Conspicuously absent from Ben-Gurion's speech was the cause of the demonstration yesterday in Jerusalem. The prime minister did not utter a single word regarding his proposal for negotiations with Germany on the matter of reparations. Politically cunning, as well as dishonest in its omission. Also unmentioned was the possibility of outlawing Herut. Perhaps Birnbaum was right and Ben-Gurion was too smart to take such a step.

Greta switched off the radio. The ensuing silence lasted but a few seconds. Then the other patrons began voicing their opinion about Ben-Gurion's speech and Begin's actions. The words *fascist, terrorist,* and *criminal* were hurled into the air. All of them were directed at Begin and his followers. Even two of the regulars whom I knew opposed negotiations with Germany expressed disgust at what had happened yesterday near the Knesset. One of them opined that Begin should be stripped of his parliamentary status and arrested.

I sat immobile, struck by the horrific realization that what had happened yesterday not only failed to sway public opinion against negotiations with Germany, but had likely done the opposite. People might still find the prospect of dealing with the Germans unpalatable, but they viewed the assault on the Knesset as a greater offense.

And I, by my heedless stupidity and unbridled rage, had contributed to this. I screwed my eyes shut and breathed deeply, trying to quell the rising tide of guilt and shame that threatened to drown me. But it was impossible to keep out the accusations flying through the air of Greta's Café. My sanctuary had been breached. I needed to get away from there, from the others. I jerked to my feet so abruptly my chair toppled, and I pounded toward the exit.

"Adam, where—"

"I have to go, Greta," I said without stopping, pushing through the door and onto Allenby Street, turning north toward my apartment.

But I didn't go there. I went further north still, to a quiet residential street inhabited by people of means and connections. To the building where Sima Vaaknin lived and plied her trade.

We had first met two years before, when I was working the murder case of a young Arab woman. Sima and I had become lovers then and perhaps something more, though I couldn't say what.

Our relationship was a strange one. We saw each other sporadically, we met solely between the four walls of her apartment, and while we had slept together and shared with each other private parts of our history, we weren't truly intimate. I did not know the real Sima, for she kept herself hidden, even while naked, and I wasn't sure how she really felt about me.

When we met, it was always at my initiative. Never had Sima sought me out, even when months had passed since we last saw each other. Yet, she had, on occasion, showed a trace of displeasure at the infrequency of our trysts, though that might have been nothing but professional pride. For she was a temptress, a skill she'd honed to perfection. She was unaccustomed to men who could withstand her charms, even temporarily.

This wasn't love, nor the promise of it. What it was, I didn't know. What I did know was that I lusted after her. But I also resented sharing her, which was partly why I stayed away. Another reason was that I was still in love with my dead wife, and being with Sima made me feel guilty, even after seven years of widowhood.

So I saw Sima infrequently and almost never planned it in advance. Sima had once told me that I only came to her when I was troubled, and running down a mental list of our encounters, I had to admit that she was mostly right.

Perhaps that was why I was heading her way now, after I'd been arrested and threatened with a lengthy prison sentence. After a man I respected showed great disappointment in me. After the prime minister of Israel accused me of trying to topple Israeli democracy. After even Greta exhibited disapproval of my actions.

I knew that Sima would accept me as I was, even in my bedraggled state. She would tilt her pretty head, cock her curvy hip, smile in triumph, and invite me in. Most likely, she wouldn't bother to inquire as to the cause of my troubles, but she might fling a biting remark about my appearance or the time that had elapsed since our previous meeting. And she wouldn't be satisfied with my being there. She would continue to reel me in, angling parts of her anatomy in a way designed to shatter any inhibition and outside loyalty. For this was a game of seduction, and she wasn't content to win by anything but the widest margin.

And she would take me to her bedroom, and there would be comfort and pleasure there. For she knew men, and she knew me, and she would give me what I needed with uncanny precision, more attuned to my physical wants than even I was. It would be a surrender but of the sweetest kind, and for a few hours, I longed to stop all fighting.

But when I got there, I stopped on the sidewalk opposite her building and looked up. The light in her living room window was yellow and electric. The one in her bedroom was dimmer, muffled by curtains and likely cast by candles. I had been a fool to come here. It was still early, an hour when a man could tell his wife he was working late, but instead come here, to Sima Vaaknin. To her large bed with its plump pillows and soft sheets. To her exquisite body with its enticing curves.

I could have stopped somewhere and called in advance, and I wasn't sure why I hadn't. My mind was swirling, and I wasn't thinking straight. Now I stared at her window like a lust-deranged boy and felt a pang of unwarranted jealousy. For Sima Vaaknin did not belong to me, and sharing her with other men was unavoidable. A symptom of her profession. I had reconciled myself to this reality. For the most part.

"You're such an idiot," I whispered to myself, and had made up my mind to go home and stay there till morning, when the candlelight in Sima's bedroom started wavering and weakening. A series of tiny flames blown to oblivion one after the next. Then her bedroom went dark.

I knew what this meant. Hastily, I retreated into the shadows afforded by a wide-canopied evergreen diagonally across from Sima's building. I did not want the man who would soon be coming out to see me. Truth was, I did not want to see him either. I only wanted to know when he was gone.

A few minutes later, he emerged. A short, rotund man dressed in dark clothes and a hat. With small steps he traversed the short stone path that connected Sima's building with the sidewalk. I was about to look away to avoid glimpsing his face when something about him—his posture, shape, movement—made me stop and peer more closely.

We were but a few meters apart, but the early evening darkness and the angle of his hat combined to obscure his features. I squinted in a feeble attempt to pierce the murkiness clouding his face, gripped by an irrational craving to know his identity.

As luck would have it, when he got to the sidewalk, he turned in my direction, still on the other side of the street but shaving the distance between us with each step.

Yet, though ever closer, his face remained blanketed in shadow. Soon he would be directly across from my position, and then I would only see his back as he walked away. I would either have to cross the road and confront him, or he would remain an enigma. I was weighing the potential downsides against the obscure benefit of quenching my curiosity when the man paused at the edge of a quivering pool of light cast by a flickering streetlamp. Bowing his head, he doffed his hat with his left hand while drawing a handkerchief from his trouser pocket with his right. As he ran the handkerchief over his forehead and cheeks, he tipped his head back, so that the wavering light played across his face.

My heart stopped. The man was none other than Baruch Gafni, my powerful and selfish client. Forehead damp with recent exertion and cheeks ruddy with ecstasy, he wore a grin of abject satisfaction, like a fat cat that had just gobbled up a songbird. Gafni was Sima's client. He had just been in her apartment, in her bed. Now he cast his eyes upward at her window, gave his pudding face a final mop, folded the handkerchief with small, precise movements, and shoved it back in his pocket. He put his hat back on and strode away, whistling.

I remained stock-still, the wind jostling the branches above me, unmooring tiny tears of rain that fell upon me from sodden leaves. I didn't move until Gafni entered a car two buildings down and drove off. Only then did I allow myself to emerge from the shadows and look up at Sima's apartment once more.

I could see her now, moving in her living room. Even from this distance, her movements were liquid elegance. Alone in her home, she remained in the character of the seductress.

But I felt no stirring of passion, no spark of desire. There was only revulsion, violent and clawing, as my stomach flipped itself over. I accepted that Sima slept with other men, but with Gafni? With this shameless creature who wished to sell his people's honor to enhance his bottom line? This was the man Sima sold her body to?

Bile burned the bottom of my throat as I pictured the two of them together. The images were much too vivid, the transaction of sex for money sordid beyond tolerance. At that moment, whatever ties connected me to Sima, that led me to return to her again and again, snapped as though severed by shears.

I turned and walked away.

8

I rose early the next day, packed a bag, ate a desiccated piece of bread I found in the otherwise barren cupboards, and went out to start working on my new case.

I bought a new hat in a shop on King George Street, then made my way to the Tel Aviv Central Bus Station, where I waited twenty minutes for the bus to Jerusalem. On the bench next to me was a crumpled copy of yesterday's *Ma'ariv*. Going through it confirmed my worst fears. Ezriel Carlebach, editor-in-chief of *Ma'ariv* and possibly the most widely read columnist in Israel, and a man who publicly opposed talking to the Germans, wrote that if there had been waverers among Mapai and its coalition partners, the violence in Jerusalem had undoubtedly pushed them firmly into the aye camp. No self-respecting parliament would surrender to a violent mob. By their mutinous actions, Carlebach wrote, Herut followers had guaranteed that the government's proposal would pass in the Knesset.

With a curse, I crushed the newspaper into a ball and flung it into a nearby trash bin.

The bus to Jerusalem was half full, but the closed windows conspired with the passengers' wet clothes to create a stifling, humid atmosphere. I cracked open a window and let the cold wind whip at my face, but was soon called into order by a heavyset woman wearing about seven layers of clothing. In a cutting tone, she commanded me to shut the window. It was freezing outside, or hadn't I noticed? I thought about regaling her with tales of December 1944 in Auschwitz, for the purpose of educating her on what being exposed in freezing weather truly felt like, but instead I demurred, shutting the window. I had fought with too many people over the past few days.

As all across Israel, the main topic of conversation on the bus was the proposed negotiations with Germany. Against my wishes, I caught snatches of talk throughout the ride to the capital.

The Knesset had resumed its debate yesterday and was scheduled to vote on the matter today. The papers predicted that the government would prevail. The police had cordoned off a large area around the Knesset as a precaution against further disturbances, none of which had materialized. Most of the rioters were still imprisoned. One of the passengers declared his hope that they'd never be released. Another told him to shut his mouth. It might have come to blows were it not for the heavyset woman, who ordered the pair to keep quiet. They were hurting her sensitive ears. Cowed by her imperiousness, the two did just that. I was beginning to like her.

The day was gray and gloomy. Rain pummeled the bus as it trundled up the twisting mountain road to Jerusalem, but it petered out as we entered the city. The bus rumbled past the Institute for the Blind and Shaare Zedek Hospital and curled along Jaffa Street before wheeling into the Central Bus Station, where I disembarked. A blustery wind stabbed cold bayonets through my coat as I showed a harried ticket clerk the address where Moria Gafni had lived and perished. He told me which line to take, and I spent ten miserable minutes waiting on a hard bench, hunched inside my raised collar, for an inner-city bus to arrive.

The bus had started its life as a truck and had since been fitted with benches that looked grossly uncomfortable. Not that I got to test any of them. There were too many people for that. Clutching a leather strap that dangled from an overhead bar, I swayed with the motion of the bus as it cut a winding path through a succession of streets, some not much wider than alleyways, before finally depositing me in front of a stationery store in the northern neighborhood of Kerem Avraham. I followed the directions the clerk had given me, and five minutes later I found myself outside a sad-looking three-story building near the center of Amos Street.

It had been a house once upon a time, but it had since been sliced and diced into apartments, two on each floor. Rain and damp had left their mark on the exterior, and someone with large feet and a disdain for cleanliness had tracked mud across the tiny lobby and up the staircase. It didn't take much to reason out the whereabouts of the culprit—the mud trail ended at a door on the second floor—but I figured the landlord or other tenants could deal with it if they wished. I had more serious business to attend to.

I climbed to the third floor and, using the key Mr. Gafni had given me, entered the apartment where Moria Gafni had slipped from life into eternal sleep.

It was a small place: two narrow rooms laid in a line, so that from the front doorway, I could see all the way to the back wall of Moria's bedroom. I pushed the door closed and stood for a moment, letting my senses do their work.

The first thing that struck me was the smell. Stuffy and musty, like a newly unearthed burial chamber. The windows, I thought, had been closed for over a month, probably since the body had been carted off.

But somebody had been here since, and recently. I could tell because the frame of the small mirror by the door carried a thin layer of dust, but the inner door handle was free of it. It was a good thing I hadn't touched it when I closed the door.

Whoever it was, they hadn't busted the lock. So either they'd picked it, or they'd had a key. I didn't think it was Mr. Gafni, but not because I trusted him to tell me the truth. The simple fact was that Gafni had no need to lie to me. He had every right to visit the apartment, and it wouldn't have seemed odd if he'd done so.

So it wasn't him. Then who? The person Moria wrote about in her note? And what had he or she come for?

Next I listened, but that taught me nothing. The only sounds originated from outside the apartment. The growl of a truck engine. A man on the street below hollering some unintelligible message. A gust vibrating the windowpanes. The apartment itself was as silent as the corpse that had recently lain in it.

On pegs by the door hung a woman's coat and a leather handbag, and I went through them both. The coat yielded nothing but a pair of knitted gloves and a woolen cap. The bag contained Moria's ID card, a pencil stub, a trifling amount of cash, a handkerchief, a receipt from Schwartz Department Store, a couple of hairpins, and a crumpled shopping list that looked weeks old and included the most mundane of products. In short, zilch.

A couple of paces and I was smack in the middle of the living room. Not much had been squeezed into it, but enough to make the narrow space feel stifling. There was a couch that could sit two, a low bookcase, a pair of chairs and a square dining table by the window. The window had frilly white curtains that were pulled back and shutters that hung open. The view offered little in the way of beauty or inspiration—just more aging residential buildings, with slack empty clotheslines strung between them, under a dispiriting gray sky.

I turned my back on the drab panorama and faced the living room once more.

Everything appeared in order. The mysterious visitor had not looted the place. They had come looking for something specific, and they had either found it, or they could not bring themselves to toss the apartment. Or maybe they feared making a racket. I doubted the walls between the apartments were thick.

I went over to the bookcase. The books were perfectly aligned, none of the spines protruding, as though they'd been lined with a ruler. All of the books were novels, all in Hebrew, mostly translated works by authors such as Charles Dickens and Charlotte Bronte and John Steinbeck. Serious stuff. Nothing as lowbrow as the Westerns and adventure novels that were the staples of my literary diet.

Gazing upward, I saw a few damp spots on the ceiling, along with several discolored patches where someone had lazily slapped paint over old ones. Cracks webbed from one corner, as though a giant spider had settled into the stone and was in the process of expanding its lair.

A squat heating stove stood by a wall, but, of course, no fire burned in its belly. The apartment was freezing, as though the walls were porous and winter had seeped in. I wondered how adequate the heating was, or if the apartment bled warmth as easily as it allowed in cold.

Shivering inside my coat, it struck me that, while Moria Gafni had lived better than many Israelis, she could have afforded finer accommodations with the help of her father. Yet she had chosen not to. Which indicated that she had been a proud woman.

The kitchen was the size of a wafer. The counters were clear, the sink clean, the drying board vacant. The trash can was empty. Was the garbage removed post-mortem, or had Moria done it prior to her death? Judging by the manner in which she'd arranged her books and the orderliness of her kitchen cupboards, I suspected she might have.

Back in the living room, I headed for a white door that opened onto a small bathroom. The water in the toilet, motionless for over a month, had grown a disgusting film of crud. Grimacing, I flushed the filth away, wincing at how loud the pipes groaned and belched.

The top shelf of the medicine cabinet contained toothpaste, a toothbrush, nail clippers, and makeup. The bottom shelf held headache pills you could buy in any pharmacy, a roll of gauze, a bottle of iodine. No real medicine. The tub was on the smallish side. It might have fitted a teenager if she was petite and wasn't keen on stretching her legs. Looking at it, I realized I didn't know how tall Moria had been. I hadn't asked her father, and why would I? What possible bearing could it have on the investigation?

But now I was curious.

I exited the bathroom and entered the bedroom, heading straight for the single narrow closet. Its door was open, revealing just two shelves and a rack. Moria's clothes lay folded and piled in perfect order. Her dresses hung straight, including two nurse dress uniforms. I unhooked one of the nurse dresses and held it up before me, estimating Moria's height by its length. She'd been a short woman. Five one or maybe two. Just right for the small tub. And about the same height as the prime minister of Israel. Shaking my head, bemused by my rambling thoughts, I returned the dress to its hanger and closed the closet. Then I turned to study the rest of the bedroom.

Apart from the closet, there was a dresser; two paintings, neither of which would have made Van Gogh tremble with envy; and a bed, somewhere between a single and a double, set tight against the near wall. Attached to the wall at the corner of the room beside the bed was a small cabinet, its door closed. No sign of the pill bottles. Either the police had taken them, or someone had thrown them away.

A large depression dented the middle of the pillow. Made by Moria's head? The blanket was bunched up at the foot of the mattress, which was bare. Someone had removed the sheet. The mattress was white. Under the glare of the overhead light bulb, I could see the spiraling outlines of the springs enclosed within.

The bed stood a foot above the floor. I peered under it and found nothing but floor tiles. I went to the dresser next, crouched, and examined the knobs on each of the three drawers. No dust. The nameless visitor had opened these. Thinking that there might be fingerprints, I left the knobs untouched, gripping both sides of the drawers to tug them open.

The first drawer housed socks and underwear, all jumbled together as though someone had pawed through them. There were also a few wool stockings, which probably proved useful during the winter months. Nothing out of the ordinary apart from two pairs of silk stockings. These weren't cheap; one could sell these. The unknown visitor had either overlooked them or decided for some reason to leave them behind.

The second drawer held a large hairbrush, a pair of scissors, four squat candles, a book of matches, and two photo albums. The top one contained photos of the dead woman. There was Moria at one of the gates to the Old City, before Jerusalem had been carved in two, her arms spread wide as though to encompass the universe. There she was again, in a public garden I didn't recognize, leaning against a tree, her expression inscrutable. A third photo showed her in profile, staring off into the middle distance, her face serious and pensive. She had lost some of the adolescent freshness that I'd noticed in the photograph her father had given me, and in its place had gained a heavy dose of grown-up seriousness, as though a set of grim circumstances had plunged her deeper into adulthood than the mere passage of time could have done.

Other photos showed her at her job, wearing her white dress and nurse's cap—reading a thermometer, holding up a syringe with playful menace, standing at the entrance to the hospital where she had worked. There were other nurses around her in the last picture, and I went over each of their faces, committing them to memory.

The next several photos showed her in the company of either or both of two women, and I flipped back to the group photo, determining that indeed the two women were also nurses and had worked with Moria. Removing the photos from their mooring, I studied their backs, hoping to learn the two women's names, but they were blank. I returned all the photos but one into the album. The last, the one that showed Moria and her two friends most clearly, I slipped into my pocket.

The second album contained older photographs. There was Moria as a child of six or seven, her smile as big as the sky. There she was as a baby, lying on a blanket, staring up with huge eyes. There were many photos of Moria with an older woman who must have been her mother. Gafni had been right: the two looked very much alike.

Speaking of Gafni, he was nowhere to be found in the album. This was no accident. He had been excised from it. I could tell because some of the photos contained bits and pieces of him—a severed hand with his unmistakable porcine fingers, a shoe tip, a sliver of trouser leg, a slice of his bald head. The rest had been cut off and discarded. The little that remained could not be surgically removed without harming the image of Moria's mother in the process.

Running a fingertip along the cut edge of a photo, I wondered

74

what had led Moria to perform this amputation on her recorded past. Could she not bear the sight of her father? Was it insufficient to sever all ties with him, and this was her attempt to expel him from her past and memory? Whatever had caused her to do this must have been terrible. No wonder Gafni wouldn't tell me about it. Gafni must have been unaware of the contents of this album. He wouldn't have left it in the apartment if he knew it existed.

In the third drawer, I found a notebook with a smooth brown cover. About half of the pages inside had been ripped out. Those remaining were blank. Was this where Moria had jotted her shopping lists? Where she had scribbled little reminders? Brushing my thumb over the surface of one of the surviving pages, it occurred to me that this was the same size and type of paper on which Moria had written her suicide note. I wished I had it with me to make sure, though the value of such certainty was unclear to me.

In addition to the notebook, the drawer held a framed diploma from the nursing school where Moria had studied, several pencils in varied stages of use, a number of empty envelopes, a strip of stamps with a few stamps missing, a sewing kit with an embroidered top, a few letters and memoranda from her workplace, and a pen. Scratching the pen across one of the envelopes left a zigzagging line of black. It might have been the pen Moria had used to write her suicide note. Had she returned it to the drawer before taking the pills? It seemed an odd thing to do just before killing herself.

Also in the drawer was a small box full of ticket stubs to various cinemas in Jerusalem—Eden, Smadar, Edison, Tel-Or, Zion, Orion. Staring at a fistful of stubs, I got an image of Moria Gafni sitting in a darkened cinema, her eyes bright, staring rapt at the flashing action on the screen. Moria, I decided, had relished the temporary escape movies offered and had wanted to cling to that feeling for as long as possible. As I allowed the stubs to flutter back down into the box, I couldn't help but think that eventually reality had proved so harsh that no escape, no matter how brief, remained possible.

Under the ticket stub box was a batch of thank-you notes written by formerly sick children and their parents. They painted a picture of a devoted nurse, kind and patient and helpful. Apparently, Moria had been good with the little ones, knew how to raise their spirits, to make them laugh despite their illnesses. She had given the children and their parents hope. What could have made a woman like that lose her own hope and choose to end everything?

The door of the bedside cabinet had a handle the size and shape of a small mushroom. Dust powdered it. Apparently, the visitor had found what they were looking for and had no need to check the cabinet. I pulled open the door and found myself staring at a pack of condoms; a glass vial of perfume; a pair of fat, partially melted candles; a pack of cigarettes; a box of long matches; and a well-thumbed English paperback with a cover that suggested a risqué plot.

I riffled through the pages of the paperback. They crinkled and spewed a dry papery scent. The pages weren't yellowed though. This was the sort of book one read in the privacy of one's home, not on a park bench on a sunny day. It was a stark contrast to the books Moria had kept in her living room, and the only book in a language other than Hebrew.

The perfume had an alluring flowery scent. Nothing discreet or subtle about it. Sima Vaaknin sometimes wore the same perfume or one very similar. I picked up the pack of condoms—open and near depleted—and wondered whom Moria had worn the perfume for, for whom she had bought the condoms. Was it a single man or several? Was the person mentioned in her suicide note her lover? Or was he her client?

Thinking about this, and about Sima, brought back the memory of Gafni exiting her building, floating high on the cloud of his recent debauchery. Gritting my teeth, I slammed the cabinet door shut.

I stood unmoving in the middle of the bedroom and allowed the cold silence of the lifeless apartment to wrap around me like a shroud. Up until a few minutes ago, what little I'd known of Moria Gafni had been nothing but surface details. Now, a deeper and more vivid picture was forming.

She had led an active sex life. She had loved to dream and fantasize. She had been a dedicated nurse. She had healed children. She had devoted her life to doing good. Yet her suicide note hinted at a bad deed she had done, had been made to do, and that had led her to choose death. What could it have been? Was it whatever had caused the rift with her father? Or was it something more recent?

Hungry for answers, I let my gaze roam around the room— skating over the white walls, the closed window, the dresser with its silver-screen souvenirs and grateful letters, the closet with its orphaned clothes—and saw nothing that hinted at the solution to the mystery. Only when my eyes completed their circumnavigation and returned to the bedside cabinet did I pause and cock my head. A sudden suspicion that something wasn't right began niggling at me.

I opened the cabinet again, picked up the paperback, frowned at it. Again I thought how different it was to the other books in the apartment. But that wasn't the only thing that was off. The rest of the items in the cabinet—the condoms, the perfume, the candles, they were all a bit too much. Like a story told in excessive detail or the way a mannequin can look unnervingly fake precisely because it is too perfect. Some lies are like that. They're like a set piece: nothing out of place, everything exactly right. Too much so.

Then it struck me that a good way to look like you've got nothing to hide is to appear to be a person who is unabashed when most people would be. Like an unmarried woman who keeps condoms by her bed where they can easily be found. And also that the best place to hide something is right next to a display of openness so stark that it allays any suspicion of concealment.

A man searching this bedroom would open this cabinet and get an instant, clear picture of who Moria Gafni was—a promiscuous woman and proud of it. He would sneer, or let loose a derisive comment, or imagine how it would feel to be in her bed. But he would not look too closely at the cabinet, figuring he had already seen everything there was to see.

And maybe that was the intended effect. Maybe there was some-thing more to be found, and right there.

With a spark of excitement, I examined each item in the cabinet in turn and found nothing new. I ran my hand over the surface, top, bottom, and sides. Just wood, a little grainy to the touch.

Then, when I had just about decided I was the victim of wishful thinking, my gaze latched onto the screws at the corners of the cabinet. I tugged on it, but it was bolted tight. Earlier, in one of the kitchen drawers, I'd seen a number of tools, including a screwdriver. I got it and loosened the screws so that the only thing keeping the cabinet from falling was my grip. I tossed the screwdriver on the bed and lowered the cabinet onto the floor.

Then I looked at the section of wall behind it and felt my jaw drop.

9

I saw a pistol. Black and menacing as a dense forest on a moonless night. Lying like a forgotten relic in a small cavity that had been excavated in the wall. Beside the gun lay two magazines. The bullets nestled within them glinted like the mischievous smile of a child whose secret had been exposed.

The manufacturer's name—COLT—was embossed on the grip in big letters. I knew the model. A Colt Auto Pocket, a .25 caliber. A small pistol meant to be carried in a pocket or a purse. No hammer, so nothing would snag when you pulled it out. The barrel was short, which would lower accuracy, but at close range, it could kill as effectively as any instrument of death, provided the shooter had a steady hand. Such as the hand of the woman who'd penned the suicide note?

For a moment, I stared dumbfounded at the weapon, trying to wrap my mind around it being in Moria Gafni's possession. What would a nurse be doing with a pistol? Why would she keep it hidden? And why, once she had determined to kill herself, did she elect to swallow an overdose of pills in lieu of blowing her brains out?

I was so engrossed with these questions that I failed to hear the apartment door squeak open, and only realized that I was no longer alone on the premises when heavy footfalls sounded from the living room. Pulse quickening, I moved fast and was at the doorway to the bedroom in time to see the man turn around from the bathroom, into which he had poked his head.

He was a big man, six feet tall and wide across the shoulders and chest. He had on workman's pants and a thick woolen shirt that stretched taut over his bulky torso. The hands protruding from the ends of his sleeves were hairy and knotty and balled into fists the size of cannonballs. He was swarthy and rough-faced and was giving me a scowl so fierce that his heavy eyebrows nearly collided above his bulging nose.

A *burglar*? I thought for a second, but then I noticed his boots. They were caked with mud. One mystery solved.

"You son of a bitch," he growled, slicing the distance between us, and I could tell he had just one thing on his mind. I would have stepped back from the bedroom doorway, but I didn't want him to see the hole in the wall and what was in it.

I wished I had the gun in my hand. I couldn't see how this would end peacefully without it. Even worse, being in the doorway meant my range of motion was limited; without being able to fully swing my arms, I couldn't throw a proper punch. The man suffered no such handicap. He pulled his right arm back and launched a sweeping roundhouse that might have taken my head clean off if it connected. Luckily, he wasn't quick, and I ducked under his swing. I could feel the air splitting as his fist sailed a couple of inches above my head.

Then came a solid thump followed by a loud howl of pain. The man stumbled backward, clutching his right hand in his left, his ugly face a mask of agony. A sideways glance showed me what had happened. A fist-sized crater marked the door jamb about the height of my head. Cracks spread from the crater like fissures in dry earth.

So much for lamenting the fact that I was standing in a doorway. I couldn't have chosen a better position.

The man was breathing hard and moaning, but he wasn't out of commission yet. The bastard was actually flexing his fingers, testing them. He must have had steel for bones.

Before he could recover further, I went at him, giving him a quick one-two punch right in the middle of his big belly. My bruised knuckles screamed, but it was worse for the other guy. The blows knocked his breath out and dropped him to his knees. I shoved him hard, toppling him to the floor, his head thumping on the tiles. He sprawled there, dazed and wheezing, cheeks blotched by lack of oxygen.

I thought about kicking him for good measure but managed to hold myself back. Instead, I went into the bedroom and put the gun in my pocket. I considered shoving it in his face just to scare the daylights out of him, but then decided a softer approach might prove better. Stepping around his gasping form, I went to the kitchen and filled a glass with water. By the time I returned to the living room, he was on hands and knees, his forehead damp with sweat despite the cold, looking up at me with a mixture of fury and wariness.

"Drink this," I said, handing him the glass. And when he didn't move, "Go on. You could use some cooling down."

He took the glass and drained it in one quick gulp. His breathing was still accelerated, but not by all that much. He was a tough one, that was for sure. I put a hand on the gun, just in case.

"Are you gonna behave, big guy?"

He glared at me, and his fingers tightened around the glass, like he was about to throw it in my face.

"Don't even think about it," I said. "Put the glass down, or I'll kick your teeth in."

He hesitated, and I could see the calculation in his eyes, trying to decide who'd be quicker, me or him. He came to the right decision and set the glass on the floor.

"What's your name?" I asked.

"Why should I tell you?" His tone was belligerent and sulky. He wasn't used to being bested in a physical fight, and he had a bad opinion of me to begin with.

I said, "It will take me no more than five minutes to find out, you know. One of your neighbors will tell me. You live on the second floor, right? Closest door to the stairs?"

His eyes grew wide. He was wondering how I knew where he lived, and what it meant.

I pointed at his muddied boots. "It wasn't that difficult to figure out. You left a trail of mud across the lobby and all the way to your door. A little inconsiderate, if you ask me."

"I didn't notice," he said, and I could hardly believe it, but he actually sounded embarrassed. This from a guy who tried to clock me before I could get a word in.

"How did you get in here?" I asked.

"Door was unlocked."

I felt like kicking myself, but instead directed my anger at him. "Why the hell did you try to hit me?"

His jaw tightened, and he fairly spat the words at me. "Because you're a thief. The worst kind. You steal from the dead."

"You think I'm here to rob the place? I'm here by permission. I have a key." I tossed it at him. "You can get up and try it. It can't be comfortable being on your knees like that."

I retreated two paces, and he got up and, after eyeballing me for five long seconds, went to the door and slid the key in the lock. His shoulders sagged as it turned. A few seconds later he was back, turning the key in his fingers, glowering at me. A vein throbbed in the side of his thick neck. I had hoped giving him the key would placate him, but apparently it didn't.

He said, "Who are you? A new tenant? I heard no one is supposed to move in until at least the end of next month."

"I'm not a tenant. My name is Adam Lapid. I'm a private investigator. I'm working for Moria's father. He gave me the key."

The man's eyebrows dipped. "What's there to investigate?"

"Moria's father was shocked by her suicide. He wants to know why she did it."

"I heard she left a note."

"She did. But there are still some open questions. What's your name?"

"Daniel Shukrun," he said, the aggression draining out of his body. "Listen, I apologize for what happened before. I acted without thinking."

He looked at me steadily as he said it, and I couldn't help but respect that. A lesser man would have been staring at his shoes. It suggested he was genuine in his remorse and that he was the sort of man who took responsibility for his mistakes. Still, when he offered me the key back, I kept my distance and told him to put it on the table. I also maintained my hold on the gun in my pocket.

"How did you know I was up here?" I asked.

"My apartment is right below this one. My wife and I heard footsteps from above, so we knew someone was here."

"And you came charging in to catch whoever it was red-handed?"

"I wanted to make sure no one was robbing the place. When I came in, I saw the bag." He indicated the bag I'd placed by the door. "I thought the burglar had brought it to carry the loot. An aunt of mine died a couple of years back, and two days later, before her family could decide what to do with her things, someone broke in and made off with some valuables. I thought the same was happening here. And when I saw you, I was sure of it."

"Why? Do I look like a criminal?"

He took a thoughtful moment before answering. "Not right now. But when I first saw you, there was a look on your face like you couldn't believe what was happening, and that you were worried, maybe even scared, about something. Like getting caught in an apartment you were robbing by a guy like me."

He said "a guy like me" in an offhand way, not bragging about his size, just aware of it and the effect it had on people. And he'd read me perfectly. I had been unnerved by finding the gun and worried about the implications of its presence.

"I was worried about the door jamb," I said, putting on a smile.

He chuckled. "Yeah. I guess I should have apologized to it instead of you." He paused, shifting his fingers. He winced a little, but they did not seem to be the worse for wear. He held them up. "I guess I got what was coming to me."

"It might have been worse if indeed there was a robber here," I said. "You never know what a criminal will do when he's caught in the act."

Daniel puffed his big chest out, looking offended. "I can handle myself just fine, don't you worry."

I raised a mollifying hand. "I'm sure you can. I've seen how hard you can punch. Tell me, is this the first time you visited the apartment since Moria died?"

"Yeah. Why?"

"Just wondering. How long have you been living in this building?"

"Six years."

"So you knew Moria Gafni for a long time?"

"About two years."

"Were you friends?"

"I wouldn't say that. But I liked her very much. My wife and I both did. Especially since"—he paused and gulped—"especially since she treated our son."

"Your son was sick?"

A flash of pain went through his eyes. He said, "It's cold in here. Why don't we go downstairs to my apartment, where it's warmer? I can make us some tea."

"All right. You go ahead. I'll come down in a few minutes."

He nodded and left the apartment. I went back into the bedroom and looked at the hole where the pair of fully loaded magazines still lay. Why keep a gun hidden away like that? It wasn't for protection because Moria wouldn't have been able to reach the weapon in a hurry. So the gun served a different purpose, likely a darker one.

I took the pistol out of my pocket and weighed it in my hand. I had come to Jerusalem unarmed. I hadn't thought I would need a weapon on this investigation. Now it appeared that I might.

I would have gone with a different gun if I had the choice, but this one would have to do. I ejected the magazine and found it loaded to the brim. I returned the weapon to my right pocket and put the two extra magazines in my left. Then I reattached the bedside cabinet to the wall.

The gun and ammunition felt heavier than they should have, as though the secrets they hinted at had weight. Which shouldn't have surprised me because secrets often do.

10

Daniel's apartment was the same size and layout as Moria's, but three souls lived there, so it felt more crowded and cramped. There was Daniel, his wife, Lillian, and their baby daughter. The baby was asleep in the other room behind a closed door. To ward off the threat of her waking up a moment before she naturally would, the three of us spoke in low voices.

The heating stove was on. It hissed and whispered and emitted a faintly acrid smell. Above it, on a clothesline strung across the living room, pristine linen diapers hung to dry. The air was warm and damp and redolent of detergent and wet linen. Lillian, a wide-hipped woman with long raven hair, stood by a towering pot in the kitchen, using a long stick to rotate the additional diapers that were undergoing disinfection in its boiling water. More pots and pails and bowls were arrayed along one kitchen wall. All were full of water, a precaution against Jerusalem's frequent water outages.

Daniel set a teapot and glasses on the dining table. The teapot was beat-up metal. The glasses were narrow and had delicate artwork painted on them. Daniel caught me eying them and said, "They were my grandparents'. They brought them all the way here from Morocco in 1903."

He told me how his grandparents, spurred by religious fervor, had taken their six children on the perilous journey from Casablanca to Jerusalem. They traveled by boat, then camel, and finally mule-drawn wagons until they reached the Holy City. They went straight to the Temple Mount upon arrival. Daniel's father was ten when his own father broke into tears on the Mount, overcome by his proximity to where the two Jewish temples—the first destroyed by the Babylonians, the second by the Romans—had once stood.

"We've lived in Jerusalem ever since," Daniel said with evident pride.

From the kitchen, Lillian commented with a smile, "Daniel talks like his family has lived here since the time of King David, when in truth they're newcomers."

"Lillian's ancestors came here fifty years before mine," Daniel said.

"A full century next year," Lillian said, wiping her hands on her apron. "Long before anyone even dreamed up the word Zionism." With the stick, she fished out the pure and soggy diapers from the pot and set them to cool in a large basin. She entered the living room and plopped onto a chair with a sigh. Daniel poured us all tea.

I took a sip. The tea was hot and sugarless, but with a strong herbal taste that I liked. I could feel my bones thawing after the deep cold of Moria's apartment.

"Daniel told me you're a private investigator," Lillian said. Both she and her husband had Jerusalem accents, melodious and earthy with pronounced vowels.

"That's right. I'm trying to learn what I can about Moria."

"It was quite a shock," Lillian said. "I couldn't believe it when I heard she was dead. It still feels like a bad dream."

"How well did you know her?"

"Not as well as we thought, obviously. And not as well as we would have liked. We used to see much more of her, and during the past year we invited her to dinner a few times, but she always declined. I think she felt uncomfortable in our company."

"Why do you say that?"

Lillian exchanged a glance with her husband. Daniel drew a

breath and said, "Because of our son. I think she found it hard to be around us."

"I don't understand."

Daniel started to talk, but his voice failed on the first syllable. His eyes welled up. Lillian squeezed his hand.

"Our son, Shimon," she said, "our firstborn, got sick two years ago when he was three and a half. He was hospitalized in Ariel Hospital, where Moria worked. That's where we met her for the first time. It was shortly before she moved into the building."

Daniel was looking to the side, and I followed his gaze to a photograph of Daniel, Lillian, and a smiling child of three sitting on Daniel's lap. The photo was black and white, but the smile on the big man's face was so bright, it shone like a sunrise. The boy looked full of life, oblivious to the disaster hurtling toward him, toward them all. Sometimes death doesn't creep up on you. Sometimes it pounces.

Lillian said, "All the nurses were dedicated, but none more than Moria. Our son loved her. His mood was always brightest when she was on shift. He got better after a while, and I allowed myself to hope, but then his condition deteriorated, and the doctor told us he needed to undergo surgery." She took a deep breath and added in a hollow voice, "Shimon died during the procedure."

Daniel clamped his eyes tight, but a couple of tears still managed to escape. He wiped his face with the back of his hand—big, clumsy swipes, as though trying to erase the pain and not just the wetness. I already liked him despite the manner in which our acquaintance had commenced, but now I felt toward him the sort of intimate kinship that only comes from shared pain. We had both lost young children.

Lillian clutched her husband's hand tighter, as though to keep him from falling, or perhaps to prevent herself from doing so. "He's with the angels," she said. "With God. Remember that."

Daniel nodded, but his balled fists indicated he was far from reconciled with the Almighty for depriving him of his son.

"Moria took it hard when Shimon died," Lillian said. "She came to the funeral, the only one from the hospital staff, and she wept openly.

And once, about a month after his death, we ran into each other on the stairs, and tears sprang to her eyes the moment she saw me. Afterward, she was distant, even a bit cool toward us."

"Do you think she blamed herself for your son's death?"

"She had no reason to. None whatsoever."

Which meant very little. Guilt is an illogical beast. There's no rhyme or reason to when it rears its head or sinks its teeth. Moria might have taken the death of a patient too much to heart. She might have even found fault in her abilities, had viewed herself culpable. But I couldn't see that as the motivation for her suicide. It did not fit the content of her note.

"I think she was troubled about something," Lillian said.

"What makes you think that?"

"I used to hear her walking around in the middle of the night, back and forth. We can hear it when someone's walking upstairs. I think she had trouble sleeping."

Like me, I thought.

"I never heard any footsteps at night," Daniel said.

"Why would you?" Lillian gave her husband a smile of good-natured reproach. "You're either working or asleep. I'm the one who gets up at night to feed and change the baby. You don't even stir when she cries."

"Any idea what Moria was troubled about?" I asked.

Both of them said they didn't know.

"Did Moria have any visitors that you know of?"

"A couple of nurses from the hospital came by every once in a while," Lillian said. "Including the one who found the body."

"Naomi Hecht?"

"Yes, that's her. She used to come by pretty frequently. I hope she had time to make it up with Moria before... you know."

"She and Moria had a falling-out?"

"I think so. A week before that dreadful day, I was walking outside with the baby when I saw Nurse Hecht enter the building. Ten, maybe fifteen minutes later, she came out, and I could tell she was distraught by her face and the way she stomped off. That was the last time I saw her until the day she found Moria dead."

"How did Nurse Hecht seem to you that day? Before she saw the body, I mean."

"Preoccupied. She was always cordial, but that day she went up the stairs without saying hello, as though she didn't see me at all."

"What happened then?"

"I went back inside. Daniel was at work. A minute later I heard a shout from above. 'No!' I ran outside and up the stairs, opened the door, and saw Nurse Hecht come out of Moria's bedroom. She was as white as her nurse's uniform."

"Was she crying?"

"No. Her face was set, I remember, her mouth tight. She held up a hand when she saw me, told me to get out. She followed me to the landing and locked the door."

"She had a key? You sure about that?"

"Positive. Like I said, she locked the door."

"What happened then?"

"I asked her what was wrong. She wouldn't answer, just asked me where the closest telephone was. One of the neighbors across the street has one, and I told her the address. She sprinted down the stairs and out of the building. A short while later, the police arrived, and Nurse Hecht showed them into the apartment. Only then did she come out to the landing and tell me Moria was dead."

"Did she tell you how?"

"Yes. I remember how she said it. Just one word. 'Suicide.' I wasn't sure I'd heard her correctly, so I asked her to repeat it, and she did. That one word again. So final and abrupt. Like a door slamming shut on a life."

Lillian shivered, and now it was Daniel's turn to comfort his wife. He patted her back with his big hand, and she smiled sadly at him. I got the feeling that they were used to being each other's rock. They had weathered the worst storm any parents could face, and they had emerged from it as strong as two pieces of steel welded together.

"Did she tell you how Moria killed herself?"

"I asked, but she wouldn't say. She just told me to go home, and I did. But I kept the door open and waited. I wanted to see what was happening. A few more cops arrived, and someone I assumed was a doctor from the bag he carried. And a while later they took the body away. I remember how small Moria looked on the gurney, a tiny bundle wrapped in a white sheet. All the neighbors stood in their doorways as the cops carried her down the stairs. Everyone was silent."

We were silent too. Even the stove had quieted. Then it let out a muffled grumble and resumed its hissing, and I asked my next question: "Is one of these women Naomi Hecht?" I was holding up the photograph of Moria with the two other nurses.

Lillian nodded, pointing at the tallest of the three women. "That's her. The other one is Anat Schlesinger. They all worked together."

"Do you remember the last time Nurse Schlesinger came around?"

"I think it was two weeks or so before that awful day. Of course, she might have come by when I was out or sleeping or just happened to have not noticed." A dash of color suffused Lillian's cheeks. "Not that I was trying to, you understand."

"Of course," I said, doing my best not to smile, thinking that Lillian wouldn't like it if I told her that nosy neighbors are often a detective's best source of information.

"We wanted to go to the funeral," Daniel said, "but we couldn't find out where and when it was held."

"Moria was buried in Tel Aviv," I said. "Her father wanted to keep the funeral small."

"Sure, we understand," Lillian said, but the glance she exchanged with her husband suggested that neither of them did.

I took another sip of tea and asked, "Apart from Naomi Hecht, do you know of anyone who had a key to Moria's apartment?"

"Would the landlord have one?" Lillian asked her husband, who rubbed his forehead thoughtfully and answered with a slow nod.

"Does he live in the building?" I asked.

She shook her head. "He doesn't live in Jerusalem at all. He has a house in Ramat Gan. He comes by once a month to collect the rent. Otherwise, we don't see him."

I asked for his name and jotted it in my notebook, but since he was hardly around, I doubted he had anything to do with Moria's suicide.

I finished my tea and asked for some more. Daniel refilled my glass. I took another swallow, a long one, knowing this was about to get delicate.

"Did Moria have any male visitors?"

Daniel shook his head, saying he never saw anyone, but Lillian was quiet and still. Only her eyes moved, a quick flick down and up.

Angling my body toward her, I said, "You've seen someone, haven't you, Lillian?"

She looked at me but didn't speak.

"You're trying to protect her honor, her reputation, and that's good. You owe her that. But it may be important for my investigation. For Moria's father to understand why she killed herself."

Lillian bit her lip, obviously torn.

"I'm not here to judge her," I said. "I know Moria was a good person. Whatever you tell me won't change what I think of her."

A few more seconds passed. Then Lillian sighed and said, "There was a man, but I don't know who he is. Sometimes late at night, I would hear footsteps on the stairs going to the third floor. Our door is right by the stairs, and you can hear everything at night when there's no traffic or people outside and everything is quiet. After the footsteps going up, I would hear voices. Just a few words, nothing I could make out, but Moria had a distinct, high-pitched voice, and I could tell one of the speakers was her. Then there would be movement in Moria's apartment, of more than one set of feet. But it never lasted very long." The implication was clear. Lillian thought Moria and her visitor had gone straight to bed. "Other times, I would hear someone descending the stairs. Also in the middle of the night."

Moria's lover leaving, she meant.

"You never told me any of this," Daniel said, in the surprised tone of a man who learns for the first time that there are parts of his wife that are unknown to him.

"I wasn't keeping secrets from you. I just didn't think it would do anyone any good if I told you."

It was clear why Lillian had not told her husband about this. It was the same reason she was reluctant to tell me. An unmarried woman was not supposed to have male visitors late at night. She was not supposed to sleep with men at all. Though, of course, more than a few did.

"How many times did you hear that?" I asked. "How often?"

She thought about it. "Once a week, maybe a bit less. But it also might have happened when I was asleep. I don't know how long it had been going on. It was only after the baby was born that I first became aware of Moria's visitor."

"How old is your daughter?"

"Dina is five and a half months old."

This meant that Moria's affair had been going on for at least four and a half months, given that she'd been dead for a little over a month.

"Did you ever talk with Moria about her visitor?"

"No. Never. What would I have said, 'I can sometimes hear you and him walking around upstairs?' Can you imagine how it would have made her feel? I don't like to think about our downstairs neighbors being able to hear us."

"Did you ever actually see this man?"

"Yes," Lillian said. My excitement spiked and then fizzled out just as quickly when she added, "But only once, and only from the back."

"From the back?"

She nodded. "It was about two months before Moria died. I'd just finished feeding Dina and put her in her crib when I heard footsteps going down the stairs. I got curious. Or maybe it would be more accurate to say that I'd been curious for a while by then, and I decided to act on it. I opened the door as quietly as I could and padded out onto the landing. I saw the man as he was leaving the building. He didn't hear me, didn't turn around. That's why I only saw him from the back."

"You didn't catch a glimpse of his face? Not even a part of it?"

"I'm afraid not."

"What did he look like?"

"I just told you, I—"

"I don't mean his facial features," I said. "I mean the rest of him. How tall was he? Was he thin? Fat? Broad-shouldered like your husband?"

"He was nowhere near as big as Daniel," Lillian said, laying an affectionate hand on her husband's. "He had a sort of narrow build. I'd say he was one, maybe two inches shorter than Daniel, but it's difficult to say because I only saw him from above."

"What color was his hair?"

"Dark. Either brown or black, but I can't say which because the only light was what little filtered in through the lobby's door and windows. The man was little more than a shadow."

"Did he have a full head of hair, or was he balding?"

She gave a shrug of desperation. "I don't know. I'm sorry, but I only saw him for a few seconds, and I was dead tired, and it was impossible to tell—"

"That's all right, Lillian," I said. "Don't worry, you're doing very well."

This was a lie. Lillian's recollection was all but useless. The sort of vague, general description that would fit thousands of men.

I wasn't ready to give up yet. This man, this lover, might hold the key to understanding Moria's state of mind. Suicide is driven by emotion. Powerful emotion. And nothing is as powerful an emotion as love. Particularly the sort of love that one has to hide, as Moria and her lover had done. That sort of love can easily turn to despair.

I tried various techniques to coax additional memories out of Lillian. I wanted some detail, a feature by which I might identify this man.

She tried. I could tell how hard she tried. But she could come up with nothing more. The night had been dark, the man a shadowy form that revealed almost nothing. Just a slender build and an approximate height, and even these impressions were suspect given the lack of light, the brevity of the sighting, the tiredness of the witness.

I hid my disappointment behind a smile and thanked her for her time.

11

The baby started crying then, and Lillian slipped into the other room to tend to her. Daniel said I was welcome to stay for lunch, but I wasn't comfortable imposing on their meager means. Especially with Gafni's retainer plumping my wallet. Besides, I had learned all I could from the Shukruns for the time being, and I was eager to find out more about Moria.

As I was stepping out, I asked him, "Is your daughter likely to fall asleep again soon? Say in the next hour or so?"

Daniel gave me a bewildered look. "Her next nap won't be for a few hours. Why?"

"Because I wouldn't want to wake her up. I'm going back upstairs now, and I'll be making some noise. I'm telling you so you won't worry."

Daniel opened his mouth, doubtless to ask me what I was meaning to do, but his wife's voice rang out, calling on him to fetch her a diaper, and we hurriedly shook hands before he turned and closed the door. I went back to Moria's apartment, this time locking the door once I was inside. Daniel's unexpected visit had ended up yielding dividends in terms of information, but I had no desire for more drop-ins by concerned or curious neighbors. I had given the place a cursory search earlier, but after finding the gun, I figured greater scrutiny was in order. This was going to take time, and I did not wish to be disturbed.

I started in the kitchen, working methodically, going through every drawer and cupboard, even looking between plates and tapping on the backboards for hollow sounds. I found nothing that shed light on why Moria had killed herself or why she had hidden a gun in her bedroom. I dragged the icebox out of its corner, but the only things I saw where it had stood were ancient dust, some loose hairs, and a couple of dead bugs.

Next came the bathroom, where I peered inside and behind the toilet tank, made sure the medicine cabinet hid no secrets, and studied the broom and dustpan that had been leaning against a corner with far more care than they deserved before setting them back in their place, feeling like a fool.

In the living room, I removed each book from the bookcase and riffled through the pages in the hope that something had been tucked between them, but nothing was. I checked inside, under, and behind the heating stove, but all I got for my trouble were blackened hands and a noseful of the acrid, burned scent of long-dead fires and spent heating oil.

After washing my hands, I examined the undersides of the table and chairs, raked my gaze over the curtains, and pulled the sofa away from the wall, finding nothing behind it. Crouching down, I ran my hand over the upholstery and then brought my face close to the padding and scoured the fabric for any unnatural stitches or seams. There were none.

Rising to full height, I winced as pain stabbed deep in my side where the policeman had kicked me. I braced myself on one of the armrests until the pain receded, then pushed off toward the bedroom.

I stood motionless for a good minute, scanning the bedroom as I had done before, hoping for a flash of inspiration similar to the one that had guided me to the gun.

No such luck. Nothing drew me to one specific spot or another. It all seemed perfectly bland and innocent. Just ordinary stuff in an ordinary bedroom. No hint of where a hiding place might be. But the gun couldn't be the only thing lurking under the mundane surface of this apartment. There had to be more. My professional instincts were screaming it. I just needed to find it.

I lifted the mattress, but there was nothing beneath it. I removed both paintings from their nails, examined their backs, and hung them again when they proved to be no more than what they seemed. I hauled the bed away from the wall, circled it, and was rewarded with the disappointing sight of the cheap bed frame and nothing else.

Despite going through them earlier, I opened each of the three dresser drawers in turn, checked their undersides, went through every item they contained, and finally looked behind the dresser, gripped by a powerful certainty that I was closing in on a second secret, another clue.

Nothing.

That left the closet. I opened its door and ran my hand through the shirts and skirts and dresses and sweaters. I removed all the clothes and set them on the bare mattress. Then I checked the top of the closet and all the shelves before returning to the clothes and spreading them out on the bed, fingering every inch of fabric.

Nothing.

Swearing under my breath, I returned to the now empty closet. I checked for a false bottom, like the one I'd installed in my closet in Tel Aviv, but there was none. Only one place left to look. It had to be there, whatever it was. Whatever else Moria had hidden. Something that would explain things. Or raise new questions.

Gripping the closet in a wide hug, I heaved. The wooden legs scraped shrilly across the floor as the heavy furniture surrendered to my pull, and I wondered what Daniel and Lillian were thinking of all the noise I was making. Maybe they thought I was not all there. Maybe they regretted inviting me into their home. I couldn't blame them if they did. With all the furniture I'd dragged, yanked, and lugged over the past hour or so, it must have sounded like I was tearing this place apart brick by brick.

I pulled until I'd gotten the closet a foot and a half from its original position. My side was hurting again, but I paid it no mind. With soaring eagerness, I peered at the now exposed back of the closet and the wall it had shielded.

The sight that greeted me comprised a blank wall and empty floor tiles. No cavities in the wall. Nothing nailed to the back of the closet. Just what you'd expect to find behind every closet in every apartment—nothing at all—but I had been expecting... something.

For a moment, I just stood there, frowning in disbelief. I'd been so sure that Moria's apartment would yield another unexpected clue that I found myself unconsciously reaching for my pocket to make sure the gun was really there, that I hadn't imagined finding it.

The cool metal against my fingertips alleviated my doubts but not my disappointment. I gazed around me again, but I had looked everywhere. This apartment had surrendered its treasure. It had no more to give.

I plodded into the living room, plopped onto the sofa, and scrubbed my hands over my face. A fierce tiredness had settled upon me, pressing down on my head and shoulders. Had the mysterious visitor taken whatever else there was to find? Or were my instincts mistaken? Perhaps my judgment was impaired. Just like it had been on the night of the demonstration when I'd mindlessly clashed with police officers outside the Knesset, which was how I got myself involved in this case to begin with.

With an acute sense of defeat, I leaned back, raising my eyes to the corner of the ceiling, where that spiderweb of cracks reigned. What had gone through Moria's mind when she'd looked upon these cracks? Did they mirror the fissures that had spread through her life, finally shattering her will to live?

I remained there for a good few minutes, the heat of my exertion deserting my body and the cold of the apartment beginning to seep through my skin.

Then the apartment door handle rattled, followed by a knock. Daniel was on the other side, a mop in one hand, a bucket in the other. He wore a sheepish expression.

"I figured since you're here, I might as well wash off the mud I left."

He came inside, set the bucket in the middle of the living room, and began cleaning.

"Find anything?" he said, moving the mop back and forth.

"No," I said bitterly. "Sorry if I made too much noise."

"Don't worry about it. You do what you need to do."

He finished cleaning all the mud, moved to the doorway to Moria's bedroom, and touched the cratered wood where his fist had landed. He made a face. "I'll need to get this fixed before another tenant moves in. Is it true that Moria's father is keeping the apartment?"

"Just like you heard, till the end of next month. After that..." I shrugged.

"So I have a little time," he said, touching the wood again.

"Know of any cheap hotels in the area?" I asked, and he thought for a moment before giving me a name and an address.

"It's pretty basic," he warned. "Not that I ever stayed there, mind you, but that's what I heard."

"I'll check it out. Thank you."

He emptied the bucket in the tub, picked up his mop, turned to leave, but then stopped and asked, "You think this man, the one Lillian saw, you think he and Moria were really lovers?"

"It seems likely."

"You think he's the reason she killed herself?"

I considered the clandestine nature of their trysts and the contents of Moria's note and gave a noncommittal shrug. "I don't know, but I suppose it's possible. She wouldn't be the first woman to kill herself over a broken heart or something of that nature."

Daniel nodded a couple of times, and a muscle flexed in his jaw. "That son of a bitch," he said.

"Let's not jump to conclusions, all right? Like I said, I don't know if this man, whoever he is, had anything to do with the suicide."

He nodded again, and we shook hands. He asked that I let him and Lillian know of any development in the investigation, and I said I would, though I had no intention to.

I returned all the furniture to its place. Then, figuring other neighbors might prove as fruitful as the Shukruns, I knocked on the other doors in the building. Moria's fellow third-floor tenant was old, half blind, and more than half deaf, judging by how loudly he asked me to raise my voice. Predictably, he had seen and heard nothing useful.

No one answered the door of the apartment that shared the second floor with the Shukruns'. On the ground floor, the first door I knocked on was answered by a man who proclaimed that Moria had committed a grave sin by taking her own life. Other than that, she'd always seemed nice. In the second apartment lived a woman who said Moria had always been polite but reserved. She respected her greatly for her work as a pediatric nurse.

"My nephew was hospitalized in her ward," she said. "My sister told me she was the best nurse of the lot."

She knew little of Moria's life. If I wanted to learn more, she suggested in a somewhat malicious tone, I should talk to the second-floor neighbor, Lillian Shukrun. "She's the sort of woman who likes to know everything, always watching, always sticking her nose in other people's business."

I did not tell her that I'd already talked to Lillian and liked her quite a bit.

Overall, my second search of Moria's apartment and talking to her neighbors had both ended in abject failure. But I was nowhere near done. I was now more determined than ever to unravel the mystery of Moria's death. To discover the identity of the person in her note. To, perhaps, grant her a measure of justice.

While I was canvassing the building, I saw that Daniel hadn't cleaned the mud in the lobby and stairs. Maybe he would get to it later. Or maybe, in washing Moria's apartment, he was repaying a debt for his dead son the only way he knew how. Either way, I felt good about leaving Moria's apartment as clean as she'd left it when she died.

12

I almost didn't find the hotel. A scrawny building, it stood near the middle of Yehudit Street, about a ten-minute walk from Moria's apartment, and sported a faded sign that blended almost perfectly with the hotel's facade—both were streaked and smudged with all manner of black and gray. Inside, there was a poorly lit lobby that smelled of damp. The walls looked as though they'd last been painted during the Crusades. Incongruously, an ornate metal light fixture dangled from the ceiling, suggesting a long-forgotten glory, though only one of the sockets housed a bulb. The man behind the counter was fifty-something, with sallow skin, a bald dome of a head, and rheumy, bulging eyes. He eyeballed me over a newspaper he'd been reading, taking in the bag I was carrying, but did not utter a word of greeting.

I told him I needed a room.

He quoted a nightly rate that struck me as only mildly exorbitant. After a bit of haggling, I gave him some money, and he handed me a key. The creased leather key fob bore the number 9 and a name: Hotel Shalem. The clerk pointed a bony finger at the stairs. "Third floor. Second door on the left."

There were five doors in total. Two on either side of the corridor and one at the end. The two doors on the right had brass room numbers. The two on the left had only faint outlines where numbers had once hung. The door at the end had neither. I pushed it open and discovered a bathroom. Basic, Daniel had said, and he'd been right. One bathroom to a floor.

My room was small and cramped. There was a chair and a dresser. No closet. Just a coat hanger with one broken hook. The bed was a single and set very low. I tested the mattress and found it sagging and lumpy but adequate. The bedclothes looked clean, but their color had dwindled with age and repeated washings. The scent of cigarettes of lodgers both recent and ancient clung to the walls and furniture and the air itself like barnacles to an unattended ship.

The window resisted my efforts to open it, but finally yielded with a grating squeak, rising halfway before getting stuck. A minute of futile heaving later, I gave up, sitting on the bed before the half-open window, a cold wind rushing into the room, coiling its chilly fingers around me.

I took out the gun and the two magazines and weighed them in my hands and in my mind. Should I take them with me or leave them here? I could stick them in my bag, but I didn't trust the hotel keeper to not go through my stuff. Then again, I did not like walking around with a gun for no reason.

Too bad there wasn't a handy bedside cabinet with a hole in the wall behind it.

I settled on pulling out the bottom dresser drawer, stashing the weapon and magazines in the small space beneath it, and then sliding the drawer back into place. Not as good a hiding spot as Moria's, but I figured it was safe enough for the time being.

I wanted to keep the window open as far as it would go to air out the room, but if it started raining again, I might return to find everything drenched. I left it open a crack and headed out.

My stomach was grumbling. It was past noon, and I hadn't eaten since early that morning. I ducked into a café on the corner that had pictures of the Old City on its walls. I ordered bean soup and bread. The soup was hot and salty, the bread dark brown and rough. I tore up the latter and dunked its pieces into the former and started eating with relish.

It was the sort of simple fare that most Israeli eateries served. Plain ingredients. Nothing fancy or elaborate. Food designed to fill one's belly rather than excite one's taste buds. Israel's strict rationing policy made it difficult to produce dishes with loftier aspirations. I wondered if in Germany, with its economic miracle, people were eating better. I had a feeling they were.

My stomach full, I ventured back onto the street. I'd asked for directions at the café, and I followed them on foot, treading sidewalks in which water pooled in cracks and depressions, walking past leafless trees shivering in the wind and shops with wet awnings. Many of the buildings here were made of local limestone, coarse and pitted, each stone as unique as a man's face, with its distinct set of grooves, furrows, pocks, and bumps. As though each stone had a personal life story. As if their past had marked them with age spots and worry lines.

This section of Jerusalem, the western, Jewish part, was less than a century old, not much older than Tel Aviv, and parts of it were not older at all. Yet these streets felt markedly different from Tel Aviv's, tenser and wary.

It might have been due to the fact that Jerusalem perched on a mountain, while Tel Aviv lounged by the sea. Or perhaps it was because, generally, Tel Aviv was a hot and sunny place, while Jerusalem was colder and rainier.

But it seemed to me that the difference lay elsewhere. While Tel Aviv looked only to the future, here the streets and buildings were burdened with a heavy history, stooped under a ponderous mythical importance. Tel Aviv was a Jewish, Hebrew city and always had been. Jerusalem was holy for three major religions and had switched hands repeatedly over the millennia.

Also, Tel Aviv had not been besieged during Israel's War of Independence, while West Jerusalem had. The Arabs had blockaded it for months, leading to severe shortages of food, water, medicine. And while Tel Aviv had been bombed from the air a number of times, it had not suffered continuous barrages of artillery as had West Jerusalem.

But above all, Tel Aviv was whole and Jerusalem broken. The eastern part, including the Old City, was now separated from the Israeli section by barbed wire, walls, and barricades, and patrolled by Jordanian troops. The old Jewish Quarter was a Nazi dream come true—*judenfrei*, free of Jews, the entire Jewish population having been expelled by the Jordanians during the war. The holy sites of Jerusalem—the Temple Mount, the Western Wall—were forbidden to us Jews. The closest one could get to them was a vantage point on Mount Zion, close to the City Line, the name given to the armistice line that sliced Jerusalem in two. From there, one could gaze upon the Old City, but nothing more, similar to how Moses in the book of Deuteronomy, prohibited by God from entering Canaan, was allowed to gaze upon the Promised Land from Mount Nebo across the Jordan River. I doubted the sight alleviated his longing.

Here in Jerusalem, unlike Tel Aviv, the enemy was close, within range of small-arms fire. And indeed, on occasion, Jordanian soldiers fired into West Jerusalem, maiming or killing Israeli citizens. Here, the precariousness of Israel was emphasized, and the threat of war hung in the air like the blade of a guillotine. No wonder Jerusalem lacked Tel Aviv's vivaciousness, its convulsive energy. There was joy in the capital, yes, cinemas and cafés and culture and children and love. But all this goodness was marred by the knowledge that the divided city was a volatile tinderbox, and that the slightest spark could ignite a conflagration of fire and death.

And now this sense of vulnerability was augmented by the question of negotiations with Germany. A question that split Israeli society much like the city of Jerusalem was split. A split that had erupted into the skirmish between protesters and police, in which I had taken part.

It occurred to me then that the Jordanian troops manning the City Line must have heard the sounds of battle near the Knesset. What did they make of it? Did they smile, laugh, imagine the Jews killing each other, doing their dirty work for them? Did their fingers twitch for the triggers of their rifles as they grew excited thinking that a country thus divided would not be able to resist another attack?

Fury growled through my veins, and I found myself swearing profusely in Hungarian and Hebrew, words that would have made my mother spank me for my own good and my father shake his head in anguished disappointment.

I cursed Ben-Gurion for putting Israel in such a position, but I could not shake the biting guilt that assailed me as well. For had I not raised my hand against Israeli policemen? Had I not participated in the internecine skirmish near the Knesset?

Stopping to fire up a cigarette, I sucked in its smoke so violently that it scorched my throat. I coughed, my eyes tearing up, and I swore again, this time naming no one, but I had no illusion as to who was the target of my expletives.

I almost threw away the offending cigarette in anger, but a shrill internal voice stayed my hand, rebuking me for my intended waste-fulness. Hadn't I lived through endless days when a cigarette was but a distant dream?

I put the cigarette back between my lips, and this time drew on it gently. Warmth spread through my chest, not taking the edge off my anger, but granting me sufficient distance from it in order to redirect its focus. Away from me and onto the unknown person who had driven Moria Gafni to suicide.

"Whoever you are," I murmured, "I'm coming for you."

13

I recognized Ariel Hospital from one of the pictures I'd seen in Moria's apartment. Four stories tall and made of fine Jerusalem stone now darkened by rain, with recessed arched windows dotting its front.

It had a low wrought-iron fence, and sculpted pillars divided its entrance into three archways. The lobby milled with people. Doctors and nurses and patients. Coughs and sneezes and chatter in Yiddish, Hebrew, and a bunch of other languages resounded throughout the large space. Underlying the wet human smell was the stringent odor of Lysol. I asked a blonde nurse where the Pediatric Ward was, followed her directions, and a few minutes later found myself standing before a counter, behind which sat a matronly nurse jotting in a file folder.

I waited for her to finish, but when a full minute passed, I cleared my throat loudly.

"What can I do for you?" she asked without raising her eyes from her scribbling.

I asked where I might find Naomi Hecht.

That made her look up. She did not seem impressed. "Nurse Hecht? Why?"

"I want to talk to her."

"Are you a family member of one of our patients?"

"No."

She pressed her lips together. "Then I don't see why you should be bothering her during her shift. Now, if you don't mind." She made a shooing gesture and resumed writing.

I leaned over the counter and waved my fingers through her gaze, forcing her eyes back to me. "I want to talk to her about Moria Gafni."

"Moria?"

"I'm investigating her death." I didn't elaborate. I just stared at her hard while drumming my fingers on the counter in a show of impatience. Sometimes, you need to look a little menacing to get people to do what you want.

"I see. But she..." She looked flustered, touched her cap. "Sorry, I didn't mean..." She laid down her pencil and darted her eyes around nervously before stopping on a nurse who had just emerged from a room at the end of the hall. "That's her. Naomi, can you come here, please?"

Naomi Hecht wore shoes with low heels that clicked on the hard floor as she approached. She was a slim woman, narrow at the hips and shoulders, and tall for her sex at five foot ten. Her hair was dark and short, flattened against the sides of her head by bobby pins and culminating in an understated curl just below her ears, exposing a long, stately neck. She moved with determined, rapid steps. In one hand, she clutched a bottle of translucent liquid; the other was clamped into a fist. On her face, she had an expression of barely restrained fury, like the rattling lid of a simmering pot.

"I tell you, Paula," she said, thumping the bottle on the counter, her indignation blinding her to my presence. "I'll never understand how that stupid man became a doctor. You know what—"

The matronly nurse—Paula—raised a silencing hand and said in a cutting voice, "We'll talk about this later, Naomi, all right?" She pointed at me. "This man is here to see you."

Naomi Hecht looked at me. She had sharp hazel eyes set deep in an attractive strong face that some would find intimidating. The sort of face that suggested this was a woman who did not suffer fools gladly. I almost felt bad for the doctor she'd disparaged a minute ago.

"Who are you?" she asked bluntly. Her voice fitted the impression made by her features; it was deep, full, and had iron at its core.

"My name is Adam Lapid," I said. "I'm a private investigator. Can we talk for a few minutes? I want to ask you a few questions about Moria Gafni."

Paula was leaning forward, listening with rapt attention. Naomi Hecht gave her a cool smile that made Paula retreat to the safety of her pencil and folder. Turning to me again, Naomi Hecht motioned me away from the counter and Paula's sensitive ears. I followed her a short distance down the hall, where she stopped and folded her arms across her chest. Clipped nails, I noticed. A slim wedding ring.

"Why would a private investigator be interested in Moria?" she asked.

"Her father hired me to look into her suicide."

"Her father?"

"You sound surprised."

"I am."

"Care to tell me why?"

She parried my question with one of her own. "What do you mean, look into her suicide?"

"Moria's father wants to know why she did it. Do you know?"

"No." Her answer was immediate and without hesitation, but I thought I caught the faintest twitch at the corner of her mouth. A sign of deceit?

"Well, would you mind answering some questions about Moria?" She didn't respond straight away, so I added, "You were her friend. Don't you want to know why she killed herself?"

Color flared in her cheeks. "You've got a lot of nerve, Mr. Lapid, you know that?"

"So I've been told. Well?"

She pursed her lips, shifted them around a bit, and I wondered what was going through her mind and why she was looking at me like I was a bundle of bad news. Her arms still folded, she glanced at her watch. "I can't talk right now. My shift ends in thirty minutes. I can meet you afterward."

Which would give her ample time to prepare, to decide what to tell me and what to keep to herself—if she had anything to hide, that is. Far from ideal, but I couldn't see a way to force the issue.

"All right. I'll wait for you downstairs."

"No, not here," she said quickly, like a command. "Let's meet in Café Atara. I can be there in an hour." Then, without waiting for a reply, she turned and marched off, snatching the bottle of medicine from the counter along the way.

I watched her go, admiring the efficient way her body moved and the shape of her stockinged calves. Then I walked back toward Paula, who wasn't scribbling anymore, but watching me with keen interest.

I flashed her a smile and asked, "Is Anat Schlesinger around?"

"My, my, you are informed, aren't you?"

"I am?"

"First you asked about Naomi, and now about Anat. Both were close friends of Moria."

"Is there anyone I missed?"

She shook her head. "Moria was generally friendly, but she was closest to Anat and Naomi."

"What did you think of her?"

She took a moment to answer. She had brown hair turning gray and full cheeks, a pair of blue eyes behind round glasses. "I was worried about her."

"You saw it coming?"

"What? No, I didn't mean that. I never imagined... What I meant was that I was concerned about her future as a nurse."

"She wasn't good at her job?"

"No, that wasn't it. Of course, she was young and inexperienced, but she had the desire to learn and to help—and those are the important things."

"So what was the problem?"

She hesitated, studying my face. "You've been through things, haven't you?"

"Things?"

"War. You've been to war, haven't you? Either here or in Europe. You're acquainted with death. I don't know why I'm sure of that, but I am. Maybe because I and most of the people I work with are acquainted with it as well."

"Aren't most people acquainted with death?"

"I suppose they are. But there are degrees of familiarity. I think yours is pretty high."

"What does that have to do with Moria?"

"Nothing. It just means that there's a greater chance you won't take what I'm about to tell you the wrong way."

"Which is?"

"That the reason I wasn't sure Moria would be able to handle being a nurse for long is that she cared far too much."

"About her patients?"

"Yes."

"Aren't nurses supposed to care about their patients?"

"They are. Of course they are. But too much caring is dangerous. You must understand, Mr. Lapid, there's no escape from suffering and death in a hospital. Not even with the best medicine, the finest doctors and nurses. It can be hard to take, especially here in the Pediatric Ward."

As if to underscore her point, the pitiful mewling wail of a small girl burst from somewhere down the hall. The sound made me flinch, triggering a vivid memory of my eldest daughter after she sprained her ankle.

"Awful, isn't it?" Paula asked, and for a second I thought she could read my mind, see my pain, that she was referring to my having lost my daughters. "Children shouldn't fall prey to harsh illnesses, yet they do. And some of them don't get better. No matter how hard you try to heal them, they wither away and die. It's impossible not to connect to them, the sweet poor things. But if you don't keep some distance, they'll break your heart. And I believe a heart can take only so much breaking."

"Moria didn't keep her distance?"

"I'm not sure she knew how. It was as if they were her children, that she was their mother, not their nurse. She would often stay after her shift, reading to the children, talking to them for hours. I cautioned her about it a couple of times, told her she would ruin herself, and she would listen attentively enough but then carry on as before."

"Sounds like she was a terrific nurse."

"Was she? The children loved her, that's for sure. But we need nurses who'll last for years. I'm not sure Moria would have. Because every time one of the children died, or ended up paralyzed, or something of that kind, it was as if Moria went into mourning."

Which fitted with what Lillian Shukrun had told me about Moria crying over her son's grave, and how she was the only nurse to attend his funeral.

"You think she might have killed herself due to the strain she was under?" I asked. "All that mourning?" Not that I seriously considered the possibility, given the suicide note.

"Before, it wouldn't have crossed my mind. Now, who can say for sure?"

"Did you spot any change to Moria's mood in the days and weeks before she died?"

"No more than the rest of us."

"What do you mean?"

"We were all shaken by what had happened to Dr. Shapira." Paula noticed my bafflement and added, "I see you're not as informed as I initially thought."

"Apparently not. Who's Dr. Shapira? What happened to him?"

"He was a doctor here in the ward," Paula said. "He was murdered."

14

"How was Dr. Shapira killed?" I asked.

"He was robbed," Paula said. "The robber shot him."

"When did it happen? Where?"

"The night of November 28. He was on his way home from the hospital. He was killed on the street."

Moria died on December 6, I thought. *Just eight days later.*

"Was anyone arrested?" I asked.

"I'm afraid not."

"Do the police have any suspects?"

"I don't think so. There's been nothing in the papers."

Which likely indicated that the police had made little progress in the investigation.

"And you're sure he was really killed in a robbery? Maybe he was shot for another reason."

Her frown disappeared, replaced by a fearful, wide-eyed stare. My question had scared her.

I hastened to put on a reassuring smile. "Please forget I said that, Paula. I used to be a police detective once upon a time. I was trained to doubt everything. I'm sure the police have it right."

She nodded slowly, but traces of her unease lingered. A minute ago, she had been leaning toward me, as though we were old friends sharing gossip. Now she had drawn herself back, her manner wary. If I weren't careful, she might decide to shut me out completely.

I tried to win back her favor. "I'm sure it was tough for you, Paula, losing a colleague like that."

"It was," she said, softening. "As you can imagine, I was stunned by his death, all of us were."

"Did Moria take it worse than the others?"

"I don't think so. In retrospect, maybe she was a bit quieter than usual, a little withdrawn, but not so much that I gave it any thought at the time. You think that's why she killed herself, because of what happened to Dr. Shapira?" Clearly, Paula found the notion improbable.

"I don't know. What was their relationship like? Were they... close?" I said, and instantly regretted the question when I saw Paula's reaction.

Turning up her chin, she lanced me with a rebuking stare. "I'm not sure I know what you mean, Mr. Lapid." But of course she did, she knew precisely, as she made abundantly clear by adding, "For your information, Dr. Shapira was married. Married with two children."

I nodded as though that settled the question, but what I was really thinking was that Moria and her lover had met in secret, and adultery was a likely reason. Also, a doctor often works nights. If Dr. Shapira had indeed been Moria's lover, he could easily have told his wife he had a shift at the hospital on those nights he went to Moria's apartment. A solid marital alibi.

None of which I could share with Paula, who was standing rigid on the other side of the counter, her lips compressed to a line as hard as the one I'd evidently crossed.

I said, "I didn't mean to imply that—"

"You didn't? Because it sure sounded like you did." Paula grabbed her pencil and folder. "You'll have to excuse me now. I'm rather busy."

"All right. But you didn't answer my earlier question: Is Anat Schlesinger working now?"

"Actually, she's off for the day," Paula said with icy satisfaction.

"And don't ask me when her next shift is. I don't think I should tell you."

"How about giving me her address?" I said, guessing the answer but trying anyway. "I need to talk to her as soon as possible."

"I don't think I should tell you that either. And now, Mr. Lapid, I want you to leave. This is a hospital, not an interrogation room." She lowered her gaze to her folder, poising her pencil over the top page in a show of dismissal. But abruptly she changed her mind, her head snapping up, and pointed the pencil at my face like a sword. "You should be ashamed of yourself. That poor girl is dead, and you seem intent on tarnishing her reputation."

"I'm intent on discovering why she died."

"By trying to dig up mud, unearth some sordid secret about her life? Not that I believe there's anything like that to find. But suppose you do turn up something, what will that accomplish? It won't help Moria in any way, will it? She's beyond help. You'll only end up robbing her of her good name."

Which brought to mind the warning I'd given Gafni, that my digging into his daughter's life might lead to him learning things about her that he would rather remain ignorant of. A warning he'd decided not to heed. But what about Moria? I had failed to consider what she might have thought of my investigation. Perhaps she would not have wanted me to go rummaging through her life. Perhaps she would not have wanted the father she detested to know anything about it.

For a couple of seconds, I was seized by doubt, uncertain of the morality of my mission. But then I remembered the note. It meant that Moria was a victim, at least in part, a victim in need of justice.

I said, "Trust me, Paula. I'm doing this for Moria."

Paula let out a mocking laugh. "Oh, I'm sure. It has nothing to do with the fact that you're being paid to ask these nasty, dirty questions."

Anger, sudden and bright, blazed in my chest. I hadn't wanted this case. I'd been forced to take it. I wasn't doing this for money. I was this close to telling Paula off, but I stopped myself. Because I realized that what I'd told her, my doing this for Moria, was possibly untrue, considering the unexplained presence of the gun and the fact that one of Moria's colleagues had been shot dead shortly before her suicide. Officially felled by a robber's bullet, but perhaps not.

Which might mean that Moria would not be served by my investigation after all, though for different reasons entirely than those I'd initially contemplated.

Slow down, Adam, I told myself. *Don't get ahead of yourself. There's absolutely nothing that links the gun you found to the killing of this doctor.*

Yet my heart had picked up, and the tingle of excitement that often accompanied the discovery of a secret or unforeseen connection was spreading down my spine.

To Paula, I said, "I'm only interested in learning the truth."

Paula sneered. "How noble of you. Just try not to ruin a dead girl's reputation while you're at it."

15

I walked east on the Street of the Prophets, chased by the wind and the echo of Paula's contemptuous words. Not far from the hospital was a café. Through the front window, I saw a guy talking into a telephone at the bar. I went in, ordered a coffee I didn't want, and waited for five minutes while he blabbered to someone in Romanian-accented Hebrew, punctuating his words with flamboyant hand gestures.

When he finally hung up, I picked up the receiver, dialed 0, and gave the operator a number in Tel Aviv. In my peripheral vision, I caught the nervous stare of the proprietor—long-distance calls were expensive—and appeased his anxiety by sliding him a few coins.

"I'll keep it short," I added for good measure. "Now how about a bit of privacy?"

He grumbled under his mustache and moved down the bar. The phone rang in a small office in the police station on Yehuda Halevi Street in Tel Aviv. After three rings, the pleasant voice of Reuben Tzanani came over the line, marred by the rustle of static.

"Hi, Ant," I said, using his army nickname. He'd gotten it during the War of Independence after carrying me, shot twice and on the brink of death, to the rear lines for the medical treatment that saved my life. This despite my outweighing him by a good forty pounds.

"Adam? Is that you? Why are you coming across so bad?"

"I'm in Jerusalem," I said, which was explanation enough. "I need some information."

"You're on a case?"

"Yes. I need to look at a murder file."

"In Jerusalem?"

"Yes."

"That might be tricky, Adam. If this is an active murder case, I doubt I could get anyone to show you the file."

"The murder occurred more than a month ago. Maybe it's not so active anymore."

"Is that your case, this murder?"

"No. I'm working a suicide. The dead woman worked with the murder victim."

"If you have any information, Adam, you should go to the police."

"I don't have anything. No evidence of any kind. All I've got is a hunch. I need to read the file to see if it's just that or something more. Can you help me out?"

Reuben thought for a moment. "I can try, but I'm not making any promises. Give me the name and date, and I'll see what I can do."

I told him the date of the shooting and that the victim's name was Dr. Shapira, then sheepishly admitted I did not know his first name. The way I had bungled my conversation with Paula, I was lucky to know as much as I did. But Reuben made no comment on the incompleteness of the information I gave him. He simply read it back to me to make sure he had it right, then asked me how I was.

"Fine," I said. "I'm fine."

"You were in the demonstration in Jerusalem." It wasn't a question as much as an attempt to verify a near certainty.

"How did you know?"

"I assumed as much." A pause, laden with static and unspoken questions, and perhaps also accusations. Finally, he asked, "How are you really, Adam?"

"I'm fine, I told you."

"You don't sound like it," he said, in that caring voice of his. This short, slim man with the spirit of a lion and a heart as pure as spring water. This man who had saved my life and was always there when I needed him.

I enjoyed talking to him, usually, but now I couldn't get off the phone fast enough. A terrible fear had me in its claws, a fear that at any second, Reuben would express his disappointment in me—joining Birnbaum and Greta and most of the Israeli public, not to mention David Ben-Gurion. Right then, I felt utterly alone, more alone than at any moment since I'd arrived in Israel.

Shutting my eyes, cold sweat blooming along my hairline, clasping the phone with fingers that had abruptly turned clammy, I said in a rush, "It's the line, Reuben. Just the line. I'm all right. I gotta go. Someone is waiting to use the phone. I'll call you tomorrow morning, okay?"

Before he could answer, I tore the receiver from my ear and dropped it into its cradle as though it were a piece of hot coal. I stood still by the bar, the voices of the other patrons streaming past my ears without registering, as though I were a stranger in a strange land and Hebrew was a foreign language.

You coward, I thought. *You miserable, pathetic coward.*

"Dammit!" I cried, forming a fist with my right hand and slamming it down on the bar like a hammer. The blow rattled my untouched coffee cup, and part of the liquid sloshed over the rim and onto the bar. Someone to my left called, "Hey!" and the proprietor stomped over, scowling. "What the hell are you doing? What's the matter with you?"

I looked at his hostile face, into his dark, distrusting eyes, and opened my mouth to explain myself to him, to plead my case to this absolute stranger. Just like I had done with Greta, with Birnbaum, and again and again during the past two days, half-consciously, with myself. But he wouldn't have understood. Not even if he despised Ben-Gurion, hated the idea of negotiating with Germany. And all the other patrons, now silent and watching, would join him in his condemnation of me.

The words died deep in my throat. I closed my mouth, my face hot with shame, and I swept my eyes across the small café, stumbling over the loaded stares of the other patrons. Without looking at the proprietor, I dug another coin from my pocket, dropped it on the bar, murmured, "I'm sorry," and staggered to the door and through it into the cold street.

16

With my hands shoved deep in my pockets, I hurried, almost running, further east, head angled down to avoid the eyes of passersby. My side throbbed with my haste. My heart pounded. My back prickled with the insane sense that the eyes of the men from the café were still on me. Only when I turned the corner onto Strauss Street did I pause, catching my breath.

It was drizzling, sharp little droplets stinging my face. I lit a cigarette, watched the smoke as the wind whipped it away into nothingness. It reminded me of the gas the police had used against us the other night.

When the cigarette was done, I tossed the stub into the road and walked on south, passing Bikur Hulim Hospital, the street descending steeply, pine and cypress trees dotting both sidewalks. I didn't need to ask for directions; I'd been to Café Atara on one of my previous visits to Jerusalem.

I stopped at the corner of Jaffa and Strauss, outside Maayan Shtub, the large clothing store, and waited for a traffic cop on an elevated platform in the middle of the intersection to signal for me to cross. On the other side of the road began King George Street.

The house on the corner, number 2, carried a plaque commemorating the founding of the street in 1924. Herbert Samuel, the British high commissioner, had attended. The plaque was in three languages: Hebrew on the left; Arabic on the right; and in the middle, English, like a buffer to stop the other two from tearing each other apart.

One night in 1948, Lehi members had changed all the street signs along King George, renaming the street King David. Following a formal request from the British government after Israel had secured its independence, the original name was restored.

Down King George was Frumin House, where the debate in the Knesset neared its end, where I prayed that honor and good sense would prevail and the government would lose the vote. It had to. Despite everything. The alternative was unbearable.

I moved on, past Yampolski Pharmacy; Allenby Café, from which wafted the scent of *latkes*; and the Talitha Kumi building, which until the Second World War had been a school for girls run by German nuns, and now hosted a variety of businesses, offices, and studios.

Approaching the corner of King George and Ben Yehuda, with Frumin House about a hundred meters ahead, I saw half a dozen police vehicles of various sizes. Ranged across the intersection and the street beyond was a mass of officers behind barbed-wire barricades, armed and watchful, ready for the resumption of hostilities, though there was no sign of any.

Suddenly, I was seized by an acute dread that one of them would recognize me from the other night. That an officer would point his finger and yell, "There's one of the bastards. Let's get him!"

But no one pointed. No one yelled. In fact, none of the cops paid me any mind. Still, I was relieved when I turned onto Ben Yehuda Street, out of their sight.

Heading east again, I realized I was tracing the same path I had the other night, only in reverse. I had walked this street as part of the crowd of demonstrators en route to the Knesset, with Menachem Begin's speech resounding in my brain.

But now the crowd was gone. There were no banners. No thudding mass of feet. No coats with a yellow star pinned to their breast.

No eyes glowing with insult, grief, and determination. There were still a few anti-government posters here and there—plastered on walls, on a noticeboard, a couple nailed to trees, all of them wet to near illegibility—but other than that, no sign of the recent upheaval, of the argument still raging.

I felt like a soldier retreating from a battlefield after a defeat. But no. It was not over yet. The Knesset had not yet decided. There was still hope.

Café Atara stood near the center of Ben Yehuda Street, at number 7. The sign above the entrance displayed a triple-pronged crown over a steaming cup of coffee, with the café's Hebrew name floating on the steam. Each of the three prongs doubled for the letter *A*, with the letters *T* and *R* printed in the spaces between, together spelling the café's name in English, a relic of the time when a sizable proportion of its clientele had been made up of British soldiers and officials.

The space inside was large, longer than wide, with a short counter on the left side and pastries under glass at the far end. And in between, a scattering of square tables that could sit four, with straight-backed chairs around them.

The café was nearly full. I felt underdressed. Many of the men wore suits and ties. Government officials, or maybe employees of the Jewish Agency, whose building was a short walk away on King George.

I found a table and sat facing the entrance. I checked my watch. I was early. There was still time for Naomi Hecht to arrive.

I ordered a coffee and drank it slowly. Atara boasted of the finest coffee in Israel, and it wasn't bad, but it didn't hold a candle to Greta's. My heart gave a twinge when I thought of Greta, how she'd looked when she said, *How could you, Adam?* after I'd told her I'd participated in the charge on the Knesset. I gritted my teeth and pushed the memory away. Naomi Hecht would be here soon. I needed to focus.

The waiter came by, asking if I wanted a newspaper, but I declined. I did not want to read any more about the government's projected triumph.

When I finished my coffee, it was already ten minutes past the appointed time at which Naomi Hecht had said she'd meet me. I smoked a cigarette, telling myself to be patient. When the cigarette was done, she'd still not arrived. The waiter asked if I wanted to order anything else. I said I was waiting for someone; she would be arriving shortly. He gave a little bow and moved off. I thought I caught a little smirk on his lips. He'd seen his share of hopeful, delusional men waiting for women who never showed up.

Maybe Naomi Hecht had never intended to come. Maybe she had made this date just to get me out of her hair. Or maybe Paula had had a word with her, convinced her to steer clear of me.

I lit another cigarette, telling myself that when it was done, I'd leave. I checked my watch again. Twenty-five minutes late. At the next table over, two men in sharp clothes were talking about the United Nations. Something to do with a resolution the Arabs were about to introduce against Israel. At another table, a man pulled out a chair for a smartly dressed woman who'd just walked in. One less delusional man in the world.

When the cigarette was down to its filter, I snuffed it out in the ashtray as though it had offended me, crushing it flat. I'd go back to the hospital, I decided, make a nuisance of myself, get Naomi Hecht's address one way or another, go pound on her door and make her talk to me. I was angry enough to do it.

Swearing softly, I rose from my chair and was digging in my pocket for my wallet when I heard a deep female voice say, "Leaving already, Mr. Lapid?"

Raising my eyes, I saw Naomi Hecht standing on the other side of the table.

Her nurse's uniform was gone. In its place she wore a knee-length dark-blue dress over black wool stockings, a brown coat that was beginning to show its age, a gray scarf she was unwinding from around her neck, and a furled umbrella hooked on a forearm. No hat, no makeup, and no smile, despite the suggested humor of her question. Without her nurse's cap and the bobby pins she'd worn at the hospital, her short black hair had more volume and body. Her skin was pale apart from under her eyes, where inadequate sleep had tinged it purple, the bruises of fatigue. I estimated her age at twenty-seven or twenty-eight, a few years older than Moria had been.

"I thought you weren't going to show," I said, pulling my hand out of my pocket and sitting back down.

"An emergency at the hospital," she said, taking the chair opposite mine. That was the extent of it. She'd given me an explanation. No apology was warranted. I studied her face, wondering if the emergency had been real. I decided it had been, or else why had she come at all?

The waiter approached. I asked Naomi Hecht what she'd like. She ignored me and proceeded to order coffee and a small pastry directly from the waiter. I signaled to him to double the order. He took her umbrella and coat and deposited them by the door, where there was a coat rack and an umbrella stand.

"You don't like me, do you?" I asked when the waiter had gone.

"You're very perceptive."

"Care to tell me why?"

"You're the detective, don't you know?"

"I think it's because of Moria's father. Am I right?"

She didn't answer. She smoothed a napkin on the table, not taking her eyes off me. Out of the hospital, in regular clothes with her hair freer, she looked less severe, but there was still something intimidating about her, something that suggested getting too close might get you burned or bitten. Her eyes, despite the natural warmth of their hazel color, had the texture of hard wood.

"Do you know why Moria hated his guts?" I asked.

"What makes you think she did?"

"He told me they didn't get along. Of course, that could mean just that and nothing more. But he also said they had barely any contact for years, which suggests a more powerful aversion on her part. But what really tells me Moria hated her father is a photo album I found when I visited her apartment this morning. She'd cut her father's image out of all the pictures. You only do that to someone you detest through and through."

The waiter served our coffee and food. The pastry was rolled like a snail's shell, with frail lines of cinnamon snaking through it. It smelled and looked delicious, but I bet that in past years, before rationing, the cinnamon lines had been thicker, the sugar and butter more plentiful. Were they serving better pastries these days in Munich and Hamburg and Bonn? Were they richer, sweeter, bigger?

Naomi Hecht stared at the food, then away at the window looking out on Ben Yehuda Street. "I didn't know about that," she said thoughtfully.

"What do you know, Mrs. Hecht?"

She looked at me. "About what?"

"You know what. Moria and her father. Do you know why she hated him?"

"Why not ask your client?"

"He won't tell me."

"I suppose he has his reasons."

"I'm sure he does."

"Why do you need to know? What does that have to do with Moria's suicide?"

"Maybe nothing. I don't know. That's the point. I hardly know anything about her life. I won't know why she decided to end it until I do."

"Why does your client care? What difference would it make?"

I hesitated. I was pretty sure Gafni did not want me to share his fear of guilt with anyone.

"Moria was his daughter," I said. "Isn't that reason enough?"

Naomi Hecht tilted her head, assessing me with her intense eyes. Here, in the subtle lighting of Café Atara, I noticed that along with the hazel, there were also golden, honey hues. She tore a piece of her pastry, put it between her lips, and chewed on it with small movements of her mouth. She swallowed, rubbed an errant crumb off her lip, and said, "You're not telling me the whole truth now, are you, Mr. Lapid?"

Involuntarily, I found myself averting my eyes from the directness of her gaze. Like a novice criminal in his inaugural interrogation. I hid my embarrassment behind my coffee cup, taking a long sip. I doubted that it worked.

Setting the cup back on the table, I said, "That's all the reason I can give."

She nodded, tearing off another piece of her pastry and eating it. I followed her example, not realizing how hungry I was until the first bit of food touched my tongue.

We ate and drank in silence for a couple of minutes, until only crumbs remained on our plates. My coffee cup was empty; hers still held a measure of brew.

The pastry had not subdued my hunger. "Want another one?" I asked, gesturing at our empty plates.

Something ignited in her eyes. "Trying to buy your way into my good graces, Mr. Lapid?"

"As if that would work," I said.

"You're right; it won't. Just so you know, I intend to pay for my food and drink."

I shrugged, trying to hide my irritation. "I was about to suggest we use some of the expense money Mr. Gafni gave me, but suit yourself." I signaled for the waiter, ordered another pastry and coffee. Naomi Hecht surprised me when she said she'd have the same.

I raised a questioning eyebrow. She pretended not to notice. Instead she said, "I understand he's rich. Moria's father, I mean."

"Stinking rich," I muttered, without much forethought, and caught a smile dancing on Naomi Hecht's lips, the first time I saw humor, however tenuous, on her face. It did something to her features, transforming them into something softer, more feminine and inviting, almost beautiful, like clay being shaped by a sculptor's strong fingers. It didn't last long, that smile, but when it vanished, a small part of its effect clung to her face like a promise or an aspiration.

"You don't like him much, either, do you?" she asked.

"Not much."

"Does he know that?"

127

"He'd have to be blind and deaf to think anything else. I doubt he cares."

"Do you?"

"Care? No, why should I?"

"You work for him."

"I don't need to like him. He's a client. Sometimes it's better not to like clients."

"Why?"

"It makes it easier to tell them things they won't like hearing."

"Do you expect to tell Mr. Gafni such things?"

I thought of Moria's mysterious lover, the condoms in the bedside cabinet, the gun hidden behind it.

"I don't know," I said. "What do you think?"

She didn't answer. The waiter arrived with our second order. He was smiling openly at me now, a twinkle in his eye. His smirk from before was ancient history. Things were going well for me, he thought. Romance over pastries and coffee. Appearances could certainly be deceiving.

Naomi Hecht drew on her coffee. I took a bite of my pastry.

"He would send her presents, did you know that?" she said, the cup clasped in both hands, gray filaments of steam rising like a gauzy curtain before her face.

"He mentioned it. What sort of presents?"

"Expensive ones. A fur coat, a radio, a refrigerator, if you can believe it. And other things, too. He would have them delivered to her apartment."

"There was no refrigerator in Moria's apartment. No radio or fur coat, either."

"She didn't keep them. Not any of them."

"What did she do with them?"

"She gave them away."

"To whom?"

"To people who needed them, that's what she said. Of course, Moria could have used them too, but she didn't want them."

"Why not give them to you? You were her friend."

"She never offered. I think she wanted to remove her father's presents from her life, and I was part of her life. The only reason I know of them at all is that I was at her apartment when the refrigerator arrived. Only then did she tell me about the presents at all."

"I see," I said, remembering my impression of Moria's apartment, that she could have lived in finer accommodations with the help of her father, but that she chose not to. I remembered Gafni telling me of all the money he'd spent trying to win his daughter's affection, and how it did no good. For once, his money had proved useless.

Again we fell silent for a spell. I studied Naomi Hecht over the rim of my coffee cup, and she studied me over the rim of hers. She had an oval face with fine cheekbones, a high forehead, and straight eyebrows. Her face was a little thinner than it should have been, like the rest of her body. Her skin was very smooth, unblemished apart from those purple bags under her eyes. There was something younger than her years in her features, and something older too. But both qualities were elusive, hard to pinpoint. I wondered what she saw in my face. I doubted there was anything younger than my years in my features. There were certainly things that were older.

There were many questions I could have asked her at that moment, but I held off. I sensed that she was considering telling me something, and I knew that any word I uttered might cause her to clam up. I waited, eating another piece of my pastry.

Finally, with an almost imperceptible nod of decision, Naomi Hecht said, "I don't know why Moria hated her father so. I wish I did."

"She never told you?"

"Never. I asked several times, but she would always shake her head and change the subject. But I do know it had something to do with her mother."

"Her mother?"

"You know about her mother, right?"

"I know that she died a few years back."

"When Moria was sixteen. But do you know how she died?"

I thought back to my conversation with Gafni. What had he said about the cause of his wife's death? He hadn't said anything about it.

Glossed over it in the flow of his speech. Which was uncommon, I thought. People usually supply such details. She died in an accident, they might say. Or of pneumonia. Something to explain the loss. But Gafni hadn't.

"No," I said. "No, I don't."

"Her mother committed suicide. She killed herself."

I stared at her. "Are you sure?"

She nodded. "Moria was the one who found her. In their apartment in Tel Aviv. Why do you look like you don't believe me?"

"It's just the shock," I said. "First the mother and then the daughter." But that wasn't it. Not all of it. The bulk of my surprise was because Gafni had kept this information from me. The reason might have been innocent, a matter of privacy, but there was a point in our conversation in which it would have been pertinent, even useful, for him to mention it. It had been when I raised the possibility that Moria hadn't actually killed herself. Gafni had offered a number of persuasive arguments as to why she had, but he had failed to mention her mother's suicide, even though that would have lent more weight to his assertion. After all, a self-annihilating tendency, like all others, could be hereditary.

The fact that Gafni had acted that way was curious. He had to have had a damn good reason for doing so.

"Did Moria blame her father for her mother's death?" I asked.

"I don't know for certain," Naomi Hecht answered. "But it would be a good reason to hate him, wouldn't it?"

I nodded, thinking, *Yes, it most certainly would.*

I said, "Do you know how her mother did it? How she killed herself? Or why?"

"No. Moria didn't want to talk about it. I don't think she planned on telling me about her mother at all. It slipped out, and I could tell she regretted it."

"How did you two meet?"

"During the war. Jerusalem was besieged. The Arabs bombarded the city. Many people died; many were injured. Moria was at the end of her training. Not yet a nurse, but pretty close. We nurses couldn't handle the workload, so nursing students were called upon to assist. Each student was assigned to a nurse. Less risk of them making mistakes that way. Moria was assigned to me."

"It must have been hard."

"Very. The siege caused shortages in everything. Medicine, bandages, even water. Conditions became more primitive with each passing day. Beyond the objective difficulties, what made it hard was knowing how to treat people but not being able to do it properly. Injuries that were treatable under normal circumstances would result in the loss of a limb or even death."

"How did Moria handle it?"

"She was terrific. Hardworking, dedicated. Not flinching even when shells were exploding nearby. I could tell she'd be a wonderful nurse."

"Paula told me Moria took things too much to heart, that she didn't know how to distance herself from her patients."

Naomi Hecht's eyes flashed. "What other criticism did the venerable Paula share with you?"

"None. She held Moria in high esteem."

The fire in Naomi Hecht's eyes abated. She drank some coffee, ran her finger along the curled cup handle. "Paula has a point. Moria did get too close. Sometimes, I worried about her too."

"Ever think she might hurt herself?"

"No," she said firmly. "Never."

"What sort of things did the two of you do together?"

"All sorts. We went to the cinema or for walks or to cafés, things like that."

"Just the two of you?"

"Sometimes. Or with another friend of ours."

"Anat Schlesinger?"

Naomi Hecht nodded. "Yes. With Anat."

"I'll need to talk to her. Can you give me her address?"

She recited it. I jotted it in my notebook.

My coffee had become lukewarm by then. I finished it in one gulp, then tapped my fingers on the table, trying to decide how to proceed. The easy questions were done. Now it was time for the uncomfortable ones.

"Do you know who Moria's lover was?" I asked.

"What makes you think she had one?"

I told her about the condoms in the bedside cabinet. An awkward smile played across her lips before she smothered it.

"I don't know," she said. "She didn't tell me."

Which wasn't surprising, given the secret nature of Moria's relationship with her lover.

"Did she go on dates?"

"On occasion. But never more than a couple of times with the same man."

"Why did none of them last?"

Naomi Hecht considered the question and answered slowly, "She had the bad luck of attracting unworthy men, I think."

"Do you remember any of their names?"

"No, I don't. I'm not sure I ever knew them."

A dead end. I said, "How did Moria react to Dr. Shapira's death?"

"Dr. Shapira? How do you—oh, of course, Paula again."

"Well?"

"How did she react? The same as the rest of us. It was a shock."

"What was their relationship like?"

She arched an eyebrow. "You think they were lovers?"

"You don't?"

She smiled her tiny, short-lived smile again. "No. Not a chance."

"Did Moria like him?"

"No, she didn't."

"Oh?" I said, thinking of the gun. "Why not?"

"She didn't appreciate his skills as a doctor."

"Was she as diplomatic as you when it came to criticizing doctors?"

It took her a second before she remembered what I was referring to. Another fleeting smile. "Much more so. Moria was better at keeping her thoughts to herself."

A woman of secrets, I thought.

"What did you think of Dr. Shapira?"

"That he was an arrogant fool. But that's nothing special. Many doctors are."

Now it was my turn to smile. "What did Dr. Shapira look like?"

"What does it matter?"

"A neighbor saw Moria's lover exit her building. I'm wondering if Dr. Shapira fits her description."

Naomi Hecht frowned. "Wouldn't it be easier to show her a picture of him? There's one in the hospital, I think."

I explained that the neighbor had seen the lover from the back, in the dark, so all I had were an approximate height and build and hair color.

"Ah, I understand," Naomi Hecht said. "Well, that's easy enough. Dr. Shapira was thin and about five eleven, six feet tall. He had black hair. Does that fit?"

"Pretty closely. You still don't think there was anything between him and Moria?"

She shook her head. "They were just two people who worked together. Nothing more."

Which was similar to what Paula had said, though Naomi Hecht had exhibited no outrage at the suggestion of romance between Moria and Dr. Shapira but found the notion amusing.

Perhaps both women were right. Maybe I was trying to force a connection where none existed.

Time for a change of subject.

"Did Moria know any unsavory people?" I asked.

"Unsavory? What does that mean?"

I searched for the right word, failed to find it, and finally settled on, "Suspicious."

Naomi Hecht narrowed her eyes, two faint lines etched between her eyebrows. "What are you getting at, Mr. Lapid?"

The gun. I was trying to understand the presence of the gun. It didn't fit. But I didn't want to ask about it directly.

"It's the note," I said. "Did you read it?"

Her face darkened. "Yes, I read it."

"What do you make of it?"

Her lower lip began trembling. It was odd to see, unexpected, far removed from her customary controlled firmness. When she spoke, her voice was husky with emotion, more than any she'd shown thus far. "That Moria was in a great deal of distress, that she was suffering terribly."

"Do you know what she was referring to, or whom?"

She shook her head, spreading both hands, palms up, in a show of resigned frustration. "I've thought about it over and over, probably a million times or more. I simply don't know. I feel that I should, but I don't."

Guilt, I thought, that insidious beast. I knew it well, my unwanted companion in the seven years that had passed since the end of the war in Europe.

"Tell me about that day," I said.

She took a deep breath, looked at her hands, then back up at me. "What do you want me to tell you?"

"Let's start by why you went to Moria's apartment."

"She didn't show up for her shift. That was unlike her. I don't think she missed a shift in two years. So I went to check on her."

"You had a key?"

"Yes."

"How come?"

"Moria gave it to me, in case she lost hers."

"You live close by?"

"A few minutes' walk. On the corner of Malachi and Zeharia."

"Okay. You unlocked the door, went inside, and then?"

"She hadn't been dead long. There was hardly any smell. I went into the living room and saw the note right away. It was—"

"Wait! The note was in the living room? Not in the bedroom?"

"In the living room. On the floor under the table. It was odd because everything else was so neat."

"The police report said the note was found on the bed."

"That's because of me. I read the note, understood what it was, and rushed into the bedroom with it in my hand. I saw the pill bottles. I saw Moria. I could tell she was dead at a glance."

"What did you do then?"

"Screamed. I screamed, but I don't remember what."

It was the word "no." That was what Lillian Shukrun had heard. The most primal, animalistic word in existence. A word of denial, of rejection, of defiance and rebellion. A hopeless word on that particular day, as on many others.

"What then?"

"I hurried to the bed, dropping the note. I checked her pulse, even though I knew it was pointless. Then I went to call for help. One of the neighbors was standing in the doorway, looking scared. She'd probably heard me scream. She told me where I could find a telephone. I called the police, and that was that."

I remembered Lillian telling me that Naomi Hecht did not cry that day, but now her eyes were glistening. I watched as a single tear escaped from each of her eyes, as her thumb caught the left one quickly, swiping it away, and how the right continued its journey unimpeded down her cheek to the corner of her mouth. Only then, with the taste of salt on her lips, did she become aware of it, wiped her cheek with her fingers, and finished the job with her napkin.

She sat like that for a minute or so, her face buried in the napkin. Her shoulders shuddered, but her weeping was oddly silent, as though she were choking her sobs so deep in her body that not a whisper of them survived.

I gave her the time she needed, waited until she lowered the napkin, revealing a face that was flushed, eyes dry but reddened. Her brief storm of emotion had roiled through her, but it had passed. She was collected again.

I said, "You told me everything was neat."

"Yes. Moria had cleaned everything. I don't know why."

"Were the windows open or closed?"

She shut her eyes, drew a deep breath. "Closed. No, that's not right. The one by the table in the living room was open a little. I remember the cold air blowing in, chilling me as I read the note."

That's how the note got under the table, I thought. Moria had left it there before going into the bedroom to die, and the wind coming through the open window had blown it off the table and onto the floor.

"Why do you think she didn't name the person in the note?" I asked.

"I don't know."

I didn't either, and it had been bothering me ever since I first read the note in Gafni's office.

I stared across the table at Naomi Hecht. The color in her cheeks had faded to a flowery pink. Her mouth was open just the tiniest bit, and it made her lips fuller. She was glancing at her watch.

"I'm sorry," she said, "I didn't realize it was so late. I need to go."

To her husband, I thought. *She needs to get home before her husband does.*

"Wait," I said, feeling a small pang in my stomach, for there was still one matter we had to discuss. "Just a couple more questions, Mrs. Hecht."

She hesitated, looked at her watch again, and gave a quick nod. "All right. What do you wish to ask me?"

"Would you say you and Moria were close?"

"Yes," she said, "of course." But there was the briefest of hesitations. I recalled what Lillian Shukrun had told me, that she thought Moria and Naomi might have fallen out.

"How about shortly before her suicide?"

A pause before she spoke. "What brought about this strange question?"

I shrugged, doing my best to feign innocence. "I just figured Moria's frame of mind must have been different given the turmoil she must have been experiencing, and that it might have affected your friendship."

Naomi Hecht studied me with those hard eyes of hers. Gone was the tenderness she'd exhibited when she told me of the day she found Moria dead. Here was the woman I had met in the hospital, the one she'd been when we began our conversation here in Café Atara—all steel and sharp edges.

"No," she said in a flat, modulated tone. "Everything was as usual." But she fiddled with her wedding ring as she said it, twisting it around and around her finger, and I became convinced, for the first time in our conversation, that she was lying to me.

I couldn't say why, but her deceit filled me with a deep, heavy, strange sadness. I held my breath, hoping she'd have a change of heart and tell me the truth. But she didn't. Instead, she said, "Anything else, Mr. Lapid?" And in her voice was that old animosity again, the one she'd shed during the course of our conversation.

"Just one more thing: When was the last time you visited Moria's apartment?"

"When do you think? The day I found her body."

"Not since?"

"No. Not since."

I tried to read either truth or falsehood in her set features, but they gave away nothing.

I said, "That's all, Mrs. Hecht. You can go to your husband now."

She flinched, perhaps in surprise at my abrupt, dismissive tone. Looking down, she appeared to suddenly become aware of how she was fiddling with her ring. She yanked her hands off the table and jerked to a stand, the feet of her chair scraping on the floor. She drew a small coin purse from her bag, unclasped it, took out some money, and laid it on the table by her plate. There was no goodbye, just a final inscrutable look and then a turning of the heel and a quick, erect march to the door, where she snatched back her coat and umbrella. She left without putting on her coat, eager to be away. I watched her through the window until she vanished from view.

17

The waiter gave me the stink eye as he cleared the table. I could guess what was going through his mind. The way he saw it, I had made a woman cry, then said something that caused her to flee the café as though chased by a pack of wolves. Not only that, but I was such a boor that I did not even offer to pay for her food like a gentleman should. And all this after he had already become invested in the success of my romantic endeavors. Perhaps I had broken his professional heart.

As he was leaving with the laden tray, a grim-faced woman came in from the kitchen. "Have you heard?" she asked him in a somber voice.

"Heard what?"

"It's done. The Knesset voted in favor of negotiations with Germany."

The waiter's face locked itself into a grimace of pain and despair. "God damn them."

I couldn't breathe. There was a stillness in my chest, as though my heart had ceased beating. "Are you sure?" I asked, disbelieving despite all the signs, the predictions, the unequivocal manner in which this woman had delivered the news.

The woman nodded gravely. "Sixty-one in favor; fifty opposed."

"God damn them," the waiter said again and emitted an anguished cry. Tears leaped to his eyes, and he brought his hands up to stanch the flow, the tray tumbling from his grasp, the plates and cups that Naomi Hecht and I had used shattering on the floor in a loud, spraying crash.

The woman laid her hand on his forearm, murmured, "Don't, Yisrael."

The waiter turned away, cursing in Yiddish, and disappeared into the back. The woman turned to me and the other customers. She offered a wavering smile. "Anyone want anything? Anything at all, I'll get it for you."

No one spoke. Rain began falling again, fat drops sliding down the windowpanes. Another waiter hurried over, spoke in low tones to the woman, then went away and returned with a broom and pan. The news spread among the tables like a ghastly rumor. A few shook their heads, a couple muttered something I couldn't catch, but none reacted anywhere close to how the waiter had. No one cried their eyes out like I wanted to. No one shouted their throats raw like I wanted to. No one overturned a table like I wanted to or hurled a chair through the nearest window like I wanted to. And I did none of those things either, for I had already committed my futile act of mad outrage the other night, just a few hundred meters away outside the Knesset, and I'd paid a price for it. Most of these people, maybe all of them, hadn't.

Then it hit me, the awful certainty that for most people this moment, which to me felt like an irreparable rupture, would pass like any other, that life would continue on its inexorable course as it always did, no matter what happened or who suffered or what injustice was done.

In less than a minute, as though to validate my fear, the café came back to life, conversation resuming all around me. At a nearby table, a woman began telling her friend about a movie she'd seen the other night. Someone laughed. A man asked for tea, and the woman who'd brought the terrible news went to fetch him some. On the way back from delivering it, she passed by my table. "You need anything, mister?"

I slowly shook my head.

"You sure? How about a glass of water?" She leaned closer and added in a murmur, "You look like you could use it."

"No, thank you," I said, but the words came out in a croak. My mouth was as dry as an old grave, as hopelessness itself. I tried and failed to work saliva into it, involuntarily swallowing, hurting the inside of my throat as though I had swallowed a piece of rough tree bark. "Yes," I managed to say. "Please."

When she brought me the water, I downed the whole glass in a single swallow. "Thank you," I told her.

"It's a terrible thing." She shook her head and sighed. "A terrible thing."

I didn't answer. What answer was there to give?

She sighed again, a what-can-you-do sort of sigh, and in that small, defeated exhalation I heard the awful acceptance of the fact that life would proceed, that we would all be dragged, kicking and screaming or indifferent or in a sort of simmering resentment—it didn't really matter how—to the following moments and days and so on, pulled by our daily duties and obligations and the necessities of life. "Can I get you anything else?" she said.

"No. Just the check."

Out on the street, people hurried past, huddled into their coats. A wicked wind flapped coattails around, ripped umbrellas from cold hands, scattered paper and debris in all directions.

Conjured by the weather, and no doubt prodded by the recent news, a seven-year-old memory I thought I'd managed to suppress clawed up from the dark depths of my mind, and instantly my entire body felt as though it were encased in ice.

It was December 1944, and I was in Auschwitz, standing in roll call as heavy, relentless snow plummeted upon me and the other miserable creatures who were my fellow prisoners.

My clothes were tattered rags, my body depleted of fat, and the wind had fangs like that of a hunger-crazed tiger. It bit and tore at my wasted flesh through my prisoner's uniform, leaching the very life out of me. And I couldn't even wrap my arms around myself for warmth. I had to stand there, at attention, or risk getting shot by the guards.

And now, in Jerusalem, I stopped in the middle of the sidewalk with the rain beating on my coat and hat, shivering all over in recollection. I clenched my jaw to silence my chattering teeth, but in my memory, my teeth of seven years ago continued their clicking stutter.

The die had been cast. Israel would negotiate with Germany. A deal would be struck. A devil's bargain. Money for blood. I wanted to scream, scream "No!" like Naomi Hecht had done at the sight of Moria's dead body. But I bottled the scream inside, my stomach convulsing with its toxic pressure.

It was done. No shouting or yelling or protest would undo it. I'd done all that and failed—and in the attempt perhaps contributed to an outcome opposite the one I desired. I had to focus on what I could do, on what was in my power. My case. The search for the person in Moria's suicide note. That, I could influence. There, my efforts might bear fruit.

I hurried east, pausing at Zion Square, where I cast a gloomy glance at the balcony from which Menachem Begin had delivered his moving oration. It was empty now.

A clutch of people was milling about the entrance to Zion Cinema. Others were streaming in and out of Schwartz Department Store. Business as usual. Life moving on.

I moved on as well. The rain hardened to sleet that bounced like shrapnel on my shoulders and head. My shoes crunched on tiny pellets of ice, and with a shudder I imagined that I was walking on fragments of bone.

I crossed Jaffa Street again, this time heading northeast, and entered Hasollel Street. On the corner opposite the offices of the *Jerusalem Post*, where in February 1948 an Arab car bomb had killed three people, I turned right and soon found myself outside a nondescript building on Heleni Hamalka Street. Here, according to Naomi Hecht, was where Anat Schlesinger lived.

It was a nicer building than the one Moria had chosen for herself. Four stories tall and dotted with tiny half-circular balconies with wrought-iron railings, all empty in this weather. I climbed the stairs to the third floor and knocked on the door of apartment 8.

The woman who opened it looked nothing like Naomi Hecht. Short, buxom, and red-haired, Anat Schlesinger was all curves and soft womanhood. Not a hard edge in sight. She possessed one of those sweet, pretty faces on which a smile looks more natural than a frown. She was smiling now, questioningly, as she said in a pleasant, lilting voice, "Hello, can I help you?"

I gave her my name and said I'd like to talk to her about Moria Gafni.

The smile gave way to bafflement. "Moria?"

I nodded. "I'm a private investigator. Moria's father hired me. He wants to know why she did what she did. Can I come in? It won't take long."

Anat Schlesinger looked me up and down, hesitant. I understood her concern. I was a strange man in wet clothes, and I was on an odd mission.

"I'm not sure—"

"Naomi Hecht gave me your address," I said.

"Oh." The worry cleared from her face. "You've spoken to Naomi?"

"Less than an hour ago," I said, putting on what I hoped was a confidence-inspiring smile, trying to banish the memory of Naomi Hecht in such a hurry to get away from me that she had neglected to put on her coat before stepping out into the cold. "She told me quite a bit about Moria, but I know you were her close friend, too, so it's important that I speak with you as well."

"Well, yes, of course. Please come in."

Inside, it was warm and homey. A heating stove gurgled in a corner of the cozy living room. White curtains were pulled back from windows that showed a patch of cloud cover and the shingled rooftop of the building across the road. Anat Schlesinger led me to a comfortable sofa and asked if I wanted some tea. I shook my head. "I'm fine. Thank you."

"I'm sorry, but we're fresh out of coffee, or I would offer you some."

"That's all right. I had some earlier." I thought of Naomi Hecht playing with her wedding ring as she lied to me. Why had she lied to me? "Who's we?" I asked.

"Huh?"

"You said, 'We're out of coffee.'"

She smiled. "I meant my roommates and I."

"How many of you live here?"

"Three. We used to be four, with two girls sharing one of the rooms, but thank God, that's no longer the case. Three's crowded enough, believe me."

"I do."

"Don't get me wrong, I like it here a lot. It's a nice apartment. Better than my previous one by far. I was lucky to find it."

"How long have you been living here?"

"Two years."

"Since around the same time Moria moved into her apartment on Amos Street, right?" I said, recalling what Lillian and Daniel Shukrun had told me.

"In the same month, actually. Which brings up a painful memory."

"Why painful?"

"Because of Moria," she said, the corners of her mouth tucking down. "Since we were both looking at the time, I suggested we look together, become roommates. Such good friends, what could be better?"

"Why didn't you?"

"Moria wouldn't. No matter how much I tried to cajole her. And trust me, I can be quite the cajoler." She laughed, both in humor and wistfulness.

"Did she say why?"

"She said she wanted to live by herself. No roommates. She worked very hard to convince me that it wasn't personal, which took some doing, but not all that much, because why wouldn't she want me as a roommate?"

"I can't see a reason."

"Precisely," she said, acknowledging my oblique compliment with a nod. "That's what I thought. Which is why it didn't require too much effort on her part to convince me it was true."

"You weren't angry?"

"A little. Okay, at first it was more than a little, because her not wanting to share an apartment with me meant that I'd have to share it with someone else, someone I didn't know and maybe wouldn't get along with. But I didn't stay sore for long; I hardly ever do."

I was beginning to believe that. Anat Schlesinger looked like the sort of person who shrugs off the small irritations of life and just carries on with the business of living it.

"Did Moria say why she didn't want roommates?" I asked.

"She told me that at the end of the day she wanted to come back to a quiet home, where she could be by herself. I can understand that. It can get pretty noisy here with three girls living together, and sometimes I just want the other two to shut up or go away and let me have a few moments of quiet solitude."

"Like you were having before I showed up?" I asked with a half-smile.

"Exactly," she said, then caught herself and quickly added, "I didn't mean—"

I chuckled. "That's all right. I wasn't offended."

"That's good, because I wasn't talking about you, I swear. I want to help you if I can. I've been a mess since Moria's death. I can't put it—her—out of my mind."

"How long have you two been friends?"

"Five years. We studied together in nursing school."

"Was she a good student?"

"Extremely. She worked very hard, almost too hard: she rewrote each paper until every word was absolutely perfect, and she studied like crazy. Which was lucky for me because she pulled me along to study more as well."

"Were you also called upon during the war in Jerusalem?"

She nodded, a shadow crossing her face. "Talk about a trial by fire. It was that, quite literally."

"Was that also when you met Naomi Hecht?"

"Yes. Though I was assigned to another nurse. A real witch. Always tearing into me, even when I didn't deserve it. Moria was lucky to have Naomi."

"Were they very close?"

"We all were."

"I understand the two of them had a quarrel about a week before Moria's death."

"Really? Did Naomi tell you that?"

I shook my head. "Someone else I talked to."

"Someone at the hospital?"

"No. Not at the hospital, Ms. Schlesinger. It's someone you don't know." Which was untrue because she had probably met Lillian Shukrun when Lillian's son was at the hospital. But I didn't see what harm it did, telling her this white lie.

"Well," she said, giving me an affronted look for not revealing my source's identity, "I never heard anything about it. Not from Moria nor from Naomi. Whoever told you they quarreled is either mistaken or they were making it up."

No, she wasn't, I thought. *And both Naomi Hecht and Moria hid it from you, their close friend.*

I said, "Why did Moria come to Jerusalem? Why not become a nurse in Tel Aviv?"

"She and her father were on bad terms. I don't know why. She wouldn't say. And her mother was dead, and Moria didn't have any siblings, so she basically had no one in Tel Aviv."

"Did Moria tell you how her mother died?"

"It was an illness of some sort. That's the impression I got. She didn't talk about her family much, and I didn't pry. I could tell it was a touchy subject."

"It was no illness. Her mother killed herself."

Anat gaped at me. "My God! Are you sure?"

"I'm afraid so," I said, thinking that Naomi Hecht had not told

Anat Schlesinger about this. Perhaps because she'd sensed that Moria wouldn't want this information to get around.

Anat shut her eyes, shook her head. Her shoulders started trembling, and then she was crying. Not like Naomi Hecht, but loudly, with hitching gasps and cracking wails, lasting a couple of minutes. When her weeping began subsiding, I dug my handkerchief out of my pocket and handed it over. She dried her face and said, "Why didn't she tell me?"

I didn't know. All I knew was that Moria had been a person who kept secrets, all sorts of secrets, which was why, I believed, she'd chosen to live alone.

"I'm sorry that I upset you," I said.

"It's not your fault. I'm just sad for Moria, all she went through. I'm glad you told me. I just wish she had. Do you think she was ashamed? Is that why she didn't tell me?"

I said I didn't know, that I wished I did. Then I asked if she felt up to answering some more questions, and she said she was.

"You think Moria wanted to get away from her father by coming to Jerusalem?" I asked.

"I'm sure that was a big part of it. I've never met the man, and it's good that I haven't, or I might yell at him or slap his face. I'm furious with him, without even knowing what he did. I'm furious because, for one reason or another, he was a lousy father, and it makes me mad on Moria's behalf." She sighed. "Maybe I'm also mad at myself. I keep asking myself how I missed the signs."

"What signs?"

"I don't know. Looking back, I can't put my finger on anything specific and say, 'This is what you should have spotted, Anat. This was a warning of what was to come.' But there must have been something, right?"

"Did Moria act as usual in her final days?"

"I think so. Maybe she was a bit more thoughtful than normal; Moria would get that way sometimes, go into her own head for a while. Maybe she was doing more of that, brooding a little, but not so much that I felt alarmed."

"Any idea what she was brooding about?"

"I thought it might have something to do with a doctor on our ward who got killed. Kalman Shapira. He got shot about a week before Moria died."

"I heard about that."

"Well, you can imagine how we all felt. Everyone was a little rattled, not just Moria."

"Naomi Hecht told me Moria didn't like Dr. Shapira."

Anat's eyebrows twitched. "She said that?"

"Yes. Is it true?"

She shifted in discomfort and admitted that it was. "One shouldn't speak ill of the dead, but he was an unpleasant man sometimes. A little too high and mighty and brusque. But that didn't mean it wasn't a shock to learn he got murdered. That's the sort of thing that happens to strangers, you know?"

Most people experienced murder that way. It was an alien, faraway thing. Until it got close, and then it was like a monster screaming at you, its snout sticking in your face.

Based on what Anat told me about Moria's dislike for Dr. Shapira, I saw no point in raising the possibility that he and Moria had been lovers. I knew that Anat would scoff at the idea. But that didn't mean it wasn't true, especially given the fact that Dr. Shapira fit Lillian Shukrun's description of Moria's lover. Moria might have been play-acting, all the better to hide the affair.

Conversely, I considered asking Anat whether Moria had merely disliked Dr. Shapira or if she had hated him, but I figured that would only upset her, and I wouldn't get an honest answer. I did not want to believe that Moria had murdered Dr. Shapira, but her disliking him made it just a little more probable.

I said, "So you can't think of anything unusual that happened a week, ten days before the suicide, something that upset Moria?"

She considered it. She still had my handkerchief in her grip. She opened her mouth as though to speak, then threw up her hands. "No, I'm sorry."

"What were you about to say?"

"Huh?"

"It looked like you were about to say something, then stopped."

She waved a hand. "I remembered something, but I doubt it's important."

I leaned forward. "Tell me anyway."

She drew a breath. "All right. But it happened three weeks or so before Moria's death. I can't see how it could be connected to her suicide." She paused, waiting for me to either invite her to continue or tell her to stop.

I gave her a nod. "Go on."

"Well, what popped into my head was an incident with Dr. Leitner."

"Who's Dr. Leitner?"

"Our boss. He runs the Pediatric Ward, one of the chief doctors in the hospital."

"What happened?"

"I was coming in for my shift when I saw Moria storming out of Dr. Leitner's office. Her face was flushed, and there were tears in her eyes. She looked both mad and sad at the same time. I asked her what was wrong, and she told me there was nothing to worry about, that she could handle it."

"Handle what?"

"I don't know. She wouldn't say. I told Naomi about it later, and she talked to Moria, but she got the same story I did—there was nothing to worry about; it was no big deal."

Anat paused, biting her lower lip. "You must understand, Mr. Lapid, Moria was a private person. She always kept a part of herself to herself. I loved her dearly—still do—and I accepted her as she was. So when it looked like she was okay, when it seemed that whatever happened with Dr. Leitner had no lingering effect on her, I let it go."

"All right," I said, thinking that Dr. Leitner and I would soon be having a chat. Then I asked, "Was Moria seeing anyone?"

"Yes."

I sat straight. "Who?"

"I don't know his name. Moria never said one word about him."

"So how do you know there was such a man?"

The smile she gave me was one part sheepishness, three parts pride. "I could tell. I'd known Moria for a long time. One day, I could tell that she had..." She paused, blushing. "Please don't make me spell it out for you."

"That won't be necessary. I understand what you mean."

"I hope I'm not shocking you."

"Not at all, I assure you."

"That's good. Anyway, one morning, when we were both working together, I could just tell that she'd been with someone. I begged her to tell me who it was, but she kept denying it, saying I was imagining things. I didn't relent, peppered her with questions, and when finally I asked her, 'Is he married?' figuring that's why she wasn't spilling it, Moria lost her temper. She said, 'Can't you get it through your thick head, Anat? There is no man.' And then she turned red and wouldn't meet my eyes, which told me I was right, that there was a man. But she was so angry that I was scared to ask her any more about it."

"Do you have any idea whatsoever who this man is?"

"No. But I think I was right: I think he's married; otherwise she wouldn't have erupted at me like that."

"Could it be someone from the hospital?"

"I suppose it's possible. But I have no clue who it might be."

"Do you know what Moria wrote in her suicide note?"

She hugged herself, as though to smother a shiver. "Yes. I can't get it out of my head. It's so grim. Poor Moria, I wish she'd opened up to me instead of... I would have helped her. Naomi and I both would have."

"Do you think this man, this lover, could be the person Moria mentioned in her note?"

Anat's face turned to steel. For the first time, she did not look soft. She pulled my handkerchief so tightly between her hands that it ripped. "If he is," she said, looking right at me without blinking, "and if I ever find out his name, I'll kill him myself."

18

Before I left, I asked Anat Schlesinger two more questions. First, whether she had a key to Moria's apartment; and second, if she'd been to her apartment since Moria's passing. She answered no to both questions. If she was lying, she hid it better than Naomi Hecht had.

It had stopped raining by the time I stepped out of Anat's building. The air was still and frigid and crisp. The cloud cover had thinned, revealing a lustrous half-moon. The road glistened under its light.

I considered going back to the hospital to look for Dr. Leitner, but it was already evening, and I doubted he'd be there. I headed back to Jaffa Street instead, lost in thought, and turned east with no particular destination in mind.

I walked on until I reached Allenby Square, where I stopped and gazed at the cement wall that bisected the square like an ugly ridged scar. The wall marked the City Line. Beyond it was East Jerusalem, under Jordanian control. The purpose of the wall was less to prevent incursions than to protect Israeli passersby from Jordanian snipers manning the walls of the Old City.

On one edge of the square, on the Israeli side, stood a building housing Barclays Bank and Jerusalem City Hall. The building carried the marks of bullets and shrapnel from Israel's War of Independence. On the opposite edge crouched Hotel Fast. Formerly owned by Germans, and at one point housing the consulate of Nazi Germany, it was now home to indigent Jewish immigrants. A victory of sorts, I supposed, though the building's German name remained in common use.

IDF positions bristled on the rooftops of several surrounding buildings. Soldiers moved about in the gloom, rifles slung across their backs. Here, by the wall, with the City Line manifested so starkly, one could smell war hanging in the air like an evil promise. It was a terrible smell—of fire, smoke, and burning flesh.

I turned back westward, away from the wall and what it signified. My head cleared a little, and I began searching for a telephone. I needed to call Tel Aviv again.

I passed one drugstore and a couple of small cafés that had no telephone. Finally, I found a public one, dumped a few coins into it, and gave the operator a number in Tel Aviv.

A man answered and asked me my business. I gave him a name. "I need to talk to him. It's urgent."

"Hold on," the man said. "I'll see if he's still around."

I waited, muttering, "Be there, you nosy bastard. Just be there."

"Hello?" a familiar voice said after a minute. "This is Shmuel Birnbaum."

I let out a breath. "Good evening, Shmuel. It's Adam."

"Adam! Please tell me you're not calling from prison."

"No such luck."

"That's a relief. Because springing you out is an experience I do not look forward to repeating."

"I'll do my best to steer clear of trouble so as not to strain your benevolence."

"That would be wise since contrary to popular opinion, my benevolence is not unbounded. Where are you calling from?"

"Jerusalem."

"Ah. How are things in the capital?"

"Cold and wet and miserable. I suppose you heard the news."

"Indeed, I have." His voice was even, betraying no hint of satisfaction in the government's triumph.

"Are you happy? Celebrating?"

A resigned exhalation. "Is that why you called, Adam? To repeat our argument?"

"No."

"I'm relieved. Because last time we had it, I nearly drove off a cliff, which is what you and your buddies were on the verge of doing to Israel two nights ago. But I'll answer your question anyway, and I do hope it will sink in. I am not happy about this decision. Neither is Ben-Gurion or the ministers or anyone else. You don't have to rejoice in doing what's smart and necessary. You just need to do it. That's the difference between being a responsible statesman and a destructive rabble-rouser. Now pray tell, why did you call me?"

"I need to ask you a question. It's about Baruch Gafni's wife."

Birnbaum was silent. In the background on his end, I could hear people talking, typewriter keys clicking.

"Are you there, Shmuel?"

"I'm here." His voice was lower, dead serious. "What do you need to know?"

"How she died, for one thing."

"She committed suicide."

"Yes, I know that. I'm wondering why you didn't bother telling me this, considering that you were just about sure I was going to investigate Gafni's daughter's death, and that she committed suicide as well."

"It wasn't my place. I assumed Gafni would tell you."

"Well, he didn't. I'm trying to figure out why. Do you know?"

"No, I don't." Now Birnbaum sounded just a little bit curious. His natural nosiness coming to life, perhaps against his will.

"What was her name?"

"Vera."

"How did she kill herself?"

"If I recall correctly, she slashed her wrists."

"I understand her daughter was the one who found her."

"It's possible. I don't remember. I'm not sure I ever knew."

"The story didn't make the papers?"

"It did, but I didn't write it, and we usually don't go into detail in such matters out of respect for the family."

"I'm sure Gafni appreciated it. He wouldn't want his reputation to suffer. It might be bad for business." I was getting angry now, my voice getting louder, my face turning hot. "Why did she do it?"

"I don't know."

"Was there a note?"

"I don't know, Adam."

"Did she kill herself because of her husband? And don't tell me you don't know, Shmuel. There must have been rumors, and I know you hear all of them."

A pause. A low exhalation. "There were some rumors, yes."

"What?"

Another pause. The background noises diminished a little, and I guessed Birnbaum had picked up the phone and moved as far away from his colleagues as its cord would allow. When next he spoke, his voice was low and cautious. "Word at the time was that Vera Gafni took her own life due to her husband's infidelity. Apparently, he was quite the womanizer."

"What about prostitutes? Were there rumors about that?"

"I don't know anything about prostitutes."

But I did. I knew about one. I gritted my teeth as the memory of Gafni emerging from Sima Vaaknin's building played in my mind.

"Did Moria know about this? Did she know why her mother killed herself?"

"I have no idea."

"Is that the truth, Shmuel? Is that the truth, or are you lying to me to cover up for your friend?" I was shouting now, shouting into the phone, and a couple passing by on the street were gawking at me. "What?" I barked at them. "What do you want?" The woman yanked the man away, looking terrified.

"Are you okay, Adam?" Birnbaum said. "Is everything all right?"

Of course it wasn't. Nothing was all right. Because a dissolute, greedy rich man was sitting in Tel Aviv on his hoard of gold and silver, already planning how to use the money Germany would be giving Israel as reparations for the six million to advance his businesses. And this man had likely driven his wife to suicide and maybe had done the same to his daughter. And no one cared. No one did anything. He had paid no price and was not going to. He had won, and I had lost. Israel would negotiate with Germany. Gafni would get his share of the take, and I would be left with this hole in my heart, this sense of wrongness, of gaping detachment from the country I'd fought and bled for. And meanwhile Gafni would live large while his wife and daughter lay dead, just like my wife and daughters.

"Adam? Are you still there, Adam?"

I shut my eyes against the sudden wetness in them. Filled my lungs with cold Jerusalem air and let it leak out of me slowly, along with the sharp edge of my fury. My fingers were aching due to how hard I was gripping the phone. I forced them loose, and it was like being freed from tight tethers, my fingertips prickling.

"Yeah," I said, suddenly weary as though I'd walked all day with no food in me. "Yeah, I'm here."

Birnbaum's tone was tender and caring. "Adam, you *meshuggeneh*, what is happening to you?"

I opened my eyes, wiped the back of my hand across them. I looked around, but no one seemed to have noticed my turmoil. Or perhaps everyone had and was pretending not to see me, to ignore my existence. "Answer my question, Shmuel."

He sighed and said, "I'm not protecting Baruch Gafni. Contrary to what you believe, he's not my friend. I don't even like him. But I deal with all sorts of people as part of my job, just as you do. Baruch Gafni is one of them. I don't know what Moria Gafni knew about her father's extramarital activities. I don't know for sure why Vera Gafni killed herself. But I do know one thing you should keep in mind. Are you listening, Adam?"

"Yeah, I'm listening."

"Good. Because you need to know that Baruch Gafni is not a man you want as an enemy. He's powerful and connected and can be quite vindictive. And he's the reason why you're not sitting in a jail cell right now. Get on his bad side, and he won't hesitate to withdraw the protection he's granted you."

I thought of Inspector Kulaski straining at the leash like a slavering dog at the sight of raw meat—only the meat was me. A blade of fear dug sharply into my stomach and up into my chest. I knew what fate Kulaski had ordained for me. Gafni's protection was all that stood in his way.

I knew that Birnbaum was right. I had only met Gafni once, but that was enough to know what kind of man he was. Going against him meant taking a huge risk, with heavy potential penalties. It was a risk I did not want to take.

But then I thought of Moria Gafni. Not the twenty-three-year-old woman with skeletons in her closet who took her own life, but the innocent sixteen-year-old girl she'd been when she came home one day to find her mother dead.

Some deaths are cleaner than others. Taking pills and lying in bed to die is neat; slicing your wrists is messy. The human body holds a prodigious quantity of blood. Open your veins and it all comes out. It spreads around farther than most people would imagine. It's a hard sight for a grown-up; for a teenager, it could leave a permanent mark. And if it's your mother whose blood it is, and if in the center of that pool of red you see her body—well, that would change you fundamentally and forever.

I thought I understood one thing now: why Moria had opted for pills instead of blowing her own brains out with her gun. She'd seen a violent suicide, a bloody scene, and her work in the war had educated her as to what gunshots can do to the human body. She'd wanted a cleaner ending for herself. A cleaner ending than the one her mother had bequeathed Moria's sixteen-year-old eyes.

"I'll take my chances," I heard myself say, the words tripping out of my mouth before my conscious mind had time to fully register their utterance.

"What does that mean?" asked Birnbaum.

"It means that I'm going to get to the bottom of this, Shmuel. I'm going to do my job. I'm going to discover why Moria Gafni killed herself. And I'll make sure whoever is to blame pays for it, even if it's Baruch Gafni."

"What are you talking about, 'whoever is to blame'?" Birnbaum said, and I remembered that he didn't know the full details. He hadn't read Moria's note. As far as he was concerned, this was your run-of-the-mill suicide.

"Never mind, Shmuel."

"Don't you never mind me," he said. His voice was alert now, his professional curiosity fully piqued. I could picture his eyes sparkling with excitement behind his glasses as he picked up the scent of a fresh story. "Come on, spill."

"There's no need to, remember? You said there would be no public interest in this case, no matter the outcome," I said, reminding him of what he had told me in his car just before I went to meet Baruch Gafni.

"I have a feeling I should revise my earlier statement."

"Do yourself a favor and ignore it. You were perfectly right, Shmuel. As you said, Baruch Gafni is not a man you want as an enemy."

"I can take care of myself, Adam."

"I believe you. And I can do the same."

"I'm not the one in danger of being locked up in prison."

He had a point. I was more vulnerable than Birnbaum. He did not have the threat of imprisonment hanging over him, and his position and connections afforded him a measure of influence and protection that I lacked.

But that didn't matter. What mattered was Paula's accusations echoing in my head. For the time being, Moria was an innocent woman who'd gone through some bad things and died much too young. I did not want Birnbaum to start nosing around this case. I did not want him digging into Moria's life. I did not want her life exposed in the pages of *Davar*.

"Be that as it may," I said. "I don't see how you could write about this, even if there was something worth writing. Gafni came to you for help. He trusted your discretion. Imagine what will happen if you end up writing about him or his daughter? No one will trust you, Shmuel. And no one talks to a journalist they don't trust."

He was quiet for a few seconds; then he let out a grunt of frustration. He knew I was right.

He said, "I also vouched for your discretion, Adam, remember?"

"I remember. Don't you worry, I'll be as discreet as possible."

"As possible?"

"Yes, as possible. As much as I can. But not for Baruch Gafni's sake, and not for yours either."

"For yourself, then?"

"No," I said. "Not for myself. I'll be doing it for Moria."

19

When I opened my eyes, the hotel room window was filled with the gray light of a January sun. I had woken late after sleeping the night through, dreamless. I had Daniel Shukrun to thank for that. I did not know why and did not care to speculate, but for me, violent days led to peaceful nights. It had been that way since the war in Europe ended.

Most other nights were filled with vicious nightmares of Auschwitz, real and assumed and imagined, memories and ghosts and human monsters that wouldn't go away or die. By charging me in Moria's apartment and falling victim to my fists, Shukrun had granted me a night of uninterrupted sleep. I was grateful, particularly because I had worried about my screams waking the other guests.

The sagging mattress squeaked as I shifted to a sitting position. The room smelled stuffy, so I opened the window, and cold air flowed in, raising goosebumps on my arms. Looking outside, I saw the cloud cover had lightened further. The air smelled clean and fresh.

I went down the hall to the bathroom and was gratified to see the faint pink hue of my urine. My kidney was on the mend. I washed my face and shaved and looked at myself in the small mirror above the sink. I looked the same as I did on any other day. Not like a man who the day before had felt as though his world had flipped over itself. Life was pulling me along, like the rest of Israel.

The lobby was empty. No trace of the clerk. Out on the street, the sun was bright and sharp, like a light beam shining through a clean pane of glass. Either the rain had cleaned the air, or my eyes needed to adjust to the sunlight after a few gloomy days.

I had breakfast at a café. Smoked my first cigarette of the day over coffee. I thought of Greta and my chessboard. I thought of Sima Vaaknin. I thought of Reuben. I thought of Moria. I thought of Israel negotiating with Germany. The food turned sour in my stomach.

I went to the hospital. Thankfully, Paula wasn't there. Nor did I see Naomi Hecht or Anat Schlesinger, though they could have been in one of the rooms or somewhere else on the premises. I asked a passing nurse where I might find Dr. Leitner, and she pointed at a silver-haired thin man talking to another nurse near the end of the hall. I walked over there and waited a few feet away while Dr. Leitner regaled the nurse with a story of a surgery he'd recently performed. Way he told it, he hadn't just fixed and stitched a boy up, he'd rebuilt him from scratch. The nurse looked suitably impressed, but I noticed her fingers were drumming on the outside of her thigh; she was eager for her boss to quit blabbing and release her.

Coming to her aid, I cleared my throat loudly and said, "Dr. Leitner?"

Leitner shot me an annoyed look, his mouth still open. I'd interrupted him mid-sentence. He was around fifty, with thinning hair, eyes like pebbles, and one of those diamond-shaped faces that taper sharply from wide cheekbones to a pointed chin.

"Yes?" he snapped.

"Sorry to burst in on your conversation." I smiled politely at the doctor and sneaked a wink at the nurse. "My name is Adam Lapid. I would like to talk to you for a few minutes."

Leitner's small mouth compressed to the shape of a hard ball. "I'm in the middle of something, Mr... eh..." He hadn't caught my name. "I'll be doing rounds in a half hour. We can talk about your child then."

"I'm not the father of any of your patients," I said. "My name is Adam Lapid, and I want to talk to you about Moria Gafni."

Leitner narrowed his eyes. His forehead was creased with wrinkles that reminded me of suture marks. "What's your interest in her?"

"I'm a private investigator. I'm working for Moria's father."

Leitner's eyebrows shot up. "Baruch Gafni?" At my nod, he said to the nurse, "Go back to work now, Sarah. I'll finish telling you the rest of the story later."

By the speed at which the nurse made her escape, I doubted she was looking forward to it.

"Let's go to my office," Leitner said, and led the way to a door bearing his name. Beyond it was a neat room with a desk, three chairs, and a skeleton propped on a metal rod in the corner. The skeleton was grinning at me, as though saying, *Now you're in for it, you fool.* It had heard its share of boring stories.

Leitner went behind his desk, smoothing his white coat before he sat down. I took one of the opposite chairs. On the wall behind the desk were framed diplomas and pictures of Leitner with various dignitaries. Leitner giving a tour of his ward to Daniel Auster, the first Israeli mayor of Jerusalem. Leitner rubbing shoulders with President Chaim Weizmann. Leitner shaking hands with David Ben-Gurion. An important man, and he wanted you to know it.

The important man was now eying me across his desk. "I must say I'm surprised to learn that Mr. Gafni has employed a detective."

"Mr. Gafni wishes to know what caused his daughter to take her own life."

"I see." Leitner nodded sagely a few times, as though in approval. "It's a question that has been bothering me incessantly as well, I assure you."

"Have you come up with any answers?"

"Alas, no," he said, adopting a tone of amiable superiority. "Of course, taking into account Moria's age and sex, matters of the heart are the likeliest reason."

"Her sex?"

"Naturally. Oh, I suppose there are some weak-hearted men who kill themselves due to unrequited love, but women are more senti- mental, more prone to emotional outbursts and illogical acts, and Moria was young and single, which increases the likelihood further."

"You think Moria killed herself because of a man?"

"I don't know for certain, but if I had to venture a guess, that would be it."

"Any idea who this man might be?"

He smiled without parting his lips. "I'm sorry, but no. I don't involve myself in the private affairs of my nurses, Mr. Lapid."

Of course he didn't. He probably knew next to nothing about them. They were good only as employees, inferior to him, and as a captive audience to his self-glorifying stories.

"Did Moria strike you as an overly emotional woman?" I asked.

"No. Not overly," he answered, and the implication was clear—he considered all women to be too emotional for their own good. Susceptible to bad judgment and hasty acts. Like a suicide.

"Did Moria like working here?"

"Very much."

The certainty of his answer surprised me. Either he knew more about Moria than I had given him credit for, or he simply assumed that all the women working under him must be happy in their roles.

"Was she a good nurse?"

"Quite satisfactory. I told Mr. Gafni as much."

"You talked to my client?"

"Certainly. I called him after the tragedy to express my condo- lences. He didn't tell you?"

"No. That was nice of you, calling him."

"It was the least I could do."

"'Quite satisfactory,'" I said, repeating his words to him. "It doesn't sound like you were that impressed with Moria's performance."

Leitner tensed. "You misunderstood me, Mr. Lapid. I meant the exact opposite. I thought Moria was an exemplary nurse. I do hope Mr. Gafni knows how highly I valued his daughter."

I frowned at him. Why did he care what Gafni thought of him?

"So no complaints?"

"None whatsoever. Moria had a grand future ahead of her on this ward. I was very distressed by her suicide. I told Mr. Gafni that as well."

"I'm sure he appreciated it," I said, and Leitner's posture relaxed.

I said, "Tell me, then, what happened that day, about three weeks before the suicide, that caused Moria to leave your office in tears?"

Leitner froze. All apart from his tongue, which flicked out to wet his lips and then disappeared back into his mouth. The question had stunned him, and it took him a few seconds to regain a semblance of composure.

"Who told you about that?" he asked. His voice was mild, as though the answer was of but minor interest to him, but in his small dark eyes, I could see the glint of anger, the promise of retribution. I bet Anat Schlesinger would be out of a job before the day was out if Leitner discovered she was my source.

"What difference does it make?" I said. "Answer the question!"

It was the first time I'd used a forceful tone with him, but I wanted to press him a little. I was taking a risk, but I didn't think it was a big one. I was Baruch Gafni's man, and for some reason, Dr. Leitner wanted to be on my employer's good side.

Leitner brushed a finger along the space between his nose and mouth. Reaching into a drawer, he brought out a pack of Nelsons, offered me one, and when I declined, lit one for himself.

He took a couple of rapid, deep drags, blowing the smoke toward the grinning skeleton, then examined the glowing tip of his smoke with a thoughtful expression before turning his eyes back on me.

"Would you agree, Mr. Lapid, that there are times when telling the whole, unvarnished truth is not only unwarranted but also cruel?"

There were such times, but I wasn't going to give him an inch until I knew more. "Go on," I said.

Leitner pulled on his cigarette again and said, "When I said that I had no complaints about Moria's work, I was not being entirely truthful. I did this because I assumed you'll be reporting what I said to Mr. Gafni." He paused, waiting for me to confirm it, but I gave no indication either way. He continued, "I felt that was the impression a grieving father should have of his dead daughter."

"And the truth is...?"

"The truth is that Moria was a good nurse. But on that occasion, and a handful of others, I had to rebuke her."

"What for?"

"For her work, naturally. I was her boss, you know."

"What about her work? Be specific."

Dr. Leitner took a final drag and mashed out his cigarette, even though it was nowhere near done. He steepled his fingers, eying me over them.

"One of our doctors complained about her. She had gotten too familiar with one of the families. The parents were running everything the doctor suggested by her, as if she knew more than him, and she did not refrain from telling them her opinion on the doctor's prescribed treatment. Even when the doctor instructed Moria to desist, she didn't."

"And you saw fit to rebuke her for it?"

"There's a delicate structure to a hospital, Mr. Lapid. When you disrupt this structure, things begin to fall apart. In this structure, doctors are set above nurses. They are the source of knowledge and authority. They know best. Nurses should obey doctors. Nurses should not contradict them before patients or their family members."

"Who's the doctor who complained about her?"

I thought Leitner would object to telling me, but he didn't hesitate. "His name was Kalman Shapira. I would gladly introduce you to him, but unfortunately, he's dead."

"I see," I said slowly, digesting this new bit of information. Here was a motive. A reason for Moria to seek vengeance on Dr. Shapira. Hardly the strongest motive for murder I'd encountered, but far from the flimsiest either. "Was this the only time in which Dr. Shapira and Moria were at odds?"

"I'm afraid not. It simply came to a head on that occasion, which is why I had to clarify to Moria the way things work here."

"You must not have minced words if she was driven to tears."

The accusation gave Leitner pause. He leaned forward, elbows on desk, fixing his eyes on mine. "I assure you, Mr. Lapid, that I spoke to Moria with the utmost tenderness and respect. As all women, she was simply emotional, that's all, which explains her sad ending. But now you understand why I thought it best for Mr. Gafni to not know of this episode. What good would it do him?"

None, I thought. Though I doubted Leitner had been as gentle as he claimed. He simply wanted Gafni to think that, in case I told him about it.

I wondered why Moria had not told either of her friends about this dressing-down in Leitner's office. Was it that hurtful? Or had she, even then, decided to avenge herself on Dr. Shapira and so wanted as few people to know about his complaint as possible?

I disliked thinking of Moria as a murderer. I wanted to discover an innocent reason for her keeping a hidden gun, for being secretive. I wanted her to be a victim, not a criminal. Maybe if Reuben came through and I read the police file, I'd discover Moria's gun could not have been the murder weapon. I hoped I would.

20

Leaving Dr. Leitner's office, submerged in thought, I bumped into Naomi Hecht. She staggered back from the impact, and I seized both her arms to steady her.

"Watch where you're going," she snapped, wrenching her arms free. She rubbed her nose, which had collided with my shoulder. Up close, she smelled of soap and chicory coffee and something medicinal yet pleasant. The bags under her eyes had darkened. Another bad night.

"Sorry," I said. "Are you all right?"

She lowered her hand and glared at me. "I'm fine. Don't you worry about me. Back to ask more questions?"

"That's right."

Her eyes flicked to the closed door behind me, and her brow creased. "You spoke to Dr. Leitner?"

"Yes."

"I trust you were suitably impressed."

I smiled. "How could I not be?"

"How indeed. Did the great doctor tell you something interesting?"

"As it so happens, he did." Doctors and nurses and visitors were

165

moving along the corridor. I took Naomi Hecht by the arm and guided her to a small alcove where we would have more privacy. "He told me about the time about three weeks before Moria died when she came out of his office crying."

Naomi Hecht's eyes blazed. "I remember that day. I don't know what he said to her, but she wasn't the same all that day and the next."

"She didn't tell you anything about it?"

"Not one word. I was so angry, I was about to march into his office and tell him off, but Moria made me promise to keep my cool."

"She probably saved your job, didn't she?"

"Probably."

"Are you always this impulsive?"

She started shaking her head, then stopped and lowered her gaze. "Sometimes."

I nearly smiled again, then remembered my own impulsiveness three days before in the demonstration, and all levity deserted me. My mind turned to what Dr. Leitner had told me and what it might mean.

"I need your help, Mrs. Hecht."

"I think I've given you enough of my time already, Mr. Lapid."

"This won't take long. I'm thinking that there must be a shift log somewhere in this ward. I'd like to see it."

"What for?"

"I want to know which nurses worked on a certain night."

"Which night?"

I hesitated. I didn't want her to know, but I was going to have to tell her which week or month I was interested in, and she was smart enough to figure it out."

"November 28."

It took a second for the significance of the date to sink in. "What are you getting at, Mr. Lapid?"

"Nothing in particular."

"I thought you were working on Moria's suicide? Or was that a lie?"

"It's the truth. That's my case."

"So why...?" She paused and glowered at me. "Are you actually suggesting that Moria—"

"Lower your voice, Mrs. Hecht."

She did, casting a quick glance around to make sure we hadn't drawn any attention. But whatever intensity her voice lost, the outrage on her face gained. "Do you really believe Moria killed Dr. Shapira? Are you crazy?"

"I'm simply gathering information."

"Like hell you are. And if you think I'll help you, you can forget it."

She turned to go, but I grabbed her arm. "I'll make you a deal, Mrs. Hecht."

Her eyebrows knitted. "What deal?"

"Get me the log, and I'll tell you what Dr. Leitner told me about why Moria left his office in tears."

Naomi Hecht stared at me so hard, I thought she was about to slap me or punch me in the face. Maybe if we weren't where other people could see us, she would have.

"If you're so sure about her," I said, "what harm could it do?"

She didn't like that logic one bit, but at length she surrendered to it with a stiff nod. "All right. You first."

I would have preferred it the other way around, but I acquiesced. She listened without interruption as I related what Dr. Leitner had told me. I admired her control: her facial muscles never so much as twitched. But her eyes gave away her internal turmoil; they were never still.

I didn't spell it out. I didn't need to. We both knew what Dr. Leitner's story meant: Moria had reason to hate Dr. Shapira. And hate is one of the most reliable motives for murder.

"Your turn," I said.

If looks could kill, Naomi Hecht would have been well on her way to death row. "Wait here," she said, and stomped off without waiting for a reply.

She was back two minutes later with a large hardcover notebook. "Here. Feast your eyes."

I opened the notebook and flipped through some pages until I got to November 28. Two nurses were listed on the night shift. Sarah Greenberg was the first; Moria Gafni the second.

"Happy now?" Naomi Hecht asked.

I handed back the notebook. "You took a peek?"

"Of course I did. As you can see, Moria was here on that night."

I did see that, but there were still some holes to plug before I could be sure she could not have committed the murder.

"What hours are the night shift?"

"From 9:00 p.m. to 7 a.m."

"This is the extent of the staff: two nurses?"

"There's also a doctor on call in the hospital, but he's not called into the ward unless there's an emergency."

"So normally, it's just the two nurses?"

"Yes."

"Are both awake throughout the night?"

A muscle moved near Naomi Hecht's mouth. "If it's quiet, one of them might catch a little sleep."

So Moria could have been awake alone at certain points during that night.

I said, "How long does it take to walk from here to where Dr. Shapira was killed?"

She knew what I was getting at. "What, you think Moria left the ward unattended and went off to shoot Dr. Shapira?"

I didn't answer.

"What if the other nurse had woken up and seen that Moria wasn't there?" she asked.

"Moria would have had some explaining to do."

"Some explaining." She let out a laugh, but it sounded hollow. "She would have been the main suspect, wouldn't she?"

"You'd be surprised at the risks people take to have an alibi."

"She didn't kill him. Trust me, Mr. Lapid, I knew Moria better than anyone. She was a pure soul; she didn't have it in her to kill anyone."

Sometime during this appeal, she touched my hand. Her fingers were cool and soft. My skin tingled at their touch. She pulled them away, leaving a strange absence.

"If you knew Moria, Mr. Lapid, you wouldn't suspect her for a second. Shooting someone, it's ridiculous. I don't think she ever fired a gun in her life."

She must have, or she wouldn't have had one hidden in her bedroom. A keen sense of pity came over me for Naomi Hecht's ignorance of her friend.

"But she did do something she never told you about, didn't she?" I said, my tone gentle, for I did not wish to hurt this woman; all I wanted was for her to help me uncover the truth. "She said so in her note."

Naomi Hecht said nothing. For a moment, I thought she was about to cry, but fury entered her eyes, not tears. She drew a lungful of air, her face became like a shield, and she looked as formidable as any woman I'd ever known. For the second time, I became sure she was going to strike me, but all she did was state, with quiet unbending resolution, "Moria wasn't a murderer. She never harmed anyone. And you're a fool for even considering it." Then she brushed past me and strode off without a backward glance.

Exiting the ward, I heard a voice say, "Thank you for saving me back there."

It was the nurse whom Dr. Leitner had tormented with his self-aggrandizing story. She was coming up the stairs.

"You're most welcome," I said, and then something clicked. "Sarah, isn't it?"

She smiled. She was a pretty little brunette with shining green eyes and plump lips. "Yes. Have we met before?"

"We haven't. I just remembered Dr. Leitner calling you by name."

She made a face. "He doesn't remember, but he's told me that story five times already."

"He must like the sound of his own voice."

She laughed. "He sure does."

"I'm Adam," I said, and we shook hands. She blushed a little.

"Well," she said, "I should get going. Back to the grindstone and all. Just two more hours to go."

There was an invitation there, but I wasn't about to take it. Her mouth compressed in disappointment, and she turned to leave.

"Wait a second. Is your last name Greenberg by any chance?"

She looked puzzled. "How do you know that? I don't think Dr. Leitner mentioned it, did he?"

"He didn't. I saw your name in the shift log. I'm a private investigator. I was hired to investigate why Moria Gafni killed herself."

"Oh." She looked startled. "I... I..." She obviously didn't know what to say and finally blurted, "Well, I don't know why she did it. Not a clue."

"That's all right," I said. "I'm actually wondering about something else. Do you remember the night of November 28?"

"November 28? That was over a month ago."

"It's the night Dr. Shapira got killed."

Her eyes went huge. "Sure I remember. I was working that night. How awful."

"The log says Moria was the other nurse on shift with you. What I want to know is whether you were asleep at some point during that night or if you were awake the whole time."

"Well, I don't remember..." She paused. "Wait a minute, Moria wasn't with me that night."

"She wasn't? But the shift log says—"

"She was supposed to work that shift, but she switched with another nurse."

A frisson of excitement started in my belly and spread over my arms. "Who did she switch with?"

The answer left me reeling.

21

Why did she lie? That was the question that ricocheted in my head as I made my way south toward Jaffa Street. Or had she simply forgotten?

No. I immediately rejected the latter option. Naomi Hecht hadn't forgotten. She was not the type to forget such a thing. She had shown me the shift log, knowing what it said, and let me believe it was true. She wanted me to think that Moria had worked the night shift when Dr. Shapira was murdered.

Why had she done so? To protect her friend? To make sure I didn't suspect Moria of this murder? Or did it mean she wasn't as certain of Moria's innocence as she claimed?

It occurred to me that I might have been justified in feeling anger toward Naomi Hecht, but there was no trace of it in my heart. Rather, I respected her for protecting her friend, even posthumously. Most friends, even close ones, would not have done so, especially considering that she'd given up her own alibi in the process.

Maybe she could just count on her husband to say she was home, if it came to that, a nasty voice in my head said, and I clenched my teeth, yanked my cigarettes from my pocket, and fired one up.

I told myself it didn't matter why Naomi Hecht had lied to me.

What mattered was that Moria had no alibi for the night of Dr. Shapira's murder. Sarah Greenberg did not know why Moria had switched shifts with Naomi Hecht, only that it had happened at the last minute, which was probably why the shift log had not been updated.

Perhaps Moria had done so purposely, to cover up her tracks, but I couldn't say for sure.

What I did know was that Moria had the three things all murderers share: means, motive, and opportunity. But maybe the police report would change that. Maybe it would show that the gun I found in Moria's bedroom could not be the murder weapon. I hoped so.

I called Reuben Tzanani from a café on Jaffa Street. The phone went unanswered. I ordered coffee, smoked a couple of cigarettes, tried his number again. No luck.

I walked east past display windows showing neckties and women's hats and all manner of other goods. I browsed the shelves in the Steimatzky bookstore without buying anything. I stood across from the Generali Building and gazed long and hard at the stone winged-lion statue on its roof, trying unsuccessfully to decipher its expression. I telephoned Reuben again, and this time he picked up.

"How are you?" he asked, still worried about me.

I told him I was fine, said I couldn't stay on the line for long, and asked if he had something for me.

"As it so happens, I do. I called one of the Jerusalem officers I know, and he connected me with a Sergeant Rapfogel. I asked him if you could see that homicide file. At first, he balked, but I vouched for you, and he said he'd see what he could do. He called me back an hour ago and said it would be fine. Why don't you call him directly and set up a meeting? I'll read you the number. You got a pencil?"

Sergeant Rapfogel had a scratchy voice and a local accent. He sounded very friendly. He asked if I was in the city. When I said that I was and added that now would be a good time for me to get the file, he apologized.

"I'm swamped, have to work late. Why don't we meet this evening, say eight thirty?"

The meeting place he proposed was a restaurant called Fink's on Ha-Histadrut Street, not too far from where I was now. It surprised me that Rapfogel wanted to meet outside his police station, but it saved me the trouble of suggesting it myself. I wanted to steer clear of Jerusalem police installations. I had no desire to run into Inspector Kulaski.

I returned to Amos Street to do some more canvassing. In the apartment that shared the second floor with the Shukruns' lived a family of six. The father was at work, the kids at school. The mother said that Moria had visited her children several times when they were sick with fever.

"She had a way with children," she told me. "They'd see her and their little faces would light up. I felt terrible the day she died. As long as I live, I won't forget the moment they took her body down the stairs. She was all covered up, but I could imagine how she looked under the sheet. I don't mind telling you it brought me to tears. I had no idea she'd been so sad."

When I left the apartment, Lillian Shukrun opened her door and peeked out. She saw me and smiled. "I thought I heard voices."

I smiled back, thinking of what the downstairs neighbor had told me about Lillian's nosiness. We exchanged a few pleasantries, and I left.

I spent three hours knocking on doors in the neighboring buildings. Asked the same questions: Had they known Moria? How well had they known her? Had they seen her with other people? Did they have a clue why she killed herself? The first twenty conversations yielded plenty of speculation but nothing concrete. But then I talked to a fifty-something woman who remembered seeing Moria arguing with a man about a week before her death.

"What did they argue about?"

"I couldn't hear them properly. My hearing's not what it used to be, and they weren't talking loudly, and I was on the other sidewalk, and I wasn't trying to listen, you know? He wasn't hurting her, so I minded my own business." She sounded ashamed when she said this, but I understood. Why get involved in someone else's mess when you don't have to?

"But you're sure they were arguing?"

"Sure I'm sure. I could tell by their faces and how they were moving their arms. Especially her. She was the angry one, far as I could tell. Then I saw her start to walk away. The man started coming after her, but she held up a hand and yelled at him to leave her alone. 'Stay away from me, Arye!' That part I heard loud and clear."

"Arye? Are you sure that was the name?"

"Sure I'm sure. Wouldn't have said so if I wasn't."

I sat very still. I had met a man called Arye recently and had promptly put him out of my mind. But was it the same man?

"Do you remember what this Arye looked like?"

She screwed up her face in concentration. "What I remember best is he was well dressed. I'm a seamstress, so I have an eye for such things. His clothes cost a lot of money. Other than that, let's see... he was thin and had dark hair. I don't remember his face."

"How tall was he?"

She puckered her lips and shifted her head side to side as she estimated in her mind. "He was taller than her. Five ten, five eleven, maybe even six feet."

It fitted. As did the thin build and dark hair and expensive attire. The man was called Arye Harpaz. I had met him on the way out of Baruch Gafni's factory.

Harpaz had met Moria, had fought with her outside her building. He was a handsome guy, and he fit Lillian Shukrun's description of the man she'd seen leaving Moria's apartment.

Her lover. I finally knew who he was.

22

Having time to kill and nothing to kill it with, and with my feet aching from all the walking and stair climbing I'd done, I went back to my hotel. I lay on the narrow bed and closed my eyes, but sleep eluded me. I was restless, my brain a jumble of careening thoughts, and I felt every lump and depression in the old mattress. My mind was going places I didn't want it to go, and the small room felt stifling and close, so I pushed myself up, more tired than I'd been before I lay down, put on my shoes, and hurried out.

Needing a distraction, I returned to the bookstore. I bought a slim paperback Western and read the first fifty pages sitting on a street bench with the din of the city in my ears. The day was clear and bright and warmer than at any time since I'd arrived in Jerusalem.

The sidewalks were awash with people. I heard Arabic and German and French and Hebrew accented in all of the above and a slew of other tongues. I saw bearded Orthodox Jews in black suits and diminutive nuns in black habits. I saw Jews from Europe and North Africa and the Arab countries to the east. I saw a line of people curling out of a grocery store advertising the sale of chicken. I saw children gaping into shop displays or chasing each other around, their laughter high and tinkling. Some of them had on clothes that were darned and patched to within an inch of their life or wore comically mis-sized hand-me-downs. Would the money Germany give Israel improve these children's lot? Would it allow parents to put more food on their plates? Would it help Israel provide proper housing to its new immigrants, many of whom still lived in tents or makeshift shacks in haphazard immigrant camps?

I had a late lunch at a café with a German name that had pictures of German landmarks on the walls. Someone was homesick for a home that didn't exist anymore.

All that German scenery made me curious as to what the proprietor thought about Israel entering into direct negotiations with his former homeland, but I held my tongue. I didn't want to ruin my appetite.

I stretched out the meal and lingered over multiple cups of coffee, reading eighty more pages. The proprietor didn't mind; the place wasn't full.

It was after six by the time I finally paid my bill and left. It was dark now, the air chillier, but the sky still clear.

I finished the book by the light of a candle in another café, where I also ate a small dinner. The bad guys were dead; the good cowboy was wounded, but he'd live. No need for compromises or deals with the devil. I left the book on the table and went out.

I got to Fink's a couple of minutes late and scanned the patrons. Not a uniform among them. I figured Sergeant Rapfogel was running even later than I was, but then a guy wearing civilian clothes motioned me over from the back.

He'd taken the rearmost table, and Reuben must have given him my description because he hadn't hesitated before calling me over. He was medium height and stocky, with cropped black hair and a mustache that obscured much of his upper lip. Light-brown eyes, a cleft chin, round face, pale skin. He flashed a broad smile and offered me his hand.

"Adam, right? I'm Mordechai Rapfogel."

He hadn't ordered yet. I guessed he'd waited for me and my

wallet. It was to be expected: he was doing me a favor; I was supposed to respond in kind.

I sat down. The place smelled of good food, good wine, and good cigarettes. This was going to cost me.

Rapfogel said, "You hungry? They have terrific food here."

"I just ate."

This news didn't faze him. "Mind if I have something? I missed both lunch and dinner. There's too much to do and not enough officers to handle it all."

"Go ahead. It's on me, okay? I'm grateful that you're taking the time to help me out."

He told me it was no trouble and finger-summoned the waiter. He ordered appetizers, a main course, and wine, which explained why he'd come in civilian clothes. It wouldn't do for a cop to be seen drinking alcohol in uniform.

The wine was an old vintage. Rapfogel was taking full advantage of my generosity.

He said, "This cop from Tel Aviv, Tzanani? He says you're a private detective."

"That's right."

"This is your case, the Shapira murder?"

I shook my head. "I'm working on something that may be related."

He waited for me to elaborate, but I didn't. When the silence got a bit too long for comfort, he said, "Fine. You don't have to tell me. But if you have something that could crack a murder..."

"If I had anything, I'd share it, don't you worry."

That seemed to satisfy him. He put a file on the table but kept his hand on it. "I can't let you take it. You'll have to read it here."

I told him that would be fine, and he pushed it toward me. As I reached for it, I caught Rapfogel staring at my hand, my bruised knuckles. I was sure he was going to ask me about them, but he didn't. I opened the file and started reading.

Dr. Shapira's body was discovered in an alleyway at five in the morning of November 29 by an early riser on his way to work. The police were called. The picture seemed clear enough.

Dr. Shapira had been shot twice at point-blank. Both times in the chest. One bullet tore into a lung; the other chewed his heart to a pulp. He didn't stand a chance and had likely died within seconds.

His wallet was missing, as was his watch. His clothes had been rifled through for other valuables: his trouser pockets were turned inside out. Even his belt was gone.

There were no defensive wounds or signs of a struggle. The victim was either shot immediately, or he had refused to hand over his belongings, and the killer had wasted no time on persuasion. The pathologist estimated that the murder occurred around midnight.

The motive seemed clear: robbery. If I were the investigating officer, that would have been the conclusion I'd have jumped to as well.

Speaking of investigating officers, reading who led the investigation made me cringe. It was Inspector Kulaski. Rapfogel noticed my reaction and asked if I was okay.

"It's just the pictures," I said, though I'd seen much worse.

Rapfogel made a face and then did a sweeping motion with his hand. "Put them away, will you? Don't let the waiter see them."

I flipped the pictures over and waited while the waiter served Rapfogel his food. "And another one of these," Rapfogel told him, gulping down his wine and waggling the empty glass. He grinned at me, wine staining his teeth red. "Sometimes you just get thirsty, you know?"

I nodded without comment and returned my attention to the file.

The pictures added little of investigative worth. Dr. Shapira sprawled on his back, arms close to his body, his head tilted to one side, his face slack, eyes partway open. Hardly any blood apart from on his shirt; a bullet in the heart makes for a relatively tidy scene.

Both bullets remained lodged in Dr. Shapira's corpse. The first, the one that ripped through his lung, got mashed against his spine and was unidentifiable. The other, the one that sliced into his heart, was barely dented. It was a .25 caliber, one that could fit any number of handguns. Like the one in Moria's apartment, the one that now nestled beneath the bottom dresser drawer in my dingy hotel room.

My heart sank as I absorbed this new evidence. I had hoped that the police file would eliminate Moria's gun as the murder weapon. It did the opposite. I was now convinced that the gun I found was the one used in Dr. Shapira's murder. Moria had killed him. I was working to bring justice to a murderer.

But why didn't she get rid of the gun before she killed herself? Why did she keep it hidden? Why write such a cryptic suicide note? Why not come clean at the end?

If the terrible act hinted at in Moria's note was the murder of Dr. Shapira, who was the person who drove her to it? Was it Dr. Shapira himself for having complained about Moria to Dr. Leitner, for making her cry? But why write a suicide note that Dr. Shapira, being dead, would never read?

"Got any ideas?" a voice interrupted my ruminations. It was Rapfogel, knife and fork in hand, talking around a mouthful of food.

"Nothing yet," I lied. My brain was teeming with questions but vacant of answers. I couldn't come up with a reason why Moria would bother writing a suicide note for a man who was already dead. A man she herself had killed. It made no sense.

The police had interviewed several of Dr. Shapira's co-workers, including Dr. Leitner and Naomi Hecht and Moria, but I could tell this had been done halfheartedly. Inspector Kulaski believed from the get-go that this was a robbery, so he didn't see the point in examining any of Dr. Shapira's colleagues too closely.

Kulaski had checked with local pawnshops, hoping the killer had tried to pawn off Dr. Shapira's watch or his wallet, which his wife said was made of leather and might have fetched a few liras, but to no avail. He'd sent inquiries to other municipalities, thinking the killer might have chosen to offload the items far from home, but this yielded nothing as well.

Next, he hauled local criminals in for questioning, hoping to stumble upon the killer, but all this resulted in was plenty of paperwork and no breakthrough. Soon, all Kulaski was left with was the hope that a new piece of evidence would miraculously present itself. I had such evidence in my hotel room, but Kulaski wasn't going to get it. Not yet, at least. This gave me a spark of *schadenfreude*, the only point of light in the dismal reality of Moria Gafni being a murderer.

The night of the murder, Dr. Shapira was on his way home from the hospital, following a surgery that had gone late. It rained but not too heavily, Dr. Shapira did not own a vehicle, and his home was but a ten-minute walk from the hospital, so the doctor made his way on foot.

He took a shortcut through an alleyway that sliced between two office buildings. That was where the murderer pounced. Two shots and Dr. Shapira was dead. He was a minute away from his apartment. It was his regular route, his wife later told the police, which meant that Moria could have been lying in wait at that particular dark and secluded spot. Or maybe she had followed him from the hospital. Either way, she'd known of his scheduled surgery, which was why she'd changed shifts with Naomi Hecht at the last minute.

The choice of location proved smart. There were no witnesses. Hardly anyone was about that late on a freezing November night. No one had seen anything. No one had heard anything, either. This wasn't surprising. A .25 caliber is a small gun, so the reports wouldn't have been too loud. And it was a winter night, cold and wet. People would have been sleeping with their windows shut, which would have muffled the sound even further. And if the two shots had come close together, people could have mistaken the bangs for a car back-firing or even a thunderclap. Either way, Moria had gotten off clean, and she'd known it, or she surely would have ditched the gun. I wondered why she hadn't done it anyway. Why take the risk of keeping the murder weapon in her possession? And why didn't she get rid of it before she killed herself?

"You look like you've swallowed a lemon," Rapfogel said. He was on his fourth glass of wine by then and slurring his words. His cheeks were flushed, and his eyes had a wet look to them. He sounded accusatory, on the verge of anger, as though he knew I was holding back the identity of the killer.

But I wasn't ready to tell the police what I knew just yet. Not until

I had the whole picture. Not until I knew why Moria had killed herself and to whom she referred in her note.

"Indigestion," I said, putting the papers back into the file and sliding it across the table. I'd read the whole thing. Now I wanted to get out of that restaurant and away from Rapfogel before he got any drunker. I had a feeling he was a bad drunk. I signaled the waiter for the bill. "I'll be fine after a good night's sleep."

Rapfogel nodded. "Sleep's the best medicine for everything. Where are you staying? A hotel?"

I nodded, taking out my wallet.

"Which one?"

"Just some hole-in-the-wall," I said. "Not a place I recommend." I didn't want Rapfogel or any other cop to know where I slept.

The waiter came over, and I held back a grimace at the bill. I dumped money on the table and slipped into my coat. Rapfogel slurped what remained in his glass and followed me out.

On the street we shook hands again.

"Thanks," I said.

"Don't mention it." Rapfogel's breath was thick with wine. He patted my shoulder. "You have a good night."

"You too," I said.

He headed one way and I the other. It was nearly eleven by then. I had a fair bit of walking to do, but I didn't mind. The streets were nearly empty, the cold having chased most of Jerusalem's residents to their beds. I lit a cigarette and tried to focus on the hot smoke I was inhaling. I just walked and smoked, paying no mind to my surroundings or the few people I passed by. Sadness flooded me because of what I'd learned, because of what Moria had done.

Leaving Jerusalem's center and entering less choice areas, the frequency of streetlights declined, and shadows permeated the sidewalks and alleyways. Somewhere a cat yowled. A loose shutter squeaked. A flurry of night birds or bats flapped by overhead. There was no traffic. Lights shone in some windows, but most were dark. There was a desolate atmosphere to these streets, as though a plague had ravaged the city and only a few disoriented survivors remained. Or maybe that was the product of my bleak frame of mind.

What was I going to tell Gafni? How would he react to his daughter being a killer? When I'd warned him he might learn things about his daughter he would regret knowing, this was one possibility I hadn't imagined.

I flicked the vestige of my cigarette into the street, took a deep breath of Jerusalem's crisp mountain air, and shoved my hands in my pockets. Which was why I was slow to defend myself when the attack came.

23

Like lightning on a summer day, it was unexpected and quick. One second I was ambling peacefully on a quiet street; the next I was under assault. The only warning was the sudden thump of running footsteps from behind and a barked command, "Get him!"

My wandering mind and my pocketed hands contributed to my slow reaction. I had barely gotten my hands out and was turning around when something hard struck me across the upper back, just below the neck.

They had picked the right spot. A stretch of dark sidewalk on a block made up of garages, small factories, and shuttered workshops. No residential buildings. No one about.

The blow pitched me forward. Somehow, I managed to block the fall and remain on one knee. I turned my head, saw two shadowy figures standing over me with cloth covering their faces. They were holding something in their hands. Clubs, short and thick. A third man, his face obscured as well, stood a little apart. By his head movements, I could tell he was scanning the street, making sure no one had witnessed the attack. Satisfied, he approached as well, similarly armed.

Waves of pain coruscated down my back and up into my head. My spine felt jarred, my muscles lacking substance. "What are you—" I started to say, but before I could finish the sentence, one of the men landed a hard kick into my stomach. The other whacked me across the back of one thigh with his club. Now I was prone, the asphalt scratchy against the side of my face. I had trouble drawing in breath. The pressure in my chest was torture. I wanted to tell them to take my money and let me be. But before I could utter a syllable, another smack came, another kick, and then another. All I could do was let out choked groans and whimpers as the assailants, all three of them now, rained blows and kicks upon me. Pretty soon, I couldn't even do that. All I did was curl a little and tuck my head in as far as I could, in a feeble attempt to protect my vital organs.

The barrage of blows continued unabated. My body was like a boiling cauldron, each popping bubble an explosion of pain. They hit my legs, my buttocks, my stomach, my back, my head. It was as though they wanted to mark every inch of me.

I wanted to scream for help, but I hadn't the air. A great pressure squeezed my head, as though a giant boot was stamping ever harder on it. My eyes were shut, but pinpricks of light exploded across the lightless backdrop of my vision. Then a deeper darkness crept in, like a black sheet pulled over a corpse on a pathologist's table. It gobbled up not just the pinpricks of light, but also the grunts of the men pummeling me and the sickening thuds of the blows as they landed. It devoured the smell of dirt and oil filling my nostrils. It consumed the rough press of the asphalt on my cheek. And finally, as an act of mercy, like a pair of wet fingers closing on a blazing candle wick, it snuffed out the pain and sucked me into a fathomless abyss into which no sensation could penetrate.

24

Pain brought me back to wakefulness. A blanket of fiery pain that engulfed me from head to toe. With effort, I pried my eyes open, but I could see nothing but a featureless, uniform brightness. *I'm blind*, a terrified childlike voice wailed in my head. *They kicked my eyes to pulp, and now I'm blind.*

But it was only sunlight dazzling me. I shifted my gaze a little, and slowly the brightness dissipated into dancing spots of red and blue and green before evaporating entirely. I saw that I was lying by a large arched window, and sunlight was splashing in directly onto my face.

The terror that gripped me at the thought of being blind vanished like water spiraling down a drain. I let out a breath, then groaned as sharp claws of agony scratched deep inside my chest.

The pain wasn't localized. It came from all over as though I were inside an iron maiden and the lid was being slowly closed upon me, spikes digging into my flesh.

My heart was hammering a demented beat. My ears filled with the furious sound of my rushing blood. It took a few minutes before the pain receded to a persistent ache, permitting thought to return.

I had no clue where I was or how I got there. I was lying in a bed, covered to my neck with a white blanket. I was sweating, but at the same time I was cold and shivering. My tongue was a heavy, sun-baked stone in my arid mouth. My nose was congested and aching, barely allowing the passage of air. My limbs were leaden. The tiniest shift of my head or arms caused a flare-up of pain that momentarily paralyzed me. I hadn't experienced such terrible agony since I had been shot twice during the War of Independence.

That memory gave birth to a realization: I was in a hospital.

Cautiously, I shifted my head sideways, wincing with each minuscule bit of movement. Two more beds. Mine was closest to the window.

I was dead thirsty. As thirsty as I had been in August 1944 in Auschwitz when the Polish summer conspired with the Nazis to torment us. It had been scorching hot then, and there had been hardly any drinking water available to us prisoners, and the Germans had worked us mercilessly.

I tried moving my tongue to wet my lips. It was like pushing a rock uphill. A pointless effort, as it held no moisture whatsoever.

"Water," I said, but it came out as a hoarse whisper, the sound barely audible. I tried to summon the strength to repeat the request, but a looming black weight pressed upon me, like a sky thick with storm clouds crashing down upon the earth, and it dragged me down with it into unconsciousness.

———

I awoke to the sound of rustling fabric. Opening my eyes, I saw a nurse making the empty bed next to mine. I must have made a sound because she stopped in the middle of stripping a pillowcase and turned toward me. She smiled.

"You're up. Good. How are you feeling?"

I was hurting all over, but I had a more urgent need. "Water," I croaked.

"Oh, of course." She hurried away and returned with a pitcher and a glass. She helped me drink in small sips. It was heaven going down my throat. With each drop, I felt myself reviving further. The nurse nodded in approval as I consumed every drop the pitcher held.

"My, you were thirsty, weren't you? Well, it's no wonder with what you've been through." She held a hand to my forehead. "You still have a fever. No surprise there either." She looked down at me, her expression kind. "Are you hungry?"

I was famished, but I wanted information more than food.

"Where am I?" I asked. My voice was nasal, like I had a cold, but I knew my nostrils were clogged due to a far more serious reason.

"Ariel Hospital."

That made me smile, which caused my left cheek to flame up. I was in Moria's hospital, though in a different ward than the one she'd worked in. Small world.

"How long have I been here?"

"Two days. It's just after eight in the morning of January 13."

"How did I get here?"

"I don't know the details, but I think someone saw you lying in the street and called an ambulance."

"What's my condition?"

She hesitated. "The doctor will be here shortly. I'll let him tell you."

"That bad, huh?"

"Actually, you were pretty lucky. It could have been much worse."

It always can be, I thought. *Until it can't.*

"You remember what happened?"

I did, but much of it was hazy. The beginning was vivid enough. The sudden sense of danger, a voice saying, "Get him!" the first blow, multiple men crowded around me. Then came the hazy part. The flurry of kicks and whacks. My attackers grunting with effort, I groaning in pain, shielding myself as best I could, unable to put up any resistance. At some point, memory ceased, and all that remained was a blank space where two days had come and gone.

"I was assaulted in the street," I said.

Her expression was sad and sympathetic. "Are you in much pain?"

"All over. But in my chest mostly. It hurts to breathe."

187

She nodded. My agony was nothing she didn't expect. "I'll get you something to relieve that."

"No. Wait. I need to use the bathroom."

"I'll fetch you a pan."

"No. I want to get up." I paused, a jolt of cold fear piercing through me. "I can walk, right? I'm not paralyzed, am I?"

"No, I don't think so. Try moving your legs," she said, and I did. They shifted. The pleasure this brought me was worth the concurrent pain.

I grinned at her, and she grinned back. She was a powerfully built woman, with thick arms and a kind, broad face.

"Help me up, please," I said.

Her mouth pursed in disapproval. "You should stay in bed, Mr. Lapid."

"How do you know my name?"

"From your identification papers. I saw them after you were brought in."

"My wallet was on me?"

"Yes. We put it in the head nurse's desk. Don't worry, it's in a locked drawer. No one will touch it."

I wasn't worried about that one bit. What concerned me was its mere presence.

"Was there money in it?"

She bridled at that, folding her arms tight across her large chest. "We don't pilfer our patients' belongings, Mr. Lapid."

"No, please don't misunderstand me," I said. "I didn't mean to suggest... I'm just surprised that the men who robbed me left my wallet behind."

Her expression thawed, and she smiled. "Like I said, you were pretty lucky."

I returned her smile, though I saw no cause for levity. My mind was churning. I'd assumed that I had fallen victim to a robbery, but robbers generally take their victims' wallets or at the very least empty them of money before leaving them behind. My attackers had done neither, which made me wonder as to their motives.

But that question could wait. I had more pressing business to attend to.

"What's your name?" I asked.

"Rona."

"Can you help me up, Rona? It won't wait much longer."

She opened her mouth, likely intending to berate me for my recklessness, but in the end, she merely shook her head in the manner common to women confronted by foolish men and leaned over me, cautiously sliding one arm under my back, grabbing me under one armpit. Her other arm curled around my calves, just under my knees.

"This will hurt," she said, her tone implying that it was nothing but just punishment for my obstinacy, and heaved. The movement stole my breath away. It was the only reason why I didn't cry out. The pain was hot and biting and bone-deep, but then I was sitting, propped by Rona's strong arms.

"Ready?" Rona said, and when I nodded, she heaved again, and this time I did make a sound, a low guttural grunt, but then I was standing, my bare soles stinging at the coldness of the floor, and step by slow step, Rona helped me across the room and into the bathroom.

At the end of this journey, no more than twenty feet in length, I was soaked in sweat. Rona wasn't even breathing hard. She must have been made of steel.

"Do you need more help?" she asked.

I shook my head. More stupid obstinacy, I thought, as I swayed a little on my feet, my stomach roiling, but Rona didn't argue. She told me she'd wait outside and left me alone. I was wearing hospital clothes, which were easy to maneuver out of, fortunately, and I urinated for a long moment. Once again, I filled the toilet bowl with red. Whatever recovery my kidney had done since the night of the demonstration had been erased, and likely more besides.

Turning from the toilet, I caught sight of myself in the mirror. My skin was flush with fever. My face was a mess of injuries. My bottom lip was torn and puffy; my left cheek bruised a violent red; half of my forehead abraded a raw pink; my right eye bloodshot and ringed with purple; my nose swollen and misshapen. No wonder I had trouble drawing breath.

But at least I wasn't blind or paralyzed. Like Rona said, it could have been much worse.

"Thank you," I told Rona after she helped me back to bed.

She tucked the blanket around me, then looked at me thoughtfully before saying, "Normally, I wouldn't have agreed to help you get out of bed—you might have fallen, and then I'd be in trouble—but something tells me you would have tried to do it on your own. You're a tough one, aren't you?"

"What makes you say that?"

She pointed at my midsection. "Your scars. I saw them when we were examining you after you were admitted. Those are gunshot injuries, aren't they?"

"Yes."

"May I ask how you got them?"

"In the War of Independence. Fighting the Egyptians in the Negev."

"You were lucky then, too," she said. "Two gunshots in the torso—most wouldn't have survived that."

"It's all relative," I answered. "The truly lucky ones didn't get shot at all."

"That's true. And the scar on your shoulder?"

"Another gunshot," I said, not sure why I was being so forthright. Perhaps I was enjoying her attention and the chance to act the strong man before her eyes now that I was so weak I could hardly stand on my own. "A grazing wound."

"But not in the War of Independence."

"How can you tell?"

"Scars age just the same as people do. This one's fresher than the other two. So is the one on your side. That one was made by a knife, I think. Am I right?"

"You have good eyes."

She shook her head. "Just experience. I've seen such wounds

before." She paused, licked her lips, making up her mind, then said, "But I've never seen anything like the ones on your back."

And just like that, all my preening enjoyment evaporated. The other scars were marks of pride; the ones on my back were anything but.

"No. I don't suppose you have," I said, regretting having been so open with her.

Her gaze was equal parts pity, horror, and morbid curiosity. It made me shrink on the inside. "They're lash marks, aren't they?" she asked.

They were. The ugly legacy of a whipping I'd received from a sadistic guard in Auschwitz. I couldn't say how many times he'd lashed me, I'd lost consciousness during the whipping itself, and the scars crisscrossed and overrode each other, making counting impossible.

I averted my gaze from Rona's inquisitive face. "I'm tired. I don't feel like talking anymore."

"Oh," she said, and I could imagine her cheeks reddening. "Of course. You should rest. Shall I bring you some food?"

My appetite had gone, but in my mind I was back in Auschwitz, where appetite had nothing to do with eating, so I said, "Yes. Thank you, Rona."

She left, returning a short while later with a tray bearing food and pills for the pain. She helped me sit again, propping me up with pillows. She dawdled after setting up my meal. "I'm sorry if my questions upset you, Mr. Lapid."

"That's all right, Rona," I said, swallowing the pills and then picking up my fork. "You did nothing wrong. And please, call me Adam."

She nodded. "Is there anyone you wish me to call, Adam, tell them where you are? Family or friends?"

"No. There's no one."

She bit her lip, turned to leave, then stopped and said, "I'm so sorry for all you've been through, Adam."

I followed her eyes as they flicked in the direction of the fork in my left hand. No, she wasn't looking at the fork, but at my forearm. Currently covered by the sleeve of my hospital shirt, but earlier exposed to her gaze.

She'd seen it. My number tattoo. And it had told her a story without my needing to provide any input. As had the scars on my back.

My body was like one of the rune stones I'd read about, the ones in Scandinavia. In lines, etchings, and chisel marks, it told the violent chapters of my life, the suffering I'd experienced, my various pains and losses.

Rona was waiting for an answer, but I had none I wished to give her. She shifted her feet, put on a fragile smile, and finally, in a regretful, chastised voice, said, "Eat now. I'll ask Dr. Aboulker to come see you a little later."

Then she was gone, and I was alone once more.

To the empty space where she had stood, I said, "Don't be sorry, Rona. I was lucky there, too."

25

The doctor came in about a half hour after Rona returned to clear the dishes. He introduced himself as Dr. Aboulker. A short, olive-skinned man in a rumpled white coat, he had a tired face and gentle eyes behind black-rimmed eyeglasses. He examined my pupils, listened to my heart and lungs, and stuck a thermometer in my mouth and noted my temperature on a chart. He asked, "How are you feeling, Mr. Lapid?"

"Like hell."

That made him smile. "Rona told me she brought you some pills. Did you take them?"

"Yes. And they help, but I still hurt."

"With your injuries, that's hardly surprising, I'm afraid. We can give you something stronger later if the pain keeps you from sleeping."

"All right. Now I want you to tell me my condition, Doctor. Be straight with me. Let's start with my nose. Is it broken?"

"Yes," he said simply, evidently willing to give me the information I wanted the way I wanted it. "I set it, and it will look better once the swelling goes down. Probably flatter than before, but not by much."

Another permanent mark of suffering, but I could live with it. "My ribs?" I asked.

"Three are broken. A couple more are cracked. It's a wonder neither of your lungs got punctured. We wouldn't be having this conversation if they had. How badly does it hurt to breathe?"

"Pretty badly. I have to remember to take shallow breaths. Not so easy to do when you need to breathe through your mouth."

He nodded. "Once the swelling in your nose goes down, it will get easier. But your ribs will take a few weeks to mend. Until they do, you'd be wise to avoid any exertion, anything that accelerates your breathing."

"I'll do my best," I said, then told him I was pissing blood. He did not seem overly distressed, which relieved me.

"That's the result of trauma to your kidneys. I checked you out earlier and found no signs of serious internal injuries or bleeding, but we'll keep you here for a few days, maybe a week, and monitor you to make sure you're all right."

"Okay. Thank you."

"You also have a fever, which is likely due to infection. We've given you medication to combat that, and it's not as bad as it was yesterday. Other than all that, you've got bruises and abrasions on your legs, arms, hips, and buttocks. Don't ask me how many; there are a lot. Painful, I'm sure, but nothing that won't heal on its own with time. Does your head hurt?"

"Yes."

"How about your eyesight? Is it clear? Any double vision?" He nodded in satisfaction when I told him I was seeing fine. "Any dizziness?"

"I had some before."

"Hmmm. That's not good. You may have a concussion. We'll monitor that as well. I hope you don't have any appointments scheduled for the next few days, Mr. Lapid."

"My social calendar is clear, Doctor."

He chuckled. "One less thing to worry about, then. Well, I'll be going now, but I'll check on you later. Oh, there's a police officer waiting in the hall. He wants to talk to you about the attack. Do you feel up to it? Can I send him in?"

"Yes. Thank you, Doctor."

He smiled again and said, "I suppose it doesn't feel that way now, Mr. Lapid, but it could have ended much worse for you. I hope the police catch whoever did this."

Dr. Aboulker departed, and for a few seconds the door to the hallway remained empty. Then a shadow fell across it, and a second later a policeman entered the room. My heart plummeted when I saw who it was.

Inspector Kulaski.

26

He strode into the room with a determined step. His back was straight, his uniform as immaculate as in our previous encounter. His cap was tucked under his left arm. His shoes clacked a foreboding rhythm on the floor.

My pulse had jumped at the sight of him; my breathing grew faster. My ribs sent flashes of pain through my midsection.

As we locked eyes, his upper lip curled. He stole a quick glance at the other beds in the room as he approached. Of the three in total, only two were currently occupied: mine and the one closest to the door. Its elderly occupant was snoring in his sleep, as he seemed to do without cease.

When Kulaski reached my bed, he stood for a few long seconds, looming over me. He had given himself a very close shave that morning, I noticed. The skin on his throat was pink where the razor had pressed too firmly in its passage, as though in his fastidiousness, the inspector had attempted to not merely shear off the offending hairs, but to pull them out by their roots.

A chair stood by the wall, and Kulaski drew it up and sat. He looked around for a place to set his cap and finally put it beside my right ankle, at the foot of my bed, as though laying claim to it. Then he smiled, and if I weren't already cold because of my fever, I would have shivered.

"I understand you had a bit of trouble the other night, Mr. Lapid," he said, his manner remote and official.

I looked at him and everything connected. Kulaski's presence in my hospital room, the fact that my attackers hadn't made off with my wallet or money, the savagery of the attack. The motive hadn't been money, and my attackers weren't thieves. The picture was clear now. Clear and terrible.

"I heard you were assaulted," he said after a few seconds of silence. There was a gleam in his eyes. He was enjoying seeing me all battered up and sick.

I hesitated. We were alone in the room apart from the snoring old man. No witnesses. And I was helpless, busted up inside and out.

He waited, a model of patience, his eyes not leaving mine.

"That's right," I said finally, feeling myself shrink under his cruel gaze and hating myself for it.

"On the street."

"Yes."

He made a few tsk sounds with his tongue, as though bemoaning the sorry state of the city he protected.

"These things shouldn't happen anywhere in Israel," he said, "and that goes double for our capital, wouldn't you say?" I didn't answer, and he continued, "Then again, perhaps neither of us should be surprised since other unspeakable, unthinkable acts have been committed in Jerusalem lately."

I couldn't help myself. Being the reckless fool, I said, "If you're alluding to the Knesset's decision to authorize negotiations with Germany, I agree with you one hundred percent."

He smiled. The condescending smile of someone so assured in his superiority, in his triumph, that he takes the ineffectual barbs of his opponent with good-natured amusement.

"I was surprised to learn that you were back in Jerusalem," he said. "I was sure you would stay far, far away."

"I have a right to go where I please, Inspector."

"Indeed you do. Still, I didn't expect it. What are you doing here, Mr. Lapid?"

"I have business in town."

"What sort of business?"

"What does that have to do with the assault I went through? Aren't you here because of that?"

"We'll get to it, don't you worry. But first, I need to make sure you're not here to cause any more trouble for the police or the Knesset."

"Rest assured, I intend no such thing."

"I'm glad to hear it. What, then, is the purpose of your visit to Jerusalem?"

"Like I told you, I have business here."

"Detecting business?" he asked. The words dripped with mockery. Some cops get that way with private investigators, whom they view as little more than nuisances. "Our previous encounter left me curious about you. I did some checking and discovered you work as a private investigator. I must say this surprised me. I didn't think you had the temperament for such work."

"You don't know me, Inspector."

"I know more than you imagine, Mr. Lapid. For instance, and this surprised me even more, I know that you used to be a policeman, of all things."

"A police detective," I said.

"But not in Israel."

"In Hungary. Before the world war."

He nodded as though I had told him nothing new. Then his face hardened, showing the first sign of anger since he entered the hospital room. "A man who once was a cop beating other cops. That's even worse than I initially thought. That's unforgivable."

I didn't argue. Partly because from the viewpoint of a cop, he was absolutely right; and partly because the old fear he'd instilled in me on our first meeting was back in force, and it had a squeezing grip on my throat.

Don't show it, I thought. *He's like a dog. Display fear and it will only encourage him to tear you into pieces, to strip the flesh from your bones.*

Kulaski hissed out a breath, venting some of his anger. He asked, "What are you doing in Jerusalem?"

"Working."

"On what?"

"A case."

"The shooting of Dr. Kalman Shapira." It wasn't a question. He knew it was so. Now I realized how Sergeant Rapfogel had recognized me. Reuben hadn't given him my description; Kulaski had. Kulaski had learned of my interest in the case. He'd approved of my seeing the investigation file. It had been a ploy to try to discover what I knew, what I wanted, but mostly to draw me in so they could attack me. That was why Rapfogel had wanted to meet so late. It might also explain why he'd drunk so much. Some men find savagery easier when drunk.

"Why are you interested in this case?" Kulaski asked.

"It may have some bearing on my investigation."

"Which is?"

"I'd rather not say."

He didn't lose his temper as I'd feared. He didn't threaten me. He said, "Does it have something to do with Baruch Gafni? He's your client, isn't he?"

I didn't reply, but the answer must have been written on my face, along with my surprise, because Kulaski smiled again.

"I told you, Mr. Lapid, I know more than you imagine. After our previous chat, after you escaped the punishment that was your just due, I called the deputy commissioner's office. I spoke to the secretary and learned who had interceded on your behalf. I sniffed around, didn't find any evidence of a prior connection between you and Mr. Gafni, and I also learned of your so-called profession. I put two and two together."

"That's quite an impressive feat of arithmetic, Inspector," I said, and was rewarded with a spasm of pain in my chest, my injured ribs reminding me that I was in no shape to be a smart aleck. But I was also angry—angry beyond good sense, perhaps—at this arrogant, cruel man for what he'd done to me. And I also felt that I couldn't be timid. I had to project strength, though that might have been a fool's errand, considering the state of my face and my obvious infirmity.

Again Kulaski kept his cool. "I couldn't see why Gafni would make an effort for a man such as you. I did some digging. I found out about his daughter's suicide. That's your case, isn't it? That's what you're working on."

"If you're so sure you know everything, why bother asking?"

"What I can't figure out is what there is to investigate. I read the file. There's no doubt that she committed suicide. Mr. Gafni never suggested otherwise."

"You're so curious, why don't you ask him?"

"I became doubly sure that was your case when I heard you were sniffing about the Shapira shooting. Moria Gafni and Kalman Shapira worked together. What do you think, Detective Lapid?" He put a derisive emphasis on the word *detective*. "You think Moria Gafni shot Kalman Shapira and then, consumed by guilt, committed suicide?"

I was silent, trying to keep my face impassive. But in my mind, one question kept repeating in a shrill refrain, *Has he found the gun? Has he found the gun? Has he found the gun?*

"I have no idea who killed Kalman Shapira," I said.

"I certainly hope not because withholding evidence pertaining to a homicide is an offense. Not as serious as those you narrowly avoided being charged with, but still no laughing matter."

"I'll be sure to keep that in mind."

He nodded a couple of times, lips primmed. Then, with frightening abruptness, his expression shifted, turning feral. His lips pulled back, showing his teeth. He sniffed loudly, wrinkled his nose, and said, "It stinks in here, you know that? You stink."

I was taken aback by the turn in the conversation. It did not seem in Kulaski's nature to stoop to such crude insults. A portion of his self-possession seemed to have slipped. His mouth and lower jaw were twitching, small incessant tics, like he had a boiling energy inside him, looking for a crack from which to erupt.

"Maybe you can't smell it," he went on, "with your nose busted up like that. But trust me, it's true. You stank the other time, too. You stank of blood and sweat, but mostly of fear. You stink the same way now, even though they washed you up good. They can't wash away the odor of fear."

He looked on the verge of losing control entirely, of shedding what remained of his calm facade and lashing out at me. I knew I would not be able to defend myself. I thought of crying out for a nurse, but even if one heard me, Kulaski would still have time to inflict tremendous pain on me before she entered the room. And if I accused him of doing me harm and he denied it, who would the nurse believe: a respectable police inspector or a patient she knew nothing about?

Kulaski shifted forward, his hand rising, fingers closing, and I braced myself for excruciating agony, opened my mouth to shout for help anyway, but then my roommate quit snoring. In the ensuing silence, Kulaski froze and looked toward the other patient. He couldn't afford to be seen hurting me.

But my roommate didn't wake. He merely let out a phlegmy gurgle, moaned, gasped, shifted a little, and resumed snoring. Kulaski blinked, his tongue flicking across his lips, and the tension in his body eased. He moved back in his chair, unclenching his fingers, composed once more. I exhaled. The moment of danger had passed. My body ached all over, as though it had been struck by phantom fists.

"Perhaps it's time," Kulaski said, "that we talk about the assault you underwent, Mr. Lapid. As it so happens, I'm the investigating officer. Can you tell me what happened?"

"Nothing you don't already know," I said through gritted teeth.

"But I hardly know anything, I'm sorry to say. There were no witnesses to the attack. No one saw a thing." He spread his hands in a what-can-you-do gesture. "I spent all day yesterday pursuing leads, but so far nothing."

He was sending me a message, telling me I had no hope in hell of seeing the men who'd attacked me brought to justice. Not that I expected any different.

"I'm sure you couldn't sleep a wink because of it," I said.

He ignored my sarcasm. "Would you be able to recognize the assailants?"

"They came at me from behind, it was dark, and they wore something across their faces."

"So they could be anyone?"

"Yes. Even you."

He chuckled, wagging his finger as though reproaching me for telling an inappropriate joke. "Just so you know, I was at the station throughout that night, Mr. Lapid. Other officers would vouch for me."

Sure they would. And he would vouch for them if called for. That was how it worked. Cops protecting each other and avenging their comrades. I had no doubt that my assailants were police officers. Told by Kulaski that I'd put one of their colleagues in the hospital and then escaped justice. And then informed that I was back in their city, on their turf, thumbing my nose at them merely by walking freely on their streets. I felt only a limited measure of anger at these men despite the injuries they'd inflicted on me. As far as they knew, I was a violent criminal who'd pulled strings to avoid paying the price for beating one of their own. I'd evaded the justice of the law, so they set out to impose an alternative brand of justice. In their shoes, goaded by the right words from the mouth of an esteemed fellow officer, I might have been persuaded to do the same.

Only Kulaski was to blame. Kulaski with his personal vendetta against me. For some reason, I had become the focal point of his unbounded rage at the demonstrators who had warred with the police outside the Knesset. As through a sniper's scope, his desire for retribution had concentrated all its firepower on a single target: me.

And, deprived initially, his fury and thirst for vengeance had only increased. At first, it was at an intense yet reasonable level. Now it was an obsession.

"Normally, the police could dedicate more manpower to the investigation of your assault," Kulaski said, speaking in a tone that would sound doleful to other ears, but in which I heard an underlying glee, "but, regretfully, many of our officers are unable to carry out their duties because of injuries they sustained defending the Knesset from you and your buddies. So don't expect any breakthroughs."

"I won't be holding my breath," I said.

"A wise decision, Mr. Lapid. A wise decision. And speaking of wise decisions, another unfortunate symptom of the large number of incapacitated officers is an increase in crime here in Jerusalem. Cause and effect, you see. Fewer cops patrolling the streets, the more dangerous the streets become. As you can personally attest." He ran his eyes over me, lingering over various parts of my face, a thin smile on his thin lips. The bastard was relishing the signs of my injuries.

He said, "Jerusalem may remain dangerous for some time, I'm afraid. The smarter, safer thing for you to do would be to return home to Tel Aviv and stay away from the capital. Otherwise, in the current situation, who knows what other calamities may befall you."

The lines sounded rehearsed. Perhaps he had practiced them before the mirror as he was scraping his throat raw with his razor. They were part of the message he'd come here to deliver. The first part was him claiming responsibility for my assault; the second was the threat of worse to come if I did not heed his warning and get out of Jerusalem and never return.

It was effective. Again pain throbbed throughout my body. Fear made each tender spot ache. I curled my fingers into fists to keep the pain from showing on my face, but that only increased my suffering, as battered muscles in my arms tightened and flexed.

"I'll take that under advisement," I said, feeling foolish to keep up the pretense of self-assurance. I was beaten, and we both knew it.

"See that you do," he said. "If I were you, I'd go back to the safety of Tel Aviv as soon as possible. Today."

I stared at him in shock. "The doctor said I should stay in the hospital for several days."

"I'm sure he has his reasons, but the doctor doesn't know every-thing we do, Mr. Lapid, does he? He doesn't know how dangerous the streets of Jerusalem can be. Or even its hospitals."

Another message. This one saying that I wasn't safe from Kulaski anywhere in the capital. Not even here in the hospital. And this time, the outcome would not be confined to a bevy of injuries. This time, I would end up dead.

Looking at the inspector, I realized with horror that Kulaski's obsession with me had crossed the boundary of sanity. He wouldn't be making this threat otherwise. I doubted he could get another officer to make good on it. Certainly not in a public place like a hospital. Kulaski would have to do the dirty deed himself.

And he would. Without compunction. I could see it in the twin gray stains of mad malice that his eyes had become.

He said, "You know, Mr. Lapid, before I came to see you, I paid a visit to the brave officer you beat near the Knesset. He's still hospitalized."

"I didn't do it; I already told you that."

He nodded as though to a stupid child. "Yes, I know. You tried to help him. In some ways, he's worse off than you are. You didn't lose any teeth." It was obvious he considered this an oversight on his part. An unjust state of affairs.

Again, it seemed like the inspector was struggling to remain in control, to not let his violent urges get the better of him. The tics had returned. The skin on his face moved constantly, as though maggots milled about beneath it.

Fear squeezed my lungs at the sight. I couldn't draw air. I knew I was in terrible danger. Only when Kulaski picked up his cap, returned it to its place under his left arm, and stood, did the pressure in my chest subside and I could suck in air.

He said, "I apologize I could not be the bearer of good news today, Mr. Lapid. But I'm glad we had this little talk, aren't you?"

"Yes," I said, relief flooding my veins. He was leaving. The immediate danger had passed. "Yes, I am."

"I'm glad to hear it." He flicked a glance toward the door of the room, at the bed where my old roommate still snored, and added, "But just to make sure you grasp my full meaning..."

And before I could react, not even cry out, he drew back his right hand and rammed his fist into my ribs.

He knew of my injuries; his remark about my teeth proved that. That was why he chose the ribs. The pain was like a volcano eruption —scorching, searing, all-consuming. It snapped me up like a leaf in an evil wind, tossed me about, and then plunged me into a black abyss of seething agony. I was blind. I was deaf. I was in a vacuum of sensation. All my senses but that of pain were devoured by the lava that burned through my chest, spreading all over me. I was choking. My brain was shooting garbled messages, warped signals, panicked by its loss of control over my body.

The disconnection from everything around me could not have lasted more than a few seconds, but it felt as though I'd been exiled from myself for years and only now allowed to return.

Above me stood Kulaski, a mad-wolf smile stretching his mouth wide. His teeth appeared to glisten. His eyes sparkled with manic joy.

My ears didn't register it, but I must have let out a loud cry or groan, because the old man was awake and calling to me. "Hey, are you okay? Are you all right?"

"Don't worry," Kulaski answered in my place. "He's fine. Just a little pain. I'll ask the nurse to bring him something."

He looked down at me again. "Goodbye, Mr. Lapid. I wish you a pleasant trip back to Tel Aviv."

27

Kulaski left me gasping for air, whimpering like a whipped dog. Naturally, he did not ask any of the nurses to bring me any pain medication. The old man did that. He shuffled out and got Rona.

She was appalled when she saw me. "What happened?"

There was no point in telling her the truth. "It hurts," I said. "My ribs. I must have made a bad movement. Can you bring me something for the pain?"

She did. I swallowed it with effort. It took a few minutes before the medication started working and I could breathe properly again.

"What happened?" she repeated when she saw the worst of it had passed.

"Don't worry," I said. "I'm fine." It was such a ridiculous statement that it might have provoked a laugh if not for the bleakness of my situation.

"You don't look fine. You look much worse than before." She touched my forehead, and her mouth fell open. "You're burning up. I'll get the doctor."

"No. Get me my clothes."

"What?"

"My clothes. Please, bring them here."

"Whatever for?"

"I'm leaving."

"Leaving? What do you mean, leaving?"

I took a breath, not too deep so it wouldn't inflame my throbbing ribs. "I'm getting discharged and going home."

"I don't think that's a good idea, Adam. Not a good idea at all."

It wasn't, but the alternative was even worse. Kulaski had told me to get out of Jerusalem today, which meant I could spend a little time in the hospital and still catch the bus to Tel Aviv. But I wasn't taking any chances that he would have second thoughts and come back. I wanted to be gone as soon as possible.

"You may be right," I said. "But that's what I've decided."

"But why?" she asked, holding her hands out in supplication, begging me to let her help me.

"It doesn't matter, Rona. What I need you to do now is get me my clothes. Please, can you do that for me?"

She kept looking at me for a few seconds. Then she shook her head and walked out. She didn't return. Dr. Aboulker did. He looked distraught, agitated, his former cool demeanor gone. He wasn't wearing his white coat, which led me to think he'd been on his way out when Rona brought him the news.

"What's this nonsense I hear, Mr. Lapid? You wish to be discharged?"

"Yes."

"You're in no condition for it," he said flatly, leaving no room for argument.

"Are you planning to keep me here by force?"

He glared at me. "I could, you know. A man in your state, I could have you committed for your own good."

"You'd have to strap me to the bed, Doctor."

He studied my face, gauging my seriousness. He didn't like what he saw. He rolled his lower lip between his teeth as he pondered how to convince me to reverse my foolish decision.

"Look at you," he said. "Your fever has shot up."

I didn't need to see a thermometer to know it was true. I could feel it. Kulaski's punch had rattled my body, thrown it off-kilter. As though his fist had injected pollution into my blood vessels, and my body was frantically fighting to kill the poison by burning it up.

"You can give me something for that, can't you?"

"Such a fever, such injuries; you need to stay under observation. It's malpractice to let you leave."

"I'll take full responsibility, Doctor."

He snorted, but utterly without humor. "Yes, I can see you're the responsible sort." I made no comment, and he continued, "You think that will help me sleep better at night if you drop dead from your injuries?"

I hadn't considered that side of things. I was moved by his concern. "I'm not going to die, Doctor. I've survived worse."

His eyes twitched toward my left forearm. He had also seen my number tattoo; he knew what it signified. He rubbed a finger across his mouth, thinking furiously. "I hope you have a damn good reason for leaving," he finally said.

"I need to be in Tel Aviv."

"Can't it wait a few days?"

"I'm afraid it can't."

"How about tomorrow? Surely it will hold till tomorrow."

"It won't, Doctor. I wish it would."

"Is there no way I could prevail upon you to remain here?"

I shook my head. "None."

"How about I list the potential risks you face if you walk out of here in your condition?"

"Please don't. My mind's made up."

He nodded, removed his glasses, and pinched the bridge of his nose. He looked as worn-out as I felt. Returning the glasses to their place, he said, "I hope you don't take this the wrong way, Mr. Lapid, but you're a damn fool."

I half-smiled. "An accurate diagnosis, Doctor. Unfortunately, it's a chronic condition."

He didn't smile back. "I hope you know what you're doing. I really do."

I didn't answer. What was there to say?

He sighed. "All right. I'll tell Rona to fetch your clothes and get your discharge form ready."

He left but returned a minute later with a syringe. "For the fever," he said before plunging the needle into me. Rona appeared with my clothes. There was no hat. I asked her about it, and she said I hadn't been wearing one when I was brought in. I took this in without comment. Two hats in the space of a week. Had to be closing in on a record.

Rona gave me a discharge form. I signed it.

"Who's picking you up?" Dr. Aboulker asked.

"No one."

"How do you plan to get to Tel Aviv?"

"By bus."

"By..." He didn't finish the sentence. He and Rona exchanged a stunned look. Both thought this another layer of my madness. The doctor squeezed his forehead, blew out air. "I understand," he said, though his tone expressed the exact opposite. "My shift just ended. I'll drive you to the bus station."

"I have to get my things from my hotel first," I said.

"All right. I'll drive you there and then to the station. At least I'll make sure you're fine part of the way."

"Thank you."

"Don't thank me, Mr. Lapid. I'm doing this to appease my conscience. I'm not sure I'm doing the right thing by letting you leave."

"It's my decision, Doctor."

"I hope it won't be your funeral as well." He turned to Rona. "When he's ready, bring him to my office, okay?"

Then he was gone, and Rona was helping me out of my hospital clothes and into my own.

It wasn't easy. Each movement of my arms ignited a shooting pain in my chest. Rona worked silently, her attitude distant and sulky. I realized that I'd offended her by deciding to leave, by placing my well-being in jeopardy.

I apologized for distressing her. "You're terrific, Rona. This has nothing to do with you or anyone at the hospital."

She smiled a little. "Thank you for saying that."

She handed me my wallet. The money was all there. As was something else. A scrap of paper had been tucked into the bill compartment. It was a newspaper clipping detailing the government's triumph in the Knesset. Kulaski rubbing it in all the way to the bone. Clenching my teeth, I crumpled the clipping into a tight ball.

"Is everything all right, Adam?" Rona asked.

"Yes. Everything's fine. Just throw this away for me, will you?"

Returning my wallet to my pocket, I realized something was missing. My hotel room key. I asked Rona about it.

"It wasn't on you when you got here," she said, looking anxious. "You think the robbers took it? Should we call the police?"

"No. That won't be necessary. I'll call them if anything's missing from my room. Let's go."

Each step proved a challenge. I was lightheaded, unsteady, and I hurt. Rona gave me her arm, and together we covered the short distance to the doctor's office in what must have been five times what it normally took.

The doctor looked up from his desk. He took in my appearance. "Are you sure about this, Mr. Lapid?"

"Yes. I'm sure."

He sighed. "So be it. I'm sorry about your clothes. We assumed someone would bring you fresh ones."

The state of my clothes corresponded with my own. Wrinkled, torn, streaked with dirt from the street where I was beaten, both they and I looked ready for the trash heap.

"They'll do until I get home," I said.

The doctor nodded. He scribbled something on a piece of paper, then shrugged into his coat and picked up his briefcase. "Ready?"

"Yes."

The doctor looked at me for two more seconds, then shook his head and said, "All right. Let's go."

We bid Rona goodbye and headed out. It was slow and hard

going. To his credit, Dr. Aboulker did not try to use my debility to persuade me to change my mind.

He had a small mud-green Fiat. The front seat would have been difficult to squeeze into under normal circumstances. I had to clench my teeth to keep from crying out as I maneuvered my battered body inside.

He drove with calm assurance and stopped outside the hotel. He peered out the window and grimaced. "This is where you're staying?"

I nodded. "First class all the way."

He chuckled. "Which floor is your room?"

"Third. Listen, Doctor, I appreciate you doing this for me, but if you'd rather not wait while I get my things, I'll manage from here."

"What do you mean, wait? Shape you're in, you want to climb three floors? I'll hop inside and get your stuff."

"No. I'll do it."

"Come on, why not let me help you, Mr. Lapid?"

"You're helping plenty, Doctor, but I need to get my stuff by myself."

He gave me a look. He was a smart guy. He probably deduced that there was something in my room, in my things, that I didn't wish him to see. Maybe he thought I had dirty pictures strewn about the bed. Maybe he thought I had illicit drugs lying around. Or maybe he figured I had contraband I'd acquired on Israel's widespread black market. I didn't care what he thought. All I cared about was going into that room and seeing if the gun was still there.

Dr. Aboulker eyed me thoughtfully, seeming to consider his next words. He said, "Are you a criminal, Mr. Lapid?"

The question took me by surprise. He probably wouldn't have asked it if I hadn't been in such a dismal physical state. "No," I said.

"You decided to leave the hospital right after that police inspector talked to you."

"He was there to investigate my assault."

"Is that all he was there to do?"

"If I'm a criminal, why didn't he arrest me?"

"Maybe you're just a suspect at the moment."

"If I was, don't you think he would have warned you and the rest of the staff?"

He pondered this. It had started raining again. Fat drops splattered on the windshield, drummed on the roof.

After a minute, he said, "You don't have a hat or umbrella, and I don't have either to give you. You go out, you'll get wet."

"So would you."

"I'm not running a fever."

"The rain will cool me down, do me good."

"I'll climb those stairs faster than you will."

"Like I said, Doctor, you don't have to wait. You've already done enough."

He kneaded the back of his neck, his jaw tight. "I'll wait, Mr. Lapid. But if you're not back here in fifteen minutes, I'm coming in to see if you're okay."

He'd parked right before the front door. Still, my hair was wet by the time I hobbled into the lobby. The clerk looked up from his magazine. His bulging eyes protruded further when he saw me.

I walked to the counter. "I'm checking out. I'm going upstairs to get my things. But I seem to have misplaced my key."

He raised his chin a tad, and a malicious smile tugged at the corners of his mouth. "There's a three-lira fine for losing your key."

I wanted to grab his shirtfront, drag him over the counter, and hurl him at the nearest wall, but I was in no condition to. So instead I took three one-lira bills from my wallet and tossed them on the counter. He replaced them with a key, then stepped back as I reached for it, as though afraid of contracting whatever ailed me. I had half a mind to cough deeply in his direction but knew that would cause me agony. So I merely picked up the key and headed for the stairs.

Before beginning to climb, I followed the rise of the dim staircase with my eyes all the way to the second-floor landing. I counted fourteen steps. No big deal. But now it seemed like I was about to scale a sheer mountainside, and I had to get to the top without falling even once.

I gripped the banister, set my right foot on the bottom step, and heaved myself upward. This simple movement, normally done mindlessly, without effort, now felt as though I were stretching my body to its breaking point. A little more pull and I would tear apart like a badly stitched seam.

By the time I cleared five steps, I was gasping for breath. After ten, my body was shaking. Twice, I was dizzy and had to grab the banister with both hands to steady myself.

When I got to the second-floor landing, I stood with my head pressed against the wall until I recovered a bit of strength. I wondered how much time had elapsed. Three minutes? Five? Maybe more?

The thought of Dr. Aboulker barging in at any moment impelled me to move on. I had another flight of stairs to climb.

This one was harder than the first. Each step a jagged shard of torment. When I finally reached the top, my heart was hammering, and an acidic lump of bile was lodged at the bottom of my throat. My legs wobbled. My chest ached. My various bruises throbbed. Each inhalation seemed to contain not merely air, but also a lick of flame that scorched my lungs. I wanted to sit down right there in the hall, but I knew that if I did, it might be a long while before I was able to stand up again.

I staggered to my room instead, unlocked the door, and went inside. I could tell instantly that someone had been there in my absence.

Kulaski and his fellow cop goons.

I swore, surveying the mess. The mattress was crooked. They had looked underneath and hadn't bothered to straighten it. My bag had been overturned. My things lay scattered across the floor. Nothing seemed to be missing, though I couldn't be sure.

My heart went into palpitations when I saw the dresser had been pulled from its place, a cake slice of blackness between its back and the wall. All the drawers were open, each to a different degree, but none had been pulled out entirely, including the bottom one, under which I'd hidden the gun. A good sign, but they might have put it back just to give me false hope. It was just like Kulaski to pull a trick like that.

The next part was difficult. Gingerly, I lowered myself to my knees as though I were made of the thinnest glass and was liable to shatter at the mildest tension. It still hurt. As did my knees and shins when I set my weight on them. My attackers hadn't spared those body parts either.

I pulled the bottom drawer, wincing as I scooched back to get it all the way out. I set the drawer aside and, holding my breath, peered at the space between the floor and where the drawer usually lay. There, right where I'd left them, lay the gun and two magazines. An exhalation of pure relief whooshed out of me. A triumphant smile spread across my face.

"Kulaski, you incompetent moron," I murmured. But maybe that wasn't the reason why Kulaski and his pals hadn't found the gun. Maybe they hadn't tossed my room to find anything, but merely to intimidate me further. To pass on yet another message. To appear stronger and make me feel weak and small in comparison. So maybe they hadn't searched too hard. They'd just made a mess and left.

My smile widened. Kulaski had no idea how close he'd been to a key piece of evidence in the Shapira murder investigation.

You don't know as much as you think, Inspector, I thought. *Not nearly as much.*

I put the gun in my coat pocket. The two magazines I buried among the clothes I gathered back into my bag. I felt safer with the gun on me, within easy reach. If Kulaski had a change of heart and tried to prevent me from leaving Jerusalem, I intended to fight.

I returned the drawer to its place—another simple task that caused me great suffering. Then I zipped the bag shut, grabbed the leather handles, and tried to stand. A swirl of dizziness clutched me, spinning the world around me, robbing my equilibrium. I stumbled, flailed around with my left hand, and luckily managed to brace myself against the dresser or I would have fallen on my face. I waited a moment until the world stabilized and, with tentative, old-man steps, headed for the door. Descending the stairs was going to be a trial, especially with one hand monopolized by the bag.

The quick thud of approaching feet greeted me as I stepped into the hall. Someone was bounding up the stairs toward me. I dropped the bag and ducked my right hand into my pocket. My fingers curled around the cold grip of the gun. My forefinger slipped into the trigger guard, pad on the trigger, ready for firing.

I was about to pull out the gun and aim it where the stairs met the hallway when a voice reached my ears: "Mr. Lapid? Mr. Lapid, where are you?"

A second later, the owner of the voice appeared on the landing, panting a little, droplets of rain in his hair.

Dr. Aboulker.

I'd completely forgotten about him. My physical discomfort and the menacing sound of approaching footsteps had wiped him from my mind. I'd been certain it was Kulaski.

I let out a breath. Released the gun grip. "Has it been fifteen minutes already, Doctor?"

"Just about," he said, frowning a little. "What's the matter? Why are you looking at me like that?"

I'm just happy I didn't shoot you, I thought, saying: "I'm happy to see you, that's all. Thank you for sticking around. Sorry it took me so long."

His frown didn't go away. "You got your things?"

"In the bag."

He looked at it, down at my feet. "Why is it on the floor?"

"I dropped it," I said. "I'm a little weak. Would you do me a favor and carry it down for me?"

He hesitated. Whatever it was I didn't wish him to see might be in this bag.

"Never mind," I said, and started to bend down to pick it up.

"Let me do it," Dr. Aboulker said, rushing forward and grabbing the bag before I could.

I thanked him, and he led the way. For some reason, perhaps because of Dr. Aboulker's presence, or maybe fortified by the reassuring weight of the gun in my pocket, I found the descent easier than the ascent had been.

"So long and go to hell," I said to the clerk, brandishing the key he'd given me before letting it fall to the lobby floor. Dr. Aboulker and I stepped out into the rain. I got into the car. He dumped my bag on the back seat, next to his briefcase, and climbed behind the wheel.

On the drive over to the central bus station, his eyes kept darting to me and then to the rearview mirror, where he could see the bag. He kept rubbing his mouth nervously, which made me feel bad.

After stopping outside the station on Jaffa Street, he asked, "Who are you really, Mr. Lapid?"

I saw no harm in telling him. Besides, now that I was on the cusp of fleeing Kulaski's domain, my anxiety had decreased and my professional curiosity was beginning to reassert itself. "I'm a private investigator. I'm working a case here in Jerusalem. A case pertaining to your hospital, in fact."

"My hospital?"

"Yes. It concerns a nurse by the name of Moria Gafni. Did you know her?"

"Not closely, no. We never worked together, but I know who she was. News of her death was all over the hospital. What does it mean, your case concerns her?"

"I was hired to discover why she killed herself."

"I didn't know her motivation was unknown."

"Quite unknown," I said with bitterness, remembering the obscure suicide note.

"Well, I'm sorry, but I don't think I can help you. I never said more than two words to her. Just hello, goodbye, that sort of thing."

"What about Dr. Shapira?"

"Kalman Shapira? He's dead."

"I know he's dead. Were you and he friends?"

"I wouldn't say friends, but friendly, sure. We used to work together before he moved to the Pediatric Ward. Why are you asking about him?"

"Two people who work together die unnaturally within a short period of time, it interests me."

A dash of fear played across Dr. Aboulker's face. "What are you implying, Mr. Lapid?"

"I'm not implying anything. I'm just gathering information. What was Dr. Shapira like?"

He didn't answer. People sometimes get that way when asked about the dead. They don't want to speak ill.

"He won't mind, Doctor," I said. "It could be important."

He scrutinized my features, looking past the bruises and swellings and trying to see the man behind the injuries. Whatever he saw must have tipped some internal scale, and he said, "He was a good doctor, a talented surgeon, but he could be a bit abrasive. He was sometimes brusque with the nurses."

"Was he the sort of doctor who'd complain about a nurse if she didn't show him the proper respect?"

"It happened. Why?"

"It confirms something I was told about him," I said. "What about Dr. Leitner?"

"What does he have to do with this?"

"He was Moria Gafni's boss. What do you think of him?"

Again he didn't answer, just stared out the rain-streaked windshield. A muscle clenched along his jaw.

"You don't like him very much, do you?"

He turned to me. "Am I that easy to read?"

I smiled. "On that issue, you're an open book. Care to tell me why you dislike him?"

"I probably shouldn't."

"Why not?"

"Leitner might become head physician one of these days. He'll run the entire hospital."

"He's that good a doctor?"

Dr. Aboulker huffed, his mouth twisted in bitter contempt. "I wouldn't let him treat my children if he was the only doctor in town."

"That bad, huh?"

He hesitated, scratching the side of his face, tapping the wheel.

I said, "Dr. Leitner will never know what you tell me. You have my word on that."

He looked at me for a moment, then said, "Leitner is one of those doctors who seem to forget that his patients are people. He treats them as though he's a mechanic fixing a machine. And he's not so brilliant at that, either."

"Then how in hell is it possible he'll become head physician?"

"Because he's good at internal politics, and, more crucially, he's a great fundraiser."

"That's more important than being a good doctor?"

"To get appointed head physician? Yes, it is. Sometimes it seems like it's the only skill that matters." He paused for a beat, then added, "Maybe I shouldn't disparage Leitner on that score. Donations are vital for a hospital. A hospital with money becomes more modern, acquires better equipment, can offer a higher level of care to its patients. A hospital needs fundraisers. But with Leitner it has always seemed to me that his main goal is not the well-being of his patients, but the fulfillment of his personal ambition. He wants to be head physician not because he believes he'll do the best job for the patients, but for the status that comes with the title, the boost to his ego."

"I see," I said, thinking that it fit my impression of Leitner.

"Do you know Anat Schlesinger?" I asked. "She's a nurse who worked with Moria Gafni."

"I know who she is, but I don't know her any better than I did Moria."

"What about Naomi Hecht?"

"Sure, I know Naomi. We used to work together." A dark cloud passed over his face. "Leitner must be stupid, not just incompetent."

"Why do you say that?"

"Because he fired her, that's why. One of the best nurses I've ever met."

I stared at him. "When did this happen?"

"Yesterday."

Soon after my conversation with him. "Why did he do it?"

"No one seems to know. One rumor says she botched some procedure, but I don't believe it. And this after he surprised everyone just two months ago by announcing Naomi will become head nurse of the

Pediatric Ward next year when the current one retires. Usually, the head nurse is much older. I didn't think Leitner had it in him to make such an unorthodox appointment; I was actually impressed. But now he's overturned his earlier decision and gotten rid of her."

I tried to think what any of this might have to do with Dr. Shapira's murder, with Moria's suicide, but I couldn't see a connection.

I racked my brain, but I couldn't come up with more questions to ask Dr. Aboulker. I held out my hand. "Thank you, Doctor. For everything."

He smiled. "You're most welcome, Mr. Lapid." Then the smile faded. "I really shouldn't have let you leave the hospital."

"You didn't have much choice in the matter."

"I suppose I didn't. My professional advice is that you go to the hospital the minute you reach Tel Aviv, but I'm not going to ask if you will. The answer might make me feel guiltier than I already do. How are you feeling right now?"

"Much better already."

"You're a terrible liar, you know that? Which makes me feel better because now I'm sure you'll keep your word and not repeat what I told you. Before you go..." He reached into the back seat and got his briefcase. He produced two squat bottles of pills. "This one's for the fever. Take three a day until it breaks. This is for the pain. Don't exceed four a day. Take the pills with food, okay?"

I put the medicine in my coat pocket. I thanked him again.

"Take it easy, Mr. Lapid. Rest. Don't exert yourself. And stay out of trouble, okay?"

28

Five seconds after I exited Dr. Aboulker's car, the rain turned into a deluge. By the time I made it into the station, my hair was matted, and water had infiltrated my clothes, freezing my skin. My ribs, especially where Kulaski had punched me, were screaming with agony.

Once on the bus, I settled into the backseat and struggled to find a comfortable way to position my body. I didn't find one. However I shifted, a different part of my battered anatomy ignited with pain.

I was also cold beyond reason. I shook, trembled; my teeth chattered. I wrapped my arms around myself, but it did no good. It was as though my body had stopped producing heat.

The other travelers looked at me once and then avoided eye contact. I looked like trouble, and they wanted to steer clear of it.

The bus ride was an ordeal. The road was rife with bumps and potholes, and I felt every single one of them in my battered and broken bones. I tried sleeping, but every little uneven patch of tarmac jolted me back to dismal wakefulness. The rain kept up most of the way, so the ride was slow and long.

The sky was gray in Tel Aviv, but at least it was dry. The air was cold and still, like a pent-up breath. I staggered out of the bus station and tried hailing a taxi. A couple veered closer, but when the driver got a look at my face, he spun the wheel and tore off. When the third one came, I was smarter. I bent my head and pretended to scratch my forehead, obscuring my face. When I slid into the backseat and the driver saw me in all my bruised glory, he gulped, but it was too late to drive off. The enemy was inside the gates.

I alleviated his anxiety by showering him with gifts; in this case, a few coins from my wallet. He drove me to Hamaccabi Street and was so relieved that I hadn't passed out or worse in his taxi that he bade me a cheerful goodbye and expressed his heartfelt hope that I would feel better soon. I didn't reply. I had too little energy. With my bag in one hand, I trudged into the building and cursed myself for living on the third floor. The climb up the stairs was a repeat of the one earlier that day in Jerusalem, only worse. The pain in my chest had increased, and I was also exhausted.

I wobbled up the first flight, stumbled up the second, fumbled with my keys, nearly dropped them, missed the keyhole several times, and finally managed to get the door open.

Inside, dizzy with pain, fever, and fatigue, I dropped the bag by the door, tottered toward my bed, plopped onto it, and fell on my back without removing my coat or shoes. The only thing I did before drowning in unconsciousness was to take out the gun. I fell asleep with it in my hand.

29

I slipped in and out of consciousness for eighteen hours. I had outlandish dreams, feverish delusions. I was visited by apparitions of the dead. I wept; I beseeched them for forgiveness; I said I longed to join them. I might have meant it, too. I'm not sure.

I shivered, burned, sweated profusely, then froze as the sweat evaporated inside my clothes, turning them damp. I hurt. The pain came in bright flashes, in powerful and clawing waves. Even in the best moments, it never went away entirely. It was a constant companion, always present, like a noise that rises and falls but is never silent.

I forgot about the medicine. My head pounded and swam, even lying down. It was impossible to form coherent thoughts. My brain was jumbled, messy, like a room after an earthquake.

My nose throbbed. It felt too big for my face—a bloated, alien, monstrous thing. I was nauseated, without appetite, submerged in a swamp of agony, illness, disorientation, and bleak imaginings.

Two things pulled me from the depths of semiconsciousness and back to the real world. The first was a series of firm knocks on my door—initially, they filled me with panic; I was sure it was Kulaski—and a voice calling from the other side: "Adam! Are you there, Adam?" The second was a painful pressure in my lower abdomen, coupled with the urgent need to pee. "Just a minute," I rasped and hurried to the bathroom, arriving just in time to avert an awkward disaster.

More blood in my urine. I flushed it down as one attempts to bury a terrible memory.

I opened the door. It was Greta. A look of horror came over her face, and her hand flew to her mouth.

"Adam, dear God, what happened?"

"Hello, Greta. I had a little trouble."

"Not so little, I think. Can I come in?"

I moved aside, and she entered the apartment. Her nose wrinkled. "We need some air in here." She opened a window, looked at my bed, and asked, "Were you expecting a burglar?"

She had seen the gun. In my rush to the bathroom, I had left it on the sheet.

"A policeman, actually."

Her eyebrows shot up. "I think you'd better tell me everything, Adam."

I massaged my pounding temples. "It's a long story. What are you doing here, Greta?"

"I was worried about you. You were distraught when you stormed out the other day, and then I didn't see you for a few days. I came over here yesterday and the day before, but you didn't answer your door."

"I'm surprised you cared enough to make the effort."

She looked insulted. "Why wouldn't I?"

"You made it clear what you thought of what I did in Jerusalem. Like Ben-Gurion said on the radio, I'm one of the terrorists who tried to topple Israeli democracy."

Greta shook her head, an expression of sadness on her face. "Oh, Adam. You're so hard on yourself sometimes, you think the rest of the world has to be the same way. Well, I'm not. If I'm disappointed in you for something you did, it doesn't mean I've stopped caring about you." She set her bag on my dining table, stepped forward, and engulfed me in her embrace, my chest mashed against her large bosom, my head in the crook of her neck. It was wonderful, like returning home after a cold, arduous journey, and tears sprang to my

223

eyes. But then Greta squeezed me a little too strongly, and I groaned and pulled away.

"What is it?" she asked.

"My ribs." I sat down heavily on one of the two chairs in my apartment, bending my head, struggling to regain my breath.

"What's wrong with them?"

"They're sore."

"Quite a bit more than sore, I'd say. And your nose, your face." She touched my cheek and then my forehead, just like my mother used to do when I was a boy. "You're a furnace, Adam. You need to go to the hospital right away."

"No hospital."

"This is no time for stubborn manliness. You're obviously very ill."

"No hospital, Greta."

"Why not?"

I fixed my eyes on hers. "You can't have a gun handy in a hospital."

That stopped her cold. She looked at the gun, then back at me. I thought she'd ask me again to tell her what happened, but she had other priorities. "If you refuse to go to the hospital, I'll get a doctor to come here."

"No."

"You can keep the gun in your pocket until he leaves."

"He may decide I have to be hospitalized. I can't risk that."

"That means you're in really bad shape. Even worse than what shows."

I thought about the blood in my urine, the busted ribs Kulaski had punched, the high fever, my bone-deep exhaustion. Greta was right. I was in a terrible state. But what scared me more than my health was the chance, however slim, that Kulaski would decide that the pain he'd inflicted on me and my banishment from Jerusalem weren't enough, that he needed to pay me another visit. Even here in Tel Aviv, he terrified me. He'd become a monster, a demon that might appear at any time, any place. And the worst thing that I could imagine was being helpless if he came after me, like I'd been in

Jerusalem. That was a scenario I simply couldn't tolerate. I needed to be armed. I had to be able to fight.

"I have medicine," I said, suddenly remembering the two bottles in my pocket. I showed them to her with almost childish pride. "This one's for the fever; this is for the pain."

Greta took the bottles from my hand and studied them dubiously. "Who gave you these?"

"A doctor in Jerusalem."

"Jerusalem? So that's where you've been these past few days?"

"Don't look at me like that. I wasn't there to protest. I was working a case."

Greta nodded, held up the pill bottles. "When was the last time you took one of these?"

Embarrassed, I explained that I hadn't taken any yet, that I'd been sleeping, and that you needed to take them with food. Greta told me to wait a minute, stepped into the kitchen, and returned with a scowl of disapproval.

"You have nothing to eat."

"I'll do some shopping later."

"You?" She snorted, shaking her head, her nest of salt-and-pepper curls dancing. "You can't even sit straight. You still have your coat and shoes on, which means you slept in them. You should have come to the café instead of here. I would have helped you."

"I didn't think you'd want to see me. I know you were angry with me. I saw how you looked at me when Ben-Gurion was speaking on the radio."

"I wasn't angry with you. I was angry with Ben-Gurion for saying such nasty things about you." She drew a deep breath. "I shouldn't have let you leave so agitated. I'm sorry, Adam."

I told her no apology was warranted. I felt foolish for assuming the worst had happened between us. Despite my fever, despite the pain, I felt happy, optimistic. I thought I'd lost Greta, and now I knew I hadn't.

"Well," she said, "first things first..." She returned to the kitchen, ran the faucet, and emerged with a glass of water. "Drink," she commanded, and I obeyed.

Back in the kitchen, she puttered about for a time, let out a triumphant exclamation, and a minute later appeared with a bowl partly filled with corn. "It turns out you weren't completely out of food after all. I found this one small can wedged behind a couple of empty tins. I put some salt on it, so it shouldn't be too bad. Eat!"

I ate. At first, my stomach seemed on the point of rebellion, but gradually it settled, and my hunger resurged. Greta supervised me quietly, nodding in satisfaction as I emptied the bowl to the last kernel. Then she refilled my glass and told me to take my medicine.

She said, "How are you feeling? And don't try to sugarcoat it. I promise I won't call a doctor even if you're at death's door."

I knew she wasn't serious about the last part, but that she was serious about the first.

"Pretty lousy," I said.

"Will you tell me what happened?"

I nodded, yawning, my eyes and head heavy. "Later, okay? I wasn't lying about it being a long story, and all I want to do is sleep."

"All right. But not in those clothes. And you should shower first. To put it delicately, you don't smell like a bouquet of roses."

I grumbled, claimed I was too tired to undress, but Greta was adamant. "I'll help you."

She pulled off my shoes and socks, then helped me out of my trousers, coat, and shirt. She gasped when she saw the bruises on my legs and abdomen. The largest and freshest was on my side, where Kulaski had hit me. It looked like a deep lake where hardly any light pierces the surface. I could tell Greta wanted to ask me about it, but she restrained her curiosity, respecting my desire to postpone the telling until later.

She helped me to the bathroom, me in my underwear, made sure hot water was coming out of the showerhead, and then left me alone. I managed to get fully naked by myself.

After the shower, with a towel around my waist, I shuffled back into the room that served as bedroom, dining room, and living room.

There I discovered that Greta had changed the bedding and was in the process of examining my clothes.

"There's blood on them," she remarked.

"All mine, I'm afraid."

She nodded, running a critical eye over my bruised torso. "I wish I could say the shower improved your appearance, but I won't lie. At least you smell better."

"Did I smell like fear before?"

"What?"

"Never mind," I said. Greta had laid out underwear on the bed, and, with her back turned, I got into them and under the blanket.

"The gun's under the pillow," Greta said. "In a novel I once read, that's where the protagonist kept it."

I smiled sleepily, my eyes shutting of their own accord. "Books can teach you the oddest things."

She moved closer. She laid her hand once more on my forehead and said, "Sleep, Adam. Everything will be fine, I promise."

30

I awoke, groggy, to the sound of a lock unlatching. Greta pushed the door open, face flushed. She was laden with bags. Seeing that I was awake, she showed me her cargo: one bag contained bread and vegetables; the other held a whole chicken.

"How'd you get it?" I asked, meaning the chicken. You couldn't get a whole bird legally, and even on the black market, it was hard to come by.

"I have my sources."

"It must have been expensive."

"It wasn't cheap."

"I'll reimburse you."

"That's not necessary, Adam."

"I insist. There's money in my wallet."

"I tell you what: why don't I put it on your tab? That way you'll feel obligated to recover so you can pay me back."

With that, she ambled into the kitchen. End of argument. I drifted off again.

When I awoke next, the mouthwatering scent of chicken soup was thick around me. It took me a second to realize what this meant: my sense of smell had returned; the swelling in my nose must have gone down.

Greta was humming to herself in the kitchen, accompanied by the sound of running water and the tinkle of cutlery. I pushed off the blanket and cautiously shifted to a sitting position. I waited for dizziness to strike and felt a burst of confidence when it didn't. I should have known better. When I tried to stand, it leaped on me, as though from ambush, forcing me back on the bed. Greta must have heard me because she appeared from the kitchen.

"What's wrong?"

"I'm dizzy. Don't worry. I'm actually feeling better."

"You don't look it." She came over, felt my forehead and tut-tutted. "Still hot. The soup is almost ready. I also put a new block of ice in your icebox and stocked it with vegetables, cheese, butter, and milk."

"You shouldn't have done all that."

"Stop that, all right? I did it because you needed me to and because I wanted to. Either of those reasons is reason enough."

I looked into her kind, gentle eyes, and felt a pleasant warmth in my chest. "Thank you, Greta."

She squeezed my hand. "Let me help you up."

I didn't argue. Once on my feet, she returned to the kitchen and I went to the bathroom. I looked at myself in the mirror and winced. My face was a mess of reds and purples, my nose a large, unfamiliar shape at its center. I was a model of defeat—a beaten, wounded soldier after a rout.

Greta had put my razor and shaving cream, toothbrush and paste on the small shelf under the mirror. Stubble grassed my face, but I didn't dare put the razor to my skin. I brushed my teeth. My gums were tender. I hadn't lost any teeth, but it had been a close call.

I shivered. I was in underwear and undershirt, and the apartment was cold. From my closet I got trousers, socks, and a shirt, and, with Greta's help, which I accepted without further attempts at bravado, worked myself into them.

"Shouldn't you be at the café?"

"Rita can mind the place for a while." Rita filled in for Greta at the café from time to time. "Sit down. I'll get you some soup."

The soup was a delicacy. Spicy and rich with potatoes and carrots and morsels of tender chicken. I ate with gusto, almost forgetting my troubles. Greta watched me with quiet satisfaction, which only grew when I asked for another helping.

Then I took my pills. And then I said to Greta, "I'm in trouble."

"I could tell that."

"If I don't work this case, I'll go to jail. If I do, I might end up dead."

"Perhaps you should start at the beginning, Adam."

So I did. I started with the demonstration. I didn't sanitize the story. I kept in all the ugly bits. I described the fight outside the Knesset, made it clear that I'd hit cops, probably injured some. I didn't shy away from Greta's gaze as I spoke. I wanted to see her reaction, even if it was a bad one. But she just nodded in encouragement for me to continue.

I told her about the fallen policeman, how I was arrested, and my first encounter with Inspector Kulaski.

"He was going to see to it that I'd spend years in prison," I said. "It was personal for him." Then I told her about the phone call from the deputy commissioner and Kulaski's vow that it wasn't over.

"I was just as gobsmacked as he was that I was being released," I said.

Next, I related to her the car ride with Shmuel Birnbaum, my meeting with Baruch Gafni, and the mission he'd given me. "If not for him, I'd still be locked up. I should feel thankful, but I don't. Probably because I dislike him so much."

Then came the investigation itself. My visit to Moria's apartment. Finding the hidden gun. Meeting Daniel and Lillian Shukrun, and the latter's description of Moria's lover. Going to the hospital, talking to Paula, and hearing about Dr. Shapira's murder. Sitting in Café Atara with Naomi Hecht, where she lied to me about her falling-out with Moria, and learning of the suicide of Vera Gafni, Moria's mother. Interviewing Anat Schlesinger. Meeting Dr. Leitner. Discovering the identity of Moria's lover. Reading the homicide report of

Dr. Shapira. Figuring out Moria killed him. Being attacked on the street.

"At first I assumed I was the random victim of a street mugging," I said. "The truth is entirely different."

Now came the hardest part, the most shameful to share—as being helpless and weak and at the mercy of brutal men usually is. I told Greta of waking up in the hospital, learning that I hadn't been robbed, and finally realizing what had happened when Kulaski marched into my room to gloat and threaten and hurt me.

"The huge bruise on my side, that's Kulaski's doing. He knew I had broken ribs; that's why he chose that particular spot."

Greta sucked in a shocked breath when I described what Kulaski had done and clasped her hands as though in prayer, fingertips against her lips.

"That's why I need the gun," I said. "In case he comes after me."

"If you stay out of Jerusalem, maybe he won't."

"That's the catch, Greta, don't you see? I can't do that."

"Why not?"

"Because if I stop working the case, Gafni might withdraw his protection, and I could get arrested. Besides, I'm already invested. I need to see this case through. I have to know why Moria Gafni killed herself."

"There's a good chance you'll never know."

"I know. You don't have to tell me that."

"You're in no shape to work a case."

"I know that, too. I'll rest for a while, don't you worry."

"How long is 'a while'?"

I smiled and answered vaguely, "A while, Greta."

She sniffed, knowing I wouldn't rest as much as I should.

"If you stay out of Jerusalem, maybe this business with Inspector Kulaski will blow over."

"Maybe. But I doubt it. His hatred of me is illogical, irrational. It's madness."

"You can ask Mr. Gafni to talk to the deputy commissioner about Kulaski."

I shook my head. "I doubt that he would or that it would work if he did. Remember that Kulaski came after me outside the boundaries of the law. Nothing the deputy commissioner can say or do would prevent him from doing so again."

"Then how do you plan on dealing with him?"

"I don't know, Greta. I just don't know."

She pondered this for a long moment but came up with no answers. "Anything else you need to tell me?"

"Not much. Just how I got back from Jerusalem." I refrained from telling her about the ordeal the trip proved to be, but I did tell her about discovering my hotel room had been ransacked, and also about Dr. Leitner firing Naomi Hecht. "It happened soon after I spoke with him, but I can't see any connection."

Greta studied my face, and a faint smile quirked her lips. "You like her, don't you?"

"Who?"

"Naomi Hecht. You like her."

"I hardly know her, Greta."

"As if that's a requirement to liking someone. Is she attractive?"

"Most people wouldn't say so, I think."

"I'm not interested in most people, only in you."

"She's married," I said evasively, and there was a clear tinge of annoyance in my tone. "She has a husband."

"Yes," Greta deadpanned. "Married women tend to."

I let out an exasperated breath. "Is this really what we should be focusing on, Greta?"

But Greta would not be budged. "Why can't you simply admit it? Why can't you just say you like this woman?"

"Because she lied to me. And not just once, either. I don't like being lied to."

"Is that the only reason?"

I took a moment before answering. "No, it's not. There's something else. Something I've avoided thinking about, maybe because I didn't want to consider the implications. What it suggests about

Naomi Hecht. It has to do with the suicide note. There's something odd about it. Something that's missing."

"What?"

"A name. It's missing a name. Think about it, Greta. Moria's suicide note is a message. A message intended for a particular person. The person she refers to in her note. She wrote it for that person to read. Then she left the note on her dining table and went off to kill herself. Do you see the problem?"

"I don't think so, no."

"How could Moria have been sure that the person she wrote the note for would actually get to read it? Maybe she was referring to her father; she could have guessed that the police would show him the note. But whatever drove them apart, it happened years ago, so wouldn't she have written his name just so he'd have no doubt whatsoever as to his responsibility for her death?"

Greta didn't answer, just nodded for me to continue.

"Since she omitted the name," I said, "it leaves just one possibility. She wrote the note for the person who would find her body. She knew who it would be. A woman she worked with. A woman who was on shift that day and would wonder why Moria didn't show up for work. A woman who had a key to Moria's apartment."

"Naomi Hecht," Greta mumbled, her mouth dropping open.

I nodded. "It almost didn't work. Moria left a window open in her living room, and the wind blew the note under the dining table. Naomi Hecht could have easily missed it. But she didn't. She read the note and knew what it meant. She knew fully."

And there it was. The unwelcome deduction my subconscious mind had supplied me during my long hours of feverish sleep. The one I should have come up with long before, but hadn't. Maybe because, on an internal level, I'd resisted it. Because I was attracted to Naomi Hecht.

"Are you sure about this, Adam?" Greta asked.

"I can't prove it, but do you see any other explanation?"

"What about Moria's lover, Arye Harpaz? Perhaps he also had a key?"

"Would you let a man you shouted at in the street to stay away from you keep a key to your apartment?"

"He might have refused to give it back."

"Then wouldn't Moria have changed her lock?"

"Not if she intended to kill herself soon after their quarrel and planned on him finding her body and note."

I shook my head. "I can't rule it out, but it's highly unlikely."

"Why?"

"There are two reasons. The first is that Lillian Shukrun, whom I told you about, was described to me as terribly nosy, constantly watchful. This isn't malicious gossip. When I visited that building again, she opened her door to see who was climbing the stairs. Moria died around midday. If Arye Harpaz found her body, there's every chance Lillian Shukrun would have seen him enter or leave. She would have told me about it."

"Maybe she was out," Greta said.

"Or taking a nap along with her baby," I agreed. "But it lowers the likelihood, all the same."

"And the second reason?"

"That has to do with timing. Naomi Hecht found Moria's body at three thirty, right after her shift ended. About three and a half hours after Moria died, according to the police report. It seems like a lot, but isn't really, when you take into account the suicide method. Dying from pills isn't instantaneous like shooting yourself in the head or jumping off a building. It can take quite a bit of time, even if you swallow a lot. You slip into a deep sleep and can remain that way for quite a while. Moria would have known this, as well as how long it would take Naomi Hecht to get to her apartment from the hospital. If she had arranged for Arye Harpaz to find her before Naomi Hecht did, she would be taking a big risk. What if he got delayed? Or came too early and found her still alive? Either way, it doesn't seem likely."

Greta spent a minute taking this all in. Then she nodded. "But why? What awful thing did Naomi Hecht do to Moria Gafni?"

"I don't know exactly, but I think it has something to do with Dr. Shapira's murder. Otherwise, why did Naomi Hecht lie to me about

Moria working that night? She didn't want me to suspect Moria of the murder. So she showed me the shift log and didn't say that she and Moria had switched shifts, that she had worked that night in Moria's place. I think she knows Moria killed him. I think she knew beforehand. Based on the note, there's a good chance she put Moria up to it."

"Dear God," Greta whispered.

"It all fits. Moria killed herself due to guilt. She wrote the note for Naomi Hecht to find. She omitted her name just in case someone else found her body first."

"But why did she keep the gun?"

"I don't know."

"And why did Naomi Hecht leave the note at the scene?"

"It might not have been a conscious decision. She took the note with her to the bedroom and dropped it when she saw Moria dead. Maybe, in the emotional turmoil that followed, she simply forgot about it. Or maybe she figured the note couldn't hurt her. After all, her name wasn't mentioned in it."

Greta's eyes were saucers of horror. "Why would she do it? Naomi Hecht, I mean. Why would she want Dr. Shapira dead?"

"Apparently, Dr. Shapira was an unpleasant man to work with. He could be especially hard on the nurses. He'd made life difficult for Moria. Perhaps he did the same to Naomi Hecht."

"Why didn't she shoot him herself? Why have Moria do it?"

"I don't know. It's a good question."

"If you're right, Adam, she's absolutely evil."

"Yes, she is."

"You need to go to the police."

"And tell them what? That I found a gun hidden in Moria Gafni's apartment and didn't report it? And who do you think I'll need to speak with? Kulaski is the investigating officer. I'll have to explain it all to him. He'll either laugh in my face or try to pin the murder on me. I wouldn't put it past him." I shook my head. "No, I can't talk to the police."

"Then what are you planning to do?"

I kneaded the back of my neck. I was tired and aching and feeling the tragic weight of this case pushing down on my shoulders and back.

"I have no proof of Naomi Hecht's guilt. I'm going back to Jerusalem to find some. Maybe then I'll have enough to risk going to the police."

"But if Kulaski finds out you're back in Jerusalem..."

"I'll need to make sure he doesn't."

"And if you fail?"

"Then," I said, "I'll likely end up in the cold ground alongside Dr. Shapira and Moria Gafni."

31

As much as I hated to admit it, Greta was right. I was in no shape to work a case. Hell, I was in no shape to go down the three flights of stairs from my apartment to street level. I was hurting all over, I couldn't draw a proper breath without my ribs screaming, I was weak and tired constantly, and I still had a fever.

Greta looked after me as well as any person could. She cooked my meals, made sure I took my medicine; she even brought me a couple of Western paperbacks to pass the time.

My fever broke two days after my return to Tel Aviv. The swelling in my nose went down. Gradually, my urine lost its redness. Still, it was only after seven days of Greta's firm yet gentle ministrations that I felt strong enough to go out.

Greta didn't like the idea. "What's the urgency?" she asked, her arms folded across her chest.

"I need to talk to my client. I told him I'd report to him a week after he hired me."

"Can't it wait until tomorrow?"

"I'm late as it is."

"You sure you want him to see you this way?"

My bruises were in vibrant, colorful bloom. Having lost nearly all traces of blue and purple, they glowed in a range of yellows, a few tinted a sickly green or a disconcerting brown. The abrasions across my forehead had scabbed over, looking like a bunch of earthworms paralyzed mid-squirm on my skin. They itched like mad, and Greta admonished me to not touch let alone scratch them.

In short, I wasn't a sight to inspire confidence in any client. But as I was recuperating, I was also growing restless. I wanted to do something. And while I still wasn't ready to go back to Jerusalem, where I might run into Kulaski, I felt well enough to see Gafni.

"Why not call him?" Greta asked. "You can deliver your report over the phone, can't you?"

I could, but I had a few questions for Gafni, and I wanted to see his face when he answered them.

I called his office from the public phone in Levinson Drugstore, on the corner of my street. The secretary answered. I gave her my name, and ten seconds later, Gafni came over the line. I told him I wanted to see him and asked when I could come by.

"Have you discovered what I hired you to?" he asked.

"Not yet. But I'm getting close. I have a couple of questions I need to ask you."

"I understand." There was a pause. All I could hear was his breathing. Then he said, "Come by at six thirty. I'll be waiting."

I took a bus that belched its way through the cold January evening to Gafni's factory. My ribs still ached, protesting with a teeth-clenching spasm when the bus driver accidentally mounted the curb on a turn.

The door to Gafni's factory was locked. The windows on the ground floor were dark. No machinery sounds. All the workers were long gone. Gafni wanted privacy.

I pounded on the door. The metal echoed. A minute later, I heard a key being turned, and Gafni pulled the door open and motioned me inside. The foyer and staircase were dim, so he noticed my injuries only after I followed him upstairs to the outer office where his secretary's desk stood.

"What happened to you?"

"I was mugged."

He voiced no concern or empathy. His only reaction was a creasing of the forehead.

"Don't worry," I said, making no effort to keep the sarcasm from my voice. "It's not serious."

He exhaled a low grunt and turned toward his inner sanctum. There, settled in his large chair behind his desk, he observed me with half-masted eyes beneath knitted eyebrows, his fingers steepled. It was his favorite spot, I bet, where he could appear as he wanted to: the successful, crafty businessman, in total control not only of his own destiny, but of that of many others as well.

I sat in one of the chairs opposite his and was about to speak, but he beat me to it. "How much?"

I didn't understand. "How much what?"

He rolled his eyes. "Money. That's what you're here for, isn't it? I imagine you don't have any after being *mugged*." It was clear by his inflection that he doubted my story. Probably thought I'd had an accomplice punch me in the face a few times.

I felt like doing the same to him, but I quelled the urge and shook my head. "Rest assured, I'm not here to squeeze you for more money. The muggers left empty-handed."

A filament of fear fluttered in his eyes. I bit back a smile. He assumed I'd done battle with multiple muggers and emerged bloodied but triumphant. I was a man to be reckoned with. And he was alone with me in a deserted building, and he had just insulted me to my face.

If only he knew the true story.

Taking advantage of his discomfort, I angled forward, planting my elbows on his desk as though I owned it. "Why didn't you tell me about your wife?"

His face lost color, and he retreated deeper into his seat. In the light that now splashed directly on his face, backdropped by the large dark windows that looked down on the deserted factory floor below, I could see the cracks in the image he strove to project. The fatigue. The worried, drawn features. The lines of mourning or guilt or both.

"Who told you about her?" he asked in a hushed yet cunning voice, no doubt already plotting his retribution on whoever had whispered his family's unsavory history in my ear.

"That doesn't matter. What matters is that she killed herself and that your daughter found her body."

"And so?"

"I'm wondering why you failed to mention it."

"To put it simply," he said, seemingly recovered from his shock, "it was not pertinent to your assignment."

"I think it was."

"It is not your place to think of such things. You are to concern yourself solely with the job I hired you for."

"Why did your wife kill herself?"

His jaw clamped like a dog chomping on a bone. "You are overstepping your bounds, Mr. Lapid."

"I heard it was because you were having affairs. Is that true?"

He let out a breath and laced his hands atop his round belly. To my surprise, his anger did not spike.

"It's not something I'm proud of, but I won't deny it."

"Is that why Moria severed all contact with you?"

He looked down at his hands, his mouth working, and nodded. "I didn't see the point in telling you."

Which wasn't why he'd kept this information from me. His motives were selfish. He simply didn't want his reputation tarnished.

I thought of the three lines of Moria's note and how they might fit Gafni's confession. *I hate you for how you made me feel.* That could describe Moria's sadness over the loss of her mother. *I hate you for what you did to me.* That could mean Gafni's responsibility for her mother's death. *I hate you for what you made me do.* This would refer to Moria finding her mother dead in a pool of her own blood.

Gafni must have run this interpretation through his mind a million times since Moria's death. I understood him better now. Understood his need to know why his daughter had killed herself, and why it drove him to hire me despite the risk of having his past misdeeds unearthed. He already felt responsible for his wife's suicide. The possibility of him being the cause of his daughter's suicide as well must have been unbearable. His need to find an alternative explanation must have been as urgent as a drowning man's desire for breath.

At the sight of him, with his bowed head and slumped shoulders, an unexpected emotion came over me: pity.

He had treated his wife badly. He had betrayed her. And this betrayal had led to her death and scarred his daughter's young soul.

But many men committed similar sins, and almost none of them suffered such brutal punishments. Gafni had lost his wife, and twice he had lost his daughter. Once when she expelled him from her life; the second time when she ended it. These twin tragedies—first the wife and then the daughter—must have birthed a terrible guilt. I knew such guilt. I knew how it could eat at a man.

So yes, despite my dislike for him, I felt pity. And this pity opened my mouth and pulled the following words from my throat: "I don't believe she killed herself because of you."

Gafni raised his head. His eyes were all questions and hope.

"The person in Moria's note," I explained, already regretting having said anything. "I don't think it was you."

He didn't move. Only his eyes blinked. Twice and slowly, like a predator lying in ambush. "Who then?"

I didn't want to tell him. Not yet. Even though I was sure I knew. Because I remembered my worry that Gafni would wreak terrible vengeance on whoever had pushed Moria to suicide. So I wanted absolute proof before I pointed the finger at Naomi Hecht.

"I have my suspicions, but I don't know for sure yet."

"So how can you be sure it's not... it's not..." His voice trailed off, and his fingers made a vague motion that might have been directed at himself.

"It's difficult to explain, but I just am," I said. "I'll be going back to Jerusalem in the next few days, and I believe that soon I'll be able to tell you who the person in the suicide note is."

Gafni looked at me across the expanse of his desk. His mouth was turned down, his lips mashed together. He didn't like my evasiveness one bit. "So basically, you can tell me nothing definite."

I cursed myself for succumbing to the pity I'd felt. I'd wanted to make Gafni feel better, but all I did was infuriate him and perhaps make him suspicious that I'd told him a lie he'd like hearing. I had to give him something concrete or he might go off on me.

"There is one thing," I said without giving the matter much thought, although, at a glance, I couldn't see the harm in it. "It has to do with Arye Harpaz."

Gafni's eyebrows shot up. "What about him?"

"What's he to you? A business associate?"

"He was a few years ago, and he'd like to be again." A cold smile bent his lips. "But he won't. I'm done with him. He's untrustworthy. You can't depend on him to keep his end of a bargain. I don't do business with men like that."

"Did Moria know him?"

He cocked his head, slitted his eyes. "Why are you asking this question?"

"Did she?"

He huffed in irritation. "Yes. Years ago, when Arye and I partnered on some ventures, I'd invite him home for dinner every now and then. And Moria would sometimes visit me at my office and run into him. I hope that answers your question. Now"—he made an impatient give-me motion with his right hand—"it's high time you answer mine."

So I did. I told him about talking to the neighbor who'd witnessed Moria and Harpaz's explosive argument on Moria's street. "It happened about a week before the suicide. Did you know they were in contact so recently?"

Gafni shook his head. His face was set, his dark eyes like lumps of coal ready to be put to flame.

"That's not all," I said, and I told him about finding the condoms in Moria's bedroom and then talking with Lillian Shukrun, though I didn't name her, and learning that Moria had a lover who would visit her apartment late at night. "She saw him once from the back, but I still managed to glean a description of him. Five ten or eleven. Lean. Dark hair. Rings a bell?"

Color started rising in Gafni's cheeks. He clutched the ends of his armrests so hard I thought his knuckles might split the skin.

"He was Moria's lover," I said. "Why they kept it secret, I'm not sure."

"Because Arye is married," Gafni said through clenched teeth, his voice rising with every word, his face turning blood red. "And because Arye knew I'd ruin him if I found out. The dirty bastard!" The expletive came out in a guttural shout that echoed around the office along with the wooden bang of the two fists he slammed onto his desk.

I flinched at his explosive reaction. I figured he might get mad, but I hadn't expected this erupted fury. Spittle dotted his lips and chin, and his eyes bounced around the room. His fists were still clenched. As hard as he'd hit the desk, they had to hurt, but he didn't seem to notice.

Finally, his gaze settled on me. "It's him, isn't it? He's the one who drove her to it."

I didn't need to ask whom he was talking about. I could have told him no, that Arye Harpaz did not cause Moria to end her life, but I knew that if I did, I'd have to explain why I was sure, that Gafni would not allow me to evade answering again.

"I don't know," I ended up saying. "Like I said, I need to do more work."

Gafni nodded, wiping his chin dry with the back of one hand. "You do that, Mr. Lapid. And finish the job fast."

32

I rested for six more days before I felt it was time to return to Jerusalem. By then, the bruises on my face had disappeared, and my forehead had shed its scabs. The large bruise on my ribs, where Kulaski had punched me, had shrunk like a pond in a drought. And like said pond, it was greenish and roughly circular in shape.

My ribs still hurt, but I'd gotten used to the pain and no longer took any pills. Still, I was in no shape to run or fight. If Dr. Aboulker knew what I planned, he would have thrown a fit.

Greta didn't. She took in my declaration that I would be returning to Jerusalem that evening in silence. Then she went to cook me a bountiful meal and stood over my shoulder until I ate it all.

I wondered if this was the equivalent of a condemned man's last meal but kept the question to myself.

I packed some clothes and put an empty bottle, a can opener, a spoon, and half a dozen cans of food inside my bag.

"Why are you taking all this?" Greta asked.

I told her, and she shook her head.

"You don't approve?"

"It's morbid."

"Do you see any other option?"

"No. I suppose you have no choice."

That left the question of Moria's gun. Should I take it with me? On the one hand, it was a murder weapon, and getting caught with it would be bad. On the other hand, if the police arrested me in Jerusalem, I'd probably be too dead to notice a murder charge.

Besides, the gun might come in handy, and not just for shooting.

So I slipped it inside my right coat pocket, putting the extra magazines in my left.

I left my apartment at nine, was on the bus to Jerusalem at nine thirty. The bus was nearly empty, which suited me fine. I huddled in my seat, leaned against the window, but I couldn't sleep. The closer I got to Jerusalem, the greater my foreboding became. Something terrible was going to happen. I just hoped it wasn't going to happen to me.

I pulled my new hat low over my face as I got off the bus in Jerusalem. I sneaked glances under its brim but saw no cops in the station. For the first time since this case started, I wished it would rain; it would make me harder to recognize. Still, night offered some cover, which was partly why I chose to return to Jerusalem this late.

The air smelled of exhaust fumes and the faint odor of someone's pipe. My skin crawled as though I were being watched, but I spotted no watchers. It was as though Kulaski was an evil spirit roving about Jerusalem, seeing everything that went on in the capital.

It was after eleven, the streets dark and cold and nearly empty, but it was still too early for what I had in mind. Most cafés and restaurants had already closed for the night, but I finally found a small bar that was still open. I chose the rearmost table, ordered a glass of wine I had no intention of drinking, and tried to read the latest paperback Greta had brought me. I couldn't concentrate on the story; I kept raising my eyes from the text to look at the front door, sure I'd see Kulaski grinning at me.

It was well after midnight when I picked up my bag and got out. It was time to go to sleep.

There was a chance Kulaski had given my name and description to all Jerusalem hotels. And if not, he might periodically check with them. I couldn't risk it. I needed someplace else to lay my head, where no one would know I was there, and I could think of just one option.

I made my way north and entered the now familiar streets of Kerem Avraham. On the corner of Malkei Israel and Amos, I paused and took a long stare into the street where Moria Gafni had made her home.

Both sidewalks were empty. Nearly all the windows I could see were dark. I counted just three lights, none of them in Moria's building. The street was quiet apart from the whisper of the wind and the pattering of small animal feet in the impenetrable shadows between buildings.

I turned onto Amos Street, scanning the windows on either side, but saw no curious faces peering out at me. At the entrance to Moria's building, I paused and listened. No sound. No baby crying, no muffled speech, no sense of movement anywhere.

I removed my shoes and padded inside, crossed the lobby, and started up the stairs. If anyone opened their door and saw me in my stockinged feet, I'd have some difficult explaining to do.

A shaft of moonlight from a rectangular aperture set into the wall bathed the second-floor landing a tarnished silver. I held my breath as I tiptoed past the Shukrun apartment. Lillian was probably asleep, but I wanted to take as few chances as possible.

I still had the key to Moria's apartment. I slid it into the lock as quietly as I could and turned it, cringing at the clicking sound the bolt made as it retracted. I went inside and closed the door gently. I waited with my ear pressed to the door for two full minutes, but it seemed no one was coming to check on the apartment. Gritting my teeth, I relocked the door. More noise, but it was worth it. I did not wish to be surprised in my sleep.

The air in the apartment was breathless and dead; the windows were shut against the cold and wind. It was gloomy, Moria's furniture nothing but obscure black humps, and I did not dare to switch on the lights. Leaving my shoes by the door, I soft-footed to the bedroom and set my bag by the closet. My gaze landed on the unmade bed where Moria Gafni had taken her own life. Greta had been right: this was morbid. But I had slept in places far more ghoulish.

Unwilling to risk making unnecessary noise, I did not make the bed. Nor did I remove my clothes. But I did take out the gun before stretching out on the same mattress where Moria had lain dead. I wanted it in my hand while I slept.

As I closed my eyes, I could sense the nightmares brewing in my subconscious. They would be especially gruesome tonight. Before I drifted off, I rolled up my handkerchief and jammed it between my teeth. It was the only way I could think of to choke off my screams.

33

I woke up early and exhausted. My sleep had been brittle and shallow and haunted. My jaw was cramped, and my throat burned, as though all the screams I'd stifled had seared my airways.

The light outside the windows was gray and sickly, just like I felt. I sat up, my feet on the floor, then jerked my head around as a cold finger ran down my spine. Of course the mattress was empty. No ghosts here or anywhere except in my dreams.

I treaded softly to the bathroom, peed, but did not flush. I remembered how loudly the pipes rumbled the last time I did.

I didn't dare go out. Not yet. Instead, I took up position by the window overlooking the entrance to the building, but stood well back so I could not be seen by any passersby below.

Beside me I had the bottle I'd brought with me from Tel Aviv, which I had filled up with water at the bar last night, and an open can of peas with the spoon I got from my bag; I didn't want to open any kitchen drawers if I could help it.

I stood for a long time before I saw anyone exit the building. It was a man I didn't know, one of the neighbors I hadn't encountered, probably. Then there was one of the women I'd spoken to and her children, school bags on their backs.

It was seven thirty when I saw the hulking form of Daniel Shukrun lumbering outside, a lunch pail in his grip. He walked south toward Malkei Israel Street and disappeared from sight.

That left Lillian. Nosy, watchful Lillian. She was the one I feared most. I hoped she would venture out soon.

Two hours passed and she didn't. My back started to ache. My ribs throbbed, reminding me that I was not fit for so much standing. But if I sat, I would have to move closer to the window to be able to see the building's entrance and near sidewalk, and then I might be seen in turn. I ate another can of food, corn this time. I drank all the water in my bottle. I wanted a cigarette badly, but I feared someone might smell the smoke from the landing.

Another hour. And then another. This was like guard duty in the war, standing watch over an empty landscape, getting so bored you half wished the enemy showed up and broke the tedium. A soldier's foolish mind.

"Come on, Lillian," I mouthed. "Go do some shopping. Take the baby out for a walk. Let her have some air, dammit."

And, as though God himself had heard my prayer, she appeared. Bundled up in a coat and pushing a baby stroller before her. She paused, started raising her head, and I took a hurried step backward, cursing. Was the woman psychic? Did she have a sixth sense?

I was too far from the window to see her now, and I worried that if I stepped forward, she might see me somehow. So I stayed rooted to my spot for a good minute, then inched forward to peek down.

She was gone.

Had she slipped back inside, alerted somehow to my presence? I moved right, caution thrown to the wind, to get a better angle of the southern portion of Amos Street.

There she was. Walking away, her back slightly bent as she maneuvered the stroller around a pair of chatting women.

I exhaled loudly and moved quickly. I had no idea how long Lillian would be gone. I flushed the toilet, had a drink of water, and got out of the apartment after checking through the peephole that no one was lurking on the landing.

I turned north, in the opposite direction of the way Lillian had gone, and left Amos Street behind me. That was the easy part of my day. Now came something harder.

————

The night we talked in Café Atara, which seemed like years ago now, Naomi Hecht had told me she lived on the corner of Malachi and Zeharia Streets. I had no idea if she was home at the moment. I also didn't know whether her husband would be there, but he was likely at work. As for her, unless she had found a new job since the day I fled Jerusalem, she was currently unemployed.

I walked through a drizzle, my spine tingling, my pulse spiking every time I turned a corner, sure Kulaski would be waiting for me, his immaculate uniform magically untouched by the precipitation and a merciless tight-lipped smile on his lips.

My palm was clammy around the grip of the gun in my pocket. If Kulaski came after me, he was in for a big surprise.

And afterward?

I preferred not to think about that.

Naomi Hecht's building was four stories tall. A departing neighbor told me she lived in apartment 6, on the second floor. A child's bicycle leaned against one of the walls in the lobby. The smell of cooking permeated the second-floor landing. Someone was making powdered eggs and beans. A potent combination.

I knocked on the door marked 6. Naomi Hecht opened it. Her face registered surprise when she saw me. She was wearing a black dress that fit her perfectly and white stockings that clung to her calves. Her only ornament was her wedding band.

The days that had elapsed since our last encounter had been cruel to her. She looked more tired than ever.

"Mr. Lapid, what are you doing—" She stopped and peered closely at my face. "What happened to your nose? And your fore-head? Were you in an accident?"

My nose was no longer swollen, and, like Dr. Aboulker had

predicted, it was flatter than before but not overly so. The skin on my forehead was tinted pink, still recovering from its abrasions.

Despite what I knew about her, her scrutiny made me self-conscious. Involuntarily, my hand went to my forehead as though to shield it from her stare. Swearing inwardly, I yanked it down and said, "Can I come in, Mrs. Hecht?"

She moved aside, and I entered a homey living room. A gray sofa, a small oval table and chairs, heavy curtains pulled back from south-looking windows, books on shelves, a thick rug. Everything tidy and neat, as though just after a rigorous cleaning.

"Shall I make you some tea?" she asked.

"I'm not here to drink."

"What are you here for?"

On a sideboard stood a number of photographs. Naomi Hecht in a pristine nurse's uniform, squinting against the sun in her eyes. Naomi Hecht in a wedding dress next to a handsome black-haired man in a suit, both of them grinning like excited children. The same man, this time in an IDF uniform, standing against a forest backdrop, somewhere in the Galilee, maybe, or in the mountains around Jerusalem.

"Is your husband home?" I asked, my eyes still on the photos, though there was a sense of vacancy to the place that made me believe she and I were the only people there.

She hesitated, cleared her throat. "No. He's not here. Why?"

I looked at her. There was a sparkle to her eyes, and her pupils looked dilated. Nervousness? Her breath was a little quick, and she was fidgeting with her wedding ring again. Her tell for deceit, or most likely, her getting ready to lie through her teeth. No doubt she was at that instant trying to anticipate my questions and preparing false answers to them.

"I know you lied to me," I told her. "I know you and Moria switched shifts the night Dr. Shapira was killed. I know everything."

Her shoulders sagged, and she dropped onto the sofa. She ran her hands over her face and kept them clasped under her chin.

"I lied to protect her," she said. "I didn't want you to think she could have been a murderer."

I snorted. "That's not the full reason, and we both know it."

Naomi Hecht frowned and lowered her hands to her knees. "What do you mean?"

She was getting better at deceit. She didn't go anywhere near her wedding ring this time.

All the lying she'd told and was still telling set off a reaction inside me. Like a match being put to an oil-soaked log, making it erupt into flame.

I whipped the gun out of my pocket, thrust my hand at her face. "Recognize this?"

She recoiled in terror, though I wasn't pointing the weapon at her.

"This is what you went to Moria's apartment to find, right? You were there a few days before we first met. You searched through her bedroom. But you didn't find this."

"I've never seen this gun in my life."

"But you don't deny going to her apartment and searching through her things."

She shook her head, her eyes dropping. "I did no such thing."

I allowed myself a smile. She was once again a bad liar. The pressure I put on her was showing. Her posture made her look fragile and afraid. Her shoulders drawn inward. Her hands clasped in her lap. Her legs pressed tight together. A smaller target, but there was no escaping the truth.

I was standing on the other side of the narrow coffee table, looming over her. I felt no pity, only anger. And not just for what she'd done to Dr. Shapira, to Moria; also, for what she'd done to me. Because, as Greta had made me admit, I liked this woman. And she turned out to be an evil killer.

"This is the gun that was used to kill Dr. Shapira," I said, fighting to keep my voice level. "I found it in Moria's bedroom."

Naomi Hecht raised her head, her face frozen in a stunned expression. "No. It can't be."

"Don't feel bad about not finding it. Moria had hidden it well. It was in a small hole dug into the wall directly behind her bedside cabinet."

"You're lying. You're making this up."

"I don't know why she didn't dump it after the murder. But you know, don't you? Otherwise, you wouldn't have gone looking for it."

"I didn't. Like I told you, I've never seen this gun before."

My hand was still outstretched, clasping the weapon. I lowered it but didn't return it to my pocket. I wanted her to still see it.

I said, "The night of the murder, you switched shifts with Moria at the last moment, so no one got around to changing the shift log. It wasn't much of an alibi. It wouldn't have stood up to scrutiny, but you hoped it wouldn't need to. If Moria did her job well, the police would think this was a robbery that turned deadly. They wouldn't look too hard at Moria or anyone else at the hospital."

I paused to let her speak, but she remained silent. She barely moved, like an animal caught in headlights, sensing impending disaster but unable to flee from it.

"It worked out perfectly," I said. "The police never suspected Moria. Maybe they looked at the shift log, but if so, they never discovered the switch. And you ended up using it to try to steer me away from Moria. To make me think it was impossible for her to kill Dr. Shapira."

"She didn't. She couldn't." Naomi Hecht's voice had risen and sharpened. Her eyes were pleading with me to believe her lies.

"Yes, she could. She wasn't working that night, and she had this gun in her possession." I waved the gun before her, and she flinched.

"She had no reason to kill him," she said.

"Of course she did. Dr. Shapira complained about her to Dr. Leitner, who in turn excoriated her in his office, making her cry. I'm sure this wasn't the only time Dr. Shapira behaved badly toward Moria. As he did to other nurses. Including you, I bet. Especially you, with how you allow yourself to openly criticize doctors. Which is probably why you ended up getting fired. Should Dr. Leitner be in fear for his life now?"

Another shake of the head. "You've got this all wrong. Please believe me, it's nothing like what you think."

"No more lies, Mrs. Hecht. I'm sick and tired of them. Why did you and Moria fight a week before she died? It was because she felt guilty for the murder, right? But I'm guessing you didn't."

She shook her head violently, saying as though in recitation, "No. No. No. No."

"Moria killed herself because of you." My voice was louder now, cutting, each word slicing into her like a spearhead. "She chose the time, knowing you'd come looking for her after she failed to show up for work. She wanted you to find her."

Naomi Hecht clamped her eyes shut, and her entire body went rigid, but then, with a cry, she broke into sobs, rocking back and forth, her shoulders quaking.

I let her cry. Did not offer a word of solace or anything with which to dry her tears. My ears throbbed with the echo of her sobs. My heart thumped with excitement. I wanted to break her, and I was getting close.

When she started to calm, I went over and sat beside her on the sofa. I could feel the heat of her body, smell the salty, sour odor of her tears and desperation.

"You'll feel better if you come clean," I said in a gentler voice, pushing down a sick feeling as I recalled Kulaski using the same technique on me. "If you admit it. I'll take you to the police station, and you can tell them everything." In truth, I couldn't do that without letting Kulaski know I was in town, but I'd figure something out when the time came. "They'll go easy on you if you confess."

Her sobbing dwindled to nothingness, she dried her eyes with her knuckles, and then Naomi Hecht turned her head to face me. Her eyes were fresh puddles, the skin on her cheeks wet and pale to near translucence, and the bags under her eyes black like the inside of a blindfold just before an execution.

Her voice was surprisingly firm and controlled. "You are a damn fool, Mr. Lapid. You know nothing about me or Moria. Absolutely nothing. And you're crazy if you think I'll confess to a murder neither I nor she had anything to do with. Now I want you to leave."

"You're making a mistake, Mrs. Hecht."

"No. You're the one who's making a mistake. I told you to leave, so leave. Get out of my home!"

I nodded slowly and rose to my feet, trying to hide my disappointment. I had thought this might end right then, but I was wrong. I slipped the gun in my coat. I said to her, "Confessing might be the safer option for you, Mrs. Hecht."

She stared at me. "What does that mean?"

"Nothing," I said, for I was not about to tell her Mr. Gafni might prove more dangerous to her than a prison term. "But I promise you this: I won't stop looking for proof. And I'll find it. And when I do, you'll pay for what you did. You'll pay for Dr. Shapira. And you'll pay for Moria, too."

34

I walked through cold rain and hot shame, though the latter perplexed me. What did I have to be ashamed of? Making a killer cry? Using a customary interrogation technique to get her to confess? Once again, I was allowing my attraction for Naomi Hecht to influence me.

I fled the rain into a café, smoked a couple of cigarettes, and ate a mediocre lunch. I could have ended the case then and there. I could have picked up the phone, called Gafni, and told him about Naomi Hecht. But then I would have had to explain to him what she'd done, what Moria had done. I didn't think he would believe me. Not unless I had undeniable proof.

And once I did? How would he take it? I didn't want to think about that just yet.

As I ate, I kept glancing at the door and front window. Would I see Kulaski walk by? Or maybe that gluttonous rat Rapfogel?

I didn't see anyone. The rain stopped by the time I had my second cup of coffee. I went out into the wet street and just avoided getting splashed when a truck bounced into a puddle, showering the sidewalk in front of me.

Choosing side streets as often as possible, I wended my way to where Dr. Shapira had met his doom. I had no idea what I'd find when I got there, but it's never a mistake to visit a murder scene.

The alleyway where Dr. Shapira had perished was a patch of wet tarmac that held no traces of the violent death that had occurred there. Someone had shattered a bottle against the ground, and glass glittered at my feet. An old chair missing a leg leaned crookedly against a wall, its wood distended and cracked with rain. A child's mitten lay forgotten and soiled in a puddle.

But no blood. No clues left by the killer. No sense of death.

What was I expecting, more than a month after the slaying? I hated to admit it, but I had no idea how to proceed. Returning to the hospital to ask more questions was risky. Kulaski might have asked one of the employees on the ward to keep an eye out for me. So how was I supposed to find the evidence that would nail Naomi Hecht to the wall? The longer it took, the greater the chance that I'd be spotted. I needed a solution fast.

Until I came up with one, I had to get off the street. It was almost three by now. Soon the cinemas would open. I went into the first one I saw, bought tickets to all three shows, and chose the farthest seat in the last row. I buried my head in a newspaper I'd picked up on the way until the lights went out and the newsreel started playing.

Ben-Gurion was being shown around a factory in Haifa. Foreign Minister Sharett was shaking hands with a bunch of European ambassadors. Miserable immigrants in an immigrant camp in the north were repairing weather damage to their makeshift homes, mud everywhere.

Then the movie started. Voices speaking American English. Images of skyscrapers and an unbelievable number of cars.

The darkness felt safe, and I relaxed slightly. I watched the movie and tried to clear my mind, hoping inspiration would strike.

It didn't.

I sat through two more screenings of the same film. I used the time to grab some shut-eye. With how tired I was, it was easy to sleep, even when the cinema hall filled up for the evening screenings.

When the lights came on after the last show, I dragged my feet toward the exit, knowing that outside would be colder and likely wetter, and that I had more time to pass before I dared go to Moria's apartment for the night.

Luckily, the night was dry, though the wind was a cold knife that whistled like an incoming bomb. I wedged my hands into my pockets and meandered aimlessly for a while. I was hungry but didn't feel like sitting anywhere after being in a chair for hours. At certain times, I again had the feeling that I was being watched, but I was starting to suspect that it was just my nerves playing tricks on me.

Then a man called my name, and I felt the bottom drop from under me.

35

I whipped around, my heart pounding in my ears, ready to pull out the gun and start blasting.

But it wasn't Kulaski. Nor Rapfogel. Not a cop at all. In my agitated state, it took me a second to place him. Then I remembered and almost laughed with relief.

Arye Harpaz. Moria's lover. The untrustworthy businessman whom Gafni wanted nothing to do with. A man I'd considered hunting down for a conversation if I ran out of ideas, and here he was before me.

He had a pretty brunette on his arm. He pulled her across the street toward me. She looked a little reluctant but didn't utter a peep. Up close, I saw his cheeks were flushed and his eyes sparkled. Hers too. Both smelled of wine and cigarettes; he also of cologne and she of some overly sweet perfume.

"Adam Lapid," Harpaz said. "Fancy running into you."

"Arye Harpaz," I replied.

He grinned. "You remember me."

I nodded. Looking around, it seemed no one had heard him call my name or cared if they did. "Indeed I do. In fact, just the other day, I was talking about you with Baruch Gafni."

That sobered him up quick. He was dressed in a dark blue coat that must have cost what some men make in two months. His trousers and shoes looked expensive too, as did his hat. He really was handsome. And about two decades older than the bored-looking brunette.

"Why were you talking about me?" He sounded wary and on edge.

"Because of Moria," I said, and saw his Adam's apple bob as he gulped.

He worked up a smile and said to the brunette, "Go to the hotel. I'll join you in a little while."

She began to protest, but he cut her off brusquely. "Go, I tell you. I have business with this man."

She pouted; she had the lips for it. It made her look even younger, innocent and vulnerable. Harpaz caressed her cheek and softened his voice.

"I don't want you to stand out here in the cold. I promise you it won't take long. Now run along, sweetheart. I'll be there before you even miss me."

The brunette flicked me an accusatory look and sashayed away. Harpaz watched her go, then turned back to me.

"Your wife?" I asked, though I guessed the answer.

His smile was a perfect blend of the boy who got caught with his hand in the cookie jar and the Casanova who enjoys nothing more than to see other men envy him his conquests.

"You can say she's a close friend of mine. My wife is in Tel Aviv, no doubt turned in for the night."

"She's very young, your friend."

"Twenty-one last month. But intriguing despite her age. You're intriguing as well," he said to me. "From the moment we first met in Baruch's factory, you interested me."

"You didn't," I said. "Not at the time."

He smiled. Perhaps he truly didn't mind the dig.

We were on Jaffa Street, people still milling about us, heading home from cinemas and late suppers.

"Let's find someplace more private to talk," I suggested.

He nodded. "There's a café down the street. It stays open late and has a back room. I know the owner."

"Lead the way."

The café was narrow and dingy and hosted just a solitary customer bent over his drink. The owner, a burly guy with a bushy beard, greeted Harpaz by name. He nodded when Harpaz asked him if the back room was vacant.

"What will you have?" Harpaz asked me.

"I'm not thirsty."

"It's on me."

"That makes no difference." I didn't want to drink with him. I didn't like him, and I wanted him to know it.

Harpaz shrugged, but I could see that my rejection had unnerved him. He recovered quickly and faced the barkeep. "Give me a good bottle of red and two glasses." To me he added, "Maybe you'll change your mind."

With the bottle and glasses in hand, Harpaz led the way to the back room and switched on the light. The room was small and held the residual smell of sweat, cigarettes, and wet shoes and clothes. Next to the rear wall was a round table bearing a couple of half-full bottle crates. Five chairs stood against one wall, striving for innocence like suspects in a lineup.

"You like to gamble?" I asked.

Harpaz gave me a surprised look.

"Those two crates are nice camouflage," I said, "but they don't look too heavy. Remove them, drag the table to the middle, right about here"—I stood directly under the overhead light fixture—"pull some chairs around, and you're all set for a nice game."

Harpaz clapped his hands. "Bravo, detective. I'm impressed." His grin returned. "I told you I found you interesting. I asked around a bit. Learned you work as a private detective."

"Why waste the time? Or is it really Baruch Gafni you want to know more about?"

He laid a hand across his heart. "Guilty as charged." He uncorked the bottle, poured himself half a glass, held out the bottle to me, and shrugged when I declined. He took a long drink.

"I also heard you used to be a cop. I hope this little set-up here"— he gestured with his hand at the room—"doesn't bother you."

"I'm not a cop anymore. It's none of my business if people want to throw their money away."

Harpaz said, "My God. How rare. An honest man. And here I thought you were angling for a little *baksheesh*."

"Maybe I'm just planning to squeeze you for a lot more later on."

He smiled. This was his expertise, wheeling and dealing, and now he thought I might after all be susceptible to his charm and money.

"Why are you so keen to learn more about Baruch Gafni?" I asked.

He took another sip of wine. "I want him to invest in a business venture. A big one. The more I know about a potential investor, the better."

"Was that why you met Gafni the same day you and I did?"

He nodded. "I showed him some papers relating to the venture."

"Let me guess, he wasn't too impressed."

Something hateful and dangerous glinted in Harpaz's eyes and then was gone. He finished his wine and poured himself some more.

"He'll come around. He just needs more convincing. The deal is too good for him to pass on." He drained his glass and refilled it. "You said you and Baruch were talking about me because of Moria." He was striving for a nonchalant tone, but I knew he was bothered by it, that this was why he had agreed to speak with me. "I'm not sure I understand."

I smiled and let the silence stretch for a few seconds. "I think you understand perfectly well."

"I assure you I don't."

He was goading me to tell him what I knew or thought I did. He was hoping it was less than he feared.

"Let's just say I don't think you and Baruch Gafni will ever do business again."

His eyes tightened, and there was that glint again. I realized it was a kind of hunger, a ravenous craving. For wealth, status, success. And that it was dangerous to stand in the way of that hunger, that Arye Harpaz was a man who'd cross many lines, break many norms, to achieve his goals.

His tone was low and suggested a threat. "And why is that, Mr. Lapid?"

"Because he knows you were sleeping with his daughter. And let me tell you, he didn't like it one bit."

Harpaz gaped at me, shocked that his secret was exposed. "Whatever gave him that idea?"

"You did. You thought you were being careful, but it wasn't enough."

"What the hell are you talking about? Careful about what?"

"Your middle-of-the-night visits. You thought no one would see you go in and out of Moria's apartment that late. But one neighbor did."

"They're lying. Or maybe you're lying. I never visited Moria's apartment. Not at night nor at any other time. Never." Not a trace of his suaveness remained now. His voice was agitated, as were his movements. Seemingly oblivious of the full wineglass in his grip, he spoke with jerky shifts of his hands, and red liquid sloshed over the rim, spattering the floor, his shoes, and his trouser cuffs.

He stopped suddenly, his face coiled into a less handsome configuration than normal. A vein throbbed at his temple, like a tethered snake. He pointed a finger at me as though he wanted to stab it into my eye. "You told Baruch this. Why did you do this to me?"

"He hired me to learn more about Moria's life," I said, guessing Harpaz had already deduced that. "Reporting about your affair was my job."

"There was no affair," Harpaz screamed, and more wine flew from the glass.

The door burst open. The burly barkeep was on the threshold, a scowl on his face. "What the hell is going on here?" he asked.

Harpaz became aware of his glass, his wine-drenched hand and sleeve. He set the glass down, wiped his hand dry with a handkerchief. "Just a lively discussion among friends," he said. "Nothing to worry about."

The barkeep looked dubious. "Maybe keep it a notch less lively, what do you say?"

Harpaz and I both nodded.

When the barkeep left, Harpaz said to me, "I don't know where you got the stupid notion that I was sleeping with that cold bitch, but it never happened. Not even once."

"A neighbor saw you, I told you."

"They're either imagining it or lying, or they saw someone who looks like me. Because I never went to Moria's building. I never slept with her."

"Why was Moria a cold bitch?"

He hesitated, then figured he had little left to lose. "Just because it never happened doesn't mean I didn't try. I pursued her all right. Used all my regular tricks and... nothing. Total rejection."

"That makes her a cold bitch? That she didn't want you? Does every woman have to fall at your feet?"

I waited, but he didn't answer. His head was lowered, and he was shaking it slowly, like a lazy pendulum.

"Why did you want to sleep with her anyway?" I asked. "I've seen pictures. Moria wasn't nearly as pretty as that woman you were with tonight."

Harpaz raised his head. His face was set, his eyes hard and calculating. "How much?"

"How much what?"

"How much money do you want to call Baruch and tell him you made a mistake, that some other guy was sleeping with Moria, not me?"

"You want me to lie to my client?"

"A hundred liras? A hundred and fifty? And you won't be lying to him, I tell you, because I never slept with her."

"Sure you didn't. And you and Moria didn't fight a week before she died? It happened on the street where she lived. Or was the neighbor who saw you two also lying or imagining things?"

"No, that truly happened. At least you got that right."

"Moria yelled at you to stay away from her. Seems to me like she was ending your affair."

"There was no affair, I tell you. Why can't you get it through your thick head?"

"Then why warn you to stay away?"

Harpaz raked both hands through his hair, then leaned on the table, his back to me, head bent and shoulders hunched. He stayed that way for a full minute, muttering to himself words I failed to pick up.

Finally, he straightened and turned to face me. Red spots of anger marked his face. His hair was in disarray, and sweat glittered on his forehead.

"Baruch was being obstinate, the lousy cheapskate. You couldn't get a lira out of him. But then I heard that he'd made a large donation to Ariel Hospital. It wasn't like him at all. It didn't take long to learn why he'd done so: his daughter, Moria, worked there as a nurse. Then I learned that this was the second time Baruch had given the hospital money. He'd done it a few months before, too. I realized he had a soft spot for her. That she could make him part with his money."

That explained why Dr. Leitner hadn't fired Moria despite Dr. Shapira's complaints. Leitner was angling for a promotion, and his fundraising was key to that. Having Moria on staff made it easier for him to lobby her father for donations. That was why Leitner had telephoned Gafni to offer his condolences, and why he had prevailed upon me to not taint the pristine image of Moria he had painted for her father. He didn't care one bit about Gafni's feelings. He only wanted to keep the money spigot flowing.

"How do you know Moria was personally involved in getting these donations? Couldn't Gafni have donated simply because she worked there?" But even as I asked this question, I recalled something Gafni had told me during our first meeting. He said he and Moria had talked a couple of times on the phone and that he had been pushing for a face-to-face meeting. That was when he said he'd spent a lot of money. At the time, I didn't know what he was referring to, and later thought I'd learned the answer when Naomi Hecht told me about the expensive gifts Gafni had sent Moria. But that was small change, probably, in comparison to what he'd given the hospital, and he'd done so at his daughter's behest.

Acid churned in my stomach at the thought of how Harpaz had tried to manipulate Moria.

"So that's why you had the affair with her? To get her father to go into business with you?"

"You're not listening to me," he said, sounding peevish and surly. "I already told you, I tried getting her into bed, but no luck."

I didn't believe him, but a good interrogator lets a suspect talk. Maybe there'd be a nugget of truth in the river of lies.

"But you didn't give up on her."

"I offered her a percentage of the deal if it came through. A lot of money. More than she made in a year in her crummy job. She said no. I offered her more, but still she refused. She wasn't interested in money. Just like she wasn't interested in me."

He shrugged to share his bewilderment with me. He was puzzled as to why Moria wouldn't jump at having the two things he valued most in the world: money and himself.

"What did you do then?"

He hesitated, which made me even more curious to hear what he had to say. What could be more damaging to his prospects than what he'd already admitted to?

"I knew Moria and Baruch did not get along. That they barely spoke, hardly saw each other. Rumor was she hated his guts, wanted nothing to do with him, while he was desperate to fix that. I thought I'd take advantage of both those emotions."

"How?"

"I explained to Moria that I could arrange things so her father would lose his investment while I made it big. She could help. Help cause him serious pain."

"You were trying to involve her in a fraud scheme," I said.

His eyes flashed. "Don't look at me like I'm something that got stuck to your shoe. You think your client is a saint? You know how many backs he's stabbed, how many partners he's used and discarded? He deserves to be on the receiving end for once. And what I planned was totally legal. Dirty, maybe, but legal."

"What did Moria say?"

"She wouldn't go for it. I tried to persuade her several times, but she wouldn't budge."

"What happened that day when she screamed at you in the street?"

"That was the last time I saw her. I followed her home from the hospital, tried again to get her to help me with her father. When we got to her street, I said to her, 'Don't you want to get back at him for what he did to your mother?' That's when she exploded on me."

I could imagine the scene, this snake pouring poison in Moria's ear, dredging up her traumatic past for his own greed. It's a wonder she didn't slap him.

"You know Moria was the one who found her mother dead?" I asked.

"Yes." His tone was flat, as though he didn't see the point of my question.

"You had to know how difficult that was for her. Yet you still used it to try to get her to do your bidding."

"I thought she'd jump at it. Baruch pushed her mother to suicide, for God's sake. That's what everyone says. I was offering her a way to get some payback."

While making yourself rich in the process, I thought with disgust. Arye Harpaz didn't care about Moria, a traumatized young woman whom he'd planned on exploiting for his benefit. He didn't care how being reminded of her mother's death made her feel. Nor did he give a second's thought to what betraying her father would do to her. Arye Harpaz cared only for himself.

Harpaz guessed none of my thoughts. He was too busy blurting out more of his own. "They say he was seeing women on the side, the ugly, bald pig. Though who they were, I don't know." He looked at me with sudden interest. "Do you?"

"Do I what?"

"Know the names of the women Baruch had affairs with?"

"No, I don't."

"But you could find out, right? You're a detective. I'll pay you well."

"Why do you care who they are?" But the answer came to me before he could speak. "You think one of them will have information you can use to force Gafni to invest in your business."

He smiled. A devil's smile. Perfect white teeth. Made to fool people.

"I tried finding out myself back at the time, but couldn't. Maybe all the women were married and were keeping their mouths shut."

Or maybe he was going to prostitutes, I thought. The affairs were just a more socially palatable cover.

"Will you do it?" he asked. "Will you find out for me?"

"No."

"Why not?"

"Because I don't want to. It's not the sort of case I investigate."

He nodded a couple of times, muttering, "Fine, fine, all right." Then a cunning light shone in his eyes; he produced a fat wallet and counted out a hundred and fifty liras. "For you. To not tell Baruch anything we talked about tonight, and to tell him you were wrong about me and Moria being lovers."

I shook my head.

He sighed. "How much? You need to be reasonable."

"You don't have to pay me anything to say nothing about tonight."

"So take the money and just clear up what you already said about me and Moria."

"No. Because I don't believe you. You're a liar, Mr. Harpaz. You use people to further your own ends, and you don't care what it costs them. I think you did have an affair with Moria, and I'm not going to betray my client and lie for you, understand?"

He stared at me incredulously. "Five hundred liras. That's my last offer, Mr. Lapid."

It was a good one. The sort of money that could tide me over for a long while. But I wasn't tempted. Not when it came from him.

"It doesn't matter how much you offer me. The answer would still be no."

He grabbed my coat. "You can't do this to me. Not to me."

"You did it to yourself." I pushed him off me and turned for the door. I was done here.

The shattering of glass alerted me to what was coming. I ducked and whirled, and the jagged bottle end streaked over my head. If Harpaz had been smarter, he would have hit me with the full bottle. Then he might have caught me by surprise.

I punched him hard. Right on the nose. There was a satisfying crunch, and then he was on the floor, moaning incoherently, blood streaming over his face.

I stood over him, breathing hard. "There's more where that came from if you ever try something like that again."

The door to the room smashed against a wall. There was the barkeep again, knife in hand. Behind him was the solitary customer, brawny and glowering.

"What the hell?" the barkeep growled.

"Mr. Harpaz attacked me and got more than he bargained for. He could use a doctor," I said. "I'll be heading off."

"Like hell you will. He's a valued customer; you, I never met before today."

"I'm just a guy who defended himself and now wants to leave. So step aside. I don't want any more trouble."

"You gonna let him talk to you that way, Mendel?" the customer said, clearly drunk beyond good sense. "In your own place?"

Mendel glared. "You make trouble in my place, you damage my reputation. You need to pay for that."

"Or else?"

"Or Mendel will cut you up some, and I'll help," said the customer, flashing crooked teeth. "And we'll take what's coming to us from your wallet, like it or not."

I nodded slowly. My fingers ached from slugging Harpaz. My ribs were full of stabbing pain from putting my body behind the punch. This had to end quickly and without more violence.

I pulled out the gun. Pointed it straight at Mendel's face. "Drop the knife and kick it here."

His face turned white, and he complied. I stepped on the blade and turned the gun on the equally stunned customer.

"You got something to say?"

He shook his head and raised his hands. Decent of him to stick them up without my asking.

"Step inside. Both of you. Go sit on those chairs there."

They obeyed. They looked like misbehaved pupils awaiting their headmaster's ruler.

Harpaz, his mouth ringed by a beard of red, raised himself on his elbows and gave me a look of abject hatred. "I'll get you for this, Lapid. I'll get you."

"You'll have to get in line," I said, not bothering to point the gun at him. To the other two, I added, "I'm going to walk out now. I'll close this door behind me. Count to five hundred and only then come out. And if I ever see either of you two again..."

I pulled the trigger.

The bullet blasted a chunk of floor near their feet. They both jumped with a yelp. The report echoed around the small room, and the air stank of spent gunpowder and blood.

I walked backward until I passed through the door and then slammed it shut. I hurried out. I didn't think they'd come after me, but you can never know with fools and drunks.

36

It was raining with rage, and I was glad. The heavy downpour had probably muffled most of the report.

I'd neglected to bring an umbrella from Tel Aviv, but Harpaz had left his by the door to the bar, and I grabbed it on the way out.

I turned the first corner I got to, and then the next, moving quickly and putting many turns between myself and the bar. After ten minutes, certain I wasn't being chased, I slowed to consult street signs and get my bearings.

It was about midnight, and the number of people I saw out could be counted on the fingers of one hand.

I headed to Moria's apartment. As I walked, I thought about my talk with Arye Harpaz. He was a creep and a liar, but could he have been truthful about the affair? Maybe Moria's lover had been Dr. Shapira after all, as improbable as it seemed. He fit Lillian's description. If he had broken things off with Moria, that would only add to her motive for killing him.

Still, it was likely Harpaz. The guy was a rake, and he'd admitted to trying to seduce Moria. Good liars know that the best lies are rooted in truth, not made up of whole cloth. And Harpaz was an experienced prevaricator.

But why not simply admit it? After all, he'd confessed to trying to cheat Gafni out of money. Wasn't that bad enough? But maybe he sensed that I disliked Gafni and thought it would be easier to bribe me to look the other way if I believed the fraud scheme rather than his affair with a much younger, and now dead, Moria.

I got into Moria's apartment as I had the previous night. It was cold and dark, and a little water had got into my shoes, so I removed my socks and spread them out on the rim of the tub.

I figured I was in for better sleep than the night before. I'd committed violence today. The nightmares wouldn't come. I was in no danger of screaming. I wouldn't need the gag.

But I was restless rather than tired. I felt like pacing but didn't dare to. I wanted a cigarette but didn't fire one up. Instead, I stood in the middle of the dark living room, the remnants of Moria's life around me like ancient relics of a bygone civilization, feeling like an archaeologist trying to decipher a murky past.

With careful steps, I moved toward the window. I looked at the roiling sky blanketed with bloated black clouds. I watched the rain strafe the buildings across the street. I recalled harder rains in colder lands and shivered at the memory.

Then my eyes drifted downward, and I saw the man.

He was standing on the opposite sidewalk, a black shape with a black umbrella. Standing motionless in a bombardment of water. I strained my eyes, but his height and build were difficult to estimate. But he wasn't fat, nor very tall. A regular guy. But why would a regular guy be standing in the middle of Amos Street in the dead of night under heavy rain?

Fear scurried up my back like a swarm of spiders. Who was this man? Had he been following me? How come I hadn't noticed him before?

Was he one of the men from the bar? A cop? I didn't think he was Kulaski. I couldn't make out his face, but his shape didn't fit the inspector's.

The man was moving. Tiny shifts at this distance. Moving his head?

Then his umbrella tilted up a little, and I realized why.

He was looking up. He was scanning the windows of Moria's building. Searching for me?

I took a quick step backward, out of sight from street level. But it had taken me a split second to react. Had I been fast enough? Had he seen me?

I swore. I took out the gun. I looked at the closed door, at the accursed window with runnels of water running down its pane like prison bars. Up until that moment, I'd felt safe in Moria's apartment, unseen and unheard, but now that illusion was shattered.

What should I do? Go down and confront him? But doing so would make a lot of noise, and I wouldn't be able to come back to Moria's apartment. I chewed my lip for a minute and then, still undecided, chanced another peek at the street.

The man was gone. Where he had stood was nothing but rain bouncing off tarmac. The street was empty.

Had he gone to alert others to my presence? Was he about to telephone Kulaski and tell him I was back in town? Should I pack my bag and flee?

But where to? There were no busses this time of night. No taxis either. I'd already ruled out hotels, and I couldn't sleep on the street in this weather.

Besides, the man might be lying in ambush, waiting for me. I was safer here.

I swore again, checked the gun, added a fresh bullet to the magazine to replace the one I'd fired in the bar.

I could stay up all night, waiting in dread, but I needed my sleep. But if someone came while I was sleeping, I might not live to regret it.

Picking up a chair, I leaned it against the apartment door. It wouldn't stop someone from opening it, but it would fall if they did. The clatter would wake me. I'd be able to fight. It wasn't ideal, but it would have to do.

I lay in Moria's bed, listening to the rain. I stared up into darkness and thought of the man and almost laughed at myself. Did I really think I'd be able to sleep with him out there?

But then my eyes drifted shut, and I drifted off, and I didn't stir till morning light invaded the windows.

37

I woke up in a fright, my hand fumbling for the gun, which had slipped from my grasp in the night. I was alone, and the sun was bright and sparkling. The sky was free of clouds.

In the living room, I saw the chair still angled on the door. I looked out the window, and there was no man across the street gazing back at me, just the ordinary traffic of people heading to work and school.

But he might still be around. If he had indeed been following me, he wouldn't be standing in the open like that in daylight.

As yesterday, I ate breakfast from a can and waited until the Shukruns went out. Daniel came first, just about the same time as yesterday, but Lillian dawdled again. It was noon when she appeared, again with the stroller, but this time she didn't pause to look back at the building.

I hurried out, doing my best not to scour the street with my eyes. If the man hadn't seen me after all, I wanted him to think I didn't know about him. It would make it easier to spot him.

Turning west onto Tsfanya Street, I walked at a casual pace, veered south onto Yona, west onto Hagai, and south again to

Yekhezkel. I used each turn to get a quick look behind me. I saw plenty of people, men and women both, but no one who stood out.

I went into a café and ordered lunch. Five minutes later a man came in and did the same. I'd chosen a table at the rear; he opted for one by the window. He sat with his back to me, perusing a newspaper, and appeared to pay me no mind. I refrained from looking directly at him, fearing he could see me reflected in the window, but snatched sidelong glances at him from time to time.

I wasn't sure, but he looked familiar. Not a long familiarity, but of a more recent vintage. It took me a few minutes to put my finger on it.

Yesterday. The movie theater. The one I'd hidden in for three straight screenings.

He'd been there. Not during the first screening, I thought, but the second. I'd noticed him because he'd come alone, like me, which was unusual, but then I'd put him out of my mind when he took a seat a few rows ahead of me and proceeded to ignore my existence.

But maybe that had just been the impression he gave.

He was of average height and build, with black hair that was thinning on top. Clean-shaven, a high forehead, a wide space between his long nose and thin-lipped mouth. He wore a dark-blue jacket and black slacks, a flat cap he put on the table next to his plate.

Could he be the man I'd seen last night on Amos Street?

The answer was yes, but so could a big chunk of the male population of Jerusalem. I had to make sure.

I asked for my check, paid it, and left. I ambled south and a block later stopped to admire a suit in a display window. At the edge of my vision I caught sight of the man, bent low over his shoe, retying its laces.

Got you, I thought, but the sense of victory was mingled with fear.

I walked on, my back prickling, knowing I was being watched. I picked up my pace, taking my shadow on a trip south and east, finally coming to Hillel Street, where I entered the open expanse of Mamilla Cemetery.

This was a Muslim cemetery, by and large, where centuries of dead rested, but I'd heard that archaeologists had found graves here dating back to Byzantine times, and that a few Crusaders were interred here as well.

The cemetery was five acres of uneven ground and in a deplorable state. Many of the old tombstones were broken or dirty or sunk into the earth at odd angles. Trees of various types dotted the large area with no order or cultivation. Much of the ground was covered by wild grass, weeds, stubby bushes, and the occasional wild-flower. The rest was mud.

I walked along a narrow path that curved southeast. The man shadowing me had a problem now. This was open ground, with few places to hide, and there were no people about. If he followed me into the cemetery, he'd be easy to spot.

On the other hand, the cemetery was large and had numerous exits. If he gave up the tail, he'd have no clue where I went. I hoped he wouldn't let that happen.

I was taking a risk. The isolation afforded by the cemetery could backfire. Not only was this hallowed ground empty of living souls but me, the cemetery was ringed by a stone wall that shielded much of it from view of passersby on surrounding streets. It was the perfect spot for a crime without witnesses. A place fit for murder.

I passed a scattering of graves that might have been from the time of the Mamluk Sultanate, though I couldn't be sure. I couldn't read the faded Arabic inscriptions.

Walking on, now fifty meters into the cemetery, I stopped abruptly to light a cigarette. Behind me, I heard the faint scrape of a shoe as someone came to a sudden halt. The man had followed me in, but he was keeping his distance. Good news on both counts. He was still on my tail, but too far to fire a gun accurately. It made me feel a little safer.

I didn't turn, though my back was no longer prickling but itching like mad. I carried on, pulling on the cigarette as though I hadn't a care in the world. Soon I arrived at a spot I remembered from my previous visit to this cemetery shortly after the War of Independence. It was a Muslim mausoleum, squat and domed, dating from the thir-teenth or fourteenth century. The man buried there must have been important to merit such an edifice, and it had withstood the eroding claws of time better than any other graves I'd seen here.

The mausoleum had an entryway topped by an ornamental arch, and inside two shafts of light slashed the dimness from windows on the opposite wall. Instead of entering, I circled the structure to the far side. Here I stopped, taking care not to block either window, dropped my cigarette, and killed it under my shoe. The trail continued on, and for some distance the mausoleum blocked it from view of anyone coming on its other side. Like the man following me.

I could hear him now. Soft-footed but not silent, approaching at an unhurried but steady pace. I got ready, counted back from ten to one, and then completed the encirclement of the mausoleum, the gun pointed forward.

My timing was imperfect; I didn't come up behind him as I'd hoped. But it was good enough. The man was eight feet away. A little far for such a small gun, but close enough so he'd think twice about chancing it. The man froze, his jaw dropping, and I closed the distance, stopping five feet away, the gun aimed at the center of his homely face.

"Who the hell are you?" I said. "And why are you following me?"

38

"Following you?" the man said, his voice quavering. "I don't know what you mean, mister. I've never seen you before in my life. I was cutting through here to Agron Street. Don't shoot me. I got kids."

"You followed me here from a café on Yekhezkel Street," I said. "And yesterday, you came into a cinema after me. Boring movie, wasn't it?"

The man swallowed hard, making a clicking sound deep in his throat. "You've got me mixed up with someone else. I didn't watch any movie yesterday."

"And last night you were on Amos Street, right across from the building where I slept." I angled the gun downward. "Now, do I have to shoot you in the knee to get you to stop lying? You feel like hobbling on a cane for the rest of your life?"

The man went green, and his hands shook. His eyes darted in all directions.

"There's no one here," I said. "And this is a small gun. The sound won't carry far. I don't have much patience. Are you going to make me count to three?"

He exhaled loudly and shook his head. "That won't be necessary, Mr. Lapid."

I smiled. "You know my name, but I don't know yours."

"I'm Yigal Ruslander."

"Are you armed, Yigal?"

"No."

"Let's make sure, shall we? Very slowly, open your coat. Good. Now lift it up so I can see your waistband. Turn around and keep those hands still."

No gun.

I told him to dump the contents of his pockets, then ordered him to go sit on his hands in the entryway of the mausoleum so he'd have nowhere to run. Keeping the gun trained on him, I crouched and opened his wallet. I learned two things: he wasn't a cop, and he had given me his true name.

I closed the wallet without touching his money and left it on the ground.

"What do you do for a living, Yigal?"

"I'm a private detective. Just like you."

"How long have you been following me?"

"I was hired on January 10, but it took me a few days to find you, not until you were back in Tel Aviv. I understand you got hurt pretty badly."

I didn't like him knowing it. "I'm fine now, so don't try anything."

He permitted himself a small smile. Now that we were talking, the acuteness of his fear had waned, but he was still sitting on his hands, his posture distinctly nonthreatening. "Don't worry. I've no desire to get shot."

"Who hired you?"

"Dr. Yosef Leitner."

This surprised me, but any other answer would have done as well.

"Why would Dr. Leitner want me followed?"

Ruslander shrugged. "He didn't tell, and I didn't ask. I've learned it's better this way. I only want to know what I have to."

"He must have given you instructions."

"To tail you. To report where you go, who you meet. He wanted daily reports."

"You did all this yourself? For nearly three weeks?" It was January 29.

"I hired a guy to help out. One of the most boring jobs I've ever done, let me tell you. For a week, I sat for twelve hours a day in a car on Hamaccabi Street, waiting for you to show your face. But you stayed in your apartment all that time. The old lady from the café took care of you, didn't she?"

That made me angry, him knowing about Greta, though I had no logical reason why that was.

"What did you tell Leitner?" I asked, not showing my feelings. For Ruslander did not deserve my anger. He was just doing a job, like I would have done in his place. If I should have been furious with anyone, it was Dr. Leitner.

"Everything. That you got assaulted and were in the hospital in Jerusalem for a couple of days, but then left for Tel Aviv. That you didn't come out for a week. After three days with nothing to report, I was sure he'd tell me to pack it up—two guys on the job, it was costing him plenty—but he told me to stay on it. I don't know what you did to him, but he's mighty irritated with you."

I didn't know what I'd done to Dr. Leitner either. I'd been harsh and brusque during our talk; I'd used a tone he was probably unaccustomed to. But that wouldn't explain him paying a private detective to follow me around.

"What else did you tell him?"

"Can I get off my hands?" Ruslander asked. "They're getting numb. I won't try anything, I swear."

I believed him. I could tell he wasn't too fond of Dr. Leitner. He wasn't going to risk a bullet for his sake.

"All right. Want a cigarette?"

He nodded, and I got his cigarettes and lighter from the ground and tossed them to him.

"Thanks," he said, lighting up. "After a week, you finally went out. Your face looked like crap. I can only imagine how you were a week before. I followed you to a factory downtown. I later learned it's owned by Baruch Gafni. That was interesting."

"Interesting how?"

He took a drag, blew out a long stream of smoke, and watched it curl up and dissipate. "I don't suppose you'd like to share what you're doing in Jerusalem."

"You're right. I wouldn't."

"But you're working for Baruch Gafni?"

"Let's be clear about something, Yigal: I'm the one getting information out of you, not the other way around."

He raised a hand, palm out. "Fine, fine. Don't get upset. I'm just curious, that's all."

"You still haven't told me why my meeting with Baruch Gafni is interesting."

He gave me a crooked smile. "Would it be worth a little something for you to know, you think?"

I broke out laughing. I was beginning to like Yigal Ruslander. "It's worth not taking a bullet to you."

"No harm in trying, right?" he said, laughing as well. Another drag, and he got serious. "The reason it's interesting is that it wasn't the first time I encountered the surname Gafni. And recently."

I felt a chill, and it wasn't because of the weather. "Is that so?"

"Yeah. But the first name wasn't Baruch. I'm betting you can guess what it was since you spent the past two nights in her apartment. Though without turning on a single light. Why not, by the way?"

I ignored his question. "How did you hear about Moria Gafni?"

"Same way I heard about you."

"Dr. Leitner?"

"One and the same."

"He hired you to investigate Moria?"

"To follow her. Learn everything about her."

"Why?"

"He didn't say, and I didn't ask. I prefer—"

"You prefer not knowing, yes, you told me that already," I said, my brain roiling with this unforeseen development. "But you must have an idea."

"Oh, it hurts my soul to admit it, but not an inkling," he said, pressing both hands to his heart, adopting an absurdly mournful expression.

I laughed. "You greedy devil. All right, there'll be a little something in it for you. Now talk, damn you."

"Leitner was looking for dirt on young Miss Gafni."

"Why?"

"Why does anyone look for dirt on anyone?"

To hold it over their head, I thought.

"What did he want from her?"

"That I don't know. And before you ask, I got no ideas, either."

"Did you find any dirt?"

"I sure did." He proceeded to tell me what it was, and much of what I thought I knew was shredded and burned to ashes.

"I don't know what Leitner did with the information," Ruslander said.

"That's all right," I told him. "I think I do."

39

On the way out of Mamilla Cemetery, walking together now, I asked him how he came to be a private detective.

"Used to be a cop," Ruslander said. "Right here in Jerusalem. Two and a half years ago, I got kicked off the force."

"Why?"

"The official reason was that I took bribes. Which is true. Most cops I know did the same, and some took far more than I did, and from worse people. And some of those cops not only stayed on the force but got promoted. Real reason I got fired was because there was an officer who had it in for me for personal reasons. A son of a bitch called Kulaski."

I stopped in mid-step. Ruslander continued a couple more before noticing and turning.

"What?" he asked.

We were close to the exit. On our right were a couple of old headstones that the wet earth was in the process of swallowing. I could smell the mud, rich and drenched, the old, decaying stones. I could feel Kulaski's punch slamming into my ribs.

"Nothing," I said and resumed walking. "What personal reasons?"

"It's because of my kid brother. He was in the Irgun. Once Kulaski heard about him, I was done for. He hates everyone connected to the Irgun or Herut."

I remembered Kulaski asking me if I were a member of Herut, how he relished telling me the party might get outlawed.

"He has cause," Ruslander went on. "The Irgun planted a bomb under the car of a British official. Someone messed up, and it went off at the wrong time. Kulaski's sister happened to be walking by. Two days later, she died from her wounds in the hospital."

"Dear God," I said.

"My brother had nothing to do with that botched operation, but it made no difference to Kulaski. He started hounding me. Tried to have me prosecuted for being on the take. Threatened to lock me up for years. But eventually, all that happened was that I got fired and lost my pension. Could have been worse, I suppose."

We stopped at the exit to Hillel Street. I fished out my wallet and gave him a five-lira note. He pocketed it without meeting my eyes and stood scuffing the tip of his shoe back and forth on the ground. "What I told Leitner, you think that had something to do with that girl killing herself?"

"I don't know."

He scrubbed a hand over his mouth. "I hate to think that it did."

"Try not thinking about it, then."

He chuckled without humor. "I guess that's the best advice anyone could give me on the subject, isn't it?"

I had nothing to say to that. "I assume Dr. Leitner knows I'm back in town?"

"Afraid so. I hope it won't cause you any trouble."

"And I hope he paid you in advance."

Ruslander laughed. "Oh, he did, don't you worry. Told me I was doing a terrific job. But I don't suppose I'll be using him as a reference anytime soon."

"I don't suppose so, no."

"That's all right. I'll make do somehow." He eyed me speculatively. "You know, apart from Leitner being angry with you, I also got the feeling you scared him."

"Good," I said. "I hope he's terrified."

I asked Ruslander a couple more questions, including where Dr. Leitner lived and what his home telephone number was. Then we shook hands, and he walked off. I stood for a while, smoking and thinking, rage boiling in my gut and questions swirling in my head. What Ruslander had discovered following Moria changed a lot, but I wasn't sure the extent of it. Even worse, I had no idea how to get to the truth.

What he'd revealed about Kulaski explained a lot about the inspector's obsession with me. By taking part in a Herut demonstration, and injuring cops in the process, I'd become a symbol of what he hated most. I was now surer than ever that Kulaski wasn't going to let my punishment be limited to a beating. His sister's death called for a harsher vengeance, and in his warped mind I was responsible for it.

I cast my gaze around Hillel Street, saw a pair of officers walking toward me. My instinct screamed at me to bolt, but luckily, my brain saved me. The two cops weren't there for me. They weren't even looking at me. One of them was telling the other a story, and it must have been funny because the listener burst into uproarious laughter. I crossed the street to avoid them, and they walked on without incident.

But seeing them still rattled me. I checked my watch. Two in the afternoon. Too early for what I planned next. I needed a place to hide for a few hours.

Arnon Cinema proved my refuge. I watched Judy Holliday fall in love with William Holden in *Born Yesterday* and pondered the unpredictable, strange nature of love.

It was five when I ventured out of the cinema and into twilight. I had coffee and a sandwich at a small place on a side street, and at six o'clock I rang Leitner's number.

His smug voice came over the line, and I hung up.

I took a bus south to Rehavia, one of Jerusalem's more affluent neighborhoods, where the streets were clean, the buildings sturdy and neat, and the passersby dressed in clothes that were still in fashion. There were more private cars around, too.

On Azza street, I entered a three-story building and climbed to the second floor. A sign affixed to the door confirmed that I'd arrived at the residence of Dr. Yosef Leitner. I knocked and waited, simmering over what Ruslander had told me, telling myself to keep calm. For now, at least.

Dr. Leitner answered the door. He was in dark slacks, a white shirt, and a tie tucked into a vest, like a businessman at the office. But incongruously, his feet were in slippers. They were blue and looked warm and soft. He eyed me with those hard pebble eyes, and his lips were pressed into a bloodless, gray line.

"Hello, Doctor," I said.

"Mr. Lapid, to what do I owe this pleasure?"

"I have a few more questions to ask you, if you don't mind."

"Of course not, but I'd much prefer if we met at the hospital. Why not come over first thing tomorrow morning?"

"I wish it could wait, Doctor, but the matter is of some urgency. I'd appreciate it greatly if you could spare a few minutes now. My client would too."

The reference to Gafni proved irresistible, as I hoped it would. Leitner wanted to remain on good terms with my client in the hope of extracting more donations from him.

"All right, Mr. Lapid. But I don't have much time. Dinner will soon be ready."

"This won't take long," I said, and with a twist of the mouth, he gestured me inside.

The living room was spacious and well-appointed. A piano stood against one wall. A few expensive glass lamps were arranged about the room. On the large dining table, a couple of bouquets of radiant flowers soaked in vases, and next to them stood a bottle of wine with a bow around its neck.

"What's the occasion?" I asked.

Leitner puffed his scrawny chest. "They're for me. It was announced this morning that I will be the next head physician of Ariel Hospital."

"Congratulations. When do you assume your new post?"

"In three months."

Atop the piano stood photos of Dr. Leitner alongside a plump, gray-haired woman and a boy of Bar Mitzvah age who not only bore a striking resemblance to his father, but also appeared to share his imperious stare.

"I'm sure your family is proud of you," I said.

A door to my right swung open, letting in the enticing scent of vegetable stew. In the doorway, wearing a red apron and an expression of surprise, stood the woman from the photos. Mrs. Leitner.

"Oh." She moved her gaze from me to Leitner. Her demeanor and tone seemed more appropriate to a housekeeper than a wife. "I didn't know you were expecting company, Yosef. Will your guest be staying for dinner?"

Leitner shook his head. "No, Ada. Mr. Lapid will only be here for a few minutes." And to me: "Mr. Lapid, let's continue our conversation in my study."

I nodded at Mrs. Leitner and followed her husband to a small room at the far end of the apartment. Leitner shut the door after us.

The study housed two chairs, a desk, and shelves crowded with books. A glass ashtray heaped with dead cigarettes stood next to a used tulip glass and a fat bottle of what appeared to be expensive cognac. The windows were shut. The sweet, woody aroma of the beverage mingled unpleasantly with that of the cigarettes, each unable to escape the other. There were no pictures of his family.

Leitner looked discomfited by my seeing the cognac. He waved a begrudging hand at the bottle. "Would you care for some?"

"No. Nothing for me."

"As you please," Leitner said, looking relieved as he lowered himself into his chair. "Now, what would you like to ask me?"

I sat in the chair before his desk but didn't speak, just riveted my eyes to his, keeping my face impassive.

Leitner shifted in his seat. "Well? Aren't you going to say something?"

I remained silent. I could see it was getting to him. Leitner wet his lips. He drew out a cigarette and soon had it burning. After a bracing drag, he said, "Listen, I don't know what game—"

I cut him off. "I met a friend of yours today."

Leitner blinked. "Oh? And who might that be?"

"A fellow by the name of Ruslander. Remember him?"

Leitner had just pulled on his cigarette. Shocked by my revelation, he choked on the smoke. He started coughing, face turning red, eyes tearing. I made no move to help him.

"Yeah, I can tell that you do. He sends his apologies, by the way; he won't be reporting on my movements any longer."

Leitner coughed one last time, then hissed out a curse. "That incompetent fool. What did he tell you?"

"A whole bunch of interesting things. He and I had a nice long chat. One of the things he told me is that you hired him. He didn't know why."

"It was for the sake of the hospital," Leitner said quickly, grabbing hold of the first lie that flitted across his mind. "I was worried your investigation might cast the hospital in a bad light. I wanted to be forewarned of any adverse development."

"The hospital is very important to you, isn't it, Doctor?"

"It's my life," Leitner stated simply, and I wondered where that absolute viewpoint put his wife and son.

"And it's very important for you to be head physician."

"Yes, and for the same reason. I can do the best job for the hospital. For its reputation, its status in Israel and around the world." He was livening up, getting into it. I could tell this was something he fervently believed in, his indispensable role in making that vision come true. But mostly, it was about himself, as Dr. Aboulker had told me.

"You forgot the patients," I said.

"Huh?"

"You mentioned status and reputation, but you didn't mention the patients. Aren't they the most important?"

Leitner cleared his throat, smoothed the front of his vest. "Of course they are. All I do is in order to be able to provide better care to our patients. Anything that harms the hospital harms our patients, which was why I thought it prudent to have you watched, just to be on the safe side."

"It's a nice story. Admirable if true. But it's not, is it?"

Leitner pushed himself straight. "I'm not sure what you mean, Mr. Lapid."

"I mean that you didn't have me followed out of worry for the hospital, but for yourself. Ruslander told me I wasn't the first person you had him follow. That a few months ago, you put him on Moria Gafni."

It had been more than a minute since Leitner had last attended to his cigarette. During that time it had built up a long column of ash that now collapsed onto the desk. Leitner swore, quickly stubbed out the offending remnant, and brushed the ash off the desk into the ashtray.

In no time, he had a new cigarette burning and was sucking on it nervously. The large pile of stubs in his ashtray told me he'd been on edge even before I knocked on his door. Probably because Ruslander had told him I was back in Jerusalem, sniffing about.

"As you can see, Doctor, I know everything. So why not do me a favor and quit lying, okay?"

Leitner flashed me a baleful look. "What is it you want, Mr. Lapid?"

"I want you to tell me everything. Omit nothing."

"What for, if you already know it all?"

"I want to hear you say it. I want to understand."

"Okay. If you must."

"Why did you have Moria Gafni followed?"

"To find out what I could about her."

"What sort of thing did you hope to find?"

"Something sordid, dirty, or criminal. Something secret and shameful."

"What for?"

"So I could get her to do what I want."

"Which was?"

"Get her father to donate money to the hospital. Which she should have done herself if she cared about the place as much as I do. Her father is very rich, but when I approached him myself, he refused to give a lira. But then I discovered that Moria was his one and only child, so I asked her to change his mind. But she refused to try. She said she had no contact with her father. I explained to her how important money was for the hospital, but she persisted in her refusal."

"It made you angry, didn't it?"

"Of course it did," Leitner said, his face a contortion of old fury. He drew on his cigarette and pointed its fiery tip at me. "I was her boss. She should have done as I asked. It wasn't much. All she had to do was talk with her father, for heaven's sake."

"Do you know why Moria wouldn't talk to him?"

"I don't care why. This was about something bigger than her little feelings."

"The hospital?"

"That's right."

"And your position in it?"

"Yes." It came out almost as a shout, fire in his eyes and a forked blood vessel throbbing in his forehead. He wasn't embarrassed by his selfish admission. In his view, it was a statement of obvious and justified fact. "I'm vital to the hospital. Without me, it will fall into decay and ruin. I put my heart and soul into it. I deserve to run it."

"But you need to bring in money for that. Donations. The more the better."

"That's right," he said, tapping ash off his cigarette. "And Baruch Gafni has plenty, and his daughter works at the hospital, so he's the perfect mark."

"Mark? You sound like a con man."

Leitner sat back, brushing off my comment. "A slip of the tongue, nothing more. I value all our generous contributors."

"I'm sure you do. So you put Ruslander on Moria. What did he find?"

"You know what."

"I want you to say it."

Leitner shrugged. A man appeasing the immature wishes of a foolish child.

"For a while, he found nothing. Moria led a boring life, it seemed. But then, one time late at night, he saw a figure entering her building. A moment later, he saw two shadows behind Moria's curtains. He could tell they were kissing.

"At first, Ruslander couldn't tell who the visitor was; he hadn't gotten a look at his face. So he waited, and three hours later, the visitor left. Only it wasn't a man at all. It was a woman."

Yes, I thought with a stab of disappointment. And I had missed it entirely. For just like Ruslander, and Lillian Shukrun too, I'd assumed it was a man. And Lillian's description supported that.

But I had met one woman who fit that obscure description as well. She was tall and slender. She had short dark hair that at night in a dim staircase could be mistaken for a man's. And she also had a deep voice. Hearing that voice behind a closed door from one floor down, it wasn't surprising Lillian thought she was hearing a man speaking with Moria, especially since it fit her preconceptions.

This woman had a key to Moria's apartment. She had lied to protect her. And I had jumped to the wrong conclusions. I had been foolish and blind. I had also been cruel and quick to cast blame.

"Naomi Hecht," Leitner said, mashing out his smoke. "She was the woman Ruslander saw. She and Moria Gafni were sleeping together. Two nurses on my ward."

Leitner's mouth warped in revulsion, and anger glinted in his eyes. It seemed that, in his mind, a double sin had been committed here. Not only were two women engaged in unnatural sexual relations, but both had worked for him. Their conduct reflected on him, and that was something he couldn't abide.

"What did you do with this information?" I asked.

"Nothing at first. I couldn't use what Ruslander saw unless I had tangible proof, and that was difficult to come by. Those two bitches were careful not to show their depravity in public. They only engaged in their disgusting acts in Moria's apartment in the dead of night behind drawn curtains. But I didn't despair. I told Ruslander to keep at it. An opportunity would come."

Leitner paused and poured himself a large dose of cognac. He threw it down and sighed in contentment.

"And it did. Moria and Naomi got careless. They were in a public garden, hidden by trees, or so they thought. But Ruslander was ready with a camera. He snapped a few good shots of them kissing. That was what I needed to get Moria to do her duty."

"To you or the hospital?"

"I am the hospital, Mr. Lapid," Leitner said firmly. Gone was his earlier anxiety. Before, he'd been afraid that I would learn something I shouldn't. Now he knew that wasn't going to happen because I already knew everything. He was free to show his true colors, to gloat over the success of his wicked scheme.

Leitner said, "Moria was stunned when I showed her the pictures, but she still refused to talk to her father about giving money to the hospital. I think she might have held firm were it not for Naomi. When I explained to Moria how publicizing those pictures would ruin her lover, her resistance crumbled. Soon after that, the hospital received a handsome donation from Mr. Gafni."

"But that wasn't the end of it, was it?" I said. "You wanted more."

"The hospital needed more. It always needs more. So I called Moria into my office and told her she had to speak with her father again. I also announced that Naomi Hecht would become the next head nurse."

"I understand she's very good at her job."

"She's not bad, but she's annoying. She has a big mouth. She constantly oversteps her mark."

"Then why make her head nurse?"

Leitner's smile was cold enough to keep meat fresh. "To add a carrot to the stick. So Moria would know that disobeying me would mean not just exposure of her lover, but also stripping her of a coveted position."

"And it worked."

"Like a charm. Mr. Gafni made another sizable donation."

"And you got the credit."

"Credit where credit's due, Mr. Lapid, or haven't you heard a word I said?"

I watched his face. He showed no hint of regret or embarrassment. He was proud of his actions. He viewed them as just. They were a means to an end, whoever got stomped along the way be damned. Moria and Naomi Hecht were less than nothing. Partly because they were troublesome women—one didn't do as she was told; the other didn't know her place—but mostly because of their affair. Leitner's morality was so twisted that he considered their romantic involvement as worse than his blackmail.

"What happened then?"

Leitner poured himself another glass. Again he downed it in one swallow. The alcohol tinged his pale cheeks pink. His expression was sour. "I wanted another donation. Moria went to talk to her father. I assumed everything would go smoothly, just like before, but Gafni threw a wrench in the works. Moria burst into my office and told me she couldn't go through with it."

"What did he want?"

"To meet her face-to-face. He was open to giving more money, but she had to meet with him. I couldn't see what the problem was."

"Did you bother asking?"

Leitner looked perplexed by the question, which was an answer in and of itself.

"How did Moria seem that day?"

"Emotional, distraught. You know how women can get over the most trifling things. She started bawling, told me she couldn't meet with her father, begged me not to force her."

"But you did," I said, my fists clenching atop my thighs. I wanted to grab him by his tie and smash his prim, smug face into his desk.

Leitner nodded. If he noticed my fury, it didn't affect him. "I wanted that donation. I needed it. The decision on the next head physician was approaching. So I told Moria to dry her eyes and obey or else."

"That was about three weeks before her death, wasn't it?"

"I think that's about right, yes."

"And she left your office in tears?"

"I offered her my handkerchief, but she wouldn't take it," Leitner said with a slight shake of his head, sharing his bewilderment at the illogical nature of women.

I could imagine the scene. Moria caught between Leitner's rock and her father's hard place. Forced to pick one of two unbearable options. Either her own well-being or that of her lover, Naomi Hecht. No wonder she had cried.

"Did Dr. Shapira really complain about her, or was that something you invented on the spot?" I asked.

"It happened. More than once. Most of what I told you was true, only it didn't happen on that day."

Like all good liars, Dr. Leitner had based his prevarications in truth. And I had believed him.

"Dr. Shapira got quite angry with Moria a few times," Leitner said. "And I did rebuke her for undermining his authority with patients."

Which meant that Moria did have motive to kill Dr. Shapira. That hadn't changed. Nor had the fact that she'd had the probable murder weapon in her possession. She was still a murderer, but that didn't change what Leitner had put her through.

"Moria didn't meet with her father, did she?" I said.

Leitner contorted his face. "She kept putting it off. I inquired about it, and she always had an excuse. Either she didn't feel well, or her father was away on a business trip, or his schedule was packed, and so on. Finally, my patience ran out, and I told her she had one week to do it. No more excuses."

"When was this?"

Leitner picked up the cognac bottle and poured himself another glass. "A few days before she killed herself." And he took a drink.

I stared at him. He drank again, oblivious to my right hand, which had slid into my pocket and closed around the grip of Moria's pistol. This was why she had kept the gun, I thought. To one day kill this filthy blackmailer, this selfish fiend. It would have been a justified killing. One I could do in her place, right here and now.

"Have you ever considered the possibility that she killed herself because of you?" I asked. "Because you demanded too much of her?"

Leitner's eyes bulged. "Too much? What was too much? To meet with her father?"

"You don't know anything about what he did to her. Why she wouldn't see him."

"I don't care why," Leitner exploded. "You think my father was easy? He was the rottenest bastard who ever lived. But if I had to see him to get something done, I would've done so without feeling sorry for myself. Moria was just a spoiled girl. A whiny brat, and depraved to boot. She didn't kill herself because of me. She killed herself because she was weak and pathetic and not right in the head."

I was on my feet without realizing it. My hand outstretched with the gun pointed at his head. Leitner reared back as far as his chair allowed, his mouth gaping.

For a long moment, neither of us moved nor spoke. Then Leitner said, "Careful with that gun, Mr. Lapid."

"Where are those pictures? And the negatives too. Give them to me now."

"And if I won't?"

"Then I use this," I said, moving the gun a little closer to him.

"You're going to shoot me with my wife in the apartment? I don't think so. Not unless you plan to kill her too, and she has nothing to do with any of this." He smiled, reading the answer on my face. "No. You don't have it in you."

I lowered the gun, the blood rushing past my ears like water from a busted dam. "I'll tell Gafni what you did to Moria. He'll make sure you lose your appointment."

"He wouldn't dare. If he interferes, I'll spread those pictures far and wide. Everyone will know what sort of woman his daughter was. It will be embarrassing for him, not to mention what it will do to her name."

"He'll go to the police. You'll be arrested for blackmail."

He laughed. "There's no proof of that. Moria is dead, and I don't think she told anyone about our arrangement. Surely not her big-mouthed lover, or I would have heard about it by now. You know, but I can always say that you're lying. I'll never be charged with anything."

He was right. The police couldn't touch him. And I suspected Gafni would choose to protect his name, and Moria's, and wouldn't take any action against him.

"He might send someone to kill you," I said. "Or I'll do it. You won't be able to hide behind your wife forever."

Leitner didn't so much as flinch from the threat. "If I die, those pictures go public. I've set it all up, Mr. Lapid. I'm no fool."

I racked my brain, trying to produce another threat or argument, but I came up empty.

Leitner smiled again, a pink patch of tongue showing between his teeth. "You can do nothing to me, and neither can your client. I'm untouchable. Inviolate. I'd have preferred to remain on Mr. Gafni's good side—I hoped he'd be open to make further donations to commemorate his daughter, but now your meddling has killed that prospect—but since I already got the appointment, it's not so important."

"Where are those pictures?" I asked him, grinding my teeth in defeat and frustration. "Where are they?" I shouted.

"In a safe place, where you can never find them."

"I'll tear this whole room apart if you don't tell me."

"Then my wife will call the police, and I'll see to it that you go away for a long time. Mr. Gafni isn't the only man who knows people. Besides, the pictures aren't here."

I was breathing hard, my face hot. "There are things I can do to make you talk. I don't have to kill you."

Leitner sneered. "You're not the only one who can make threats, Mr. Lapid, and I'm in a better position than you to follow through on them. Nothing bad will happen to anyone I care about if something bad happens to you. But you care about Moria, don't you?" He leaned forward, examining my face with glittering eyes, and huffed out a laugh. "You do, I can see it. And maybe even about Naomi. Though, heaven help me, I cannot see why. The first was a depraved woman, the second that and worse because she also betrayed her husband. I thought of firing her for a long time, but I ended up doing it because of you. You sticking your nose where it didn't belong and making trouble. It felt good to finally be rid of her."

Before I knew it, my hand was up, the gun pointing again at Leitner's head, my finger putting pressure on the trigger. If he hadn't raised his hands, if he hadn't looked so scared, I think I would have shot him; I was mindless with rage. He must have seen it on my face. He must have known he was a heartbeat from death.

"Listen to me," I said, my voice low and vibrating, as I sought to control my fury. "I'm giving you until tomorrow at noon to hand over those pictures and negatives. I'll be waiting for you at Zion Square, just outside the cinema. If you don't show up, I'll be back. You got that?"

His hands were still up, his face colorless and static. It took him a long moment to answer, but he finally said, "Yes. Yes, I understand."

"Good." I pocketed the gun. "I'll bid you good night, then. Enjoy your stew."

40

I went over to Naomi Hecht's place, but she didn't answer her door. Maybe she was working. But no, I'd forgotten: Naomi Hecht was currently unemployed. That left her husband. She must have been with him.

In Studio Cinema, I watched Bette Davis and Robert Montgomery in *June Bride* but couldn't keep track of the plot. My mind kept bouncing about, flashing pictures that overrode those on the screen. Arye Harpaz with blood on his face. Naomi Hecht crying and then ordering me out of her apartment. The photos of Dr. Shapira dead in the street. Leitner with his hands up as he saw death in my eyes.

Mostly I thought about Leitner. The evil bastard was right. He had the upper hand. I couldn't touch him, and I didn't think Gafni could either. Not while Leitner had those pictures. And I couldn't make him give them to me. My threat at the end of our meeting was as hollow as Leitner's conscience. My only hope, and it was as flimsy as old paper, was that I'd put enough fear into him that he'd fold. Maybe I had looked crazy enough. I'd have my answer the next day at noon.

After the movie, I had a small dinner, then wandered about until midnight before heading back to Amos Street for the night.

It had rained while I was in the cinema, and the pavement glistened, reflecting the moonlight. The wind was faint like a caress, but its fingers were cold, making me shiver. The street was empty and quiet. Shadows clung to walls like murky nets waiting for an unsuspecting prey. The windows around me were dark like the empty eye sockets of a skull.

In the lobby of Moria's building, I removed my shoes as I'd done on the previous two nights, then began the ascent to Moria's apartment. The building was silent around me, the coldness of the floor penetrating through my socks.

The moon was almost full, the sky clear of clouds, so just like the previous night, light splashed onto the second-floor landing through the aperture in the outside wall. Just as I was passing through it toward the next staircase, a faint creak came from behind me, followed by a single hushed utterance: "Psst."

I froze, my heart leaping to my throat, then turned to look behind me.

Standing in her quarter-opened doorway, just her face and the left side of her body visible, was Lillian Shukrun. She motioned me toward her with urgent movements of her hand.

It took me a second to respond, so shocked was I at being spotted. I had been so careful. I hadn't made a sound. How on earth did she know I was there?

As I approached, she opened the door wider to let me inside her apartment, then closed it silently the second I was in. The interior was dim, illuminated by moonlight and the faint glow of a streetlamp a little further up the street. The stove wasn't burning, so it was cold. The room smelled of milk, detergent, and the faint tang of urine-filled diapers. As on my previous visit, washed diapers hung on a line in the living room, alongside various articles of clothing. Lillian was in a misshapen gray robe, and her hair was in disarray. She pressed a finger to her lips, then held up a stopping hand while she peered out of her peephole at the landing I'd just vacated.

Turning, she whispered: "The baby is asleep. We need to keep quiet."

"Where's your husband?" I asked, matching her volume, wondering what was going on and starting to get a bit worried too. Lillian looked distraught, perhaps even scared.

"He's working tonight. He won't be back until morning. I hate being alone at night, I just hate it, but he has to work." Her eyes jerked about, going to the closed door, then up to the ceiling, then back to me. Her brow creased. "Why are you holding your shoes?"

I glanced down at the shoes clasped in my hand and blurted the first thing that came to mind, "I stepped in a puddle, and water got in them. I don't like walking around in wet shoes."

She nodded, too agitated to give my answer much consideration or she probably would have seen through my lie. "Were you going to Moria's apartment?"

"Yes." Then, feeling that the hour demanded an explanation, I added, "I know it's late, but something came up in the investigation that I had to check right away."

Again she nodded. Her eyes went to the ceiling again and stayed there. "It's a good thing I was awake, then."

"Why is that?"

"Because someone's up there."

"What?"

"Someone's in Moria's apartment. I was nursing the baby, and I heard footsteps."

I gazed up. The ceiling was a grayish plain with patches of shadow and darkness eating away at the corners. There was no sound of movement from above. Nothing at all. I looked at Lillian. She was worn out. The baby must have been keeping her up at all hours. Could she have imagined it? Mistaken one sound for another? Maybe it was something carried over from a dream that the baby had interrupted. "Are you sure?" I asked.

"Absolutely." She grabbed my arm tightly. "I heard it as plainly as I hear you now."

Her certainty was compelling. My scalp began tingling. I'd been foolish to return here. Moria's apartment was no longer safe since there were people who knew I had slept there. Ruslander was one; Dr. Leitner another. "When did you hear the footsteps?"

"At first, about a half hour ago, after I finally got the baby calmed down and was putting her in her crib. They continued for a short while and then stopped."

"So maybe whoever was up there has already left."

She shook her head. "They haven't, or I would have heard them and seen them, too. After the footsteps had stopped entirely, I stood by the door, looking out. I wanted to see who it was when they came down so I could tell my husband, and the police if need be. That's how I saw you."

So it wasn't a burglar. Because a burglar would have made more noise searching Moria's apartment. They wouldn't have sat still in the dark.

I felt like giving Lillian a big hug and a wet kiss on both cheeks. I also had half a mind to wake up the neighbor who'd maligned Lillian for her nosiness and tell her she should not think ill of her watchful neighbor. I didn't know who was up in Moria's apartment, but I was dead sure they meant me serious harm. Lillian's keen senses and watchful nature had saved me from walking into an ambush.

Could it be Leitner himself? It was possible, but he didn't seem the sort who would dirty his hands with blood. But maybe he had hired someone and told him to expect me here after midnight, the time I'd crept into Moria's apartment on both previous nights.

Or maybe it was Kulaski, though I didn't see how he'd know of my stay here.

"Is there just one person up there or more?" I asked. "Could you tell?"

"Just one, I think," Lillian said. "Judging by the footsteps, I'm pretty sure."

That was good news. But not good enough to get me to go up there, where someone might have a gun trained on the door, ready to shoot me once I stepped inside. Still, facing a single opponent was better than having to deal with a bunch of them.

But that was something for later. For now, I had to be patient and cautious. I needed to know who was up there before I decided what further steps to take.

"Thank you, Lillian," I said. "I'll take care of this. You should head back to bed now."

"I don't think I could sleep while he's up there," she said, hugging herself.

"You need your rest. Your daughter may wake up again at any time. She'll need you."

Lillian mulled this over. She glanced at her door, and I knew her natural curiosity was pulling her toward the peephole.

"I'll be heading out now," I told her, "but I'll be waiting for him when he comes down. I'll come back and tell you who it was."

She looked at me, her tired eyes searching my face. "You'll do that?"

I almost laughed. Her need to know was so powerful, she might stay up all night to satiate it, but I wanted her prying eyes closed in slumber. "I promise."

She sighed, massaged her forehead, giving in to her physical need for rest. "All right. Thank God you're here. I can barely keep my eyes open."

I patted her shoulder. "I'll be heading out. Lock the door after me and go to sleep. Tomorrow, I'll come back and tell you everything."

I stood on the landing until I heard the snick of the lock turning. I glanced up at the dark staircase leading up to the third floor, where my unknown adversary lurked, but I headed in the opposite direction. Letting the enemy choose the battlefield is usually a deadly mistake. I was going to be the one doing the choosing.

Out of the building, I clung to the shadows on that side of the street, hoping whoever was in Moria's apartment hadn't seen me through the window when I had gone in, and that he couldn't see me now. My plan hinged on it.

I stopped three buildings up the street, and there I waited. The temperature had dropped, and the wind had strengthened. My breath came out as whitish vapor, and I was shivering despite my coat. A cigarette would've warmed me up nicely, but the glow would have given me away. At least it didn't rain.

I had no idea how long I'd need to wait, but I didn't think it would be hours. Soon, the person in Moria's apartment would conclude I wasn't coming that night and leave. With how cold the apartment got, they must have been freezing like I was. The thought made me grin.

The minutes trailed by. I kept my eyes on the doorway of Moria's building. My hand was on the gun, fingers caressing the grip. I wiggled my toes inside my shoes, a trick I'd learned back in Hungary, a way to improve circulation and pump some warmth into my feet. It had served me well in Auschwitz, and it was much colder there than in Jerusalem.

Less than an hour after the start of my vigil, a figure exited Moria's building. At first, I couldn't make out who it was; the figure was merely a moving lump of blackness. But I could tell by its shape that it wasn't Leitner.

As the figure came closer, even before light from the streetlamp hit his face, I knew who it was.

My nemesis. Inspector Kulaski. There was no mistaking that bearing and gait.

Fear struck deep in my chest. My ribs began aching. How had he found me? Was he here alone? The street seemed deserted. I'd seen no one during my wait.

Kulaski was in dark civilian clothes. His expression was tight, like he had indigestion. I guessed he hadn't enjoyed waiting for a quarry that failed to show. It was about to get worse for him. He didn't know it yet, but he was the quarry now.

Him being there, and in civilian clothes, eliminated all vestige of doubt. He had come here to settle matters with me, and he knew that a witness would remember a police uniform. He probably had something to cover his face with as well, like when he and his cronies had jumped me in the street. Once he had finished me off in Moria's apartment, he would have concealed his face as he made his getaway. It was still a risky move, especially since Moria's apartment was on the third floor, but Kulaski was beyond reason when it came to me.

A wave of unalloyed hatred engulfed me. This man had tried to lock me up for a crime I didn't commit. Later he had me beaten half to death. And then he had come to my hospital bed and punched me where I hurt most. Tonight, he had come to kill me. All because of what had happened to his sister, something I had nothing to do with.

If I let him go, he would simply try again another time. There was no escaping it: it was either him or me.

I pulled out the gun, held it pointed down by my thigh. I didn't want to confront him just yet, fearing that Lillian's inquisitiveness had overwhelmed her fatigue and she was right then peering through her window at the street.

I let him come and then pass by me; he was staring rigidly forward and didn't see me hunching in the shadows.

As he passed, I crept up behind him, pointed the gun at his back, and said, "Stop right there, Kulaski."

The inspector whipped around. His face registered surprise, but it was subsumed by fury: his eyes didn't widen in fear but tightened to slits, and his entire face bunched up. Rage came off him like steam off a boiling cauldron.

"Get your hands up," I said, moving slowly toward him and stopping five feet away.

He didn't obey. "You shouldn't have come back to Jerusalem."

"I said, 'Get your hands up.' Don't make me repeat myself."

Still he didn't comply. "But you can't keep from causing trouble, can you? Like the rest of you Herutniks. You're just a common criminal."

"You're one to talk. First you assault me in the street, and then you break into an apartment to ambush me. Not exactly following police procedure, are you? Now raise your hands, damn you. If I have to ask you again, I'll shoot you."

He sneered. "No. You won't." And then I felt it. The hard jab of metal at my back. Even through my shirt and coat, I sensed the small hard circle of a gun's muzzle.

Then a familiar voice in my ear. "Drop the gun, Lapid. It's over."

41

Before I could overcome my shock, Kulaski stepped forward and wrenched the gun from my hand. He shoved it painfully under my chin, his face so close I could not escape his hot, sour breath.

"You're not just a troublemaker; you're also stupid," Kulaski said. His lips were stretched back, his teeth like sharp stones in the moonlight. He pushed the muzzle harder into my throat, and I tried pulling my head away, but there wasn't anywhere to go with a second gun pressed into my back.

Kulaski grabbed my hair, yanking it hard. "I told you not to come back, you idiot. I guess what I did in the hospital wasn't enough to make that sink in." His face was taut, and I was sure he was going to shoot me then and there.

The man behind me had the same thought. "Easy, Inspector. Let's stick to the plan."

Sergeant Rapfogel. He was the man who'd come up behind me without my noticing. I'd been so careless, I could have killed myself. But I didn't think I'd get that chance. Kulaski would take care of that first.

Kulaski nodded. "All right. Cuff him."

Rapfogel took his gun away, and I was about to try something desperate, but Kulaski read the intention and grinned. "Do it and your brains will litter this sidewalk."

I didn't resist as Rapfogel jerked my hands back and closed the cuffs around my wrists. Then his gun returned to the small of my back.

"Let's go," he said. "And don't try anything."

They led me to a car a few buildings up the street. I'd noticed it before but had seen no one inside. Rapfogel opened the rear door, and Kulaski pushed me inside. He slid in beside me, gun pointed at my midsection. Rapfogel got behind the wheel.

Kulaski said, "How did you know I was waiting in Moria Gafni's apartment?"

"I could smell you," I said, my insides like water swirling down a drain—all weightless and dwindling. I was cuffed and powerless in a car with two armed men with murderous intent. I was done for, hopeless, impotent. All I could do was hurl insults.

Kulaski smiled, his eyes bright. "You're funny. Isn't he funny, Sergeant?"

"Hilarious," Rapfogel muttered. He lifted a bottle of wine off the passenger seat and took a long swig. I noticed the bottle was less than half full. Just like last time, Rapfogel needed the alcohol for what came next. He started the car, put it in gear, and eased away from the curb, going at a moderate speed.

"Who told you I was sleeping there?" I asked.

"Dr. Leitner." Kulaski laughed. "You didn't expect that, did you? The look on your face... it's priceless. The same day I visited you at the hospital, I asked him to let me know if you ever returned. He called me a few hours ago and told me where I could find you. He sounded quite angry with you."

"Did he tell you why?"

"I didn't ask."

"It's because I found out he was blackmailing Moria Gafni."

Kulaski's expression didn't shift. "Cut it out with your lies. I'm not going to fall for them."

"Did you stop to wonder how he knew where I was sleeping? It's because he hired a private detective to follow me. This is my third night back in Jerusalem. There's a reason why Leitner didn't call you yesterday."

"I don't care. What's important is that I have you now."

Did Leitner know what Kulaski intended to do to me? He must have because it wouldn't do him any good to have me arrested. He needed me out of the way permanently. He needed me dead. His knowing Kulaski's mind suggested a deep acquaintance between him and the inspector. Perhaps even friendship.

"How do you know Dr. Leitner?" I asked.

"He treated a relative of mine a few years ago."

"Your sister?"

Kulaski grabbed the front of my coat, his austere face all harsh angles and rigid lines. "What do you know about my sister?"

"That she died before her time. I'm sorry for your loss."

"Right, I'm sure you are. She died because of you and your Herutnik buddies, you Irgun terrorists. It was your bomb that killed her."

"I had nothing to do with that. I'm not a member of Herut, and I've never been part of the Irgun."

"More lies. You were in that demonstration. For the rest of my days, I'll hound you guys."

The streets were nearly empty, the city asleep around us. Rapfogel drove the car down wet roads, and soon we were on Jaffa Street, heading west. With one hand on the wheel, he put the bottle to his lips again.

"Quit that already, will you," Kulaski said. "You'll drive us into a building."

"I'm fine," Rapfogel answered, putting the bottle aside and wiping his mouth. "I can handle much more than this bitty bottle." He laughed, looking back at me. "Last time you paid for four glasses, remember? And it didn't slow me down any."

"Keep your eyes on the damn road," Kulaski barked as the car began to drift. Rapfogel whipped back, gripping the wheel with both hands and righting the car.

"Where are you taking me?" I asked, shifting in my seat. The cuffs were cutting into my wrists, and I tried in vain to find a position that would ease the pain.

"We're throwing you out of Jerusalem. And this time, I hope you'll stay out." Kulaski didn't look at me as he said this, and the lie was so obvious that I had the crazy urge to laugh.

"Where's your buddy, the third guy who beat me?"

"He couldn't make it tonight." The statement was mundane, but by his tone and the way his mouth tightened, I could tell Kulaski was angry. Not at me, but at the unnamed third officer. Maybe he didn't have the stomach for what Kulaski and Rapfogel planned. Maybe he was open to a beating but drew the line at cold-blooded murder.

We were near the city limits now. The buildings flowing past my window dark and brooding hulks of Jerusalem stone, the sidewalks empty of souls like my body would soon be empty of mine. No cars on the road to witness our passage.

It got darker when we exited Jerusalem. Just the stars and moon and the twin beams of the headlights slicing through the darkness ahead.

"Why not let me out here?" I asked for no useful reason. "We're out of Jerusalem, aren't we?"

"A few more minutes," Kulaski said. "It won't be long now." Rapfogel merely drank more wine.

We neared a bend, and Rapfogel slowed to a crawl. He leaned forward, peering out the window. "There it is," he said, and turned onto a narrow dirt road cutting between tall trees. We bounced over ruts and potholes for a few minutes, and then the trees spread out, and the road spilled into a clearing. Rapfogel stopped and jerked up the handbrake, but left the motor running, the lights burning bright like two tongues of fire. "We're here," he said, then drained the bottle before tossing it onto the floor.

Kulaski opened the door and climbed out. "Let's go, Mr. Lapid. Final stop."

I didn't move. I was covered in cold sweat, and my breath was fast and off tempo, like my lungs had lost their natural rhythm.

Kulaski leaned into the car. "Don't make us drag you out. Be sensible for once."

"You're a son of a bitch, Kulaski."

His lips curled wickedly. "Not half as much as you, Lapid. Now get out!"

I did. Standing in the clearing, I noticed that Kulaski was holding a different gun, having pocketed Moria's after he got out of the car. His gun was bigger, familiar, but with my brain panicked and jumpy, I couldn't put my finger on the model. But it wasn't standard police issue. Over by the front of the car, Rapfogel held a gun, too, also a nonstandard issue.

It figured. You didn't use your regular guns for a murder. You used pieces you confiscated on one of your cases. Then you disposed of them, and there was nothing that could point to you.

I looked around me, my heart stammering. Nothing but dense trees and darkness between them, and the empty ribbon of dirt on which we had traveled here. No noise apart from the hum of the vehicle and the vague sounds of forest nightlife. The fresh smell of trees and shrubs crisp and pleasant. The moon a bleached unblinking eye in a black sky.

A beautiful night, but that didn't make it a good time to die. I recalled all the times I'd come inches from death but somehow survived. A few times in Hungary before the war, many more in Auschwitz and Israel's War of Independence, and several times since. But I couldn't see how I'd make it through tonight.

I couldn't fight. I had no weapon, and my hands were cuffed. I could run, but I wouldn't get far. I was in the middle of the clearing, the trees a few meters away. No cover between me and them, and long before I would get to them, a bullet would get to me.

"You should have signed that confession when you had the chance," Kulaski told me. "You should have taken your punishment like a man."

"I didn't beat that cop."

"It doesn't matter anymore. Now step away from the car and move that way."

I didn't budge, so Kulaski grabbed me by the arm and hauled me, struggling ineffectually, to where the headlights shone brightest, and I was reminded of the searchlights that scoured the grounds at Auschwitz at night, the armed guards who shot anyone they felt like.

With Kulaski close, I searched for an opportunity to strike him, but with my hands useless, I couldn't do much, and Kulaski kept me at arm's length. Finally, he gave me a shove, and I stumbled a little but managed not to fall. Now he was six feet away from me, and whatever chance I'd had was gone.

Rapfogel had another bottle and was guzzling more wine. His face was flushed, and his brow glistened with perspiration, unlike Kulaski, who was cool and calm.

Now they'll do it, I thought. I had just a few seconds to live. Groping for a way to stave off death, I said the first thing that came to mind.

"Did Kulaski tell you I'm under the protection of the deputy commissioner?" I asked Rapfogel. "That's why he had to let me go."

Rapfogel frowned at his superior. "What's he talking about?"

"Nothing. Don't listen to him."

"If I die, the deputy commissioner will wonder why. He'll want answers."

Rapfogel tugged Kulaski's sleeve. He was slurring now. The wine was getting to him. "Is he telling the truth? Does he know the deputy commissioner?"

"No, he doesn't. He's trying to fool you. Now put that damn bottle away, and let's get this over with."

"There'll be cuff marks on my wrists," I said. "When they find my body, they'll know cops killed me. They'll come for you, Inspector. And for you, Sergeant."

Rapfogel looked nervous, but Kulaski just laughed. "By the time they find you, the animals will have eaten all the evidence." He raised his pistol. "Enough talk. No last words for you."

"I know who killed your sister," I blurted, my stomach so cramped it was hard to stand straight.

"What did you say?" he asked, staring at me without blinking.

"I know who planted the bomb that killed your sister. I know who constructed it." I had no idea if those men had been caught. I was betting my life that they hadn't.

"Who are they? What are their names?"

"You have to let me go."

"I'll shoot you if you don't talk," he shouted. His face was turning red. His gun hand shook a little. The tendons in his neck stood out like taut ropes. This was the reason we were here; this was why he wanted to kill me. His sister. He couldn't punish the men who had caused her death, so he took it out on anyone connected with the Irgun or the political party affiliated with it, Herut. Now I was dangling his wildest dream before his nose: the chance to get even with those directly responsible for his sister's death. I was hoping the temptation would make him careless.

"Shoot me and you'll never know. You'll go to your grave without knowing."

"Who are they?" he screamed, and somewhere in the trees behind me, a bunch of startled night birds took flight.

"They live in Jerusalem," I said, feeding the furnace of his desire. "You can be at their homes in under an hour. If I tell you the addresses."

I could see it in his eyes: the moment he snapped. Then he was sprinting toward me, a frenzied yell gushing from his throat like lava from a volcano. His gun was in one hand; the fingers of the other were curled like talons. "Tell me, or I'll—"

I didn't let him finish. When he was a step away, I tucked my chin into my chest and lunged forward to meet him, ramming the top of my head into his face.

I connected with bone and heard it crunch and break. Kulaski and I flopped to the ground right next to each other. He was knocked out, his nose and mouth bloodied. The top of my head hurt like hell, and my vision swam a little, but I bit my lip to clear it up. From the corner of my eye, I saw Rapfogel gawking at the unexpected scene, the wine bottle discarded and dripping at his feet. Then he lifted his gun to fire, but Kulaski and I were so close, he had to be careful not to hit his friend.

Kulaski had dropped his gun when I hit him. I rolled to it, earth exploding near my face as Rapfogel fired, and then I grabbed the gun awkwardly in my cuffed hands, struggling to fit my finger onto the trigger. I rolled again, small stones and acorns digging into my back and stomach, as another shot rang out, and then two more. If Rapfogel had been sober, I doubt he would have missed me.

Rolling onto my stomach, Kulaski's gun in my brittle grip and pointed in Rapfogel's general direction, I pulled the trigger over and over, shifting my hands to cover more ground, howling an incoherent battle cry, firing without aim or sense until the magazine was spent.

I fired eight bullets. Seven of them missed. The eighth bit through Rapfogel's shoe and masticated his foot. He screamed, crashing down, gun discarded and forgotten as he gripped his ruined foot with both hands.

I rolled to Kulaski, who was beginning to stir. I didn't have much time. I had to get free before Kulaski came to or Rapfogel stopped wailing long enough to remember that more than his foot was at stake here tonight.

I wormed my fingers into Kulaski's closest pocket, praying that was where he kept his keys, and fumbled around until my fingertips touched metal. I tugged the key ring out and undid the cuffs. The instant they fell off my wrists was one of the most exhilarating moments of my life.

I knelt by the stunned inspector and, digging through his pockets, found Moria's gun and a fresh magazine for Kulaski's pistol. He came to as I was rummaging, and for the first time I saw sweet fear in his eyes. He tried to shove my hand away, so I smacked him in the mouth, and he screamed with agony. "Doesn't feel so good getting hit on an injury, does it?" I said. I pocketed Moria's gun, reloaded Kulaski's pistol, and aimed it at him. "I am truly sorry about your sister," I said, and shot him in the center of his face.

I turned to Rapfogel. The shot I'd just fired seemed to have reminded him of the danger he was in. Grimacing, his foot a red mess, he scrambled for his fallen firearm, but I was faster.

"Please," he whined, tears streaming down his ashen face. "Please don't shoot me. It was Kulaski. He ordered me to."

"I know," I said soothingly. "You had no choice."

"Please take me to the hospital. My foot hurts so bad."

"I need you to tell me something first. What is the name of the third officer who took part in my beating?"

"Revivo. Sergeant Gideon Revivo."

"Why isn't he here?"

"Kulaski didn't tell him about tonight. Gideon stopped him from going too far when we jumped you. Later told me Kulaski was crazy, out of control. He was right. I should have listened. Dear God, my foot..."

So I was right about Kulaski being mad at the third man, I thought. "Who else knows you were coming after me tonight?"

"We told no one. Take me to the hospital, and I won't breathe a word of what happened tonight. I swear I won't."

"I know," I told him. "I know." Then I put a bullet between his eyes.

42

Rapfogel's wallet held fourteen liras. I took them all. "That's for the wine," I told his corpse, and put the wallet back, holding it with my handkerchief to avoid leaving prints.

Kulaski only had one lira on him. "You weren't only crazy, but cheap too," I muttered, and took the single bill.

I dragged both bodies into the woods, careful not to get any blood on me. I didn't bury them. I had no shovel, but even if I had, I wouldn't have made the effort. If what Rapfogel had told me was true, and I was sure it was, no one knew what he and Kulaski had been up to that night. No one could prove I was here.

I wiped the dead men's guns clean, as well as Kulaski's keys and the magazine I'd loaded into his pistol after shooting Rapfogel's foot. I threw both firearms into the trees in one direction, Rapfogel's cuffs and Kulaski's keys and empty magazine in another. I also picked up all the spent shell casings and scattered them in the undergrowth.

Back in the clearing, I kicked dirt over blood patches, obscuring the scene. Someone else might come by, and I didn't want them to know what had happened here. I also brushed away any footmarks that led to where I'd put the bodies. The longer it took to find them, the better.

I wiped off the section of the backseat where I'd sat on the ride over. One good thing about being cuffed is it prevents you from leaving prints all over the place.

That was everything. All that remained was getting out of there. I sat in the driver's seat and got the shakes. I stared at my fingers; they were trembling like naked tree limbs in a gale. I shut my eyes and took deep breaths until the shaking ceased. But still I didn't drive off. I looked through the windshield at the empty clearing, getting used to the idea that I was going to survive this night. I started laughing and didn't like the manic edge to it. I forced myself to stop, mumbled, "So long, you bastards," and drove out of the clearing.

Back in Jerusalem, I parked the car on a dark stretch of road on a side street. I wiped off the wheel, the door handle, and anything else I might have touched. I left the keys in the door. Anyone wanting to take the car for a ride could be my guest.

For the second time that night, I took off my shoes and went up the stairs to Moria's apartment. I wasn't worried about Kulaski anymore, but I still didn't want Lillian to hear me. I was too tired for explanations.

She didn't open her door. I hoped the baby had let her sleep.

Kulaski had picked the lock on Moria's door. If he'd left any tell-tale signs in the process, I couldn't see them in the gloom of the landing. If Lillian hadn't stopped me, I would have walked into his trap completely unprepared.

Inside, there was no sign that the inspector had been lurking there. Tired beyond belief, my ribs aching from rolling around on the hard ground of the clearing, my head throbbing where it had connected with Kulaski's face, I padded to Moria's bedroom, took off my grimy, muddy clothes, and flopped onto the bed. I plummeted into sleep a second later.

When I awoke, the sun was shining on my face. My watch said it was almost eleven. The sky was a startling blue, and, if you ignored the biting cold, you wouldn't have guessed it was winter.

No longer feeling the need to hide my presence, I got into Moria's tiny bathtub and scrubbed my skin raw. I put on fresh clothes, shaved, and drank multiple glasses of water in the kitchen. My coat was muddy from all the rolling around I'd done yesterday. I scraped off the mud over the toilet and flushed it away.

I did all this quickly, knowing that if Lillian was home, she might be getting frantic hearing all the noise I was making. Once I was through, I went down and knocked on her door.

"Was that you in Moria's apartment?" was how she greeted me.

"Yes."

"Thank God. I was getting worried."

Dina, Lillian's daughter, was awake, sitting in her crib with a rattle in her hand. She looked at me with huge curious eyes. I smiled at her. She smiled right back.

"I was just having tea," Lillian said. "Do you want some?"

I said I did, and we sat at her table with our steaming cups.

"She's beautiful," I said, gesturing at Dina.

Lillian smiled. "She's a handful, but a beautiful one for sure. See how she looks at you? She's so curious, wants to know everything."

"I wonder who she gets that from."

Lillian laughed, blushing a little. "Guilty as charged. Some of the neighbors hate me for it. I know it's a bad habit, but I can't help myself."

"It sure proved useful last night."

She looked at me. She had the same eyes as her daughter. "What happened? Did you find out who was up there?"

"A burglar," I lied. "I waited for him on the street and caught him as he was leaving."

"What did he steal?"

"Nothing much. There wasn't much to steal. I put it all back."

"It's a good thing you came."

"And a very good thing you were up and alert. Thank you for that, Lillian. From the bottom of my heart, thank you."

She smiled. "I guess my bad habit isn't so bad after all. What's going to happen to the burglar? Will he go to jail?"

"No," I said, and drank some tea. "I let him go with a stern warning and a couple of slaps. He's just a kid. I didn't want to get the police involved. It would ruin his life." I'd prepared this lie in advance, fearing that Lillian's curiosity would compel her to go to the police and ask about my made-up burglar.

"A kid?"

"Fifteen years old. He heard Moria had died, so he figured the apartment would be empty. Easy pickings, like what happened with your husband's aunt."

Lillian's eyebrows bunched closer. "Daniel's aunt? What do you mean?"

"The aunt who died a few years ago. The one whose apartment was burglarized shortly after her death."

Lillian's bewilderment deepened. "You must be mixed up, Adam. None of Daniel's aunts are dead."

I gave her a look. "Are you sure?"

"Of course I'm sure. You think I'd forget something like that? Whoever gave you the idea that Daniel had a dead aunt?"

He had. The day he'd attacked me in Moria's apartment. He'd said he thought I was a thief looting a dead woman's apartment, like what had happened to his aunt.

"Oh," I said with a wave of a hand. "I guess I got confused with someone else." But I didn't. Daniel Shukrun had lied to me, and I needed to know why. "Where is Daniel, by the way?"

"At work."

"I thought he worked last night."

"He did. He works two jobs. A couple of nights a week as a watchman in a factory downtown, and during the days at his uncle's locksmithing business. He gets so tired sometimes, poor dear."

"Daniel's a locksmith?" I asked, a terrible suspicion beginning to take root.

"A very good one. He's going to take over the business in a couple of years, and then I hope he won't have to work nights anymore."

Snippets of past conversations began flitting around my brain. Then I recalled something Lillian had said when I asked her and Daniel if they knew who had a key to Moria's apartment. Lillian had turned to her husband and asked if the landlord had one, and Daniel had rubbed his face as though to hide his expression and nodded.

"Did Daniel install the locks in this building?" I asked.

"Yes. Three years ago the landlord replaced all the doors; the old ones were so poorly made they were rotting. Daniel and his uncle put in all the locks. How did you know?"

"I was just wondering," I said, hurrying to drink more tea. The liquid, which minutes earlier was sweet, now tasted bitter.

Daniel Shukrun had lied to me. And he had installed the lock on Moria's door. Which meant there was a good chance he had a key or could make one that fit.

"Is everything all right, Adam?" Lillian asked. She was peering at me worriedly.

"Yeah. Everything's fine." I worked up a smile, but it felt crumbly and slippery on my lips. Because nothing was fine. Once again, all I'd been sure of had been overturned and scattered, and a new certainty had emerged. One that I was finding it hard to wrap my mind around.

I finished my tea and set the cup back on the table. "Lillian," I said, "I have a few questions to ask you."

43

The locksmithing store was on Shamai Street. I walked there through crisp winter air and a fog of my own thoughts. I thought I knew everything now. The terrible truth was laid bare like a mutilated corpse that had long defied identification, but which had just yielded its name.

But that was not what troubled me most. A bigger problem was Dr. Leitner and what I should do about him.

The man had sent Kulaski to kill me. Against all odds, I'd survived, but Leitner was free to try again, and I might not get so lucky next time. I had to deal with him, but he had an ace up his sleeve—the pictures of Moria and Naomi Hecht.

Leitner had told me that if he died, the pictures would go public. They would ruin Moria's name posthumously and bring shame upon Naomi Hecht. I didn't want either of those things to happen.

I could carry out my threat and force him to give me the pictures, but that was easier said than done. I'd need to grab him, take him someplace isolated, and it might take a while to break him, and I did not relish the necessary process.

It might not work even if I did everything right. What if the pictures were in a bank and only Leitner had access to them? In that case, breaking him would be pointless.

Another way was to threaten his family. But it wasn't something I wanted to do, and I got the impression that Leitner cared for them much less than for his career.

I was at an impasse. As long as Leitner had those pictures, I couldn't go after him. But I had to go after him or keep looking over my shoulder for assassins.

Submerged in these somber thoughts, I was crossing Zion Square, cutting through a milling crowd of people next to Zion Cinema, when I heard a woman call my name. I stopped, looked around, saw no familiar faces. The voice came again, closer now, from the south, its owner hidden by the blinding sun.

I shielded my eyes and saw her mincing toward me with hesitant steps, her small bag hanging on one forearm, her hands clasped before her. She kept casting nervous looks around as she neared.

"Hello," she said. "You cannot imagine how glad I am to see you, Mr. Lapid."

"What are you doing here, Mrs. Leitner?"

Ada Leitner still brought to mind a housekeeper despite not wearing an apron. There was a servile quality in the way she held herself, a natural contraction of her body, as though to take up less of someone else's space.

"I... I didn't know where else to try," she said. "I heard you tell my husband that you'd be here at noon. I was worried you wouldn't be able to make it, that you'd be... Well, never mind, you're clearly not, thank God. I just hoped you'd be here."

"Is your husband here?" I asked, searching the crowd for him while keeping an eye on her. Was this a trap? What if she had a gun in that handbag? Was she as cold-hearted as her husband?

"What? No, of course not. I'd rather not think what he'd do if he knew I was talking to you."

Her face had a fearful cast, but underneath flickered a different sort of emotion. Determination? Hope? I couldn't be sure, but it was brittle. Then I remembered what she said a moment ago, hearing me tell her husband I'd be here at noon.

"Were you eavesdropping on my conversation with your husband yesterday?"

Her cheeks flushed, and she gave an abashed nod. "When I saw you two in the living room, I could tell it was serious by my husband's face. He's been on edge these past few days, but he won't tell me why, and I thought you might have something to do with it, so I listened through the door."

I didn't know what to make of this. I repeated my earlier question, "What are you doing here, Mrs. Leitner?"

She licked her lips. "Can we go somewhere quiet to talk? I'd rather not discuss this on the street."

We found a small café that was half empty despite the hour. We took a rear table, and I ordered us two glasses of tea, but when I brought them to the table, neither of us made a move to touch them.

I waited. This meeting was her initiative. I'd let her talk first.

Away from the prying eyes of the multitudes on the street, Ada looked more assured and confident. I spotted the instant she shattered the last shackles of hesitancy as she reached into her bag and drew out an envelope.

"Here. Take it."

Inside was a cylindrical object and something flat and rectangular. I reached under the flap and slid the contents out. A roll of film and a stack of photographs. My breath caught in my throat as I recognized the two women in the topmost photo: Naomi Hecht and Moria Gafni.

I flicked my gaze at Ada, but she had her eyes on her hands, so I returned my attention to the photo.

There was nothing salacious about it. Just two women walking through a park, sharing a smile. They looked like nothing more than good friends; they weren't even holding hands. In none of her other pictures had I seen Moria so happy. As for Naomi Hecht, she looked joyful and vibrant. Her face looked younger than I'd ever seen it, and it took me a second to realize why—there were no bags under her eyes.

The next picture was similar. As were the following four. Then, after a picture from the rear showing the two women entering a dense copse of trees, the tenor of the images changed.

There were eight photos, partially obscured by low branches, each showing Moria and Naomi Hecht kissing passionately. The pictures left no room for doubt or alternative interpretation.

I lowered the final photo, stacked it with the rest, and put them and the roll of film back in the envelope. I said to Ada, "Why did you bring these to me?"

"I heard nearly everything you two said to each other. What Yosef did with these photos, what he forced that poor nurse to do, it was wrong. Evil. I only wish she were still alive."

Me too, I thought, especially now that I knew Moria hadn't been a murderer after all. Just a pure-hearted victim with tremendous bad luck.

"Where did your husband keep these?"

"In a small safe in his study. Only he and I know the combination."

"So he'll know you were the one who took them."

She nodded, gulping. "Yes. He will."

"You're taking a big risk, aren't you? Why? Just because what your husband did was bad?"

For a few seconds, she said nothing. Then she showed me another photo, an older one, ten, twelve years old, judging by how much younger she looked in it.

"That's me and my son, Moshe. He's three years old here. Doesn't he look like me?" He did, and I told her so. "He's fourteen now, and he doesn't look like me at all. He's a copy of his father."

She stated that last fact with aching bitterness, and I remembered the photo of the three of them on the piano in Leitner's apartment. How the boy resembled his father not only in features, but also in manner and bearing.

"We used to be so close, Moshe and I, when he was little. Now he barely notices me, but he worships his father. Every day, he grows a little more like him. And not just physically. He's adopting more and more of my husband's immorality, his ruthless ambitiousness. I'm losing my son bit by bit. Soon it'll be too late, there'll be nothing of me left in him, and he'll be as evil and selfish as his father. I can't let that happen."

"I'm sorry to hear that," I said. "But what does that have to do with you giving me these photos?"

She leaned forward, her eyes bright and animated. "You were pointing a gun at my husband, weren't you? I heard him telling you to be careful with it."

I looked around us. There was no one at the neighboring tables. No one had heard her question. "And if I was?"

"You can't imagine what a thrill I felt when you threatened to shoot him. I was praying you'd do it. But then Yosef said you wouldn't dare because I was in the apartment, and you relented. I cursed myself. Why couldn't I have been out?"

"Let me get this straight, you actually wanted me to shoot your husband?"

She nodded. "More than anything. It would have freed me, freed my son. I would have been able to change him back to the sweet little boy he once was. But Yosef, damn him, he had the photos to protect him. I heard him threatening that they'd be released if he died."

"So..." I began, still not sure where she was going with this.

"So," Ada said, and I noticed her posture was better, lending her height and an aura of power. "Now there's nothing to stop you."

"You brought me these pictures so I'll kill your husband for you?"

"Yes," she said, and there was a simple, fragile strength in that short utterance. A strength that her husband might have squashed and stifled and nearly killed over years of bad marriage, but not quite. And accompanying that strength was a filament of courage that allowed her to state her wish without averting her gaze. "He'll be alone in the apartment all evening. I'm taking my son to visit my sister. We won't be back until nine."

"Why don't you kill him if you hate him so much?"

She wrung her hands. "I thought about it a thousand times. I pictured it in my head. But I can't. I'm not sure I'd be able to go through with it. And I don't know how to do it without getting caught."

"You could hire someone."

"I wouldn't know where to find him. But if you want money, I can—"

"I'm not a hired killer, Mrs. Leitner, so save your breath."

She flinched, shrinking back to her customary subservience. "I'm sorry... I didn't mean to... I..." She swallowed, seemed to find some internal reservoir of resolve, and said in a rush, "If you don't kill him, he'll kill you. When you were late coming to Zion Square earlier, I was sure you were dead."

"What made you think that?"

"I heard him talking on the telephone after you left. He said you were back in Jerusalem and were sleeping in an apartment—I didn't catch the name of the owner. Yosef told the man on the other end that he wanted you dead. He sounded so angry."

Kulaski. Leitner had been speaking to Kulaski.

"Do you know who your husband was speaking with?"

She shook her head. "He didn't say his name."

That was good. Because soon reports of two missing cops would hit the newspapers, and I didn't want Ada to think that I'd killed them.

But what of her husband? When he didn't hear from Kulaski, he'd start to worry. And when it became public that Kulaski was missing, Leitner would know I was responsible. He might hire someone else to kill me, or he might send the police after me, anonymously most likely. It wouldn't lead to a conviction—I'd covered my tracks well— but I might get arrested and jailed until it all cleared up. And maybe in jail, I'd get stabbed or otherwise meet an untimely death.

I tapped the envelope thoughtfully. "Are these all the photos?"

"That was everything there was in the safe."

I nodded and put the envelope in my pocket.

"How will you get by if your husband dies?"

"We have savings, we own our apartment, and I can sell a few things if need be. I don't care if I have to live more modestly. I just want him gone so he doesn't ruin our son. Please, you have to do it today. Otherwise, he might look inside the safe and realize the photos are gone. He'll know I took them."

Looking at her anxious face, I swore inwardly. Ada was putting me in a terrible position. I wasn't ready to go after Dr. Leitner today; I had no plan. But if I waited, he might hurt his wife once he learned the photographs were missing. He might even kill her. And I felt that I owed her for bringing me the pictures.

"Why not go away for a while?" I said. "Get away from Jerusalem?"

She shook her head emphatically. "My son won't agree to join me. And if Yosef discovers I took his photos, he'll poison him against me, and I won't be there to explain why I did it. My son will think I ruined his father, our family. I couldn't bear that."

I scoured my mind for a solution but found none. What aggravated the problem was that the time window Ada suggested was problematic. Most people are at home and awake during the evening before nine o'clock. Dr. Leitner's building would be full of neighbors. Killing him and getting away unseen would be difficult, and I'd already used up my share of luck last night.

"Please, Mr. Lapid, you have to help me." Ada paused, then added what I already knew to be true: "You don't have a choice. Either you kill my husband, or he'll soon kill you."

44

I made Ada Leitner no promises, just thanked her for the photographs and left. I wasn't sure what I'd do come evening. I had another matter to deal with first.

I found Daniel Shukrun at his uncle's locksmithing business on Shamai Street. The place was crowded with locks and keys of all sizes, and the smell of oil and metal thickened the air.

Daniel was alone at the front of the shop, bent over a counter, peering at a key-cutting machine.

"Hello, Daniel," I said, and caught the flitting glitter of fear in his eyes as his head swept up and he saw me.

"Adam," he said, smiling awkwardly, wiping his hands clean on a cloth, "what... what are you doing here?"

"Is your uncle here?" I said, looking through an open door behind the counter, seeing more tools and equipment but no movement.

"He went home. Didn't feel well. Why?"

Instead of answering, I turned to the street door and flipped the Open sign to its opposite side. Turning back, I reached into my pocket and brought out the gun that I'd once thought was Moria's.

"Because of this," I said.

He blanched, and a massive exhalation fled his lungs, as though he'd been holding his breath for weeks. He leaned heavily on the counter. A big man bowing under the weight of uncovered secrets.

"How did you find out?"

"I learned none of your aunts are dead."

He looked at me blankly. "My aunts?"

I reminded him of what he'd told me after I punched him in Moria's apartment. "A pointless lie. You could have just said you heard noises and came to check. You didn't need to embellish."

He made a helpless gesture with his hands. "I got nervous. I really did think you'd come to rob the place. I was furious with you, and I was worried you'd find the gun."

"That's why you came back to wash the mud off the floor, isn't it? To sneak a peek into the bedroom and see if I'd removed the bedside cabinet?"

"Yes."

"I should have realized it soon after," I said, more than a little angry with myself, "when I saw you didn't bother washing the lobby or stairs. I thought you cleaned the apartment because of Moria, that you felt beholden to her. But you didn't care for her one bit."

He shook his head forcefully, and his expression turned imploring. "That's not true. I admired her. I was grateful to her."

"Then why stash a murder weapon in her apartment?"

"It was the only place I could think of. I couldn't keep it in my home. Lillian notices everything."

"Why not keep the gun here in the store?"

"My uncle likes rearranging stuff. Every once in a while, he moves everything around. Besides, I wanted the gun close to home so I could reach it in a hurry."

It sounded flimsy. Daniel's motivation was likely different and selfish. He didn't want the gun anywhere connected with him in case the police found it.

"Why Moria's apartment? Why not one of the others in the building?" I asked.

"She lived alone, and she worked long hours, including several nights a week, and it was easy to find out when she was on shift. And

I knew when she was in. When I'm home, I can hear every step someone takes in her apartment. It was the perfect place."

"Weren't you worried Lillian would hear you up there?"

"I hardly ever went there, and I always chose a time when Lillian was out or fast asleep. There's also the fact that the other neighbor on the third floor is old and nearly deaf and blind. He wouldn't see or hear me go into Moria's apartment."

"Didn't you stop to think of the trouble Moria might find herself in if the police found that gun in her apartment after you killed Dr. Shapira?"

"Why would they suspect her? She was a woman who wouldn't hurt a soul."

"Because she worked with him, and because she and Dr. Shapira had locked horns several times. He tried to have her fired. He disapproved of her habit of undermining his authority by talking directly to the parents of patients. Like she did with you. Lillian told me about it. She said Moria had warned you that the surgery Dr. Shapira recommended for your son was risky, an experimental procedure, but that Dr. Shapira insisted on doing it, and you relented."

A paternal wave of rage coiled through Daniel's features. "He assured us it would go without a hitch, that we had nothing to worry about. We later learned it was the first time he'd performed such a surgery. He wanted the acclaim of being the first surgeon in Israel to do it. My son died because of him."

"Is that when you decided to kill him?"

He shook his head. "First we went to talk to him. If he'd only apologized, explained himself, showed some remorse, that might have been the end of it, but instead he was very rude to us. He behaved as though we were a nuisance. So we went to the head of the ward, Dr. Yosef Leitner, to complain. I thought he'd fire Dr. Shapira. Instead, he backed him fully. He told us Dr. Shapira was a respected surgeon. He was very angry that we were bothering him at all. It didn't seem to matter to him that our son was dead. Lillian was crushed. She didn't get out of bed for weeks."

You must have been crushed too, I thought, *but like men the world over, you kept it shoved deep inside you, where it festered, spawning a hatred so keen it had to be satiated.*

"You planned this for a long time, didn't you?" I asked.

He nodded. "There were weeks in which it was the only thing I could think of. At first, it was just a powerful desire for vengeance, but I didn't think I'd act on it. But it grew into something harder, sharper, like a tumor I had to cut out or it would kill me. So I started planning how I'd do it. It wasn't easy, but I managed to buy a gun. I told myself I'd wait a year before I used it so the guy I bought it from wouldn't connect the shooting to me."

"You had a lot of patience."

"Waiting was hard, but I wanted to get away with it." His eyes met mine, but there was no animosity in them, only resignation. "If you hadn't come along, I would have."

"I'm sorry for what happened to your son, Daniel. And I wish Moria were still alive so I wouldn't be here."

"Me too. She was a good woman. Did you find out why she killed herself?"

"It'll take too long to explain, and I'm not here for that."

"No." Daniel sighed. "I suppose you're not."

"You said you planned to wait a year, but it took you nearly two to kill Dr. Shapira. Why so long?"

A wavering smile lived and died on Daniel's lips. "Lillian was pregnant, and then Dina was born, and I hoped the new child would help me get over the death of the old one. But she didn't. The urge to get even kept growing. So I resumed planning. I'd tell Lillian I was working at night, and I'd wait outside the hospital and follow Dr. Shapira home. I did this for several months; I wanted there to be no mistakes. I decided winter would be the right season for the killing. Most people are at home, so there would be less risk of witnesses. I decided to make it look like a robbery so the police wouldn't think the killer was after Dr. Shapira specifically."

"You did a good job," I said. "Taking the belt was a nice touch."

Daniel didn't seem to have heard me. He was back on that night, reliving the realization of his dreams of revenge.

330

"It was very cold. Waiting outside the hospital was difficult, but I'd made up my mind. I was determined to go through with it. I followed Dr. Shapira through a light rain. There were barely any people about. Off in the distance there was a lightning storm, and I remember thinking how perfect it was; maybe the shots would be mistaken for thunder.

"When we got to the alley, I closed the distance between us and tapped him on the shoulder. He turned, surprised, and I could tell he recognized me. Maybe he even guessed what I was there to do. He opened his mouth, but I didn't give him the chance to speak. I fired the gun twice. He fell without uttering a sound. I hurriedly took some of his things and got out of there."

There was no remorse in his voice. In Daniel's eyes, this was a justified punishment. An eye for an eye.

I said, "The day we met in Moria's apartment, you sent me to that fleabag hotel because you weren't sure if I'd found the gun, right?"

He nodded.

"Did you install the locks there as well, like you did in your building?"

"Who told you about that? Lillian?" I nodded, and he heaved a breath. "Yes, I installed the locks in that hotel. Cheap, generic locks. I still had a master key. I could get inside any room without trouble. After you left our building, when Lillian was out with Dina, I went upstairs to Moria's apartment. I discovered you had the gun."

"So you searched my hotel room for it?"

"Yes, but I didn't find it. You must have had it on you."

Another clue I'd missed. I was sure Kulaski had lifted the key from my pocket during the beating he and his buddies had given me, but it must have fallen out when he took my wallet to put that newspaper clipping in it. Thinking I'd outsmarted Kulaski had offered a glimmer of satisfaction on that day of pain and terror, and it had also blinded me to the truth, that it wasn't Kulaski who searched my room, but the only other person who knew I was staying there. Daniel Shukrun.

"Why go to all that trouble?" I asked. "Why did it matter that I had the gun? I didn't know it was yours."

"There was something about you that worried me. I was sure you'd somehow connect the gun to me. Besides, it wasn't easy to get it, and I wanted it back."

"What for? Why did you keep it at all? Why didn't you throw it away after you killed Dr. Shapira?"

Daniel hesitated, looking thoughtful. "You can't prove any of this, can you, Adam?"

"You're right; I can't. But the police probably could. If they had a reason to suspect you, they'd start digging into your life. They'll learn you didn't work the night Dr. Shapira was killed. Maybe they'll find someone who remembers seeing you following him some night. Maybe they'll find the guy who sold you the gun. The police can do things I can't. But they might not have to go to all the trouble. They can bring you in for questioning. They can lean on you hard. I'm not sure you'd be able to handle a forceful interrogation."

Daniel's throat worked. Fear dominated his face, but soon it was supplanted by anger. "He deserved to die, Adam. He killed my boy. For a little prestige, he lied about his surgery and killed him."

Lillian had told me this already. She had been angry too. She had even expressed joy that Dr. Shapira was dead, and then was embarrassed to have done so. I thought of Lillian, who had saved my life. I thought of her daughter, Dina. I thought of their son, dead because Dr. Shapira viewed him not as a boy in need of healing, but as a means to further his professional standing.

I couldn't blame Daniel for killing him. In his place, I might have done the same. I wouldn't have hidden the gun in Moria Gafni's apartment; that was cowardly and wrong. But the right punishment for that sin was not a murder conviction.

"Please don't go to the police, Adam. Give me a few days, and I'll turn myself in."

"What would a few days get you?"

"I need to do something first."

"What?"

He didn't answer, but I thought I understood. "Why did you keep the gun?" I asked again.

"What does it matter now?" His tone was dejected, empty of hope.

"Just answer the question, Daniel."

"Because I had another use for it."

"Who?"

"Dr. Leitner. I was going to kill him too."

That was the answer I'd expected. I looked at Daniel, this big hulk of a man with coarse features and an ocean of sadness in his heart. I knew how he felt. I'd lost children too, and I'd taken revenge, but that revenge hadn't been complete. It couldn't be. But Daniel's revenge could. It might cost him everything, but he needed to carry it out just the same. He would die a slow death on the inside if he didn't.

The decision made itself for me. I still had the gun in my hand. His gun. I ejected the magazine, took out my handkerchief, and wiped the weapon and magazine clean. I did the same with the two extra magazines. Then I placed them all on the counter.

Daniel looked at me in puzzlement.

"I don't know about Dr. Shapira," I said, "but Dr. Leitner certainly deserves to die. Not just because of how he treated you, but also because of something awful he did to Moria. Something I can't tell you about. I'd kill him myself, but I think you want to do it, don't you?"

His jaw tensed. A feverish light sparked in his eyes. "More than anything."

"I can't give you a few days, Daniel. I can't even give you one. Dr. Leitner will be alone at home this evening until nine o'clock. He has to die today. Don't ask me why; just accept it. Do you understand?"

"Yes."

"There's a chance you'll get caught, or worse," I said, and suddenly thought of what either of those outcomes would mean for Lillian and their daughter.

"I know."

"How will your family manage if that happens?"

"My extended family will help. And Lillian will understand why I had to do it."

He sounded completely sure of it, and I didn't argue. In some ways, Daniel Shukrun was already lost to his wife and daughter, even if they weren't aware of it yet. I felt like screaming at him that he still had much to live and be free for, that he hadn't lost everything, but I didn't think it would make any difference to him. "If you do get caught," I said, "and you say anything about me, I'll deny it. Is that clear?"

"I won't breathe a word about you, Adam. I swear it on my son."

I looked at him. He was standing erect, his back rigid and straight, his meaty hands lumped into fists. His expression was one of unmitigated determination. Like a soldier about to go into a crucial battle, ready to give his life for the worthiest of causes.

A wave of relief and shame came over me. Relief that the killing of Dr. Leitner would not fall to me. Shame that I was sending Daniel in my place.

As if reading my mind, Daniel's rough lips turned at the corners. "Don't feel bad, Adam. I want to do this. I need to. I'm grateful you're giving me the chance. I want that bastard to know he's going to die because of what happened to my son."

"I won't turn you in if you don't do it," I said. "You can just walk away."

"I can't," he said, and I could tell by his voice that it was true.

"And you're sure you'll do it today? I need to know. If you can't, I'll do it instead."

I half hoped he'd take me up on my offer because I was suddenly gripped by a terrible premonition that Daniel Shukrun was heading toward disaster.

Daniel's expression didn't waver. "Yes. Yes, I'll do it. I have to be the one. I'll kill Dr. Leitner today."

45

I left Jerusalem soon after. I wanted to be gone before Daniel went to kill Dr. Leitner. I called Gafni's office before boarding the bus, but there was no answer. I wanted to inform him that the case was over, that I'd failed, that I wouldn't be working it anymore. Maybe he'd get angry, but that didn't matter. Kulaski was dead. I didn't need Gafni's protection anymore.

Back in Tel Aviv, I had dinner at Greta's Café. I planned on staying after closing, to sit with Greta and tell her everything, but she had to leave early that evening. "We'll talk tomorrow," she said, cupping my cheeks with her hands. "I'm so glad to see you back and well."

I watched a movie at Allenby Cinema, then went home and fell into a troubled sleep. At some ungodly hour, I awoke into darkness, certain I'd heard gunshots, but it was only the boom of thunder. Rain started falling. It drummed on the roof like an army of hard-shelled insects demanding entry. I huddled under my blanket and thought of Daniel and prayed that he'd done what he promised and got away with it clean, but somehow I doubted it.

It took me a long while to fall asleep again.

At the café the next morning, I surprised Greta by asking to hear the news bulletin on the old, scratchy radio. She turned it on, and I listened intently as the anchor ran through a list of important items that did not interest me in the slightest.

Toward the end of the bulletin came the report I'd been waiting for. Somberly, the anchor reported that last evening in Jerusalem, a respected doctor by the name of Yosef Leitner had been murdered in his home. The killer, whose identity the police had not yet revealed, was fleeing the scene when he ran into a patrol car. The two officers inside the car shot and killed him.

I closed my eyes, bowing my head, and asked for forgiveness from Daniel and from Lillian and their daughter, Dina. I shouldn't have let him do it. I should have been the one.

Yet I knew that Daniel had been truthful when he told me he needed to do it himself. That was why he had thanked me for the opportunity. I also knew that, for Ada Leitner's sake, Dr. Leitner had needed to die yesterday. There'd been no time to plan things carefully. I was guilty of nothing, but guilt was what I felt. Not a new emotion, but the press of it on my shoulders and soul was now heavier.

I called Baruch Gafni's office, and again there was no answer. This was odd. A sense of wrongness gripped me, of some unknown calamity that had happened.

I waited an hour and telephoned again, telling myself that if this call too went unanswered, I'd go to the factory and see what was going on.

But the phone was picked up. A woman's voice, thick with tears. "I told you already: I don't want to talk to any reporters. Stop bothering me."

"I'm not a reporter," I said quickly, perplexed. "My name is Adam Lapid. I need to speak with Mr. Gafni."

A whimper. A short bout of weeping. My confusion deepened. "Mr. Gafni isn't here," she said.

"When will he be in?"

"How should I know? Maybe never." She sounded a bit hysterical now.

"What do you mean, maybe never? Where is he?"

"He's in jail," she wailed into the phone. "Mr. Gafni's in jail."

46

His lawyer arranged the meeting. I went to the jail, and the guards let me in with no trouble. It seemed Gafni still had some pull, though I doubted it would last for much longer.

A potbellied guard with acne scars and a nightstick on his belt led me down a dank hallway with cells on one side. The smell of mildew, concrete dust, and urine permeated the frosty air. Some of the bars were rusting, and the walls were a demoralizing unpainted gray.

Gafni had the last cell all to himself. There were two bunks, and he lay on the lower one with an arm thrown over his face as though to shield his eyes from some unbearable sight.

There was a chair by the hallway's end, and the guard dragged it noisily a few feet before the bars. "Sit here," he told me. "Don't go near the cell, and don't try to hand him anything. I'll be right there, watching."

There was the other end of the hallway, where there was a guard station consisting of a table and a couple of chairs. The guard would have to strain his ears if he hoped to catch anything Gafni and I said to each other, but he had a clear line of sight.

I told him he had nothing to worry about, and he responded with a curt nod and retreated to his post, his key chain rattling. Gafni hadn't stirred. He looked dead to the world. Maybe a part of him wanted to be dead for real.

I sat in the chair. "Mr. Gafni," I said, and had to repeat myself louder a couple of times before he shifted, slowly pulling his arm off his face before pushing himself to a sitting position. He blinked unfocused eyes in my direction, as though surprised to see me there, or maybe unsure whether his new environment was real or a nightmare.

Already it had started taking its toll on him. He still had on his regular tailored clothes, but they looked old and as though they had been made for another man. Stubble dirtied his face, and his features were slack and worn-out and pallid. His head hung forward and his chin dipped, his back rounded like a man two decades his senior.

Jail is a sledgehammer. It dents and flattens even the sturdiest men, and it can do so with terrifying speed. I'd seen it firsthand and experienced it too.

"Mr. Lapid," Gafni said, straightening his back for an instant before slumping again. "I didn't think you would be here so soon."

"I came as soon as I heard you wished to see me. You should thank your lawyer for setting it up so quickly."

Gafni nodded. "He's a good man. Expensive, but worth it. He won't come out and say it, but he thinks I've gone crazy, I can tell. He may even be planning to argue that in court when the time comes. You think I should let him?"

"It may be your best bet."

"Do you think I'm crazy?"

"I don't know. Why did you do it?"

He looked surprised by the question. "Why do you think? Because of what you told me that lowlife did to Moria."

I stared at him, dumbstruck. He didn't seem to notice. His eyes took on a strange light, and his lips curved into a warped smile, which made me think his lawyer's judgment wasn't that far off.

"It was so easy," Gafni said. "He was so stupid and greedy; the minute I told him I wanted to go ahead with his foolish business scheme, he came running to me like a dog."

I could imagine it. Though hadn't Harpaz suspected something was off? Was he so money-hungry or desperate that he'd forgotten what he'd told me, what he must have believed I'd relayed to Gafni, though in the end, I didn't get around to? Didn't he know that there was no chance in hell Gafni would ever deal with him again? Or was he, the inveterate con man, blinded to the trap he was entering by the intrinsic belief in his boundless powers of persuasion, common to all men of his ilk?

"You should have seen him," Gafni went on. "So hopeful. I'd left the street door unlocked for him, and I could hear him bounding up the stairs, a spring in his step. He had on the widest smile when he came into my office. The sort of smile he must have used on the poor women he seduced." Gafni paused for a second, eyes locked on the memory, his lips twisted with hatred for his victim. Regaling me with his tale had invigorated him. He sat straight, his gaze razor-sharp, the cast of his features firmer and younger. Reminiscent of how he'd been when I first met him—the business magnate with overwhelming confidence and full control of his destiny. But the effect was ruined by the bars between us, slicing his image to strips.

"He wasn't the pretty boy I'd always known," Gafni said. "His nose was bandaged, and he had trouble breathing. Someone had clobbered him good and proper."

"That was me," I murmured.

"You?"

"Yeah," I said heavily, remembering the crunch Harpaz's nose had made as my fist connected with his face, then him on the floor with blood coating his mouth and chin.

Gafni clapped his hands and barked out a laugh. "That's beautiful. I must say, Mr. Lapid, hiring you has exceeded my expectations. I wish I had my wallet on me so I could give you a bonus, but I'll ask my lawyer to arrange it. You've more than earned it."

"But..." I began, but didn't finish my sentence. For what purpose would telling him the truth serve? Would Gafni benefit in any way from knowing Arye Harpaz had not been Moria's lover? That she, in fact, had been engaged in a love affair with a female coworker?

"No bonus is necessary," I said.

Gafni held up a magnanimous hand. "I've decided, and I'll hear no more about it. Now, where was I? Ah, yes, I was telling you about the smile Arye was flashing as he came into my office. It vanished awfully quick when he saw the gun." He made a gun with his right hand and stared at it as though it were the real thing, his lips pulled back, showing small teeth and pink gums. He was reliving the moment, intoxicated on the memory. It made me cringe, all the pleasure he derived from remembering his act of murder.

"I could have killed him right then and there. I'm a pretty good shot. I've owned a gun for years, and I practice regularly. I could have put one in his chest and called it a day, but that would have been too good for the slimy snake. Much better than he deserved."

"So what did you do?" I asked. A sense of incipient horror had come over me. For I bore at least some responsibility for this killing. Gafni's motive was my erroneous report that Harpaz had been Moria's lover.

"I shot him in the knee," Gafni said, in a tone of even contentment, as though reporting on the signing of a routine contract, not the slaying of a man. "Then, when he was on the floor, blubbering and wailing, I told him he should have kept his filthy hands off my daughter. Between his sobs and whimpers he denied it, the liar, so I shot him in the other knee. There were bone fragments and blood everywhere, drenching the papers he'd brought over for me to sign. And I signed them all right. With my bullets and his blood."

"And then?" I asked when he stopped, the question leaving my lips of its own accord. For a part of me wanted to hear not one more word, to get up now and leave and never return. But I knew I'd be glued to this chair, in this moldy, depressing hallway, until the story was finally laid to rest.

"Arye lost consciousness from the pain," Gafni said, oblivious to my discomfort and horror, "but I wasn't done with him yet. I poured a bucket of water over his face. That woke him up. Then I ordered him to apologize for ever laying a finger on Moria, for being in her... in her..." He had trouble finishing the sentence, then clamped his eyes shut and forced it out. "In her bed. Again he denied ever touching her, and I shot his right hand and then his left, the two hands that touched my Moria. Finally, I shot him in the crotch. I still had one bullet left, and I thought of ending it, of putting the last one in his head. But no. I didn't want it to end that quickly. So I just sat on the edge of my desk and watched him while he wept and wailed and bled and begged for mercy. Until he could do none of those things anymore, or anything else for that matter. Only then, I telephoned the police and told them to come."

The silence that followed this confession was as oppressive as the walls and bars around us. The air itself was harder to pull into my lungs and then push out again.

I thought of Arye Harpaz—lying, deceitful, manipulative Harpaz. He had planned awful things, tried to exploit Moria to further his ends, and he had even tried seducing her, which was what Gafni had killed him for, what I'd told Gafni Harpaz had succeeded in doing.

I was responsible, but I felt only a smidgen of guilt over Harpaz. He had been a man without scruples. A man who had used others. He had planned to defraud Gafni. There was justice in Gafni killing him instead. And Harpaz had also sworn vengeance on me. Who could say what form that vengeance might have taken? Perhaps even murder. Now that threat was erased. At least on that score, I could breathe easier.

But the manner of his death both horrified and perplexed me. This was more than simple retribution or punishment. This torture was incongruous with a father angry at a man who'd seduced his adult daughter.

"Why did you want him to suffer so much?" I asked.

Gafni's eyes fluttered. He seemed to be in some other place, and it took him a second to look at me. "What?"

"Why didn't you just kill Harpaz? Why did you need to torture him?"

"He deserved it," Gafni stated simply.

"But why? Just for sleeping with Moria? She was a grown woman. It's not such a terrible thing, is it?"

Something rippled on his face. He brushed a hand along his

mouth and chin, closing his eyes and then reopening them. "She killed herself because of him. He's the man in the note."

"Why do you think so? I never told you that."

His face darkened. "You never told me anything about that, did you? What good are you? Maybe you don't deserve that bonus after all." He pushed out his lip and gazed around his cell with a bewildered expression, as though seeing it for the first time. Then he deflated like a pierced balloon, only silently, losing what he'd regained while in the throes of his killing tale, and returning to the hunched, weathered old man he'd been when I'd first roused him from the bunk.

"Who else could it be?" he said in a sullen voice, looking at his kneading hands. "Who else?"

I didn't answer. There was even less point in telling him the truth now than earlier in our conversation. Besides, I felt no obligation whatsoever to be honest with him. Because Gafni did not deserve the truth from me. Because, and I had no idea why, Baruch Gafni had just lied to my face.

47

I stood across the street from the building, just as I had done some weeks before, gazing up at her apartment. But then it had been night, and now it was day, and no light shone in her window.

I didn't want to go up there. I didn't wish to see her. But I knew I would do just that. As I had done several times before, though always with a different purpose in mind.

Wishing to postpone the moment, I got out my pack of cigarettes, then swore when I couldn't find my lighter. A mother walking past with a little girl in tow shot me a disapproving look; she didn't like my language. The girl, a rosy-cheeked beauty of four or five, looked over her shoulder at me, and I gave her a wink. She smiled in return, and it made me feel better. I shoved the cigarettes back in my pocket and crossed the street.

I knocked on her door. She opened it with a broad smile on her perfect lips. She had on a red dress that emphasized the swell of her hips and the bloom of her breasts. Sheer stockings through which flawless caramel skin peeked.

Her hair was pulled back apart from a pair of ringlets dangling teasingly on either side of her face. Her large dark eyes sparkled with triumph. It had been a while since I'd come by, yet here I was again. A man with a need on her threshold. Just as it should be. The natural order of things.

But my need today was not the sort she was accustomed to. Sima Vaaknin was in for a surprise.

"Adam," she purred, subtly shifting her stance to enhance the already-considerable allure of her curves, "so nice to see you again."

"Hello, Sima."

She pouted, though her eyes remained mischievous. "Why the serious tone and the long face? Aren't you happy to see me?"

"Can I come in?"

Instead of answering, she leaned a little forward, studying my face. "Something's changed about you. It's your nose, isn't it? It's different."

"It got broken in a fight."

"I like it. It fits your face," she said, not asking whom I'd fought with, or why or when. That was the nature of her interest in me. It waxed and waned according to some mysterious internal logic I never understood.

She moved aside, and I brushed past her, catching a tantalizing musky scent that wafted from her hair and skin.

In her living room, I remained standing while she kicked off her shoes and reclined on her sofa, pulling her legs at an angle beneath her. Her breathing had deepened, a show of excitement, but I suspected that was mere artifice, one of the many tools of seduction she could employ with unsurpassed expertise. Show a man that you desired him and he'd forget the tidy sum of money he would soon be parting with for the pleasure of your company.

"There's coffee in that pot," Sima said, fluttering her fingers at the coffee table. "I just made it not five minutes ago. Have some. It's very good."

I could believe it. Its aroma left no room for doubt as to its quality and authenticity. This was real prime coffee.

Then I noticed there were two cups on saucers by the pot.

"Are you expecting someone?" I asked.

"No one in particular. But I've learned it pays to be ready for company. You can never know when someone will drop by. Like you did." She ran a light hand over her calf, curling her stockinged toes. "Don't worry, Adam. No one will disturb us."

"I'm not here for that, Sima."

She arched an eyebrow. "You mean coffee or—"

"Both."

That made her frown momentarily. Bewildered by the curtness of my reply, perhaps. But she wasn't about to surrender just yet. In fact, judging by the curve of her lips and the twinkle in her eyes, she found pleasure in my resistance.

She rose from the sofa in a fluid movement, glided around the coffee table, and came to stand so close to me that every cell in my body glowed with her warmth. Gazing up at me from under her lashes, she put her hands flat on my chest. "Let's get you out of your coat so you can be more comfortable." She moved her hands to my shoulders, under my coat, and started drawing it off.

I grabbed her forearms and pulled her hands off me. "I said I'm not here for that."

Sima's eyes grew to brown pools of childlike dismay. This wasn't supposed to happen. I wasn't playing my part. She stepped back and looked at me in puzzlement and hurt.

"What are you here for, then?"

"Information."

"What information?"

"About a client of yours."

"I don't discuss my clients. Would you appreciate my discussing you?"

"These are special circumstances. They relate to the death of a young woman."

"What young woman?"

"The daughter of Baruch Gafni."

"I didn't know she'd recently died."

"He didn't talk about it with you?"

Sima didn't answer. She returned to the sofa, poured herself coffee, and took a dainty sip. "How did she die?"

"She killed herself. Pills."

Sima looked relieved. "I was sure you were going to say she was murdered and you suspect Baruch of killing her. How old was she?"

"Twenty-three."

"So young. Why did she do it?"

"I don't know. That's what I'm trying to find out."

"I can't help you. Baruch never talked about his daughter."

"What did he talk about?"

"I don't think I should tell you."

"Please, Sima. It's important."

"What sort of information are you after?"

"I don't know," I said. "But I assume he must have talked about himself while he was with you. He would have wanted to appear the big man in your eyes. He must have revealed things about his life. Maybe he even told you things he never told anyone else. I'm sure many of your clients do."

"Like you did, you mean? About your scars?"

I nodded awkwardly as the scars on my back started prickling. "Yeah, like I did."

A hint of a smile floated across Sima's mouth. She'd noticed my discomfort, and it pleased her. A little payback for my rejecting her.

"Well?" I said.

Sima took another sip and tapped the rim of her cup with a forefinger. "You're asking a lot, Adam. My clients rely on my discretion. If Baruch found out I talked to you, I'd lose him as a client."

Anger flared in me. She was worried about money while I was working to decipher the death of a young woman.

"I wouldn't be expecting him to visit anytime soon," I said. "He's in jail. For murder."

"But you just said—"

"It's not his daughter he killed."

"Who, then?"

"A man called Arye Harpaz. You know him?"

"Never heard that name in my life. Baruch never mentioned him. Why did he kill him?"

"Because he believed Harpaz was his daughter's lover."

"That doesn't sound like a good reason to murder someone."

"I think so too. That's why I'm here, to see if Gafni told you anything that might explain his actions."

Sima puckered her lips, thinking it over while looking as if she were offering her mouth to be kissed, though this time I thought the effect was unintentional.

Finally, she shook her head. "There's nothing about Baruch that would lead me to believe he would be capable of murder. Compared to other clients, he was quite ordinary. Sweet, even."

"Sweet?" I said, hardly believing my ears. "In what way?"

"It's how he's still in love with his wife. She's been dead for years. He misses her terribly. It's not a common thing for me to meet men who actually love their wives."

"This is Baruch Gafni we're talking about? Are you sure about that?"

She gave me an affronted look. "Of course I'm sure, Adam. I never get men mixed up. Why the doubt?"

"Because I talked to Gafni about his wife recently, and nothing in his manner or tone indicated he feels any love for her. By the way, did he tell you she committed suicide?"

Sima breathed in sharply. "He said she died of cancer."

"She slashed her wrists. Gafni admitted she did it because he was a philanderer. Did he tell you about that?"

"No."

"And you think he's sweet. Maybe you don't know men as well as you think."

"Don't blame me for not solving your case, Adam," Sima said evenly, then notched her head. "Or is there another reason you're angry with me?"

There was. I was disgusted by her sleeping with Gafni, and to make matters worse, it now seemed that she was actually fond of him. I dropped onto a chair and raked my fingers through my hair, nails scraping my scalp in frustration. This was shaping up to be another dead end, and a particularly unpleasant one at that.

Sima's lilting voice filled my ears. "It shouldn't surprise you that Baruch talked differently about his wife with you than he did here with me. Many men are different here. It's a place where they can show parts of themselves they keep hidden from the rest of the world. Isn't that true for you?"

I didn't respond. I wanted to get out of there, but for some reason, I didn't budge.

"Baruch was that way. Here he could do things he wouldn't have been able to with any other woman. He could be with his wife again."

I raised my head. "What do you mean?"

Sima lifted her chin, her mouth set in a proud line. "You want to know why Baruch came here? What he had me do? I'll tell you, my darling Adam, since you so desperately wish to know, and I always aim to please you. What Baruch did was have me act as his wife. Pretend to be her. So he could imagine her in my place, in his arms. When we were in bed, he would call out her name. 'Moria, Moria.'"

A cold, slimy blob of horror settled in the pit of my stomach. A fist of bile thrust up my throat and hammered at the back of my mouth.

"He said Moria?" I asked, my voice weak and hoarse.

"Yes. His wife's name. Now you understand why I—"

"Moria wasn't his wife," I said in a cutting tone. "Moria was his daughter."

Sima froze, shock written all over her lovely features.

"Yes, Sima. That's right. That wasn't Baruch Gafni's dead wife you were pretending to be. It was his daughter, Moria. The one who killed herself."

I shut my eyes tight as a horrible clarity hit me, like light thrown into a deep well where a body had long been hidden.

Arye Harpaz had told me he didn't know any women who'd had an affair with Gafni, and now I knew why. There hadn't been any. Gafni had allowed that rumor to spread, maybe even started it, to hide a worse truth. A truth that caused him to gruesomely kill Harpaz for the sin of being Moria's lover. Gafni couldn't stand that because he had sexual feelings toward Moria. That was why Vera Gafni had killed herself. It was the reason Moria had broken off all contact with her father. Why she had refused to see him, why she'd wept when Leitner had informed her she had to, or he'd expose her and Naomi Hecht.

Blackmailed by Leitner, she'd managed to bring herself to ask her father for money over the phone; not for herself, but for the hospital. But when she asked a third time, Gafni had demanded a meeting. This was too much. He was her devil, the man who had taken away her mother and much more besides, and she couldn't imagine being in the same room with him. Worse, he might interpret it as the harbinger of forgiveness and closer relations to come.

Like Germany would interpret Israel's agreement to enter into direct, face-to-face negotiations, I thought.

"You took his money," I said to Sima. "You played into his sick fantasy and took his money for it."

She fixed her eyes on me, her face free of emotion and so beautiful that for a moment I forgot my fury and disgust with her and wanted to pull her to me, to dive into her and be taken out of this world for a spell.

"Would it have been better," she said, "if I didn't? If, instead of here, he'd gone to satiate his depraved need elsewhere? With his daughter for real? Or with some other girl?"

"Don't act noble. You did it for the money."

"I'm not acting. I never act with you, Adam. Not where it counts. Of course I did it for the money. It's my profession. It's what I do. You paid me too, remember?"

"Not for something like this. I'm nothing like Baruch Gafni."

"I didn't know, Adam," she said, and there might have been a hint of pleading in her voice. "I didn't know what he's like. And as for his money, why should I feel bad for taking it? Would it have been better if it stayed in his pocket? A man so evil, why not take what you can from him?"

Moria didn't. She never accepted her father's gifts or encouraged him to give her more. But Sima was right. She hadn't known. I didn't want to ask her if she would have sent him away if she had.

I rose to my feet. "Goodbye, Sima."

"Goodbye? Why are you leaving? Stay with me, Adam."

"That's not what I came for, Sima. I told you that already."

I started to turn, but her voice stopped me. "You'll be back soon enough."

I looked at her. She was still reclining, but her body was anything but relaxed. If I had to describe her expression in one word, that word would have been fear.

I shook my head. "No. I won't."

"You won't be able to stay away." The words were confident, but there was a desperate edge to her voice. The voice of someone who's lost control of a situation and doesn't understand how or why.

I said nothing more. Just left.

Out on the street, I looked up at her window. She stood there, staring down at me, a gorgeous woman behind glass. Sunlight bathed her through the pane, giving her a burnished look, like a copper statue polished to a high gloss.

She didn't wave and neither did I. After a minute of immobile, mutual gazing, I lowered my eyes and walked away without looking back.

48

The next day, Gafni's lawyer came to Greta's Café. A short, smartly dressed man with a neat mustache, he offered me a dry hand and an envelope. "Mr. Gafni instructed me to give you this," he said, and left.

Inside the envelope were six fifty-lira bills. My bonus, apparently. I put it in my pocket. I didn't want this money, but I figured I'd find a use for it.

"More coffee, Adam?" Greta asked, holding a pot.

I checked my watch. I was going to Jerusalem again today, but I still had some time. I nodded, and Greta poured.

The previous evening, I'd told her all that had happened since I returned to Jerusalem following my injuries. She shivered as I described my close escape from Kulaski's vengeance, got angry when I related Leitner's blackmail of Moria, and became doleful when I explained about Daniel first killing Dr. Shapira and then, at my urging, doing the same to Dr. Leitner before falling to police bullets. She urged me not to feel guilty for anything but knew that was precisely how I felt.

"What about Moria?" she had asked me last night. "Do you still think the person in her note is Naomi Hecht?"

"Yes. But not for the same reason, obviously. Neither Moria nor

Naomi Hecht had anything to do with Dr. Shapira's killing. But they were lovers, and they did have a fight shortly before Moria's suicide. Maybe that had something to do with it."

"Can't it be Dr. Leitner?"

"Then why didn't Moria name him in the note? Moria knew Naomi Hecht would find her body. She knew Naomi Hecht would read her note and understand it. But she didn't want anyone else to."

Greta shook her head. "Such a terrible thing to have weighing on your conscience."

It was. Naomi Hecht must have been riven by guilt. I knew what that was like. Such guilt is hell. That explained the dark bags under her eyes. No wonder she wasn't sleeping well.

As I drank my coffee, I perused that day's newspapers. There was still no sign of the two police officers who had disappeared in Jerusalem a few days before. I'd been half-expecting a visit from Gideon Revivo, the cop who had participated in my beating but balked at murdering me, but he never showed, and neither did any other policemen. I was in the clear.

Another report connected the murder of Dr. Leitner with that of Dr. Shapira; the police said the same gun was used in both killings. The reporter, God bless him, wrote about Daniel's dead son and hinted at the possibility of medical malpractice on the part of Dr. Shapira. It would not exonerate Daniel in the public eye, but it burnished his memory just a little.

I was putting on my coat when a potbellied man with a bald head and a freckled face entered the café.

"Hello, Adam," Shmuel Birnbaum said. "Going somewhere?"

"Jerusalem. My bus leaves in forty minutes."

"That's too bad. I was hoping to speak with you over the fine coffee in this establishment. But why don't I give you a lift to the central bus station instead, eh?"

Parked at the curb was the same blue Morris Eight he'd driven the day he collected me from the Jerusalem jail. We got in, and he turned the ignition.

"You've heard about Gafni?" he asked.

"I visited him in jail yesterday."

"What on earth possessed him to do such a thing?"

"Why not ask him?"

"His lawyer won't permit it. Says his client is emotionally unable to answer reporters' questions. Word is he's planning an insanity plea."

"Good luck to him."

"What do you think? Is Gafni crazy?"

"How would I know? I'm no expert on craziness."

"You talked to him. How did he seem?"

"I can't talk about that, Shmuel. He was my client."

"Was? Not anymore?"

"I finished working for him yesterday, but that changes nothing. I still can't tell you anything."

Birnbaum smacked the steering wheel in frustration. There was a story here, and he craved it like other men crave money or women or status.

"The police say Gafni made Harpaz suffer, prolonged his death," Birnbaum said. "So maybe he is crazy."

"Maybe."

Birnbaum shot me an angry look. "Can you at least tell me how you got your nose flattened?"

"I'd rather not."

"Was that also part of the job you did for Gafni?"

"In a manner of speaking."

"In a manner of speaking? What does that mean?"

"It means I can't tell you, Shmuel. Now lay off me."

We drove a few minutes in silence. Then I said, "It seems like you were right. Herut hasn't been outlawed."

"Ben-Gurion did the smart thing. As he usually does."

I looked out the passenger's side window at the passing street. "I still think it's wrong to negotiate directly with Germany over reparations, to take their filthy money."

"But you don't sound as inflamed as you were the last time we spoke about this."

I thought about the envelope in my coat pocket. The envelope with Gafni's money in it. The good that money could do to someone who needed it. "A lot has happened since then."

To his credit, Birnbaum didn't ask me what.

I said, "I do love this country, you know? Even when it does things I detest."

"That's as good a definition of a patriot as I've ever heard," Birnbaum said with a wry smile. He parked near the entrance to the central bus station and laid a hand on my arm.

"I told you this the last time we spoke, Adam, and I'll say it again now: no matter how much money the Germans will give us, we shall never forgive and we shall never forget. Not your family, and not all the rest. And we won't let the world forget either."

My throat had constricted. I had to clear it to speak. "I hope you're right, Shmuel. I hope to God you're right."

He squeezed my forearm, his hand pressing my number tattoo through my sleeve. Then his lips crooked in a mischievous grin. "Are you sure you can't spare this poor little reporter a story with some meat on it?"

I laughed. "I'm afraid not. But I'm sure the Gafni case will give you much to write about."

"It sure will. In fact, I have already written a column about it. But I still need to edit it to make sure it's perfect." He held out a hand. "Have a good trip, Adam."

I shook his hand. "Thank you, Shmuel."

49

I knocked on her door. Her voice came through ragged and raw. "Who is it?"

"Adam Lapid."

Silence. Then: "Go away."

"Please, Mrs. Hecht, I'd like to talk to you. I'd like to apologize and explain."

"I don't want your apologies or explanations. Just leave me alone."

Pressing my hand flat to her door, a peculiar ache in my chest that had nothing to do with injured ribs, I said, "I was wrong and stupid, and I'm so very sorry. I know what you and Moria were to each other. I know why you lied to me."

A longer silence. Then: "Do you still think Moria killed herself because of me?"

This time, the silence was mine.

"Go away, Mr. Lapid." Her voice cut through the door and stabbed into my ears. "Go away and don't come back."

I walked away with hunched shoulders and a heavy heart. An odd weight pressed on and inside me. That was the end of something that had never started. Naomi Hecht was out of my life for good.

I headed to Amos Street and went into Moria's building. Voices sounded from the Shukrun apartment. Men and women talking in somber voices. Someone weeping. The shiva for Daniel Shukrun in its hardest stages—the manner of his death no doubt augmenting the family's shock and grief.

I didn't knock. I didn't think I'd be welcomed. Lillian had given me the address to the locksmithing store on the same day her husband killed Dr. Leitner. It wouldn't take much for her to deduce that I had something to do with the disaster that had befallen her.

There were no mailboxes in the lobby; the residents must have gotten their mail at a nearby post office, but I did not know where it was. I decided to go search for it when a woman entered the building. She was older than Lillian, but the similarity between the two left no room for doubt. They were sisters.

I verified this impression and asked if she might deliver something to her sister. "After the shiva," I said. "When things calm down a bit."

"Why not give it to her yourself?" she asked.

I said I'd rather not and handed her the envelope containing Gafni's bonus.

Before I could react, she tore the flap open and peered inside. Her eyebrows shot up. "What is this?"

"Something to help Lillian and Dina get back on their feet."

"But why?"

"I knew Daniel, and I owed him very much. Can I count on you to give this money to her?"

She bristled. "I won't be stealing it, if that's what you're worried about." She looked at the money again and shook her head. "It's too much."

And too little just the same, I thought. "She'll find good use for it, I'm sure."

"She'll want to know who gave this to her. What's your name?"

"My name's not important. Could you pretend your family collected this money for her?"

She nodded. There were tears in her eyes. "All right. I will. God bless you, whoever you are."

I ate at a small café on Malkei Yisrael Street. On the table to my right lay yesterday's edition of *Davar*. I picked it up and flicked to Birnbaum's column. He wrote about Israel's relationship with the United States. He really had a way with words, I thought as I finished reading and picked up the coffee cup, bringing it to my lips. All the editing he did paid off big.

I froze, my mouth full of hot coffee, my tongue stinging.

Editing. That single word resounded in my head like the tolling of a giant bell. What had Birnbaum told me? He'd said he needed to edit his column to make it perfect.

That memory conjured another. Anat Schlesinger telling me what Moria Gafni had been like as a student.

Feeling as though I'd been struck on the head by a lightning bolt, I gulped down the coffee in my mouth, grabbed my coat, and ran out of the café.

I sprinted up the stairs all the way to the third floor, the key to Moria's apartment in my grip. I was so excited, I had to focus on steadying my hand to fit it into the lock.

I went straight to the bedroom, to the dresser. I couldn't remember which drawer it had been in, so I yanked all three open and went through them top to bottom.

It was in the third drawer. A simple notebook with a brown cover and half of its pages ripped out. I remembered that the first time I saw it, it had occurred to me that this notebook had the same paper as Moria's suicide note.

She rewrote each paper until every word was absolutely perfect, Anat Schlesinger had told me, and I hadn't given it a second's thought. Only now, my heart thudding and my fingertips sliding eagerly over the scratchy pages of Moria's notebook, did the significance sink in.

With shaky breath, I tore out the top page and held it to the light streaming through the window. "Yes!" I cried out, seeing what I'd hoped to see.

Then I got to work.

50

"I told you to leave me alone," Naomi Hecht shouted through her door.

I brought my face close to the wood. "Moria didn't do it because of you. I can prove it. Let me show you. Please open the door, Naomi."

Ten long seconds passed. Then the door swung open. "I think that was the first time you used my first name," Naomi said.

I pulled in a breath. Naomi looked very tired and very mournful yet also very beautiful. "You may be right. I'm not sure."

"I think it was," she said, frowning slightly. "But that's not so important, is it? You have something to show me, you said."

"Yes. I do."

"Come in, then."

In her living room, we sat together on the sofa. She wore a white dress reminiscent of her nurse's uniform, which was appropriate despite her having lost her job, given what I knew of her daily activities. I glanced at her wedding photo, my chest tight with sadness and shame now that I knew the truth.

I showed her the notebook. "I found this in Moria's bedroom. See? About half the pages are missing, torn out. I should have picked up on it the first time I saw it. I can't believe I missed it."

"Missed what? I don't understand."

"Look at these pages. They're the exact same type of paper as the one on which Moria wrote the note you found."

"And so?"

I related to her what Anat Schlesinger had told me of Moria the student. "I was sure you were the person Moria wrote about in her note because it included no name, and because Moria had arranged her death so that you would find her body. But the piece of paper you found that day wasn't her suicide note at all. It was merely a draft; one of many, I bet. Just like she did as a student, Moria rewrote her final message many times until it was perfect."

Naomi's eyes were bright hazel circles of astonishment. "Are you sure?"

I nodded. "Here's how I think it happened. You remember how neat Moria's apartment was? As though she cleaned it before ending her life? Yet you found what you thought was her suicide note on the floor, under the dining table."

"That's right."

"Until today, I thought Moria had left the note on the table, and the wind coming in through the nearby open window blew it to the floor. Now I think it happened another way. I think Moria had a bunch of drafts on the dining table, and one of them, the page you found, fell to the floor, and she didn't see it. She threw the rest of them out."

Naomi's breath turned shallow and quick. "So where is the final note?"

"By the time Moria died, the actual suicide note was no longer in the apartment. There's a strip of stamps in her dresser, and some of the stamps are missing. I can't prove it, but I think she mailed her suicide note. She never included the name of the recipient in her drafts because she didn't need to. There's no need to rewrite a name."

I showed her the page I'd examined in Moria's bedroom. It was blackened with lead. "This was the top page remaining in the notebook. I went over it with a pencil. It brought out the indentations left when Moria wrote her final note. Here. Read it."

Naomi peered at the page. "But there are two people mentioned here, not one."

"Yes. There are."

"How can that be? What does it mean?"

"Again, I can't be sure, but I think Moria wrote and mailed two notes. Identical but for the recipients. The first is addressed to her father; the second to Dr. Leitner. Both men did horrible things to Moria and caused her great anguish, but it was only when the two combined in a particular way that she gave up on life."

"What did they do?" Naomi asked. "I know Moria hated her father, but what did Dr. Leitner do to her?"

I told her about Gafni's twisted love of his daughter and how that led to her mother's suicide; about how Dr. Leitner had blackmailed Moria to lobby her father for donations; and how, finally, Gafni had demanded a face-to-face meeting with his daughter, and that this Moria could not stand.

"Here are the photos Dr. Leitner's detective took," I said, giving her the envelope Ada Leitner had given me. "And the negatives. You should be the one who decides what to do with them."

With quivering fingers, Naomi opened the envelope and flipped through the photos. With each passing picture, her eyes turned wetter, until tears started sliding down her cheeks, as bright as crystals.

"It's too bad that son of a bitch is dead," she said when she finished looking through the photos, her face fierce despite her tears. "I would have liked to tear him apart with my bare hands."

I thought of Daniel Shukrun, dead after exacting his final vengeance. "I don't think Moria would have wanted you to languish in prison or be killed by cops. Not even for that."

Naomi wiped her cheeks dry. She put the photos back in the envelope and kept hold of it like a treasure.

"What about the gun you found in Moria's apartment?"

I explained about Daniel Shukrun. Dr. Shapira's culpability in the death of his son. How Daniel chose to hide the gun in Moria's apart-ment as a means of distancing himself from the shooting. His wish to complete his quest for revenge by killing Dr. Leitner. My shame in letting him go through with it.

Naomi reached over and squeezed my hand. My skin tingled at her touch. "It was his decision, Adam. It wasn't your fault."

I nodded, hoping that one day I'd be entirely convinced of that.

A minute of silence elapsed. Then I asked, "How did it happen? You and Moria, I mean."

Naomi drew back her hand and started fiddling with her wedding band. I followed her gaze to her wedding photo. "You know about my husband?"

"I know he lives in a convalescence home."

A sad smile tugged at Naomi's lips. "Convalescence for some, maybe. Not for him. He got injured in the war. January 1949. Shrapnel pierced his skull. It did incredible damage. It's a wonder he survived. But maybe that's the wrong way to put it because most of him didn't. He's alive, but nothing of him remains. Just a physical shell. The man inside is gone."

"I understand you visit him daily," I said.

"I do my best."

"It must be hard."

Pain coursed through her features. Her voice was frayed and resigned. "It's been three years. He shows no improvement. The doctors say he never will. But he lives, and I'm his wife, so I do what I must."

I looked at her. At her strong face that merely hinted at a much greater internal strength. She was an informal widow, trapped in continual, unceasing mourning and duty, her husband dead in essence if not in body.

Naomi sighed. "Three years is a long time, Adam. The loneliness gets difficult to bear. From time to time, a man would show interest, and I'd get tempted by the promise of warmth and touch, but I didn't want to betray my husband. Then, one day, Moria revealed her feelings toward me, and I just let go. In my mind, because she was a woman, I wasn't being unfaithful to my husband. At least that's how it felt in the beginning. Do you understand?"

She was looking right into my eyes, and in the depth of her irises swirled the maelstrom of emotion that had been her life these past three years. "Yes," I said. "I understand. When did it begin?"

"Seven months before Moria died. I ended it a week before. That was the fight you asked me about. I lied because I wanted our relationship to remain a secret." A pause. "Moria took it very badly. When I found her body, the note, I couldn't help but blame myself."

"Why did you end it?"

"Gradually, the lie I'd told myself, that this wasn't infidelity, lost its hold on me. My guilt became too great."

"Why did you never stay the night at Moria's? A friend sleeping over, it wouldn't have raised eyebrows."

"Moria had bad dreams, and she would talk in her sleep. One time, after we... well, when I was with her, she fell asleep, and she spoke of her mother. She didn't speak clearly, but I understood her mother had killed herself. I asked her about it when she awoke, and she became agitated, like she'd spilled some big secret. She had never talked about her mother before, and she wouldn't then either. Nor would she speak of her father, but I got the impression that Moria's hatred of him had something to do with her mother. After that time, Moria never allowed herself to sleep in my presence again."

This also explained why Moria hadn't wished to be Anat Schlesinger's roommate. Moria had secrets all right, but they were related to her dark past, not the gun I found in her apartment.

"Did Moria also have relations with men?" I asked.

Naomi shook her head. "Moria wasn't interested in men. Only in women."

"There were condoms in her bedside cabinet."

Naomi's smile was weak and tragic. "That was a joke, a ruse. She used to laugh about them. If anyone suspected her tendencies, she said, she'd show them the condoms and that sleazy, awful book she got from God knows where. 'Better to be seen as promiscuous with men than in love with a woman.'"

"Is that what she was, in love with you?"

"Yes. She told me she loved me many times."

"And you?" I asked, my heart beating fast and hard.

"I loved her, yes, but not in the same way. Not romantically. Moria helped fill a void in my life. She helped to dispel my loneliness. But I'm not like she was. I can't love a woman that way, not completely." Her eyes glistened with fresh tears. "She should have told me about Dr. Leitner. We would have found a solution."

"She must have worried you'd do something rash. She was trying to protect you."

Naomi was quiet for a long moment. Then she said, "That sweet, poor girl. She knew me so well. I can't help but think that if I hadn't broken things off, Moria would have found the strength to carry on despite everything."

"Don't blame yourself," I said. "Moria didn't. Even if you two were still together, she would have acted the same. Caught between her father and Dr. Leitner, she saw no other way out."

"Why didn't she write me something to explain, to let me know I wasn't to blame?"

"I don't know. I so wish I did, but I don't. But I do know you were the best thing that ever happened to her, Naomi. I saw it in the pictures. That's still true, no matter how your relationship ended."

Naomi burst into tears, covered her face, and sort of toppled toward me. I held her tight as she shook against my shoulder. She cried for a long time. Partly in sorrow, and partly in relief, I thought. She now knew she hadn't driven Moria to suicide. The burden of guilt had lifted, at least most of it. Now she could begin mourning in earnest.

We stayed that way even after her tears ceased. I wasn't sure how long; time seemed different.

When she pulled away, Naomi looked embarrassed, and my arms felt empty. She got up to wash her face, returning a few minutes later, looking drained.

"There's something I don't understand," she said. "Why did Moria's father hire you to investigate her death if he had the note she mailed him?"

"He didn't. I don't know why, but it never reached him. It wouldn't be the first time a letter got lost in the mail."

"And Dr. Leitner?"

"I'm pretty sure he got his note. When I asked him if he thought Moria killed herself because of him, he got very upset and blamed her in the crudest language. Maybe he did have a conscience somewhere under all that ambition."

"What will happen to Moria's father?"

"He'll go away for a long time. Either to prison or the insane asylum."

"Good," she said. "I hope he dies locked up."

I did too. For what Gafni had done to his daughter, he deserved not being free ever again.

"He took a big risk hiring you, didn't he?" she asked.

"Because I might discover what he did to her?"

"Yes."

"He must have figured Moria wouldn't have told anyone about it. And, apart from her and him, no one else knew. It was only by accident that I discovered the truth. Also, I think he truly loved her—a sick, twisted love, but love all the same—and he couldn't stand the thought that she'd killed herself because of him. The chance of learning someone else was to blame was worth the risk."

"Are you going to tell him the truth?"

"Moria would want me to. But I'll wait until after his trial. Let him get his sentence first." I didn't tell her I was worried about how Gafni would take it. He was deranged enough to want to kill the messenger, and he had more than enough money to pay someone to come after me. I wanted a little rest before I had to deal with that.

Changing the subject, I said, "Naomi, there's one more thing I need to know. Did you visit Moria's apartment a few weeks after her death?"

Naomi nodded. "I lied about that too."

"What did you take?"

"Nothing. During our relationship, Moria wrote me poems. I gave them back to her when I ended things. I went to her apartment to look for them, but I didn't find them. She must have thrown them out." A pause, a deep inhalation. "I'm sorry I lied to you, Adam."

"That's all right. I understand why you did it. I'm sorry for jumping to the wrong conclusions, for blaming you for... well, for everything."

A twitch of her lips. "I suppose I brought it on myself with all my lies." She gave me a direct look. "There's something here, isn't there, Adam? Between the two of us?"

"Yes," I said. "Yes, there is."

"I felt it on the day we first met."

"I think I did too."

"But I can't do anything about it. I wish I could, but I can't. Please tell me you understand why."

An image of her husband, crippled and mute and blank-faced, caught between life and death, flashed before my eyes. I had to clear my throat before I spoke. "I do, Naomi."

"If I could, would what I did with Moria change things?"

I thought about it and shook my head. "No. I don't believe it would."

Naomi's smile was both happy and sad. She gripped my hands. Her pulse thrummed through my skin, in perfect rhythm with mine.

We sat like that for a long, peaceful while, our fingers clasped, communicating wordlessly yet deeply, knowing it would soon be time to say goodbye.

Thank you for reading *A Death in Jerusalem*!

Want to read more Adam Lapid?

Read *The Unlucky Woman*, an Adam Lapid short story.

Please review this book!

Reviews help both readers and authors. If you enjoyed *A Death in Jerusalem*, please leave a review on whatever website you use to purchase or review books. I would greatly appreciate it.

AUTHOR'S NOTE

Dear reader,

Thank you for reading *A Death in Jerusalem*. I hope you enjoyed it. I would like to tell you how I came to write this book and provide more historical details of the fascinating time in which this novel is set.

On January 7, 2021, I watched footage from Washington, DC, where the day before a group of protesters had stormed the Capitol Building as part of a demonstration against the election of Joe Biden as President of the United States.

With amazement, I watched history repeat itself. I was at the time busy writing the early chapters of *A Death in Jerusalem*, which begins with the storming of the Knesset in January 1952.

Long before beginning *A Death in Jerusalem*, I knew that I would write an Adam Lapid novel set in that time. I knew that Adam, a Holocaust survivor who lost his family in Auschwitz, would be incensed by Israel's intention to negotiate with Germany for reparations.

The political struggle over negotiations with Germany, which peaked in the violent demonstration outside the Knesset, was one of the most volatile moments in Israeli history, a time in which the country appeared on the verge of coming apart at the seams. Menachem Begin's fiery speech, parts of which I literally translated from Hebrew and included in this novel, might easily have served as a declaration of civil war. It is only by luck, or providence, that Israel avoided such a fate.

The issue of reparations arose much earlier. Even before Israeli independence, various Jewish organizations considered the matter, and Israeli officials discussed it as early as 1949. Many favored reparations but rejected any direct contact with Germany; Israel's government voted against direct negotiations in 1950 and again in 1951. Instead, Israel tried working through the western Allied powers, mainly the Americans, who at the time occupied West Germany.

This approach failed utterly. Western powers, wishing to prop West Germany as a bulwark against communism, were reluctant to place further financial obligations upon it. To get reparations, the government of David Ben-Gurion would have to deal with the Germans directly. Israel's dire economic situation forced Ben-Gurion's hand, and Israel and Germany commenced secret discussions in 1951.

These discussions bore fruit. In September 1951, West German chancellor Konrad Adenauer gave a historic speech in the West German parliament, the Bundestag. Adenauer declared that indescribable crimes against Jews had been committed in the name of the German people, and that while only a minority of Germans participated in these crimes and most abhorred them, these crimes demanded material reparations. He said Germany was willing to resolve the issue with Jewish and Israeli representatives.

In December 1951, the Israeli government voted in favor of direct negotiations with Germany on the matter of reparations. Public opposition was fierce and widespread. Things reached a boiling point in January 1952, when the matter was laid before the Knesset, which is when this novel begins.

As I wrote in the novel, the Knesset approved direct negotiations with Germany. These negotiations culminated in an agreement in which Germany agreed to give Israel three billion German marks over a twelve-year period, which would be used to procure German goods and products. These reparations were to compensate Israel as the representative of the Jewish people and a country where many Holocaust survivors settled after World War II.

This agreement had wide-ranging effects on Israel's economy and German-Israeli relations. German reparations helped Israel avert financial catastrophe and brought about years of robust economic development. Israel and West German cooperation deepened across many spheres, and full diplomatic relations were established in 1965. The Israeli public's boycott of Germany has withered with time, and today the two countries enjoy close economic and diplomatic relations.

The aftermath of the violent demonstration described in this book was as Shmuel Birnbaum predicted. David Ben-Gurion proved magnanimous in victory. Herut was not outlawed, and none of the demonstrators who were arrested that day was ever charged with a crime. All were released in the following weeks and months.

Menachem Begin, who a few months before the demonstration was on the cusp of retiring from politics, continued serving as the leader of Herut. In 1977, he became Israel's sixth prime minister and later was awarded the Noble Prize for Peace for signing Israel's peace agreement with Egypt. No one in 1952 would have imagined such an outcome for Begin.

David Ben-Gurion continued serving as Israel's prime minister until 1963 (with a short interlude in 1954-1955). Ben-Gurion used to say that he didn't do what the people wanted, but what he thought the people needed. In 1952, he did just that.

A Death in Jerusalem is the first Adam Lapid novel set primarily in Israel's capital. Researching how Jerusalem was in 1952 was both illuminating and fascinating. Apart from historical accounts of the city and its landmarks, my main source of information was my mother-in-law, Froumit Tandet, to whom this novel is dedicated.

Froumit was born a few months after the events of this novel and grew up in West Jerusalem. She described to me in detail the tenor of Jerusalem's streets and its people. She lived in a building just behind

Frumin House and remembers seeing members of Knesset arrive for work. Menachem Begin, she told me, pinched her cheek once on his way into the Knesset chamber.

Dear reader, I hope that you enjoyed *A Death in Jerusalem*. If so, I'd appreciate it if you took a moment to write a review on whatever website you use to purchase or review books. Thank you.

As for the future of Adam Lapid, I've already begun writing the next book in the series, and plan to write more after that.

If you're a member of a book club and wish to discuss *A Death in Jerusalem*, you will find suggested discussion questions after this author's note.

As always, if you have any questions or feedback, please write me at Jonathan@JonathanDunsky.com. I also invite you to join my author's page at Facebook.com/JonathanDunskyBooks.

Before we part, I'd like to say a big thank you to Otilia Rossetti and Jeannie Blau for their kind help in the editing process of this novel. I would also like to thank Stacey Levy for her generosity and support.

That's it from me, dear reader. Until the next book, I bid you farewell.

Jonathan Dunsky
Israel, February 2022

BOOK CLUB DISCUSSION QUESTIONS

1. Do you think Israel made the right decision to negotiate with Germany for reparations for the Holocaust? Discuss the moral, financial, and historical arguments and implications.

2. Discuss David Ben-Gurion's decision to not prosecute the demonstrators? Did he make the right call?

3. Shmuel Birnbaum tells Adam Lapid that loving your country even when it does things you detest is as good a definition of a patriot as he has ever heard. Do you agree with this statement? If not, suggest another.

4. Ben-Gurion pushed for negotiations with Germany despite fervent public opposition. When should a leader do not what the people want but what he thinks they need? Can you give other examples of such decisions?

5. Discuss the character of Menachem Begin. On the one hand, the leader of the Irgun and the catalyst of the storming of the Knesset; on the other, a man of peace who signed Israel's peace agreement with Egypt. How did *A Death in Jerusalem* change your view of Begin, if at all?

6. Between 1949-1967, Jerusalem was a divided city, with access to Judaism's holiest sites blocked to Israeli Jews. How did the descrip-

tions of a divided Jerusalem make you feel? Have they influenced your opinion of the current status of the city?

7. Several characters in this novel resort to vigilantism. When do you think vigilantism is warranted and just? Where do you draw the line?

8. Apart from Adam Lapid, who was your favorite character in *A Death in Jerusalem*, and why?

9. Ben-Gurion ordered the police defending the Knesset to refrain, at all costs, from using their firearms. Discuss this order by Ben-Gurion. How might history have changed if not for this order?

10. Discuss the topic of reparations. Can they ever resolve a historic wrong? Can they be a means for reconciliation and greater understanding between former persecutors and victims?

11. Today, Israel and Germany enjoy close relations. How do you feel about this? What lessons can be applied from this historical development to other conflicts?

12. Discuss the character of David Ben-Gurion. Has reading *A Death in Jerusalem* changed your views of Israel's first prime minister? If so, in what way?

13. Putting yourself in Adam Lapid's shoes, can you see yourself taking part in the assault on the Knesset? What does it say about Adam's character that he participated in it?

14. What do you think about Naomi Hecht? Discuss her character.

15. What themes did you identify in *A Death in Jerusalem*?

16. If you wished to recommend this book to a friend or family member, how would you describe it?

ABOUT THE AUTHOR

Jonathan Dunsky lives in Israel with his wife and two sons. He enjoys reading, writing, and goofing around with his kids. He began writing in his teens, then took a break for close to twenty years, during which he worked an assortment of jobs. He is the author of the Adam Lapid mystery series and the standalone thriller The Payback Girl.

f facebook.com/JonathanDunskyBooks

Made in United States
Troutdale, OR
04/18/2024

19263540R00216